Secret Valentines

"Camille." I whispered the name.

Dare I move? She might flee. Dare I speak? I might frighten her. Besides, it wasn't my place to address her.

What emotion did I read in her face? Recognition? Confusion? . . . Pleasure? Hope?

I sat up, as cautious as one in the presence of a fawn, mesmerized by the incredible beauty and gentleness of its nature . . . my chest filled with an exhilaration that made my heart trip . . .

—from "Primrose Lane" by Katherine Sutcliffe,
National Bestselling Author of *My Only Love*,
Once a Hero, *Miracle*, and *Devotion*

Secret Valentines

Katherine Sutcliffe

Rachel Lee

Kate Freiman

Sherry Lewis

JOVE BOOKS, NEW YORK

SECRET VALENTINES

A Jove Book / published by arrangement with
the authors

PRINTING HISTORY
Jove edition / February 1997

All rights reserved.
Copyright © 1998 by Jove Publications, Inc.
"Primrose Lane" copyright © 1998 by Katherine Sutcliffe.
"A Secret Cupid" copyright © 1998 by Susan Civil-Brown.
"For C., Who Changed My Life" copyright © 1998 by Kate Freiman.
"Send Me No Flowers" copyright © 1998 by Sherry Lewis Brown.
Book design by Casey Hampton.
This book may not be reproduced in whole
or in part, by mimeograph or any other means,
without permission. For information address:
The Berkley Publishing Group, a member of Penguin Putnam Inc.,
200 Madison Avenue, New York, New York 10016.

The Putnam Berkley World Wide Web site address is
http://www.berkley.com

ISBN: 0-515-12226-2

A JOVE BOOK®
Jove Books are published by The Berkley Publishing Group,
a member of Penguin Putnam Inc.,
200 Madison Avenue, New York, New York 10016.
JOVE and the "J" design are trademarks belonging to
Jove Publications, Inc.

PRINTED IN THE UNITED STATES OF AMERICA

10 9 8 7 6 5 4 3 2 1

Contents

Primrose Lane

Katherine Sutcliffe

Prologue

What sweet irony that I should wind up on Primrose Lane, where every fence and oak and spray of musty gray moss roused from my lethargic memory thoughts of happier, carefree days; days when I ran barefoot upon these sandy lanes and thumbed my nose at life and consequence. Once, I had hidden beyond the cascading greenery and watched the coming and going of the inhabitants of Primrose Farm, hoping against hope for a glimpse of the prettiest girl in Baton Rouge, Louisiana: Camille Philips. Blond hair, blue eyes. As graceful as a willow branch stirred by a gentle wind. I always imagined that her lips would melt beneath mine like warm chocolate.

What a glorious and dangerous game it was then. Me, the town bad boy, infatuated with the Primrose Princess. That's what the folk in my neighborhood called Camille in those days. Not out of disrespect, of course, but because she lived in the finest house in the state and bought her clothes in New Orleans. Often I would fly as fast as my legs would carry me down the wooded path to Primrose, imagining that perhaps *that* day would be *the* day that I gathered up my courage and presented myself and my adolescent fantasies to her. I rehearsed them over and over in my head, fear pressing in on me as if assassins were crouched behind every dense copse waiting to pounce and end my moronic aspirations. Yet, great as my trepidations were, I could not keep from traversing the path and drinking in the smell of verdant, rotting vegetation and hearing the birds whose raucous cries seemed to mock my anticipation. Try as I might, however, I neither proclaimed nor showed myself upon her doorstep. Instead, like a coward, I crouched behind three-hundred-year-old oaks and stared like a simpleton at the bedroom window that I imagined to be hers—that was *after* I placed bouquets of primroses near the front door; I lived in fear that someone other than she would find them.

Once, in February of '27, I made a card of construction paper that I pilfered from school and I wrote upon it: "To the most beautiful girl in the world. I would give you my heart and soul if you would have it. Signed with limitless adoration: Anonymous." Then I pasted onto the card dried primroses that I had pressed between the pages of my mother's Bible months before. I hiked through the woods with the valentine tucked within my coat against my heart and I left it propped against the front door, along with a chocolate bar I had stolen three days before from Carver's Pharmacy. For two hours I huddled in the bushes, my fingers and toes and ears stinging from the cold as I waited for her to discover the card. With a huge sense of relief and dread, I watched her brother Don retrieve it. He turned it over and over in his big rough hands, and I held my breath in fear, for certainly he would not be pleased to know that white trash was leaving Camille a valentine on his doorstep. He raised his gaze to the very place where I so naïvely thought I was well hidden, and his eyes stared directly into mine an eternal moment before he disappeared into the house. *He knows, he knows!* my mind screamed, and I fled Primrose Lane as fast as I could.

From that moment on I avoided Don Philips at every opportunity. If we found ourselves on the same side of the street, I crossed to the other. If he came into Tobias Clark's Mercantile, where I worked part-time, I made certain to remain hidden until he paid for his purchases and left.

I stayed away from Primrose Lane after that. I ushered in my manhood indulging in petty crimes, bootleg whiskey, and loose girls who were as hungry to consume life as I. Sure as I knew there would never be another girl I cared for more than Camille Philips, I knew that I was headed for trouble the moment I took Rhonda Lee Horan's virginity in the back of her brother's black-and-white squad car. Cliff Horan was deputy sheriff in those days. Everybody in the parish feared him. Like a good coon dog, he had a way of sniffing out troublemakers with uncanny accuracy, and God help you if he took a dislike to you. He didn't care for white trash or Negroes, and since I was deemed white trash I suspected that I was going to pay dearly for soiling his little sister. Never mind that she was the instigator of our indiscretion. Only a fool would have proclaimed Rhonda Lee Horan a whore. I might have been stupid in those days, but I wasn't a fool.

Therefore, when I was jolted from sleep one night in August of '30 by a half-dozen men with clubs, who all stood about pounding my body to a pulp, I knew I was done for. Only one thing saved me: the possibility that Rhonda Lee could be with child. The idea of marrying Horan's sister was more frightening than the thought of being fed to gators and I prayed every day that I festered in Horan's stinking jail that Rhonda Lee would get her period. But what bothered me most was the idea that somehow Camille Philips would learn about my idiocy.

Not that it would matter. I doubted that she would give the information more than a fleeting moment's consideration. I was a nonentity to her.

Still . . . I suffered.

Feeling much older than my nineteen years, I grieved over the idea that I had somehow been unfaithful to her. I paced the oven-hot little cell while my mind spun with images of her collapsing to the floor, weeping in sadness, wailing her abject misery over my intimacy with another. But always the vision faded with her reaching out in forgiveness, a tremulous smile on her soft red lips, her love shining like crystalline tears in her eyes.

After a month of incarceration I learned that Rhonda Lee

and I were not to be parents. I was released from jail just two days before Deputy Horan was elected sheriff. Three days later I was arrested again, this time for armed robbery of Tobias Clark's Mercantile. Everybody in Baton Rouge knew I didn't do it, but it didn't matter. I had pissed Horan off and he was going to make certain I regretted my foolishness one way or another, even if he had to incarcerate me for a crime I had not committed. I was hauled before a judge who was obviously as crooked as Horan and given three years of hard labor on Horan's chain gang.

I was busting rock up on the River Road when I first heard about Camille—how she was found out near Bixby's Dairy, raped and beaten and near death. I went crazy that day and nearly pummeled a Cajun inmate named Max to death with my sledge—all because he spat on my shoe. Guess I was hoping someone would shoot me. I simply didn't want to live in a world without Camille. My Primrose Princess, as they called her then. . . .

Chapter One

We were hungry, but the entire country was hungry. The collection of thieves and malfeasants on Sheriff Horan's road gang survived on one meal a day. But we were thankful. We were better off than a great many others, and therein was a source of trouble for us. There were a hell of a lot of folk across the country who weren't happy that criminals like us were reaping the benefit of work and food while enjoying a roof over our bodies at night and pillows on which to rest our heads. And even if we *were* forced to hold our boots together with twine and resin and patch our shabby soles with tire rubber, just like the rest of the country, at least we weren't barefoot. I'd heard recently that so much stink had been raised that the Civil Works Administration had embarked on a program of road and park maintenance that would take us off the road gangs and slam us back in jail to rot in idleness while the free unemployed were put to work laying down asphalt.

Personally, I would have hated to see that happen. Life on the chain gang wasn't so bad, at least for me; I was in heaven, or a version thereof. We were busting rock on Primrose Lane, smack in front of Primrose Farm, with a bird's-eye view of Camille's bedroom window.

The enormous smoldering sun lay on the horizon like a dissolving orange suffused with blood that afternoon in August 1933. Robert Ewing, who published the *New Orleans Stakes*, surmised that the unusual sunsets were the result of the terrible dust storms plaguing the more northern states. His readership considered the idea insane and thought Mr. Ewing should focus his concerns more on what the governor was doing to help the plight of the starving children inhabiting his great city instead of dwelling on the color of the idiotic sun. Still and all, Mr. Ewing was probably right. If the storms could deposit grit on ships two hundred miles out in the Atlantic, dumping dust over the Louisiana horizon wasn't so far-fetched an idea. The hard truth was, over the last year the air had been a hell of a lot harder to breathe. Not six weeks before, an inmate had dropped dead next to me while working the road. One minute he'd been complaining about having a hard time breathing, the next he was dead as a frying pan. The prison doctor had attributed his demise to dust pneumonia. I had been sorry to lose him, as he was the only friend I had to whom I could talk openly about my dreams of someday presenting myself to Camille.

Ah, *Camille*. She still haunted my every waking and sleeping minute. At times, I thought that I must surely be going insane with the need to see her again, to declare that I had cared for no other since the day she had walked across town to present a basket of food to my mother—charity, certainly. But more than that to apologize over her sister-in-law's unfair dismissal of my mother, who had scrubbed Primrose Farm's floors for the past several years. If I lived to be a thousand I would never forget watching through a window as Camille, with tears in her eyes, wrapped her arms around Mother and pressed her soft pink lips onto Mother's weathered cheek. I was transfixed by the sight: Camille standing amid our poverty, the Primrose Princess, adorned in her clean, starched dress, a thin pearl necklace around her throat, her generosity and goodness as iridescent as her beauty, holding my mother's ragged form in her arms, softly sobbing her heartfelt regrets. In that moment my infatuation had turned to love: blinding, consuming, wrenching. The essence of her kindness became my passion, indeed, my obsession. No other woman could hope to compete with Camille, though I searched; God, how I searched, but always they came up short.

As my youth raged into manhood I ached desperately to topple Camille's icon image that I carried in my heart and mind; but there was no escaping the reality. It was there constantly, blazing across the *Baton Rouge Gazette:* articles of her volunteering her time to the Good Shepherd Hospital or to this or that foundation. It was there as she sang in the church choir on Sunday and Wednesday nights. When my mother died, the only flowers, other than mine, to adorn her grave were those left with the card: *My heartfelt condolences: Camille Philips.*

But that was before the horrible occurrence out by Bixby's Dairy that had shaken all of Baton Rouge to its very foundation. Indeed, the entire state of Louisiana had mourned. Mr. Ewing of the *New Orleans Stakes* had driven all the way from the city to offer his condolences—going so far as to volunteer a reward for any information regarding the identity of the animal who had so abused Camille. He'd declared that the perpetrator of such a crime was as detestable as Bonnie and Clyde and when caught ought to be hanged by the neck until dead. Personally, I longed to murder the bastard with my own hands.

But the guilty party was never caught; eventually the crime against Camille was eclipsed by the escalating worry over the sorry state of the economy. Now, as I stood with my feet planted firmly on Primrose soil, I had to know if the rumors passed on by men coming and going through Horan's jail had exaggerated Camille's . . . illness. Imagine my exhilaration the morning I looked up at the grand but deteriorating house adorning Primrose Lane, and focused my eyes on her image.

Camille appeared at her window, allowing me a glimpse of her pale face for the first time since she had arrived home from the institution. Her brother Don had sent her there, to the Alexandria Sanitarium, nigh on three years before—once she had recovered from the crime committed against her. Don had felt inclined to shelter her from the gossip by sending her away. But now that she was back, rumor flourished anew. Camille Philips was indeed crazy as a Betsy bug and silent as a mute. Instead of Primrose Princess, the whole of Baton Rouge now called her "Dummy."

"You gonna stand there and gawk at that idiot all day?" Marion Dressler whispered in my ear. "Dep'ty Carr is gonna whip you good if'n you don't snap to. He done looked down here twice, and he weren't happy."

"I ain't afraid of Deputy Carr," I returned and stepped away. "Just mind your own business, Marion, and I'll mind mine."

"That dummy ain't your business, and that's for sure. You go ogling Philips's sister and you're liable to get us—"

"Shut up." I swatted at him as if he were a mosquito buzzing 'round my gritty neck. "I'll kill any man who calls her dummy, and that includes you."

"I'm just sayin' that Philips will git us throwed out to Mosquito Alley if you stir up trouble. I declare he's gone crazy as his sister."

"What do you know about it?" I turned away from the house and surveyed the stark and shabby perimeters of Primrose Farm. "Any man would go crazy to lose all this. I remember when his fields were exploding with cotton."

"This whole countryside was explodin' in cotton. Philips ain't the only man to suffer. In case you ain't readin' the *Stakes,* the whole country is starvin'. Hell, up in Oklahoma folks' entire farms been buried under dust. Heard tell half the population has up and moved to California."

"When you ain't got much to start with you don't hurt so much when it's gone. On the other hand, those who lived like kings feel the hunger all the more."

I kicked a rock and looked back at the house. Camille remained framed by the window, her vacant stare making me a little nauseated. I don't know why, but I had the gut feeling that if I could only touch her I could somehow heal her.

The front door opened and Don's wife Dixie stepped out on the porch. She wore a flimsy orange frock with a black silk stole draped over her shoulders. An Empress Eugénie hat perched on her head like a parrot, hiding her bobbed black hair. Every man on the gang stopped what he was doing and stared, waiting. Sure enough, Dixie made a show of slowly dragging up her dress hem and adjusting her hose garter, giving us all a lingering glimpse of her knee.

"Now that's what I call a woman," Marion breathed. "I wonder if Don Philips knows how lucky he is."

"I reckon we couldn't tell Don nothing he doesn't already know about her," I replied. "A woman like that is pure trouble and heartache."

"Don't tell me you wouldn't have a go at her if you had the chance."

"I ain't ever gonna get the chance and neither are you, so there's no point in festering about it."

Dixie straightened and eased down her dress. Someone in the house called out her name, but Dixie chose to ignore him. She sashayed down the steps as if she were Lady Astor and made a beeline toward us.

Don exploded from the house. His face was purple as he paused on the ledge of the front porch and watched his wife priss toward the lot of sweating convicts. "Dixie, don't you walk away from me when I'm talkin' to you."

"You're not talking, Don. You're yelling," she tossed back.

"You're my wife, goddamn it. I mean to talk to you face to face."

"I declare that man's temper grows meaner by the day." She flashed the row of gawking, scrubby inmates a smile and adjusted the stole on her shoulders. The thin veins on her neck stood out slightly and her face appeared very white under the blotches of rouge on her cheeks. "Truth is, I've been meaning to come talk to you boys for a while now. I always said it pays to be sociable."

With the hobbles around our ankles causing us to stumble, we closed in like drones around a queen bee, no matter that Deputy Carr yelled for us to get back to work and her husband simmered where he remained on the porch, his big hands clenched at his sides. Most of us hadn't smelled a woman in years; even those of us born with a modicum of common sense and moral decency weren't about to let such an opportunity slide. But even as I pushed close enough to Dixie Philips to smell a hint of talc and sweet cologne I could not help but look beyond her to Don's face, to the wild misery and knowledge that hollowed out his eyes. The base and shameful instinct that she had roused in me vaporized like mist at the image he made: shoulders slumped, jaw slack, one hand clutching his shirt against his chest. I suddenly despised Dixie Philips; I despised myself for desiring a woman like her. Hell, a woman like her was the reason I was in jail in the first place.

I shuffled to a stump near the edge of the road. I sat there, elbows on my knees, disgusted by the sight of a woman as supposedly highfalutin as Dixie Philips flaunting herself to a bunch of convicts while her husband looked on. The buzzing of my fellow inmates, along with Deputy Carr's agitated threats to beat the first man to put a hand on the ''lady'' dwindled to a pinpoint as Don turned his agonized gaze on me. As on that day so many years before, when he had discovered that it was I who had delivered the anonymous valentine to his sister, the intensity of his recognition and acknowledgment made my heart skip a beat—only this time, I couldn't run like a coward into the swamps.

''My, my, but I do believe my eyes are deceiving me. That's not Myra Norton's boy, is it?''

Dixie looked right through the pressing bodies of my sweating companions and focused on me where I sat on the stump and mopped my brow with my forearm. My belly balled up with dread and anger and I was forced to take a deep gulp of the gritty air before replying. ''Yes. I'm Myra Norton's boy.''

''Myra's little Joey? That skinny little Joey who used to steal eggs from my henhouse?''

The inmates guffawed and elbowed one another. I only shook my head. ''I'm called Joe now, Mrs. Philips.''

Her eyelids went sleepy and she smiled with one side of her colored mouth. ''You've grown up,'' was all she said.

''Yes, I have. I'm twenty-two now.''

''Twenty-two. My, my, how time flies. Twenty-two and all grown up. A man now. Tell me . . . Joe. How is your mama these days? I suspect she's not too pleased that her boy is breaking rock for Sheriff Horan. She always said she expected you to do big things. I suppose robbing Toby's Mercantile is just about as big as you can get.''

"Your memory is short, I guess. My mama is dead, Mrs. Philips. She died four years ago.'' My jaw going hard and my eyes narrowing, I locked gazes with her and added, "I thank heaven every day that my mother isn't alive to see me doing time for a crime I didn't commit. I expect that if she hadn't dropped dead of a heart attack, her grief would have probably killed her.''

"Myra dead? Why, I had no idea. My condolences to your father. Oh . . . I forgot—again. Silly me. Your father ran off with that floozy who worked at Ed Cohen's gas station out on River Road, what, six, seven years ago?''

"Ten,'' I said through my teeth, "and you damn well know it, Mrs. Philips.''

Her penciled eyebrows lifted. She smiled, then moved close enough that her knee brushed mine. The hot, heavy air suddenly swirled with her smell—cologne tinged with feminine sweat—and despite my best attempts to divert my thoughts, my body went as hard as the sledge handle at my feet.

"You got a fire in you,'' she murmured low enough so the others couldn't hear. "You always did. I'm wondering just how hot it burns.''

"It'll be a cold day in hell before you ever find out . . . *Mrs.* Philips.''

She stared at me a full half minute, the flirtation in her eyes replaced with a coldness that made my skin crawl. Turning away, she glanced back only once, her eyes as glassy as two polished marbles.

I waited for Dixie to announce to everyone that my mother had scrubbed her floors back in '27 and '28. Dixie had always taken great pleasure is letting everyone in Baton Rouge know who she employed . . . and who she fired. Even as a kid I could never figure out how a family's life could be destroyed over the breaking of a simple teacup.

I glanced at the big white house and noted that Don Philips had retreated indoors. Then my gaze traveled up again to the window where Camille remained standing, her hands lightly pressed to the glass. She appeared to look directly at me, and I experienced a stab of familiar longing in my gut. My entire world became focused on her beautiful face, and a fierce anger filled me as I realized that, at long last, Camille Philips was looking *at* me. Not around me. Not beyond me, or over me, but *at* me. And here I sat, with chains coiled around my ankles, my hands bloody from busting rock.

I was dreaming of Camille when Marion woke me. Her melancholy and misty image metamorphosed into his grizzled, unshaven, pockmarked features as I struggled to open my eyes. "Is it dawn already?" I yawned and glanced toward the slit of a window near the ceiling. I couldn't wait to return to Primrose Lane . . . to see Camille again. I had dreamt throughout the night that I had laid my hand upon her head and healed her. The sudden realization that it had only been a dream drove a pain through my chest that made me groan.

"Naw," Marion muttered, then lay down on my bunk beside me, his lips near my ear. "I've been thinkin'," he whispered.

"Not much you haven't. Not if you've woke me up before daylight." My stomach churned with hunger and I cursed under my breath.

"I've come up with a plan to get us out of here."

I moved my head farther from his, then rolled, turning my back to him. "Go to bed, Marion, and quit thinkin'. I get tired of your thinkin' all the time."

"You know how that Philips woman has been prancin' about us lately, flashin' her gams and pissin' off her husband? I've noticed that Dep'ty Carr has got a real hard-on for her. Hell, he can't see nothin' but her when she's around. I've been thinkin' that soon as he gets distracted, we jump him—"

"You're crazier than I thought."

"We knock him on the head and take the keys—"

"And spend another ten years in this stinkin' hole? That's if we're lucky. Most likely Sheriff Horan would toss our carcasses to the gators for even contemplating a jail break. Just get away from me, Marion. My stint in this slime pit is over in another three months."

"You think Horan is gonna let you just sashay back to that shotgun shanty down in Hooverville you call home? He's got it in for you, Joe. He's gonna make you suffer for what you done to his little sister."

"I didn't do nothin' to her that another twelve guys haven't done since I've been in jail, and I'll tell him so."

"You do that. I'll make certain they carve those last words on your tombstone. I'm tellin' ya, boy: whispered word is that Horan's got plans for you. If you was smart, you'd get the hell out of Louisiana while you still got the legs to do it."

A door opened in the distance, allowing dim gray light to flow along the walk between the cells. Marion slithered smoothly as an eel out of my bunk and returned to his own. With my blanket pulled up to my chin, I lay in the semidark, senses tuned to the hollow ring of footsteps nearing my cell. I peered through the slits of my lashes at Horan's feet as he stopped outside my door.

"You. Boy. Git yo' lazy ass off that bunk and get dressed. You and me are takin' a ride."

There was no use in pretending not to hear him, so I tossed back the blanket and dropped my feet to the floor. I caught a glimpse of Marion's eyes as they reflected the light from the hallway. He looked at me as if I were already a corpse.

After slipping on my clothes and waiting for his assistant to shackle me, I preceded Horan out of the building, where I was shoved into the backseat of his car. The sun was just coming up as we sped along River Road, which skirted Baptiste Bayou. I refused to look toward the swamp with its intimidating murkiness and choking cypress trees, but with each bounce of the car Marion's words tapped upon my consciousness. Many a man had gone missing in the bayou. Many a woman, too.

I met Horan's gaze in the rearview mirror. His eyes had the appearance of a crocodile's, yellow as Mississippi mud. He grinned. "What's wrong, boy? You look like a snappin' turtle just caught hold of your balls."

I glanced at the chains around my ankles and wrists. No doubt about it, if the sadistic bastard decided to pitch me in the bayou then and there I wouldn't stand a snowball's chance in hell of surviving. "Mind telling me where we're headed?" I replied as casually as I could.

"Well now, if I thought that was any of your business I would've already told you."

"Seein' that it's my ass you're haulin' down this road like a bat out of hell, I reckon it *is* my business."

"You got a smart mouth on you, Norton. But you always did. You're just like your old man. That sorry som'bitch went out of his way to piss me off."

"That why you buried him out there?" I nodded toward the blurred bayou beyond the road; then my gaze slid back to his, briefly, before jumping to the sight of his big freckled hands gripping the steering wheel so hard his knuckles looked on the verge of popping right through his skin.

"You accusin' me of killin' yo' daddy?"

Horan's eyes narrowed with an expression somewhere between guilt and fury. The sick notion that the whispered rumors of my daddy's disappearance might be true rolled over inside of me.

"Well?" he sneered.

I shrugged. "Guess it don't matter one way or the other, does it? Maybe you killed him and maybe you didn't. Maybe it's true that he ran off with that slut Sally Pyle. Either way, he wasn't around to beat up my mother anymore. It saved me from killing him myself."

"If anybody killed your old man, boy, it was probably them damn bootleggers he ran with. And don't tell me you don't know what I'm talkin' about. You're as guilty of runnin' liquor as he was. Why don't you just come out and admit it?"

"And give you a reason to lock me up again?" I grinned and shook my head. "I might have been born poor and dumb, but I sure as hell ain't stupid. Fact is, soon as I'm free, I'm breakin' from this stinkin' town for good."

"Big talk. You and your old man was always full of it. Always smooth-talkin' the ladies—"

"Can't help it if we were born good-lookin' and charmin', Sheriff. Then again, if the 'ladies' round here didn't have the morals of alley cats, men like me and my daddy wouldn't have no fun at all, would we?''

Horan slammed on the brakes, causing the car to skid sideways and stir up a thick cloud of dust. He hurled himself partly over the seat and grabbed my throat, cutting off my air and driving me back into the cushion so hard my windpipe felt crushed.

"Filthy bastard. You callin' my sister an alley cat? Huh? Are you? Talk to me, you arrogant hyena. I'll rip out your fuckin' tongue.''

I tried to swallow, but my Adam's apple caught on his finger and wouldn't budge. In some corner of my mind where I was still rational enough to reason, I suspected that I had, at last, allowed my hot temper and razor-sharp wit to get the better of me.

At last, Horan released me. He sank back down in his seat while I drank in air and fought back the sense of nausea rising up my burning windpipe. Horan drove like a madman, skirting the edge of the road, careening on two wheels, barely missing a cow that had wandered through a break in a fence before racing over the dilapidated wagon bridge spanning Napoleon Creek. I thought about killing him, then and there: of just throwing my wrist chain around his fat neck and giving him a taste of what it felt like to choke to death. But I had been truthful in my comment: I might be dumb but I'm not stupid. Stupidity would have sent me to my grave right along with Horan. So I braced myself while Horan's tantrum spent itself.

As we left River Road and the countryside brightened under the rising sun, I breathed a silent sigh of relief that Horan obviously had no plans of disposing of me in the bogs—at least not that morning. It was then that I noted the surroundings, as familiar to me as the back of my own hand. I looked harder through the window, my breath a fog on the glass as we turned onto Primrose Lane. Ahead, Camille's house loomed on the horizon—a vision swathed in sleepy golden shafts and cascades of green. After a week of busting rock along Primrose Lane, the anticipation of seeing Camille again wasn't unfamiliar. It surged in my breast like a Fourth of July rocket.

Chapter Two

I stood in the grandiose foyer, only vaguely listening to the buzz of heated conversation coming from beyond the closed cypress doors directly in front of me. Only in my wildest imaginings did I ever think I would venture over Camille Philips's threshold, and when I *had* dreamt of such a moment it certainly had not materialized in an image of me drowning in my own sweat, my wrists and ankles shackled with chains.

Where was she? Would she sweep into the room at any moment and find me there, frightened as a nervous schoolboy, terrified of standing face-to-face with her at long last?

What was I doing here? Why had Horan brought me here? Had he somehow cracked open my skull and allowed my moronic fantasies to come pouring forth like trouble from Pandora's box? Perhaps he'd decided that the cruelest vindication he could heap upon me was to drag me before Camille and announce that I loved her. I visualized them all standing shoulder to shoulder around me, pointing and laughing and shaking their heads: *What hilarity! Imagine little Joey Norton from Shantytown, whose mother once scrubbed these very floors, having the audacity to contemplate a future with the Primrose Princess!*

The doors opened. Dixie Philips looked at me with high color on her cheeks. Sheriff Horan stood behind her, grim and obviously agitated. My first thought was that Dixie had brought me here for a reason: to retaliate for my snubbing her the day before.

"I brought you here today for a reason," she announced. "Don and I have been discussing with Sheriff Horan the possibility of a work release program for one or more of his prisoners. Against my better judgment, Don has chosen you. The sheriff isn't too happy about it, obviously, nor was I—until I saw you yesterday and realized you had turned into quite a . . . specimen." She licked her lower lip and looked me over. "I do believe you'll do nicely for my . . . needs."

"You're telling me that you brought me here to work?"

"I am."

"Here, on the grounds, and in the house?"

"I am."

I looked past her to Horan. His jaw looked as knotted as mangrove roots.

"You'll be living at Primrose," she went on. "In exchange for your food and board, you'll work. No more busting rock. Isn't that nice?"

Remaining silent, I glanced around the foyer. My gaze locked on a framed photograph of Camille. She smiled out at me, as she had in my more adolescent daydreams.

"Well?"

"All right," I heard myself say in a monotone of disbelief.

The hum of semiconsciousness buzzed in my head as Horan stepped forward and removed my shackles. Reality ebbed and flowed, and I wondered if I were really back in my jail cell still asleep and dreaming. All I could do was stare down at the seemingly radiant photo and think: *My God, I'll be surrounded by Camille's presence day and night.*

Horan moved into my line of vision. His face became the entire universe, his eyes two burning pockets of hatred. "I'll be keepin' my sights on you, boy. If you so much as pick your nose I'll be on you like white on rice. Do you understand me, boy?"

I nodded and bit back my overwhelming urge to spit in his face.

In a lower voice, he said, "I ain't done with you yet, Norton. Me and you got a score to settle. I ain't about to let some no-account white filth do to my sister what you done and get away with it."

Finally, Horan backed away and looked toward the front door where Dixie was waiting, her smile smug and taunting. Without another word, he left the house, the chains I had worn on my wrists and ankles for nearly three years swinging like pendulums from his hands. Dixie followed him to the car, leaving me to stand isolated in the foyer, my heartbeat so loud and hard that the air pulsated around my temples. I wanted to retch, but not here. Camille might see me.

God, God, her presence surrounded me and the urge to flee swallowed me. What would I do when I came face to face with her at last?

Someone touched my arm, and I jumped.

Dixie smiled up at me, though it was not a friendly smile. Neither were her eyes friendly. Her mask of makeup hid the creases in her face well from a distance, but standing that close she looked painted as a clown.

"He's gone," she said. "You can relax now." Her hand trailed up my arm; her fingers kneaded my shoulder. "You're hard as a brick, Joey. I guess all those long hours of busting rock have made a man of you."

"Why have you really brought me here, Mrs. Philips?"

She shrugged. "I told you. We need help around here, and thanks to the sorry state of the economy we can no longer afford to employ a man to keep up the grounds. Utilizing our overabundant source of prisoners was my husband's idea. I was opposed to it at first. After all, a lady of my class hardly desires to surround herself with trash. But that all changed yesterday, when I discovered you out front busting rock for Sheriff Horan."

I gave her a thin smile. "So after all these years you're gonna make me work to pay for those eggs I stole."

Her head fell back in husky laughter as she touched my hair with her fingertips. "You were a pretty child, Joe. You've made a handsome man. I always did like the way your hair streaked with sunlight in the summer. And those curls . . . how they always coiled slightly over your brow and temples, as if they were windblown. Odd how they magnify your masculinity. You're enough to make a woman lose her breath.''

I stepped away, just far enough that she couldn't touch me.

Laughing to herself, Dixie caught my arm and ushered me toward the parlor. Leaving me standing at the threshold, she moved gracefully to the far wall of French doors. The morning sun spilled through the window panes and made her body into a ghostly silhouette as she turned again to face me. ''You have a sense of humor. Good for you. We need some laughter around this dump. Since the farm went belly up soon after the crash it's been like living in a funeral home. And there's also the tedious situation with Camille. You *do* remember Camille, don't you?''

I swallowed hard and nodded. I didn't dare allow the effect her name had on me to show on my face.

''I assume you heard about her . . . accident.''

''What happened to Camille was no accident,'' I pointed out.

Dixie averted her eyes and shook her head. Her voice became thick with bitterness. ''Had she not been playing hooky she wouldn't have gotten herself in trouble.''

''I hardly think she went looking to get attacked.''

''You sound like my husband, always defending precious Camille. Camille can never do wrong. She virtually lights up a room when she enters it. Well . . . not anymore. What happened to Camille left her with the mental capacity of a worm. If Don had any kind of backbone he would have left her at the sanitarium, where she belongs. Instead, she skulks about this house like a phantom. I fear she's going to drive me as crazy as she is.''

An odd look came and went across Dixie's features; then she drew herself up and focused hard on my face. ''It'll be nice to have someone halfway intelligent to talk to again. You won't mind if I rely on you for passing conversation now and again . . . will you? This place is about as entertaining as a soup kitchen.''

''I imagine Mr. Philips wouldn't care to have his wife socializing with the likes of me.''

"He'll whine, of course. He always does. But then he whines about everything. When he's not whining he's lying up in his bed like an invalid. Hell, at times he's not even capable of making it down the stairs. Therefore, I'm perfectly free to entertain myself any way I please."

"Is Mr. Philips sick?"

"According to some people. That quack physician of his seems to think Don's heart is bad. I don't buy it. I think he's just depressed. He's financially ruined. We live in poverty these days which is a far cry from the gilded halls of mansions and vaults of money he once promised me."

I looked around. "This doesn't look too bad from my perspective. Besides, you shouldn't take destitution too personally. It's not like you were the only family to be hurt the last few years."

Dixie strolled toward me, her mouth a flat line. "I didn't bring you here to act as my conscience, Joey boy."

"Why *did* you agree to bring me here, Mrs. Philips?"

She moved past me and stopped at the doorway, regarding me up and down before shrugging. "Maybe I want to make up for firing your mama like I did. Then again, it's not as if she didn't deserve being let go. That cup and saucer she broke had been in my family for a hundred years."

"Bitch," I said under my breath, and Dixie grinned.

"You hate me, don't you, Joey boy? It's all right, you know. It's natural for white trash to envy us. The few times I saw you with your mama you looked at me as if I was a pissant that you'd like to squash. You were a child, yet the only human being I know who could make me feel as low as a maggot just because I employed your mama to scrub my floors. It's something about your eyes, I think. Indigo blue. Deep as dark wells. Those eyes tell the world just exactly what's going on inside of you, Joey boy . . . what you're thinking; what you're feeling. Right now you'd like to kill me, wouldn't you?"

"No, ma'am. You're not worth getting hanged over."

She didn't so much as blink; she just lifted her chin the slightest bit and turned away.

•   •   •

Pearl Jones, a Negro with the stature of a small mountain, showed me to my living quarters—after she wrapped her big arms around me and squeezed so tight I nearly passed out. She had worked for the Philips family for forty years, as had her parents and grandparents before that. More than once she'd scrubbed floors next to my mother. On more than one occasion she had sneaked me peppermints and lemon drops, and an occasional oat cake. And after Dixie had fired my mother, Pearl delivered an occasional meal to our doorstep. She'd supplied the bundles anonymously, but we knew who had left them. Nobody in the entire parish could cook as well as Pearl.

We walked down an overgrown path, toward a cluster of ramshackle outbuildings made of logs that were chinked with mud. Their corrugated metal roofs radiated the summer heat like the inside of a woodstove.

"I never would have thought to see you in no chain gang," Pearl said.

"I didn't rob Toby's Mercantile, Pearl. Everybody in this town knows Horan set me up. Toby gave me my first job—even helped out my mother after Dixie fired her. No way in hell would I have stuck a gun in his face and robbed him."

"Ever'body knowed you to be innocent, hon. Mr. Don himself tol' me not six months ago dat he thought you been railroaded by Horan. It just a right shame dat d'judge didn't see it dat way."

"He's Horan's first cousin."

Pearl grunted and dabbed her sweating face with a red bandanna. "You was messin' with Horan's sister, Joe. What did you expect?"

"Hell, I don't know. You know me, Pearl. I got a crazy streak that runs through me now and again. I'm a lot like my old man in that way, I guess."

"Ain't nobody as crazy as yo' daddy." She chuckled and shook her head. "He had the principles of a tomcat, but he sho' was good-lookin'. Ain't a woman in dis parish or any other who wouldn't have minded to cozy up to him on a cold night."

"By the sounds of it, every woman in this parish did exactly that," I replied.

"Never you mind. Dat's all in d'past now, may his and yo' mama's souls rest in peace."

We stepped into the rustic domicile with its dirt floor and solitary window. The air smelled stagnant. Cobwebs fluttered in the corners and deserted wasp nests hung like paper stalactites from the overhead beams.

"Home sweet home," I muttered under my breath.

"Better dan Horan's jail cell, I 'spect."

"Not much."

Pearl walked to the cot against the far wall and jerked off the soiled pillow and sheets. She mumbled to herself, something about not fit for white trash and she had a good mind to tell Dixie as much. With her big arms wrapped around the dirty linens, Pearl then focused hard on me, where I remained near the closed screen door, shoulder propped against the wall and my hands in my pockets.

"I got a bad feelin' 'bout all dis. I 'spect Dixie done brought you here for a reason other dan prunin' her bushes."

"I got a feelin' you're right, Pearl."

"Dat woman never do anything widout a reason, and it's usually bad. By d'looks of ya, and d'way you done filled out dem britches, I'd say I know what she's got in store fo' you."

"She's going to be in for a real disappointment then. We both know there's only one woman on this farm I care for."

"You still bad on Camille, Joey? Aw, don't even bother to answer. It's written all over yo' face. Won't do you any good, boy. You know she ain't been d'same since d'incident."

"I'd hoped the rumors were exaggerated."

"She ain't spoken a word since Mr. Don found her out at Bixby's Dairy. It's as if somethin' just took hold of her throat and won't let go. It's 'bout to drive Dixie crazy."

"Dixie's already crazy."

"And gittin' crazier by d'day. Dat's what bothers me most. She want to send dat child back to dat crazy house. I tol' Mr. Don dat if he do dat, Miss Camille will die fo' sure. Lawd, she ain't but a shadow of herself as it is."

"I know. I've seen her . . . through the window. If I could get my hands on whoever hurt her I'd kill him for sure."

"I 'spect whoever done dat is long gone."

"Maybe. I've had a long time to sit and think about what happened, and the idea that she was attacked by some stranger just doesn't feel right. It ain't as if Primrose Lane is crawlin' with outsiders . . . is it? I'm thinkin' she knew him or she never would have gotten close enough for him to catch her."

Frowning, Pearl moved past me and kicked open the screen door with her foot before looking around. "What's done is done, Joe. No need stirrin' up d'past. Mr. Don couldn't take much more stress—not as bad as his heart is dese days. Lawd he'p us all if he was to up and die. Now git yo'self washed. Pearl is gonna fatten you up and put a gleam back in dem blue eyes."

I soon learned that my responsibilities were limitless. I was to keep the grounds, take care of the livestock, which were dwindling daily, and handle any and all repairs around the house. My first assigned chore was to clean the chicken coops. As I stood outside the fetid pen, it occurred to me that freedom lay stretched out before me—beyond the deserted outbuildings and animal paddocks. There were no shackles on my ankles any longer. No guard stood behind me with an itch to blow my brains out if I so much as stumbled. There was only the sun baking down on my shoulders, and the wind in my face.

Freedom. The word rang like chimes in my head. The muck fork fell from my hands and my legs began to move with a will of their own. Before me the land undulated like green waves, beckoning. Faster and faster I moved, my body tense as I anticipated the retribution of the guards—reminding myself there were no guards—run! *Faster!* Until my lungs burned. Until my legs felt as if they were ripping apart in pain. I leapt one fence, then another. I tripped and stumbled, then ran again, faster, until the world was a green blur. I struck out across the vast, grim, weed-infested furrows where cotton had once grown as thick as snow drifts—where once I had hidden and watched dozens of sharecroppers pluck the fluffy bolls with their callused fingertips and shove them into coarse sacks that draped from their stooped shoulders. I ran until Primrose House was nothing more than a tiny dim shape on the horizon; then I fell to my knees and dug my fingers into the rich, black dirt, knowing even as I gasped for breath in the shimmering heat that I would return to Primrose for one reason . . . and one reason only.

My legs felt heavy as stones by the time I dropped onto the shaded grass just yards from Primrose House. Lying on my back, breathing deeply of the magnolia-scented air, I was barraged by memories—when Primrose was the finest plantation in Louisiana. How long had it been since I had last smelled the magnolias?

I realized in that moment that someone stood on the veranda above, looking down at me. My breath caught.

"Camille." I whispered the name.

Dare I move? She might flee. Dare I speak? I might frighten her. Besides, it wasn't my place to address her.

What emotion did I read in her face? Recognition? Confusion? . . . Pleasure?

Hope?

I sat up, as cautious as one in the presence of a fawn, mesmerized by the incredible beauty and gentleness of its nature. I swept the blades of grass from my damp body and raked my fingers through my disheveled hair. My mouth felt dry. My chest filled with an exhilaration that made my heart trip.

Her hand lifted briefly. Had she waved?

I scrambled to my feet and dusted leaves from my knees. I hastened to button my shirt, then tucked it into my trousers. The need to speak to her made me shake, and the ache to scramble up the rose trellis and at long last touch her cheek overwhelmed me.

"Is she why you came back?" asked the masculine voice behind me.

I spun around, prepared to defend myself if necessary. Hands fisted, legs spread, I glared into Don Philips's eyes and felt my heart contract. How long had he been there, watching me watch his sister?

Don sat in a garden chair, one leg crossed over the other, a broad-brimmed straw hat tugged down to shield his eyes, which looked as faded as old denim. He had the look of a man much older than his thirty-five years. His skin resembled leather. His hands were gnarled and scarred by the sharp cotton husks he had cultivated since he was old enough to plow. He regarded me no differently than he had those years ago, when he had discovered my valentine card to Camille propped against his front door. There was a knowledge there that made my face burn with discomfort—only this time there could be no escape.

"You could have kept running, you know. Hell, the swamps beyond my land are havens for men who have the desire to lose themselves. There have been times, when the reality of life threatened to drown me, that I've thought of running there myself."

"I'm not anxious to get shot in the back by Sheriff Horan," I replied matter-of-factly. "And I never much cared for getting swallowed up by quicksand."

"There's more than one kind of quicksand that can swallow up a man, boy. Best you be learning that while you're young. Although judging by the way you look at my sister, I suspect you already know that."

I backed away and nervously opened and closed my hands.

Don rubbed his chest as a look of disquietude came and went over his features, then he shook his head. "It's hell loving a woman—especially the ones who have the capability of looking right through you. I often think they take pleasure in the misery they cause us."

"Camille's not like that," I argued. "She would never intentionally hurt anyone. Everyone who knew her loved her. They still do. She's the kindest girl in this entire parish."

"People call her an idiot."

I took a threatening step toward him, my fists slightly raised. "No one calls Camille an idiot."

"Then what *do* you call someone who neither hears nor speaks . . . who walks through life like a zombie?"

I looked up toward the balcony where Camille had stood earlier. Thank God, she was gone.

Turning on Philips again, my anger heightened, I said, "Camille is not an idiot. I don't believe it. A man with any sense of compassion and love would lay down his life to protect her name and reputation."

"Love has nothing to do with this, Joe."

"Love has everything to do with it, Mr. Philips."

He regarded me without blinking or speaking, then he left the chair and walked to the back porch steps. His hands in his pockets, he stared down at his muddied and patched boots as if lost in deep thought. "Never think for a moment that I don't love my sister," he finally said. "But occasionally we all have to make choices. You just made one of the biggest choices you'll ever make by choosing to return to Primrose. You could have kept running, but you made the choice to live up to your responsibilities, not to mention your feelings for Camille." He smiled wearily. "Don't look as if someone just goosed you with a cattle prod, boy. I knew you were sweet on my sister before you ever left that valentine on my doorstep. Me and your mama talked about it occasionally, when Dixie didn't have her scrubbing commodes or floors. Sometimes, when the air was too damn thick to breathe and Dixie was off attending her club functions, I'd invite Myra to sit with me a spell on this very porch. We'd drink iced tea with mint sprigs and discuss worldly matters. Sometimes she'd weep a little over the fact that a boy with your intelligence and sense of goodness would never get the chance to make something of himself. She knew she could scrub floors until she was ninety and never save up the money to send you to the university. She suspected that eventually trouble would come looking for you—and by the looks of things, it did."

"I didn't rob Toby's store, Mr. Philips."

"If I thought for a minute that you had, I wouldn't have brought you here, Joe, to live and work on Primrose."

Don turned his blue-denim eyes on me again, then laid his heavy hand on my shoulder. In that instant the lines in his face softened, and his lips turned up ever so subtly. "I made your mother a promise that I aim to keep: I told her once that if there was anything I could ever do to help the two of you in any way, that I would do it." With a short laugh, he added, "I trust neither of us will regret it."

As he wearily mounted the steps, I followed, bringing him to a stop as I said, "Are you going to send Camille back to the hospital because she's sick, or because Dixie has threatened to leave you if you don't? Camille's not crazy. And she isn't dumb. If you allow Dixie to send her back to Alexandria you're as guilty of destroying Camille as the bastard who attacked her.''

His head snapped around and he stared at me with blood-shot eyes, but just when it seemed he might explode, the anger suddenly drained from his body. Without another word, he entered the house.

Sprawled on my cot, sweat running down my sides, I thought of Marion, curled up on his rock-hard little slab of a bed, dreaming of freedom. With my belly full of Pearl's fried chicken and biscuits, I thought the only thing that could make that moment any better would be to have Camille at my side.

I groaned and covered my face with the pillow.

Don't think about her. Stop believing that you're her savior—that you were brought to Primrose for a reason and that reason was to rescue her from Dixie's cruelty and Don's indecisiveness.

My mind drifted and I was back in my cell again, doing my best to ignore my empty aching belly, attempting to sleep in the cloistering perimeters of my dingy little hole that smelled of sweat and urine. Voices came to me, booming like distant thunder, pounding with anger and threats. Others joined in until the hot night teemed with howls that sounded like coyotes yapping over a kill. I saw myself leave my cot and walk to the wall of rusted iron bars, gripping them in my hands so fiercely that my fingers ached. I stared down the dimly lit corridor of cells and shouted, ''Shut up! I want to sleep, damn you. Just shut the hell up!'' Then out of the darkness loomed Sheriff Horan, a gun in one hand. He pointed it straight at my head and pulled the trigger.

The dream shattered like exploding glass. I sat up in bed, gasping for breath, my arms thrown up to shield my head. A moment passed and I opened my eyes.

No cell. No Sheriff Horan.

But there were voices: high-pitched, yowling like raging tomcats. Amid it all was music—blasting, a cacophony of shrieking instruments that made the air vibrate against my ears. I rolled from bed and pulled on my pants, stepped into the scented night air and shivered as it wrapped around me. Barefoot, I ran through the damp grass toward the house, dodging the pools of light spilling through the open windows, drawn toward the escalating sounds of anger punctuated by Bing Crosby's singing "Brother, Can You Spare a Dime?"

The louvered French doors leading to a veranda surrounded by wisteria and honeysuckle vines were open. I sidled up next to the door and looked in just as Don Philips grabbed his wife by the shoulders and shook her.

"I won't have you talking about Camille that way, Dixie. I won't have you treating her like she's no-account and stupid."

"I'll treat her any damn way I want. If you don't like it, then get her the hell away from here. Why should I tolerate some dummy upsetting my lifestyle? I can't walk down the streets and hold my head up because everyone in this stinking town is pointing and talking about the 'Dummy of Primrose Lane.' They laugh at us, Don. I simply won't abide it any longer."

"You got no say-so in it, Dixie. Camille is my sister and Primrose House is my home. It has been for two hundred years and that ain't going to change because you can't handle a little gossip."

"A little gossip? You're as stupid as she is if you think we aren't an object of ridicule in this town."

"If there's any ridicule of us, Dixie, it's because you continue to sashay around dressed like a floozy and spending money we don't have while the rest of the town is having to steal just to feed their babies."

Dixie laughed softly and pressed her partially clothed body closer to Don's. She drew his hand across her breast, then down her stomach to the dark shadow between her legs. "I thought you liked the way I dress, darling."

"You got no business dressing like that for anyone but me. I can't stand the idea of other men desiring you."

"But that's what attracted you to me in the first place, isn't it, sweetheart? You liked the idea of flaunting me in front of your friends. It made you feel like a big man."

He pulled her hard against him, his fingers digging into

her bare arms. "Damn you, Dixie, I know what you're trying to do. But it won't work this time. I ain't agreein' to ship Camille off again until I'm certain there is nothin' more we can do for her."

Dixie shoved Don hard, her face becoming savage. "I'm damn tired of my life being controlled by your sister. Every time I look up, she's staring at me with those crazy eyes. Fact is, darling, I'm damn tired of you. I'm tired of your false promises of how glorious life is going to be living at Primrose Farm. I've got news for you, big man—living on this farm is hell, and marriage to you is even worse."

Don's face turned white. He sounded like a man choking. "Don't be talking like that, Dixie. You don't mean that."

"Yes I do," she hissed. "I mean every word of it. Why don't you just do us both a favor and give me a divorce? Let me go, Don. If you really love me you won't condemn me to a life that will only destroy us both."

"Never. We vowed till death do us part and I ain't a man who goes back on his word to God. Besides, soon as this depression is over, things will be good again, for the farm and us as well. Once we have money again you'll see things differently."

"Fool. We'll never have money again."

"We will if you'll quit buying on credit."

"I have to get something out of this stinking marriage. I'm not about to give up what I've got just to spare a bunch of beggars their feelings."

"We ain't got anything anymore," Don shouted. "It's gone, Dixie. The only thing that makes us any different than anyone else is this house. Hell, the way you keep spending we won't even have that much longer. I'm just one step away from having to go on relief, and you know what that means: the government puts a lien on this house. I won't be known as a freeloader and bum."

Dixie laughed. "My goodness, you *do* have a penchant for embellishment, don't you?"

"How the hell am I supposed to pay that bill I just got from Loraine's Dress Shop?"

"I need those clothes."

"Why? So you can look pretty for those fancy men in

their fancy cars who drop by the Gator Shack to see you wait tables?''

"*They* have class. *They* appreciate me. *They* look at me like I'm a woman instead of some drab little housemaid.''

"Don't you be talkin' like that, Dixie. You know I think you're the prettiest woman in all of Louisiana. I always have. There ain't a day I don't count my lucky stars that you're mine.''

"You got a funny way of showing it.''

"What am I supposed to do? If I had it to give, you know I'd give it. I always did.'' Don laid one hand against the side of Dixie's flushed face. "I love you, Dixie. You're the most important thing in my life. I'm not sure what I'd do if I thought I might lose you to someone else.''

"That kind of talk scares me.'' She shoved his hand aside and backed away.

"It's just fair warning, Dixie. I'd just as soon see us *both* dead than to see you with another man.''

"I'll say this one more time . . . if you truly love me, you'll send your sister back to the sanitarium where she belongs. She frightens me. You know she never cared for me in the first place.''

"Camille ain't dangerous, Dixie.''

"Are you certain? Who knows what's going on in her head? She could be holed up in her room right now planning on ways to get rid of me.''

"No. No.'' He shook his head adamantly. "Not Camille. She's not like that. She's not capable.''

"Are you willing to risk my life on that assumption?''

I turned away as Dixie went up on her toes to press a kiss on Don's lips. It was then my gaze locked on Camille.

She huddled in a cluster of honeysuckle near the veranda. Reality became a vortex swirling into a solitary point of light, illuminating her haunted eyes. Her fear and pain struck me like a cudgel, before her raw emotions were replaced by the vacancy of her affliction; then she dove into the bushes and scrambled for escape.

I pursued her without thinking of the possible consequences.

I caught her as she attempted to mount the back porch

steps. She fought wildly as I carried her through the dark toward my house. "Hush," I said. "I swear I won't hurt you. Be still and stop struggling."

Kicking open the screen door, I dragged her over the threshold just as she tore herself away and fell hard onto the floor. She made a sound like a whimpering dog as she attempted to dive past me for the door.

I pulled her to her feet and up against me, wrapping both of my arms around her as she beat my chest. "Stop it, Camille. I won't hurt you, I swear to God. I want to help you. Please, listen to me . . ."

Holding her tighter, cradling the back of her head with one hand, I pressed her face against my shoulder and rocked her against her will. "Don't be afraid of me, Camille. I'm not like those others. I don't want them to send you away. They won't if I have anything to do with it."

Little by little, her struggling eased. I continued to hold her tightly—so tightly—as if she could somehow absorb the strength I felt in my body at that moment. As she gradually melted against me and her trembling subsided, I closed my eyes, shaken by the realization that, at long last, I was holding Camille in my arms.

Chapter Three

I regarded Camille's emotionless features, and her eyes that were no longer wide with fear. Her lids heavy, her lips slightly parted, she stared through me as if I were vapor. As I tipped up her chin with my finger, I lightly bathed the tear streaks from her cheeks and allowed myself to smile with the realization that her skin felt as smooth as I had always imagined. I traced the curvature of her jaw with my fingertip, and noted the darkness of my skin against hers. Her pale hair was as soft and fine as angel's breath.

"You're beautiful," I whispered. "Like dawn fire on a golden pond. I suppose I'll die an old man still believing you're the prettiest woman God ever created."

Turning away, I took an uneven breath before laughing to myself. "You can't imagine how many times I've wanted to tell you that. I rehearsed it over and over in my mind all these years, never quite getting it right, at least in my own mind. Now I've said it, and it wasn't so hard or scary, after all."

Her presence hummed like electricity around me. My skin burned. My senses roused to dagger points of pain as I dropped into a cane-seated chair against the far wall and raked my hands through my hair. I didn't dare allow myself to stay near her. I didn't trust myself not to purposefully take her in my arms again.

Submerged in night sounds and the heavy perfume of dew-laden magnolias, I floated in her silence. I was content, for the moment, to wrap myself up in her companionship, to absorb every minute detail of her face and body: the texture of her skin, the moistness of her mouth, the whiteness of her eyes, the way the lamplight reflected from her honey-colored lashes. Yet as I sat there, adrift in the sublimity, the realization came to me that moments before she had wept. That her eyes had snapped with fear. That she had huddled in the bushes outside that veranda with the intent of listening to Dixie and Don's conversation . . . and understood it.

Cautiously, I pulled my chair closer to her. She did not so much as blink as I placed one fingertip lightly upon her lower lip. "I can remember when these lips smiled. There wasn't a time when I saw you that you weren't smiling. I think you even smiled at me a time or two. I could never be sure. But I hoped . . .

"I suspect they could smile now, if you tried. Will you smile for me, Camille?"

I held my breath and waited. The silence and heat of the night pressed in on me, causing my body to sweat and my mouth to go dry. I searched every little nuance of her face, desperate for any sign that I had reached her.

"I know you can hear me. If you were oblivious to reality, like the world believes you are, you wouldn't have been hiding in those bushes, listening to Don and Dixie argue about you. There wouldn't be tear tracks on your face now. You wouldn't have been trembling from the possibility of their sending you off to the sanitarium again."

Sliding my fingers through her hair, curling my hand around her nape, I drew her closer, so close that the need to touch my lips to hers filled me with an ache so intense I began to shake. Her skin smelled like roses, her breath like mint.

"What are you hiding from?" I whispered. "What are you frightened of? I won't hurt you. I would never hurt you."

The minutes ticked by and still she gave no sign of having acknowledged me. At last, I took her arm and helped her to stand. I walked her through the dark, to the back door where I reluctantly left her standing on the porch, her face as white as the moon overhead.

By noon of the next day the temperature had grown miserably hot, the air suffocating. I did my best to focus my thoughts on the previous night. My frustration mounted as I recalled Camille's unwillingness to rouse from her torpid state. Why could I not shake the feeling that there was more to her withdrawal from reality than was apparent on the surface?

I cut the overgrown hedges lining the path to the gazebo that overlooked a lily-crowded pond. I had removed my shirt hours before and my skin was fast becoming flushed by the sun's intense rays. The flesh on my hands and arms bled from the ragged, razor-sharp edges of rosebushes and cattails crowding the gazebo. As I paused momentarily to wipe the blood from my hands, I heard a rattling in the weeds and looked up.

Camille stood in a small clearing beyond the gazebo, her gaze locked on me, her eyes bright. For an instant she was the Camille of years ago, her face radiant, her expression open and inviting. We regarded one another across the deck of the gazebo, neither of us moving, my mind whirling with a thousand reasons why she would be here, watching me. Was her very presence not an open invitation to somehow try to communicate with her again? Were not those luminous blue eyes, which had reflected little more than complete lifelessness in my presence the night before, now flashing with a kind of boldness that made my heart quicken?

"Hello," I called softly.

She flinched and stepped back, as if she might flee.

"No! Don't go. I was just thinking about you. About last night. About how much I enjoyed talking to you."

Slightly tipping her head, she looked me up and down, her brows knitting as she regarded my naked torso. I snatched up my shirt, which I had tossed over the gazebo rail, and dragged it on, drawing it closed over my chest. Immediately

it became blotched with sweat and streaked with the blood
from my hands and arms. As I fumbled with the buttons, I
grinned and shrugged. "I wasn't expecting company. Obviously. Guess I've been working around that lot of cutthroats
at the jail too long. One has a tendency to forget after a while
that there might be a lady present. You can bet there aren't
any ladies like you down at Horan's hellhole. I guess you
already know that I'm on Sheriff Horan's road gang . . . or
was. I saw you staring at me one day from your window."

I crossed my arms and propped my shoulder against the
gazebo. My throat felt as tight as a fist as I attempted to act
as nonchalant as possible in her company. Though she made
no indication that she understood a solitary word I was saying, I felt deep in my heart that she did. Why else would she
be there? Her happening upon me in this remote area might
have been happenstance, but I doubted it.

Scanning the overgrown pond and the scaling garden
house, I said, "It's a real shame to see this gazebo deteriorate. I always thought it was the prettiest, most serene place
on Primrose Farm. I recall a time when you used to sit there
on that bench and eat cucumber sandwiches. You wore a
magnolia behind your ear. You'd toss bread crumbs to the
fish. Occasionally you'd read from a book. A time or two
you came here with boys. You made them sit all the way
across the gazebo from you so they wouldn't get the wrong
idea about your character. I always imagined sitting here with
you. I hate cucumbers, but I would have stomached them
just to be able to share your sandwich."

I swallowed, shifted my weight, and gripped my arms
more tightly across my chest. "You probably wonder how I
know so much about you. I used to walk my mother to work
every morning. She used to keep house for Dixie—back six,
seven years ago. Maybe you remember her . . . Myra Norton?"

Watching Camille closely, I waited for some flicker of
recognition. Still, there was nothing. "You probably never
noticed me. You were always so busy with your friends and
volunteer work." I grinned. "I used to go to church on
Wednesday nights, along with half the other boys in Baton
Rouge, just to hear you sing. I don't think any of us cared

much about what the preacher had to say. I always sat in the very back pew. I don't suppose the others would have cared much to have the likes of me joining them.

"I stopped coming around after Dixie fired my mother for breaking a china cup and saucer. You were kind enough to bring food over, hoping it would tide us over until my mother found other work. I remember that you wore a pale yellow dress that day, and a strand of pearls . . ."

The whir of insects pulsated in the hot air as my mind drifted back to the day my mother had arrived home from work early, her weary eyes red and swollen from crying, and announced that she no longer had a job. Filled with outrage, I had threatened to storm into Dixie's fancy dining room and pulverize every one of her goddamn china dishes. Only one thing had kept me from it . . . the prospect of somehow hurting Camille.

Closing my eyes, I took a deep breath and did my best to relax. I focused on the heat baking down on the back of my neck, the heavy air that seemed to slide as thick as cane syrup into my lungs, the solitary bee buzzing from one butter-yellow water lily to another. At last, I cleared my throat and ran one hand up a step rail, causing bits of peeling white paint to drift like snowflakes to the ground. "It's a real shame letting something so beautiful go to ruin. I suspect that with a little care she'd be just as pretty as she was back when you shared cucumber sandwiches with the fish. Maybe that's what I'll do on my time off. I'll peel away this old paint and cut away these cattails; maybe replace a few floor-boards so you don't fall through. If you've got nothing better to do, maybe you'll come down and keep me company . . ."

I looked to the place where Camille had been standing; she was gone.

There was a noise behind me, and I turned on my heels, coming face to face with Dixie. Her eyes were round, as cold as crystallized limestone.

"Where the hell have you been?" she demanded. "I've been calling for you for the last half-hour."

"Hedging," I replied. "Just like you told me."

"I meant the hedges down the front drive. Jesus, I was just on the verge of sending for Sheriff Horan."

"You might try being a little more specific, Mrs. Philips."
I reached for the hedge clippers.

"I could still send for him," she added spitefully, "if I
thought you were up to no good."

"Now what would give you that idea, Mrs. Philips?"

Pursing her lips, she regarded me with a keen sense of
speculation, her gaze inching its way from the top of my
head to my knees and up again. "You were talking with
someone," she finally said. "Who was it?"

"Camille."

She slapped my face. "I'll send you back to rot in that
disgusting pit of criminals for lying to me, Joey boy. Now
tell me who you were talking to."

With my cheek burning and my teeth clenched, I didn't
so much as blink as I looked her straight in the eye and
repeated, "Camille."

"Camille is an idiot. No one talks to Camille. And do you
know why? Because they could get more response out of a
mud brick, that's why. If I have my way she'll be out of
here by the end of the month and back in that damn sanitarium where she belongs."

I attempted to step around her. Her nails sank into my arm
as she grabbed me. "If it wasn't for me you'd be out front
with your felonious friends breaking your back busting rock.
You'd be smelling like a cesspit instead of soap. Your belly
would be gaunt and growling instead of packed with Pearl's
biscuits and cream gravy. That's right, Joey boy, I can send
you back to Horan's pit of snakes if I so desire. So you'd
better be nice or you'll regret it." She smiled and stepped
closer—so close that the tips of her breasts brushed my chest
and the scent of her heavy perfume wrapped around me in
a nauseatingly sweet cloud. "Play your cards right, Joe, and
maybe I'll talk to Horan about springing you early."

"What the hell are you up to, Dixie?"

"Maybe I want to make up for what I did to your mama."

I laughed and shook my head. "You don't strike me as
the kind of woman who would lose a minute of sleep out of
guilt."

"Maybe you don't give me the credit I deserve." She ran
one hand up my shoulder, lightly tracing a finger along the

line of my jaw. "Or maybe I just like you, Joey boy. Maybe I like the way you look in a pair of britches. You fill 'em out real nice. You've grown up to be quite a man, haven't you?"

I shoved her hand away. "If you're wanting a man between your legs, Dixie, I suggest you go look for your husband."

"And what if I tell you that unless you cooperate I'll send you back to jail?"

"Mrs. Philips, I'd rather rot the rest of my life in that hole than spend one minute in your bed."

Her eyes widened briefly, then narrowed. "You've got a lot of brass for a kid whose mama scrubbed my commodes. You're a lot like her, I think. All full up of dignity even though she was good for nothing more than sanitizing my bathrooms. You can see where her dignity got her." Laughing, she turned away and walked partially up the path before pausing and looking back. "By the way, you stay away from Camille. If you so much as sniff her way you'll regret it. Now get your tight little ass into some clean britches and bring up my car. It seems my husband isn't feeling up to driving me into town and suggested that you might like to do the honors." Her lips curling, she added, "Just don't go getting any ideas of using my car to take a quick trip over the state line, Joey boy. In Sheriff Horan's parish, car stealing is just one step away from murder. I suspect you'd be caught before you could reach Mississippi."

I waited until Dixie had disappeared beyond the overgrown hedge before turning back to the place where Camille had watched me earlier. I couldn't shake the feeling that she was there, somewhere, listening, and that she had seen everything that had transpired between me and Dixie.

I waited for Dixie outside McCormick's Furniture and Appliance, my stomach as tight as a fist and the sense that I was fast becoming overwhelmed by my freedom making my head pound. For the last three years I had known little other than my jail cell or the road on which I had been busting rock. My only companion had been my cellmate or the men working on either side of me on the road gang.

As I leaned back against Don's '29 Duesenberg convertible coupe, feeling the heat of the sidewalk ooze up through the thin soles of my shoes, I watched the faces of men and women as they moved like zombies up and down the mostly deserted sidewalks. They faintly resembled people I had known, but just as the business façades showed signs of disrepair, and despair, Baton Rouge residents reflected the threadbare and weary mask of desperation . . . and hopelessness. They looked straight through me as they clutched their meager parcels to their bosoms and went about their daily struggle to survive their mounting destitution. Their poverty showed in the droop of their shoulders and the look in their eyes—furtive, expectant, and resentful as they regarded the highly polished brown-and-yellow convertible parked at the curb. The car's orange stripes and wheels, along with its glossy black fenders, shouted Dixie's pretentious display of wealth.

Hot and weary of the wait, I stepped into McCormick's, hesitating as the stagnant air flooded over me. The dim light made my eyes ache. I was forced to squint to see Dixie in the back of the store, perched on a countertop, skirt hiked and exposing rolled stockings just below her knees. She swung her legs in rhythm with the music playing on a nearby radio.

"Joey!" she called, and waved. "Come see what I've just bought."

Hands in my pockets, I moved across the room. A rake-thin man grinned at me from a cubicle cluttered with file chests and a desk. The light bulb swaying at the end of a wire spat out only enough illumination to hollow the clerk's face with shadows. "Nice sound, ain't it?" he declared. "Can't beat an Atwater for quality. Take a gander at the cabinet. Solid walnut. You won't find another radio this nice outside of New Orleans."

I listened to a Glenn Miller song, then I looked at Dixie. "I suspect Don won't be too happy about it."

"Don's never too happy about anything these days. If I waited until Don was happy about something I'd be waiting for the rest of my life."

"A person could buy a lot of food or decent clothes for what that'll cost you."

"I have twenty-six clean and pressed dresses in my closet this very minute. I don't need more clothes. What I do need is something—or someone—to alleviate the tediousness of my life."

"Is that what I am . . . your attempt to 'alleviate the tediousness of your life?' "

"You're a smart boy. What do you think?" Flashing the clerk a smile, Dixie said, "Have the radio delivered to Primrose this evening."

The clerk nodded as Dixie slipped from the countertop and took hold of my arm, wrapping it around her waist as she slid up against me. As her body moved to the music I was caught between the desire to strangle her and the rousing lust that turned my disloyal body hot and as hard as stone. I moved with her until the song ended and a man's voice boomed out his thanks to Glenn Miller, then proceeded to invite people to stay tuned for the next program, sponsored by Quaker Oats Cereal—the cereal for sound minds and wholesome hearts.

Dixie waited tables at Thibodaux's Catfish and Gator Shack every Friday and Saturday night. Partially obscured by cypress trees and perched on the marshy banks of the Bayou Goula, it was a four-room shanty that served poor-quality food to the passersby on their way to New Orleans. Conrad Thibodaux ran poker games in one of the back rooms. Out back of the shack, just inside the line of cypress and mangrove trees, he cooked bootleg whiskey and ran biweekly cockfights.

Conrad seemed pleased to see me when I followed Dixie into the joint. He limped over to me and slapped me on the back. "Ho damn, me Joe man, you be done wid Horan, *oui?*"

"Naw," I told him. "I'm on work leave."

"Dat's a dog shame. You gon' be out soon, *oui?*"

"*Oui.*" I grinned. "Soon."

Sticking his grizzled old face close to mine, he frowned and motioned toward Dixie, who was tying an apron around her waist and flirting with a suited man sitting alone at a table. "You be Dixie's boy now?"

"No." Moving away, I tried to change the subject. "Damn, Conrad, you'd best take it easy on that bootleg. One whiff of your breath and every G-man in the parish will be banging on your door."

He chuckled and nudged me toward the back of the room. "You hongry, Joe man? You want Conrad to fry you up some tail and puppies?"

Stepping into the kitchen, I hesitated as the smell of grease and raw gator took my breath away. A giant Negro stood over a plank table heaped high with cornmeal and skinned catfish, his black skin glistening with sweat and the light from nearby kerosene lamps as he adeptly rolled fish in the meal, then dropped them into the vat of roiling grease.

Conrad swept up a handful of hush puppies from a pottery plate and dropped them into my hand. "You come wid me, boy-o. Come wid Conrad an' I show you what we got fo' sale tonight."

"I know what you got for sale." I laughed and bit into a puppy. The hot, moist cornmeal steamed in my mouth as I followed Conrad out the back door and down the footpath cluttered with rusting plow parts, chicken wire, and robust fighting cocks tethered to thinly plaited horsehair ropes. The ground beneath the old trees was damp with rot and overgrown by moss as we fought our way through the undergrowth, coming at last to a barely standing shanty built over the scum-covered water of the Goula. The hot, still air hummed with the sound of bloodthirsty mosquitoes as I stepped over an alligator hide and ducked under a rope of drying laundry.

"Wait," Conrad whispered. He disappeared into the shanty, then appeared again moments later, a mason jar of clear liquid in one hand. Motioning toward an overturned crate, he grinned. "Joe man sit a spell, *oui*? Catch up on old times. Maybe Conrad tawk Joe man into runnin' a load fo' me tonight?"

"What happened to Amos? He's the best runner in the business."

"Amos done got himself busted by Horan out near Bayou

Sorrel. Horan shot him four times in the back of his head.''

I sat and reluctantly accepted the jar, holding it up to judge the clarity of its contents. "Nice," I said.

"Nice?" Conrad chuckled. "Nice my ass. Joe's papa would call dat plenty good."

"Papa knew his bootleg all right."

"Drink."

"Can't do, Conrad. I'm working at Primrose now. I got a chance to make my way out of Hooverville once and for all. I can't take the risk of getting found out by Horan. If he caught me running bootleg, getting shot in the head would be the least of my worries."

"I'll pay you fifty dollar to run dis load to Lafayette to-night."

Fifty. "Business must be good."

"Conrad make you a rich man quick. You buy dat special gal somethin' pretty, *oui?*"

I looked hard into the mason jar. The smell of the liquor made my eyes water. Bending near, Conrad crooned, "Joe man still sweet on dat princess, *oui*? Fifty dollar go a long way in winnin' dat girl's appreciation. Joe man be buyin' her much candy and roses."

"*Prim*roses," I replied thoughtfully, then sipped the booze cautiously. It hit my stomach like ignited kerosene. Squeezing my eyes shut, I shook my head. "*Jeezus*, Conrad. This shit tastes like gasoline. You trying to kill off your customers or what?"

Conrad cackled and slapped his leg. "Joe man like Conrad's ambrosia, *oui*?"

"Yeah, I like it. But not enough to get my butt in trouble again."

Conrad put one finger under the jar and nudged it toward my mouth. "Go on, boy-o. One more sip and we tawk agin."

"If you think you're going to get me drunk enough to run this stuff to Lafayette, you're as crazy as you look, old man."

"Drink." He grinned and winked. "Den we tawk, boy-o. Den we tawk."

Chapter Four

At exactly four o'clock in the morning, I stood below Camille's bedroom window and shouted at the top of my voice, "Camille! Camille Philips, wake up! I got something I want to say to you. Camille! Dammit, Camille, I know you can hear me. And I know you can understand everything I'm saying to you."

The French doors of her bedroom opened slightly. Her face appeared, white in the moonlight.

I waved a bouquet of primroses that I had plucked just minutes before. "I got something I got to get off my chest, Camille. I got to do it while I'm drunk or I won't ever do it."

She moved to the balcony rail and looked down. The night breeze played with her long blond hair and caressed the cotton gown she wore. A rush of emotion swept through me, choking off my breath and causing my world to spin like a top. "I love you," I confessed so softly I was certain no one but myself could hear. "I've loved you since the moment I first saw you ten years ago. You've owned my heart and soul for so long I can't remember ever not loving you. I—"

Someone slapped his hand on my shoulder and spun me around. I stood face to face with Don Philips.

"Just what the hell do you think you're doin', boy? Camille! You get back in bed now, you hear?"

"Stop talking to her like she's a moron." I shoved Don away, dropping the primroses in the dirt. "I've come here to take her away from this hornet's nest. She ain't ever going to get well with you and that crazy wife of yours yelling at each other all the time."

"And just where the hell do you intend to take her—back to Sheriff Horan's jail?"

I dug into my pocket and withdrew fifty one-dollar bills. I waved them under Don's nose. "I'm a rich man tonight. I've got enough money here to stake me and Camille long enough for me to find a job."

Cursing under his breath, Don shook his head. "I'd ask you where you got all that money but I got a hunch already. You've been running moonshine again for that nut Thibodaux, ain't you?"

"What if I have?"

"Boy, you're drunker than I thought. There ain't a job between here and Canada, unless you think running moonshine for Thibodaux is going to build my sister her dream house. Just who is going to take care of her after you're busted by Horan and a lot of government men? Or maybe you've decided to look up Bonnie and Clyde. I hear they're looking for a good driver these days."

"I'm going up to Shreveport and getting on with Standard Oil."

"Wake up, Joe. You ain't getting on with Standard Oil. You ain't getting on with nobody except Horan. You know what he does to runners when he catches them? You want to end up like your old man—bait for gators?"

"You keep my old man out of this. I ain't my old man and I never will be. I won't ever treat Camille like he treated my mama. Now get out of my way. I'm going up those stairs and I'm taking Camille out of here. I'm taking her someplace where she don't have to listen to no more of your and Dixie's talk about loony bins and crazies." I took a swing at Don's head. He ducked. I swung again; then his fist came up to connect with my jaw and my world went as dark as the gathering clouds overhead.

I swam in an ocean of soft darkness and a faint scent of magnolias. Over and over I dreamt of Camille looking down at me from the balcony, her pale hair rippling like silver waves in the wind. Her comforting presence wrapped around me and eased the pounding in my head.

Little by little reality intruded. As I struggled from my stupor, I lay very still, recognizing the sound of light rain on a car roof. Where was I?

At last, I opened my eyes. Blurry images faded in and out of my vision as I did my best to focus on the face above me. Camille?

I sat up, staring first at Camille, then at our surroundings. We were in the backseat of Don's Duesenberg, parked down the road from the Gator Shack. Don sat behind the steering wheel, staring at the ill-lit shanty through runnels of rain on the windshield. Camille, still wearing her nightgown, huddled inside the blanket her brother had thrown around her shoulders. The rain cast teardrop shadows on her cheeks as she stared at me with wide, uncertain eyes.

"You sober yet?" Don asked.

"My head hurts like hell."

"Sorry I had to slug you like that, but I reckoned it was time I had to knock some sense into you."

"Mind telling me what the blazes we're doing here?"

Don focused again on the shanty. "A man can only take so much, Joe. I 'spect I've taken just about all I can take and hold on to what little dignity I still have, which ain't much, not since this damn depression has robbed me of my livelihood, not to mention my manhood. Do you know what it's like to be the first failure since my great-great-granddaddy first built Primrose?"

Sliding closer to Camille, I gently tucked the blanket more snugly over her chest, then smiled. "What is she doing here, Don?"

"Wasn't my idea." Partially turning, he stared over his shoulder at me a long time before speaking again. "It was

Camille's. She wasn't about to let me haul your tail off without her.''

Sitting back in the seat, I watched Camille's expression closely, noting that her gaze never wavered from mine. There was a touch of emotion in her eyes that had not been there the night before. ''What am I doing here?''

''I wasn't about to have you dragging my sister off to Shreveport while I was gone.''

Looking beyond him to the Gator Shack, I said, ''I got a feeling there's more to my being here than that.''

Don took a deep breath and relaxed against the seat. He stared out through the rain-drenched windshield, his big, rough hands gripping the wheel hard. ''Dixie didn't come home again last night. I was scared to death that I would come here and do something I'd regret later. I was hoping you would stop me.''

''She's not worth getting yourself killed over, Mr. Philips.''

''I know that. But I can't help myself. Loving a woman can make a man behave in ways he's not proud of.''

Rubbing my jaw, I glanced at Camille. Her hand lay on the seat between us. The ache to reach for it made me shiver. I knew all too well what loving a woman could do to a man—especially when the woman didn't love him back.

''I blame myself for what's become of Dixie,'' Don continued. ''Had I been the kind of husband she thought she was getting, she'd be home now instead of doing God knows what with God knows who. I made her a lot of promises that I didn't keep. Not that I didn't want to. . . . Thing is, she wanted a socialite for a husband and all she got was a farmer. Now I ain't even that anymore. A woman like Dixie expects to live in a certain lifestyle. Hell, I can't even buy her a new hat these days.''

Laying my hand near Camille's, I swallowed and steadied my breathing. Her eyes were large and luminous, her lips slightly parted and . . . faintly smiling.

''When you love a woman, Joe, you want to be able to give her the world.''

''Right,'' I replied softly. ''I guess it takes more than fifty dollars to keep a woman in luxury.''

We sat in silence, listening to the rain patter on the car, our body heat painting a fog on the windows. I finally gathered the courage to take Camille's hand in mine, then waited without breathing for her to yank it away. She didn't. My heart constricted and my throat went dry as she curled her fingers around mine and tucked our hands under the blanket. Sitting there in the dark before dawn, my shoulder pressed lightly against hers, I wondered what I had done in my miserable life to merit such a miracle.

The front door of the Gator Shack finally opened and the same suited man I had seen sitting at a table when I'd dropped Dixie off the previous afternoon stumbled out into the rain, his arm slung around Dixie as they splashed through the muck toward the stranger's Ford. Don made a sound in his throat, then calmly opened the door, stepping out into the downpour.

I laid my hand against Camille's cheek and turned her face toward mine. Her eyes reflected concern. Her lower lip quivered. "You don't need to be witness to this type of sordidness," I told her. "A man's humiliation is hard to take any time, but having his heart torn out by his own wife must be tormenting. I'm sure if he had a choice in the matter he wouldn't want you to be here. Now lay your head here on my shoulder and close your eyes. Try to think of happier times—back before everybody saw their dreams disintegrate into dust—way back, before your own life came crashing down around you. Those were real good times, Camille. I never saw you when you weren't smiling. I envied every boy in school who so much as sat beside you in the schoolroom."

Sliding my arm around her, I pulled her close and pressed a light kiss to her cool forehead as she nestled against me. Only then did I reluctantly look out through the rain as Don stumbled back toward the car, dragging Dixie with him. Behind him, the stranger sprawled facedown in the mud beside his Ford.

Don flung open the car door and shoved Dixie down on the seat. Splattered with mud, her hair plastered to her head and dripping water, she drunkenly muttered obscenities before realizing Camille and I were huddled in the backseat.

She glared at us with raccoonlike eyes just as Don got in the car.

"What the hell are they doing here?" she yelled. "Ain't it enough that I have to contend with you? God, it's got to where a woman can't have any fun at all without being humiliated in front of her friends. Jeez, did you have to go and hit him so hard?"

"He's lucky I didn't kill him," Don snapped, then drove the Duesenberg out into the slick gravel road. "A man's got a right to claim what's lawfully his, especially his wife. I've had just about as much of your behavior as I can take, Dixie. If you go back to Thibodaux's one more time, I'll—"

"You'll what? Kill me? Do me a favor, darlin'; kill me and get it over with. I'd rather be dead than be stuck for the rest of my life being married to some damn dirt farmer who ain't even got a pot to piss in any more. I'll bet your granddaddy is rolling over in his grave right now because of what you've become."

"That's right. I *ain't* got a pot to piss in any more, which is why I sent back that radio you had delivered yesterday afternoon."

Dixie flung herself on Don and began to hit him. The car careened wildly, barely missing a line of cypress trees and a fencepost that materialized through the rain. I was forced to grab her by the hair and yank her back.

Hissing like a cat, she clawed my arm and spat in my face before crying, "You ungrateful young shit. How dare you? I'll see you're sent straight back to Horan's hellhole for this. You just watch me."

"Fine," I said. "You do that. But I'm not about to let you get Camille injured or killed, not to mention myself or Mr. Philips. Now sit there and shut up before I belt you a good one."

Her eyes wide with stunned amazement, Dixie stared at me with her mouth open before sinking back into the seat, her expression one of blatant loathing and vindictiveness. Don's gaze locked with mine in the rearview mirror, and although his eyes reflected his approval and appreciation, the cold fear crept through me that I had just ruined my chances of remaining on Primrose Lane.

• • •

Dawn had just fingered its way through the falling drizzle as I carried Camille up the winding staircase to her room. Her head on my shoulder, her little body still cloaked by the blanket, she felt light as a feather in my arms.

I found my way to Camille's room and kicked the door closed behind me, shutting out the sound of Don's and Dixie's angry voices below. Swallowed by the quiet, I stood in the diluted dark, holding Camille against my chest as the damp dawn breeze rushed through the open French doors to flutter the bed canopy, as gossamer as fairy wings. I rested Camille amid butter-yellow counterpanes and plump feather pillows dressed in eyelet lace. She appeared to be sleeping; I allowed myself to study her exquisite face, which looked as pale as one of the many china dolls lining the shelves on the walls. The overwhelming sense of loss expanded inside of me as I thought that I might never see her again. That because of my rashness to protect her and Don, I might have jeopardized not only my remaining at Primrose, but Camille's remaining as well. The thought of her rotting in some sanitarium for the rest of her life filled me with a kind of violent anger I had rarely experienced. I wanted to kill Dixie Philips with my bare hands.

As the room brightened ever so slowly, I backed away from the bed and regarded my surroundings. Along with the many china dolls, all with real human hair in different shades of red, yellow, and brown, there were miniature dishes made of painted metal and tiny china tea services depicting bouquets of primroses.

Sensing someone behind me, I turned. Camille stood within the flow of wind through the door, her hair sprayed out over her thin shoulders as she raised one hand and beckoned me closer. Dare I? Could I trust myself not to sweep her into my arms and hold her, as I had fantasized for so many years?

I gave her my hand and she took me to a wooden chest placed in the far corner of the room. She fell to her knees, her gown pooling like moonlight around her. The top of the chest creaked as she opened it, releasing a musty scent of cedar that roused memories of my mother's own cedar box, where she'd stored her only good table linens. More than once, she had hidden me there from my drunken father.

But there was no terrified child coiled up inside of Camille's cedar chest, only layers of doll clothes and stacks of cherished books. Camille reached deep into the chest and withdrew an object that she held close to her breast for a long minute. Finally, she turned her face up to mine; her eyes were big and her normally pale cheeks were kissed by color. I hardly noticed when she slipped something into my hand. I moved into the pale light to better see it: a valentine card, with pressed primroses and a boy's untidy handwriting.

I read aloud softly, ''To the most beautiful girl in the world. I would give you my heart and soul if you would have it. Signed with limitless adoration: Anonymous.''

I took a deep, unsteady breath before slowly lifting my eyes to hers. ''After all these years . . . you still have it.''

Camille smiled.

The rain cleared as I sat in my room, my head in my hands as I awaited the ramifications of my actions with Dixie. I expected that at any moment Sheriff Horan would show up to physically drag me back to jail, if he didn't kill me first. The image of Amos Paquin with the back of his head shot out made my stomach queasy, and I groaned.

Exhausted, I fell back on the bed and closed my eyes. My thoughts swirled like confetti in the wind as I did my best to ignore the intensifying heat and the humidity that made my body bead with sweat. I did my best to focus on the memory of Camille's face and the extreme joy I'd experienced, learning that she still had my valentine—and that she now knew who had sent it, and approved—but the joy lasted only until the fear of Dixie's threat closed around my throat, so that I was forced to fight for every breath. As I drifted to a fitful sleep, another image wormed its way into my dreams . . . an image of Marion Dressler crawling into my bunk and whispering into my ear: *Take Camille and run.*

I wondered what sort of cruel game Dixie was playing when she sent word later that morning that I was to prune the hedges out by the road where Horan's inmates were working.

Their hoots and jeers greeted me as I walked down the gravel drive.

"If it ain't Dixie darlin's newest lover boy. Hey, Norton, does she look as good with her clothes off as she does with 'em on?"

"If you can't cut it with the lady, tell her to give me a call."

Marion elbowed his way through the crowd, his eyes wide as an owl's as he looked me up and down. "Jesus, Joe, when you didn't come back to the jail I thought Horan had done you in already. Here you are, pulling work leave for Philips. Oowee, ain't you lookin' sharp for a jailbird. Look, boys, I do believe he's wearing clean clothes. You had a bath, Joe?"

I looked away, back at the house, fully suspecting that Dixie would be watching, relishing in my self-consciousness. Sure enough, I caught a glimpse of her at a window, a drink in her hand and a smirk on her face. She was up to something; I could feel it in my gut.

"What they feedin' you, Joey?"

"You don't want to know," I replied, rubbing the sweat from the back of my neck.

Marion shuffled toward me, the chains around his ankles catching on a tree root and causing him to stumble. I jumped forward and caught his arm, and was struck by the nauseating stench of his body and breath as he thrust his face up to mine. The realization that I had looked and smelled as badly only days before made my stomach turn. The possibility that I would be thrown back with this lot of losers filled me with revulsion and dread.

"This is perfect," Marion whispered. "You can put in a good word for me with Dixie. You know, convince her you need help—"

I tried to push him away. He clung to my arm with the strength of ten men. His face looked feral.

"You owe me, Joe. You owe me big time. I'm the only friend you had in this pit of snakes."

"I don't owe you squat, Marion. Now leave me alone and let me get on with my job."

"Ain't you got proud all of a sudden?"

I attacked the hedges with a vengeance, my sight fixed on

Dixie's image in the window, my anger and frustration mounting by the minute. What was she up to?

Marion sidled up to me. "I'm bustin' out tonight, Joe."

"I don't want to know about it. Now just get the hell away from me before I call Deputy Carr."

"This is your last chance, Joe. Git out while you can."

"What's that supposed to mean?"

"Dixie and Sheriff Horan are up to somethin'. She was at the jailhouse yesterday. I seen 'em talkin'—"

"Shut up, Marion. Just shut up."

He gripped my shirt and turned me around. "They was sittin' out in his car for over an hour. I could see 'em out the window. And guess what, Joey boy . . . part of that time they was real cozy, if you know what I mean. Real cozy. Now it's all makin' sense, Joe. Why Dixie chose you for work leave . . . and why Horan allowed it, hatin' you like he does. Think about it . . . you'd be the last person he'd do any favors for."

My gaze flew back to the house, and to Dixie. Her face looked as emotionless as marble as she continued to watch me. Then she allowed the curtain to fall, blocking off my view of her.

Deputy Carr shouted then for Marion to get back to his work before he took a whip to him. Marion grumbled under his breath and spat on the ground, sneering, "I'm liable to wrap that whip around his scrawny neck before I check out of this hell hotel. See you around, Joe. Good luck. I suspect you're gonna need it."

Chapter Five

Throughout the morning cars and trucks came and went up Primrose's driveway. I took special note of the McCormick's Furniture and Appliance truck. Resting in the shade of a willow tree, I watched as a pair of burly Negro men unloaded the same radio Dixie had purchased yesterday—the one Don had returned to the store the same afternoon. Not long after, Lilah May Benchly of Lilah's Ladies' Apparel arrived, her arms laden with hat and shoe boxes as she climbed Primrose's front steps. Lilah May had changed little in the years since my mother had done alterations for Lilah's clients. Knowing Lilah as I did, I suspected that the prices for the goods she had personally delivered to Dixie weren't going to fit into Don's nonexistent budget.

Come midafternoon I managed to find respite from the sun beneath a sprawling three-hundred-year-old oak, where I rested and thought about my conversation with Marion. Why couldn't the world just leave me the hell alone and allow me to experience a little of the joy I should be feeling over my relationship with Camille? I didn't want to consider the idea that Marion might be right. I didn't want to think that at any moment Horan was going to show up and drag me back to jail—or worse, put a bullet in my head. I simply wanted to lie here in the deep shade and relish the cool grass on my sunburned back and allow my dreams of Camille Philips to flourish into a possible reality. I wanted to fantasize about the life I would build her away from Primrose . . . if she would only give me a chance.

I sensed someone near and sat up.

Dressed in a flowing cotton frock printed with pale pink daisies, her hair swept back from her flushed face, Camille stood amid a backdrop of blooming magnolias, her feet bare, her features expectant as she regarded me. She held a sweating glass of iced tea sprigged with mint leaves. For a moment I could think of nothing to say, so swept away I was by her beauty—and the fact that she had obviously searched me out.

Finally, I said, "Is that for me?" and pointed to the glass of tea.

She nodded and approached.

I spread my shirt next to me on the grass before taking the iced tea. "Sit here," I told her. "You don't want to get grass stains on your dress."

After a brief hesitation, she eased down on the shirt, curling her bare feet up under her skirt. She watched me closely, and I realized she was waiting for me to drink. I gulped the cold tea down, then sighed. "That's about the best iced tea I ever drank, Camille. Did you make it?"

Lowering her eyes, she nodded.

Tipping up her chin with my finger, I grinned. "Just for me, I hope."

She nodded again as pale color crept over her cheeks.

I skimmed the cool condensation off the glass, then touched my fingertip to her lower lip. Her tongue swept out to catch the icy bead of water, lightly brushing my finger and causing my entire body to go as rigid as the tree trunk at my back. When I finally found the ability to speak again, my voice sounded as rough as gravel.

"You shouldn't be here with me, Camille. I don't think Don would like it. As much as I want to share some time with you, I suspect it should be in the company of your brother. Not that I'm not trustworthy . . . I am. I just don't want to do anything that might get on his or Dixie's bad side. Not for my sake—hell, I've been in one kind of trouble or another since I was a boy—but right now you have to focus on getting well, and you can't do that if Dixie is screaming at you about hospitals and such."

She shifted nearer; I moved away.

A glint of mischief flashed in her eyes as she pursued me, but as I made a move to get to my feet, she grabbed my arm and hung on tenaciously, her expression going from amusement to intentness in an instant. Sinking back against the tree, I swallowed hard, catching my breath as she lightly placed her hand upon my cheek and smiled.

I could not move.

I could not breathe.

As if she were blind, Camille studied my face with her fingertips: my eyes, my nose, my lips. She ran her hand lightly through my hair, traced my ear with one finger, until shivers ran like electricity up and down my back.

"God, oh God," I whispered. "Princess, you don't know what you're doing to me. I don't think I can take much more of this or I'm liable to do something I'm going to regret like hell."

She swept my lower lip with her thumb. I grabbed her wrist and held it away, my eagerness to escape my predicament making me more forceful than I had intended. I would have thrust her aside, but something in her expression stopped me. With her lips parted, her body straining toward mine, she tried desperately to speak.

Holding my breath, I took her face between my hands. "What is it, Camille? What are you wanting to say to me? You don't have to be afraid. You can trust me. Speak to me, sweetheart."

"Miss Camille!"

Camille scrambled away and I jumped to my feet as Pearl crashed through the hedges, snapping twigs and crushing wild mint under her feet. "Lord a'mercy, child, I been lookin' ever'where fo' you. You gots to come back to d'house right now, y'hear? Mr. Don in a real bad way—"

"What's happened?" I asked, helping Camille to her feet.

Pearl took Camille's arm and proceeded to escort her toward the house. "Dat woman has done gone and got Mr. Don in a real state dis time fo' sure. I done sent fo' Doc Leavy, but I ain't sure it's gonna help none. I ain't seen Mr. Don dis bad ever."

Nearing the house, I fell back, reluctant to follow until Camille looked around and reached one hand toward me. What little color that had earlier kissed her cheeks had gone as gray as cold ashes.

Taking a deep breath, I followed.

I carefully stepped over the splintered Atwater Kent radio, made my way around the scattered piles of crushed hats, all still sporting Lilah May's price tags, then toed aside an open box containing only one shoe. The room resembled a house I'd seen once that had been ripped asunder by a tornado.

Pearl stood amid the refuse, brown lips pursed, her hands on her hips as she shook her head. "I don't rightly know what Mrs. Philips was thinkin' to go an' buy all dis, knowin' how Mr. Don feel 'bout spendin' money right now."

"I got a feeling Mrs. Philips got the kind of reaction she was hoping for," I replied.

With a shake of her head, Pearl headed to the kitchen for a broom, leaving me to kick the mounds of hats and shoes into a solitary pile and think back on the last few hours, as Don Philips had fought to survive his latest heart attack. I wondered if he would have struggled so hard had Camille not been there to remind him that his responsibilities ran much deeper than Primrose and his wife.

There came knocking at the front door. I walked into the hallway to see a short, bald man wearing a stiff-collared shirt that cut into the rolls of fat around his neck. Staring at me through the screen door, he mopped his sweating brow and waited for me to greet him. I didn't, and he finally said, "I'm here to see Mr. Philips."

I looked around for Pearl.

"I have a four-thirty appointment," he announced.

Sliding my hands into my back pockets, I walked to the door and regarded him speculatively. He had removed his suit coat. His shirt was blotched with sweat stains under his arms and across his fleshy belly. He held a briefcase in one hand, and the idea flashed through my mind that he might possibly be from some hospital, come to take Camille away.

"Mr. Philips isn't seeing anyone right now," I told him in a surprisingly authoritative tone.

"But we had an appointment. I drove all the way from New Orleans."

"Who are you?"

"Dutton. R. J. Dutton. He'll know who I am."

"Yeah, well I told you—"

"Mistah Dutton! Lawd, suh, come right on in." Stepping around me, Pearl shoved open the screen door, inviting R. J. Dutton into the house. "Mr. Don tol' me just this mo'nin' that you would be droppin' by."

He regarded me pensively, if not outright suspiciously. "I've brought some papers for him to look over, Pearl. He mentioned that his wife is normally out of the house on Saturday afternoons . . ."

"Yes, suh, Mrs. Philips be down at the Ladies Auxiliary on Saturdays. Come on back. I'll see if he up to talkin' with you a spell."

"Has he been ill?"

"Ill as can be, Mr. Dutton, but not too ill to see you, I 'spect."

I watched Pearl escort R. J. Dutton down the corridor to the back parlor, where Doc Leavy had ordered Don to reside during his recuperation. I followed for a short distance, my imagination running wild with possible reasons why a man from New Orleans would drive all the way to Baton Rouge to see Don—especially in this insufferable heat.

Pearl tapped softly on the closed door, then ushered the stranger into the room. Muffled voices came to me as I leaned against the wall, my arms crossed over my chest, my need to see Camille again not allowing me to budge from my station. I had not seen her since Pearl had rushed her to Don's side.

The door opened again and Pearl stepped out, allowing the flow of soft conversation to spill into the corridor. I caught a glimpse of Camille, sitting near Don where he reclined on a bed.

Attempting to step around Pearl, I said, "I want to see Camille."

"No suh. Lawd, ain't no way you goin' to see dat girl right now."

"Who is that man and why is he here? If he's come to take Camille away—"

"He ain't 'bout to do nothin' of d'sort. Now best you git back to yo' own house afore Mrs. Philips comes home. Dere's been enough upset on dis farm for one day. I won't be havin' Mr. Don gittin' riled up agin."

The door opened suddenly. R. J. Dutton peered at me through thick spectacles that made his eyes look owl-like. "Mr. Norton?"

I nodded.

"Mr. Philips would like for you to join us. Please, come in."

Stepping into the room, I was struck by the vision of Don's flesh—blue and cold as china. Camille sat near him, looking like a frightened orphaned child as she gripped his still hand. At my entrance, she slid from the chair and ran to me. Flinging her arms around my neck, burying her face against my chest, she clung to me fiercely and wept softly.

I rocked her back and forth, oblivious to Philips and Dutton as I savored the feel of her body against mine. Then and there I made the decision that I would fight with my last breath to keep R. J. Dutton from taking her away.

"She's understandably upset," Dutton remarked. "Poor child. Perhaps it would be best if she left us alone for a while. Just until we've finished our discussion."

"You can both go to hell." I held Camille tighter. My face went hot as I met Don's weary eyes. "I'm sorry. I know this can't be easy for you, and I know you're ill, but I won't stand by and allow you to do this to Camille."

"What are you talking about?" Dutton asked.

"You came here to take her away, didn't you?"

Dutton exchanged looks with Don, who briefly closed his eyes and took a deep, rattling breath. "Camille's not going anywhere, Joe. Not right now, at least."

"Then what's this all about?"

"Sit down and we'll tell you."

Reluctantly, I sat on a settee, Camille beside me. Her hand felt cold in mine; her eyes were swollen and red.

Dutton withdrew a sheaf of documents and handed a stack to Don, then to me. Across the top was printed: VENICE OIL AND GAS COMPANY.

For the next hour, I listened as R. J. Dutton did his best to persuade Don Philips to allow Venice Oil and Gas to drill on Primrose property. I did my best to follow along with the printed words, but the legal terminology made my head swim. At last, Dutton mopped his brow again and shrugged. "The long and short of it is this, Mr. Philips. Venice Oil and Gas believes your farm is sitting on a field that we call a dome. The dome itself is salt. That bed of salt normally traps major pockets of oil. We'd like to search out that possibility, but we cannot drill unless you give us the right to do so. As I've stated in our previous meetings, we're willing to pay you for that right."

Don shook his head. "I told you, Mr. Dutton. I'm not selling you my farm."

"We don't want your farm, Don. We don't want to lease it. We simply wish to lease the mineral rights to your property. Please, the longer you vacillate on this issue the greater the risk of your . . . well . . . of your becoming so ill that you . . ."

"Just come out and say it, Dutton," Don said. "Before I die. Hell, you and every damn creditor is pounding on my door these days afraid I'm going to die before you get something out of me."

"You're not a well man," Dutton pointed out.

"If you lot of buzzards would leave me alone I'd feel a lot better."

"I'm just doing my job, or trying to. You're making this awfully difficult for me." Looking at me, Dutton opened his arms and shook his head. "Reason with him, Mr. Norton. He obviously respects your opinion or he wouldn't have brought you in here."

I slowly got to my feet, regarding the papers in my hand a moment longer before walking over to Don. Bending near his ear, I whispered, "I don't imagine that I should be here, Mr. Philips. This should be discussed with your wife—"

"Dixie doesn't know anything about this, Joe," he replied as quietly. "I don't want her to know about it. Not yet. You understand, don't you?"

"I hardly think I should be here—"

"I need someone who can think clearly, and who cares about what happens to Primrose and Camille after I'm gone."

I shook my head. "Don't talk that way. You're not going to die anytime soon."

"She needs someone who cares for her as deeply as I do. There's no one else in this town I'd trust with her welfare."

My mouth suddenly dry, I said, "What are you talking about, Mr. Philips?"

"I knew the moment I saw your disgust for Dixie's behavior that I hadn't been wrong over the years to believe in your character. As I told you before, I made a promise to your mother and I aim to keep it."

Dutton moved up behind me. "Mr. Philips, if you desire to wrap this up before your wife returns, I suggest we go on with business."

For a brief moment, Don's eyes drifted closed, then he reached for my arm and squeezed it weakly. I turned back to Dutton, confusion causing the room to appear slightly out of kilter as I focused on Dutton's face. Somewhat unsteadily, I said, "Let me get this right. You think there is oil in the ground under us and you want to drill for it."

"Correct."

"If he leases you the mineral rights to this land, then you own the oil."

Dutton frowned and reached for his handkerchief.

"What, exactly, do you pay Mr. Philips for leasing his land?" I asked.

"One dollar an acre for a three-year lease. That's a total of three hundred dollars in his pocket." Squaring his shoulders, Dutton added, "A fair price, I believe. I'm sure three hundred dollars would go a long way in satisfying your creditors."

"If Don decided to drill himself, the oil would remain his, wouldn't it?"

"Undoubtedly. However, judging by what I've heard

around town I highly doubt a bank, or anyone else, would lend him money . . . even if they had it to lend.''

"There's no cause for you to get insulting," Don joined in.

"I'm sorry, but facts are facts. This is not a good time for anyone, but a man such as yourself . . . Well, to see everything your family has built over generations go to rack and ruin must be especially hard.''

"What if you do strike oil, Mr. Dutton? Who reaps the reward besides Venice Oil?" I asked.

Dutton cleared his throat and tugged at his shirt collar. "The partners, of course."

"Partners?"

"Individuals who put up a share of money to cover the cost of drilling.''

"So everybody in this deal makes out except Mr. Philips. That doesn't sound like a good business to me, especially since it's his oil.''

Sweat beaded on Dutton's brow as he sat down next to Camille. "Very well. Venice Oil might consider offering you a percentage of the take.''

"How much?" I asked.

Dutton shrugged. "Oh, say . . . one percent.''

"Not good enough.''

"Two.''

"Try again.''

"Really, Mr. Norton—''

"I said, try again.''

"Fine. Three.''

"You're wasting Mr. Philips's time.''

"You're a brash young man," Dutton exploded, then said to Don, "I really see no reason why you and I can't come to some understanding ourselves.''

"Joe's doing fine," Don said, grinning weakly.

Lips thinned, Dutton refocused on me, his foot tapping impatiently on the floor. "You know, gentlemen, we could go to the next farm and make the same deal. I'm certain Mr. Cox would leap for joy at the prospect of pocketing a few hundred dollars.''

"If the Cox farm was sitting on this so-called dome, I

suspect you'd be there instead of here right now,'' I said, tossing the contracts onto Dutton's lap. "You'd be doing your best to get old man Cox to sign those papers.''

Taking a deep breath, Dutton relaxed against the back of the settee. He looked first at Don, then at Camille, finally at me, and nodded. "I've been authorized to offer you eight percent of the profits and no more.''

"Eight percent!'' Don raised up in bed, his face turning purple. "You goddamn crook. You came in here with the intent of taking every bit of this deal for Venice Oil, didn't you?''

Dutton shrugged and looked sheepish. "It's my job, Mr. Philips. My company expects me to get the very best deal for the least amount of money I can. Would you sell your cotton for a penny a ton if you thought you could get a dollar for it?''

A moment passed before Don laid back on his pillow. Exhausted, he steadied his breathing before focusing again on Dutton. "Tell me something, R. J. If I do this thing, what happens if . . . when . . . I die?''

"Then your wife receives the benefits, of course.''

There was silence; then Don made a noise in his throat that sounded like an animal in pain. Camille jumped up and ran to him, grabbed his hand, and gripped it to her breast as Don rolled his head from side to side, doing his best to contain his distress. "I'd rather die a pauper than leave her a solitary penny,'' Don said.

Removing his glasses, Dutton carefully cleaned them with his handkerchief as he studied our faces. "You might consider divorcing her,'' he offered.

"I don't think you understand, Mr. Dutton. If I could make myself divorce Dixie I would have done it a long time ago.''

Dutton held his glasses up to the light, then replaced them on his nose. He reached for his briefcase. "Then you have a big decision to make, Mr. Philips. If my company is right, you're sitting on enough oil to eventually make you, or your loved ones, incredibly wealthy. It's up to you, to whom you wish to pass that wealth.''

Moving toward the door, he paused and looked back.

"You have a lovely sister, Mr. Philips, who apparently cares for you tremendously. You might think of her future . . . and what happens to her upon your death." Nodding to me, he smiled. "It's been a pleasure doing business with you, Mr. Norton. You might well have a future in this business if you play your cards right."

He left the room. I followed, catching up to him on the front porch steps. "I gotta know, Mr. Dutton: Just how certain are you that there is oil on this property?"

"My company is not in the habit of spending money needlessly these days. Were our partners not confident that below this dome we'll strike a reasonably sized field, they would keep their money tucked safely away." Dutton tossed his briefcase through the open window of his car, then opened the door.

"Tell me something," I said. "If a person was interested in becoming a partner in such a venture . . . what would he do?"

"That depends on whether or not there was room for another partner."

"Is there?"

Dutton smiled. "Interested in getting into the oil business, young man?"

"Maybe, if you've got the need for one more partner."

"It takes money."

"I've got money."

He peered at me over the top of his glasses. "You're a very lucky man indeed, Mr. Norton. Just how much do you have to gamble on such a project?"

"I was under the assumption that this venture was virtually risk-free."

Dutton chuckled, then closed the car door. "Young man, nothing in life is absolutely risk-free."

"I've got fifty dollars, Mr. Dutton. Will that buy me a percentage of that oil?"

He regarded me impassively a long moment before saying, "I suspect fifty dollars is a great deal of money for a man such as yourself."

"It's all I've got in the world."

"It won't buy you much. Maybe one percent."

I dug into my pocket and withdrew the roll of dollar bills Thibodaux had paid me for running his moonshine. I handed it to Dutton. "I'm trusting you'll treat me fair."

Dutton regarded the money thoughtfully before sliding it into his pocket. "I'd appreciate any help you can give me concerning Mr. Philips and his . . . situation."

I nodded. "I'll do what I can."

Chapter Six

I made certain that Camille was occupied by Pearl before returning to Don's room. I wouldn't have her upset more than she already was, and frankly, I didn't trust myself to fully control my anger. Judging by the look on Don's face when I reentered the room, he knew exactly why I had returned. The belligerent set of his jaw was enough to tell me that reasoning with him wasn't going to be easy.

"Divorce her," I began. "She's no good for you, Mr. Philips, and she's sure no good for Camille."

"My marriage to Dixie ain't any of your business, Joe."

"You made it my business by inviting me to participate in your negotiations with Dutton, not to mention to safeguard Camille's future."

"Divorce is not easy for a man, not when he loves his wife. But you're too damn young yet to realize that."

"You don't love her, sir. You're obsessed with her. I'd even go so far as to say you hate her. But you're a proud man. You've lost just about everything your family has built . . . you don't want to lose the last thing you can call your own . . . and that happens to be Dixie."

"Get out," Don muttered. "I'm sorry I ever brought you into this."

"Not until you stop and think what this could mean to Camille. If Venice strikes oil while you're living, there will be enough money to get Camille the help she needs right here at Primrose. If they strike and you're dead, Dixie will use that money to get rid of Camille for good."

"Not if I stipulate in my will—"

"Do you think she's going to give a damn about some stupid will? She doesn't care what you think or how you feel while you're alive; imagine what will happen when you're dead."

"Then I won't sign the goddamn papers at all!" His face turning beet-red, Don gasped for a breath and fell back on his pillow.

More softly, less angrily, I asked, "You would give up an opportunity to restore Primrose to its grandeur—all because you can't accept that your marriage to Dixie is over? I can't believe you would put Camille's welfare in Dixie's hands. What is it going to take to make you see that you and Camille will be much better off without Dixie in your life? She wants a divorce, man. Give it to her so you can at least enjoy the time you have left."

Don looked weary and resolute. Thoughtfully, he said, "I can't imagine what Dixie could do to make me give her up."

"Carrying on adulterous affairs isn't enough? Driving your good name and reputation into the ground isn't enough? The cruelty she inflicts on Camille should make you want to kill her."

"She loved me once."

"She loved your money. She loved living in the finest house in Louisiana. She loved wearing fancy clothes and eating off fine china. Love is consuming. Love is gracefully accepting the good along with the bad. Love is wanting to give that special person everything you can possibly give. It's not tearing away at someone's soul."

Don turned his eyes to mine. "Is that how you feel about Camille?"

"Yes. I'll do everything in my power to keep Dixie—or you—from hurting her more than she's already been hurt."

"How do you propose to do that?"

I took a deep breath. "I'll marry her."

"Marry? You would sacrifice your life for a woman who can't even speak to you?"

"It's no sacrifice, Mr. Philips. It would be the realization of a dream."

Don smirked. "The fact that I may be wealthy soon has nothing to do with it, I assume."

"Unlike Dixie, I don't give a damn about your money. I'd be willing to marry her today if you'd allow me."

Closing his eyes, Don lay like a rag doll amid the rumpled sheets, his once-strong body a shadow of its former self. "Why should I allow my sister to marry a penniless man, Joe?"

"You forget, Mr. Philips. We're equals now. You're just as penniless as I am."

Don's body went rigid; then he slowly opened his eyes and looked at me. "You've grown up a lot since you left that valentine card to Camille on my porch. I liked you then, and I like you now. Your mother, God rest her soul, was a decent, honorable, hard-working woman . . . but despite my promise to her, I don't think I would want Camille strapped to a man with so little future."

I did my best to swallow back the rise of hot anger in my throat. "You would commit her to an asylum for the insane before you would give her over to a man who loves her for who she is . . . not *what* she is?"

"I have the age, wisdom, and experience to know what is best for my sister," Don pointed out.

My hands clenching, I moved to the bed. "Mr. Philips, if you had any kind of wisdom at all, you wouldn't be lying in that bed right now. You wouldn't have allowed Dixie to put you there. You can't do anything about the depression, sir . . . but you sure as hell can do something to stop her from killing you by degrees."

I left the room and stood in the dark corridor, fighting my temper and the sudden sense of helplessness I felt over my inability to help Camille.

Camille moved toward me through the shadows, her face

as pale as the dress she wore. I couldn't look at her; it hurt too damn much.

She touched my arm and my burning anger vaporized. I took her into my arms and held her tight—so tight I could feel her heart beating against mine. Then it came to me: the resolution of my problems. One way or another, I wasn't going to allow Dixie to destroy the woman I loved.

Nightfall. Restlessly lying on my bed, I listened to the whir of river sounds and tried to breathe evenly in the stillness. I had done my best to communicate with Camille that I wished to meet with her at my room just after midnight. Had she understood? If so, would she come? Would she suspect that my reasons for coercing her here were less than scrupulous?

Where was she?

I rolled from the bed and paced, glancing now and again to the bundle of clothes and canned goods in the corner. I'd taken a number of Don's shirts and britches, as well as several of Camille's dresses, from the clothesline and helped myself to a good portion of pig I'd found curing in the smokehouse—going so far as to leave a note of apology to Pearl. I'd wrapped them all in a blanket and proceeded to convince myself that I was doing the right thing—the *only* thing—I could to save Camille from Don's stupidity and Dixie's cruelty.

Damn, damn.

"Come on, Camille. I know you understood me. Come on before it's too late."

My frustration and nervousness mounting, I made for the door. I would take her away by force if I had to.

Kicking open the screen door, I came face to face with Camille. The breath left me in a rush and I took her in my arms. She clung to me as I buried my face in her fragrant hair.

"You came" was all I could manage.

She nodded and I was flooded with a sense of jubilation as tears came to my eyes. "You *do* understand me, don't you?"

Pulling away, she turned her exquisite eyes up to mine and smiled. Taking her face in my hands, I searched her features—her golden lashes and crystal-blue eyes, no longer glazed with numbness. I kissed her, tentatively at first, testing like one wading into unfamiliar waters. As her lips parted beneath mine in invitation, I soared with a consuming hunger, a dizzying, spiraling elation of having finally reached heaven and discovering it was everything I'd imagined . . . and more.

What sweet agony I felt, forcing myself to back away. "Come inside, Camille. I have something to tell you."

I opened the screen door and followed her in. She noticed the bundle of clothes and food immediately and spun toward me, her face a mask of panic. She grabbed me with a force that belied her frailty and shook her head.

Smiling as steadily as possible, I whispered, "It's all right, sweetheart. Don't be frightened. I want you to listen closely and try to understand what I'm about to tell you. I'm leaving. Going away. I'm taking you with me."

She frowned and touched my cheek. Again, she shook her head frantically and reached for my hand. She wrapped her fingers around my wrist as if they were shackles.

"I won't go back to jail, Camille. I can't. I can't take the risk of leaving you here alone. Not with Dixie ranting every minute about recommitting you to an asylum. The idea that Don could die and leave you in Dixie's care while I'm in jail maddens me. We'll leave the state. I'll find work somewhere. I'll dye my hair, grow a mustache, anything to keep Horan from finding me. And who knows . . . maybe there really is oil under us. If so, you won't need Don's money. I'll build you a house that will put Primrose to shame."

The panic on Camille's face faded. She flung herself against me like a child, holding me fiercely, shaking with some emotion I could only guess at.

"It's going to be all right," I told her. "I've loved you since we were children. I'll love you when we're old and gray, and beyond, forever. Nothing or no one will ever hurt you again. I swear it."

The screen door flew open behind us. I shoved Camille aside and turned, expecting to confront Don or Dixie. Instead, I stared straight into Marion Dressler's delirious eyes.

"Jesus," I whispered. "What the hell are you doing here?"

"What does it look like?" Marion bent double, his hands on his knees as he struggled to breathe.

I glanced at Camille. She crouched next to the wall, visibly trembling as she watched us.

Stooping to better see Marion's face, doing my best to contain my mounting rage, I said through my teeth, "I asked you what you're doing *here?* At Primrose?"

Marion looked up at last, assessing me, then Camille, before smirking. "Here we all thought you was pokin' Dixie when all the time you were goin' at the idiot."

I grabbed him by his grubby shirt collar and slammed him so hard against the wall that the mud fell in hard clumps to the floor. My face in his, I said, "I told you once that I'd kill any man who disparaged Camille. I meant it."

Marion swallowed. "Sorry" was all he managed.

Taking a deep breath, I slowly released my grip on his shirt. "Damn you, Marion. I told you a dozen times that I have no intention of running with you. So what the hell are you doing here?"

He looked past me to Camille, then to the bundle on the floor. "Seems to me the two of you were about to check out of this place yourselves. Well, I don't blame you for preferring her company over mine, Joey boy, but I'm tellin' ya to your face you're in enough trouble without addin' kidnappin' to your record."

"What are you talking about, Marion?"

Marion shoved past me and walked to the door. Agitated and nervous, he ran his sweating hands repeatedly up and down his hips. "Bastard," he mumbled. "I'm out of here anyway, so what the hell?" Marion looked around, his expression one of resoluteness. "I ain't here by chance, Joe. I didn't bust out. Horan let me out."

Confused, I shook my head. "I don't understand."

"I told you they were up to no good."

"Who?"

"Horan and Dixie." Marion ran one hand through his hair and took a quick look out the door, as if anticipating something was about to happen. A cold stab of uneasiness began to seep through my chest as he turned back to me. "You've been set up big time, boy-o. They knew they'd have no trouble talking you into this work program. Dixie's known all along that you've been sweet on Camille since you were a kid."

"Get to the point."

"The point is . . . they set you up to take the rap for Don's murder."

Camille gasped and made a noise in her throat that sounded like a rabbit dying. Her eyes wide, her knees drawn up to her chest, she twisted her fingers in her hair and rocked back and forth. I fell to my knees beside her and tried to take her in my arms. She resisted and began to openly cry.

Marion bent over me. "Horan came to me, knowing you and me were tight. He also knew I'd had just about as much of him as I could take. He told me he'd look the other way while I disappeared if I'd help him. I'm ashamed to say that I agreed."

I gave him a go-to-hell look, then tried again to calm Camille. My desperation mounted as I watched the all-too-familiar dullness creep back into her eyes. "Camille," I whispered urgently. "Camille, don't go. Listen to me—"

"You listen to me," Marion declared as he fell to one knee beside me. "The plan was this. Horan would arrange for me to escape. I was to come here and encourage you to join me. But in the meantime Dixie would be up at the house killin' her husband."

My heart in my throat, I looked at Camille. Her eyes were glazed, her face white as moonlight. "God, God," I cried and gripped her to me. She felt as lifeless as a rag doll; I suddenly experienced so great a pain in my heart that I couldn't move. "This isn't fair," I groaned.

"Don's death would be explained this way: You and Don got into a fight over Camille. He threatened to send you back to jail, so you killed him. You ran. Horan and his dogs caught up to you and he was forced to shoot you to save himself. You take the blame for Don's death; since you're dead you can hardly deny it. Dixie then gets away with murder. She gets her hands on Primrose. She has her freedom and therefore can do whatever the hell she wants with it."

Marion shook his head. "Ain't you listenin' to me, Joe? Don't you give a damn that Horan is on his way here right now with every intention of killin' you?"

Turning my gaze to his, I said, "Are you telling me that Dixie is at the house right now—"

"Killin' her husband. That's what I'm tellin' you, boy-o."

Standing, I said, "I want you to take Camille away from here. You hide her good. Whatever you do, don't allow Horan or Dixie to know where she is."

"You runnin', Joe?"

"No, I'm not running. If Horan wants me, he's going to get me. But first I got a bone to pick with Dixie."

I left the house, allowing the door to slam closed behind me. For a moment, I stood in the dark, aware of nothing but the rush of disbelief and fury that consumed me. In my mind, all I could see was Camille slipping away from me again, and Don, lying in his bed and helpless as Dixie killed him.

I struck off running toward the house, stumbling to a stop as I broke through the hedges in time to come face to face with Horan and his hound. With a shotgun tucked under one arm, the other holding back the frenzied dog, Horan glared at me through the shadows before realizing who I was. "Well now, look who we have here."

"Sorry to blow your plans to hell, Sheriff, but I have no intention of running. Just like I have no intention of allowing Dixie to kill her husband."

"Marion has a big mouth. Seems a man can't trust anybody these days. Oh well, I'm thinkin' you're a bigger fool than I thought, Joe. Hell, even your old man had the brains to at least *try* to outrun me. Not that it did him any good. It's just that shooting a moving target is more sporting . . . and it's a lot less messy."

Crack! The night was shattered by gunfire.

I recoiled and stumbled back, believing at first that Horan had shot me. Then through my daze I realized Horan had not pulled the trigger after all. The gunfire had come from inside the house.

Horan chuckled. "Looks like you're too late, boy. My darlin' Dixie has just become a widow. What a shame. Imagine Don tryin' to help a no-account white trash loser, only to have the sorry jailbird turn around and kill him. I suspect the entire town will applaud my mowin' the murderin' scum down in a hail of bullets.

"Go on, boy: run. Who knows, maybe you'll make it. But I doubt it. If my aim is bad, there's always old Blue here. I've seen him drag down a man and tear his throat out in a matter of seconds. Tell you what, I'll even count to ten before comin' after you."

I didn't move, just glanced at the dog, growling deep in its chest.

Horan shook his head. "Hell, I'll kill you standin' right there. Makes no difference to me."

The silence shrieked in my ears. My heart beat so hard and fast that it seemed my entire body vibrated. The overwhelming instinct to flee made me want to vomit.

In a softer voice, Horan said, "Where's the girl, Joe? Where's Camille?"

"How the hell am I supposed to know that?"

"She's with you, ain't she? Don't look so shocked. Dixie checked out the dummy's whereabouts before puttin' our little plan into action. We can't have any witnesses, can we?"

"What about Pearl?"

"Dixie gave Pearl the night off. It's just the three of us, Joe. You, me, and Dixie."

"Don't forget Marion. He won't let you get away with this."

Horan smiled, and his laugh was chilling. "By now Marion has seen to it that Camille won't be intrudin' on anybody else's privacy . . . ever again."

My heart stopped. My knees nearly buckled. God, oh God, I had fallen into their trap after all. Instead of saving Camille, I had literally handed her over to the son of a bitch. Like an automaton, I slowly turned my back to Horan and began walking.

The hound howled in fury.

I walked faster and deeper into the dark, my breath lodged in my throat and my heart hammering in my ears. The thought that Horan would kill me at any second didn't occur to me. My only thought was Camille. My beautiful Camille.

My Primrose Princess. I had at last held her, kissed her, soared to the summit of fantasy come true and found it more glorious than I had allowed myself to imagine.

I knew the moment that Horan released the dog. I struck out running, knowing even as I crashed my way through the hedges that I could not outrun the killing beast.

The dog hit me full force from behind. I landed hard on my face, the animal's teeth sinking into the back of my neck and ripping. My ears were full of the sound of its gnashing as I struggled wildly to protect my throat, only to have my arms lacerated time after time. But in that moment, I didn't care. If Camille was dead, I wanted nothing more than to join her.

"Back, Blue!" Horan yelled, and the monster reluctantly withdrew. Lying in my own blood, pain shooting like a firebrand throughout my body, I looked up at Horan as he raised the shotgun and pointed it at me.

A scream shattered the night.

Camille materialized from the darkness, her eyes wild— not with fear, but with fury. "No!" she cried and flung herself onto me. Cradling my head in her arms, she rocked me and wept.

"Well now, what do you know," Horan said in a low, cautious voice. "The dummy finally speaks."

Tears streaming down her face, Camille slowly turned her furious eyes up to his. "I've remained silent long enough, Sheriff. But I'm not frightened of you any longer. What more can you do to me than you've already done?"

He laughed. "I can kill you."

"You killed me the day you raped me."

I struggled to sit up, my anger overriding my pain. Searching Camille's face, I said, "It was Horan? He was the man who attacked you?"

"I was unlucky enough to happen upon him and Dixie. They were in my brother's bed. . . . I ran. Horan came after me. At first he said he only wanted to reason with me, and I believed him. He took me to the outskirts of Bixby's farm. . . . Afterward, he threatened me. He said if I told a solitary person about him and Dixie . . . and what he'd done to me, he'd kill my brother and me as well. How better to protect my brother than by playing the idiot?''

"Are you telling me that Dixie has known all along that Horan raped and beat you?'' Don stepped out of the shadows, a gun in one hand, Dixie in the other. Horan made a move to raise his shotgun, but Don pointed his revolver at him. "I've still got enough life in me to pull this trigger, Sheriff. Surprised? Dixie has always been as transparent as water. When she gave Pearl the night off I knew somethin' was up. I was ready for her when she came creepin' into my room. The gun fired when I jumped her from behind.''

Dixie squirmed around to face him, and her look became comically slumbrous. "But Don, darling, I would never have gone through with it. Surely you know that.''

"Dixie. I might have forgiven you for anything, even trying to kill me . . . but the idea that you've known all this time that it was Horan who attacked my little sister turns my stomach . . . Sweetheart, if it's the last thing I ever do, I'm going to see us divorced and the both of you in jail.''

She floundered momentarily before spitting, "Where the hell is Marion? He was supposed to have killed the spoiled little brat.''

"You should know better than to trust a piece of no-account white trash like me, Mrs. Philips.'' Marion stepped through the wild-growing shrubs, his expression one of smug pleasure. He walked up to Horan and grabbed the shotgun from him, then grinned. "Just think, Horan, if you're lucky you might even git to spend some time with me while you're in jail. I'll put in a good word for you with the boys.''

Camille slid her arm under my shoulder and helped me sit up. I was bleeding all over, but numb to the pain. I was lost in her eyes and in her smile. I loved her. God, how I loved her.

Camille and I were married the next month. Although Don's health continued to deteriorate, he attended the ceremony, Pearl helping him in and out of the little chapel near the river. Of course, Camille was beautiful and radiant, an angel with flushed cheeks and sparkling eyes, the afternoon sunlight playing in her hair. At long last, she was mine. I thought my heart would burst with happiness.

Don's divorce was final three weeks later. That night, he called Camille and me into his office and announced that he had drawn up papers giving us Primrose Farm. Later, he pulled me aside and told me that R. J. Dutton had sent word that drilling had begun. He gave me the sheaf of legal papers, which he had also signed over to me and Camille. With a weak chuckle he added, "Consider it a wedding gift. Who knows, maybe something will come from it someday."

Don died two months after that. We buried him in the family plot that overlooked the towering oil rig standing like a sentinel in the middle of what once had been Don's best cotton field. Less than forty-eight hours later, R. J. Dutton appeared on our doorstep with the happy news: Venice had just struck what they believed to be the biggest oil find in all of Louisiana and Texas combined. Camille and I celebrated by driving all the way to New Orleans. She bought me a new shirt. I bought her a wedding ring.

On Valentine's Day she kissed me good morning and whispered in my ear: "We're going to have a baby."

For hours, I walked alone over the vast farmland, thinking back over my life and recalling those times I had waited in the cold or rain in hopes of getting a glimpse of Camille. I drove into town and spent hours wandering the shops, looking for just the right valentine gift that would proclaim my great love for her and the child growing inside her. And then it came to me. . . .

I huddled in the bushes, my fingers and toes and ears stinging from the cold as I waited for Camille to find the card, decorated with pressed dried primroses, that I had propped against the front door. When at last her curiosity drove her out onto the front porch to search for me, I held my breath as she discovered the valentine and retrieved it. A smile crossed her face as she read it:

> *To the most beautiful girl in the world.*
> *I would give you my heart and soul if you would have it.*
> *Signed with limitless adoration:*
> *Anonymous.*

A Secret Cupid

Rachel Lee

Chapter One

"Dad?"

Reverend Michael St. John looked up from the financial papers he was reading in preparation for tomorrow's vestry meeting. His thirteen-year-old daughter stood in the doorway of his study and smiled.

"Got a minute?"

He wondered at her hesitation when she knew full well he always had a minute for her. Since her mother had died from cancer five years ago, he'd gone out of his way to make minutes for her. Lately he'd sometimes had the panicky feeling that he wasn't going to be enough for a girl on the edge of growing up, but he didn't have any idea what to do about it. Maybe this was one of those subjects that was going to leave him feeling inadequate, and maybe his daughter knew it.

"Sure," he said, closing the folder and sitting back to give her his full attention. "But if you want to go on a date, you're going to have to wait a couple of years."

She giggled and came into the room, a lovely, coltish creature who reminded him of her mother more with each passing day. He felt a pang of sorrow, and pushed it aside.

She dropped into the chair facing him, and draped one denim-clad leg over the arm. One of these days he was going to have to say something about sitting like a lady, but he was amazingly reluctant to do so. He preferred her the way she was, unself-conscious and comfortable with herself.

He waited, then finally said, "What is it, Tory? I promise not to bite your head off."

Victoria Evelyn St. John giggled again. "You never bite my head off."

"Sometimes I chew on it."

"True. But only when I'm bad."

"So are you being bad?"

"I don't think so. It's just . . ." She trailed off, eyeing him uncertainly. Then in a rush she asked, "Dad, why don't you ask Ruth out for dinner?"

"Ruth?" he said, hoping his expression remained bland.

"Yes, Ruth. Your secretary, Ruth. She'd be perfect for us."

To say he was floored would have been an understatement. In the five years since Evelyn had died, Tory's main contribution to his nonexistent love life had been to utterly disapprove of any woman in whom he displayed the slightest interest. Not that that had been a real problem, because he'd never been seriously interested in anyone. Evelyn's death had left a gaping hole that he had just about despaired of ever filling.

But he sensed that he needed to feel his way through this cautiously. He was aware that Tory and Ruth had developed a good relationship in the six months since Ruth had come to St. George's, and he didn't want to say anything that Tory might take as a criticism of her friend. Not that he wanted to criticize Ruth. Ever.

Seeking more time, he said, "So you think Ruth is perfect?"

Tory shook her head. "Nobody's perfect, Dad. But she really likes me, which those other women didn't."

"Those other women were merely occasional dinner dates. I'm human, Tory. Sometimes I just need to get out for an evening with an adult female."

His daughter nodded seriously. "Of course you do. It's like me going out with friends."

"Exactly."

"But those other ladies didn't really like me, Dad. And face it, having a daughter is a liability for you."

He was shocked, as much by her surprisingly adult perception of the situation as by the perception itself. "Tory, believe me, I couldn't possibly be interested in any woman who thought you were a problem."

"I know." She nodded with certainty. "But it does narrow the field for you."

He almost choked. "So . . . ah . . . you're saying Ruth is my only option because she likes you?"

Tory shook her head vehemently. "No! Don't be silly, Dad. Ruth is really neat. I just love her. And she seems to really like both of us. So . . . well . . . she's an option, right? And I wouldn't mind having *her* for a stepmother."

"I'll keep that in mind."

"So are you going to ask her out?"

He couldn't evade it any longer. "No. I'm afraid not."

"But why not, Dad? She's really kind of cute, isn't she? I mean, I know she's not beautiful like a movie star, but—"

"Her looks have nothing to do with it," he said quickly, suddenly afraid of where this might lead. "She is, as you say, cute. I even think a lot of people would consider her pretty."

"Then what's wrong with her?"

"Nothing's wrong with her." He had to struggle to keep exasperation from creeping into his voice. This just didn't feel like the kind of conversation he ought to be having with his daughter. "But she's my secretary."

"So?"

"Honey, it might make Ruth uncomfortable if I asked her out."

"Why?"

"Because she works for me. What if she wants to say no, but is afraid I might get angry with her or fire her?"

"You'd *never* do that!"

"But she doesn't necessarily know that. And even if she

took the chance, she'd still be uncomfortable. It wouldn't be fair to her.''

''But . . .''

He silenced her with a shake of his head. ''I'm sorry, honey, but they've even passed sexual harassment laws to prevent this kind of thing, because it makes a woman so uncomfortable. I wouldn't want her to start wondering if she should find another job.'' He smiled wryly. ''I need her too much.''

Tory looked as if she wanted to argue, but after a moment she closed her mouth. ''Okay. It has to be your decision.''

He regarded her uneasily. She didn't usually capitulate so quickly when she wanted something. In fact, she could be a pest sometimes, but he'd always let it go because he wanted her to be persistent, and didn't want her ever to feel she didn't have a right to ask for something. But this . . . No, it was too easy.

But she was already rising, tossing her long brown hair over her shoulders and shoving her hands into her jeans pockets. ''Am I making pizza tonight, or do you want to cook?''

''Pizza sounds great, and I need to get this report done for the vestry.''

She wrinkled her nose. ''Oh, no. Tomorrow's the meeting, right?''

He nodded, amused. ''We can meet at the church if you'd prefer.''

''No, it's okay. I don't mind making coffee and brownies. I just wish they'd stop treating me like a kid.''

''Most of them knew you when you were born.''

''But I'm thirteen now.'' She tilted her head and grinned. ''It gets a little old hearing how much I've grown again when it's only been a month since the last meeting and they see me every Sunday in church, and every Wednesday at service.''

''I think,'' he said dryly, ''that they just don't know what to say to you.''

''Probably. An awful lot of people don't know how to talk to kids. But Ruth does.''

On that parting shot, she left, walking just the way her

mother had when she'd had the last word. He found himself grinning.

On the way to her room, Tory grabbed the phone book from the kitchen and took it with her. Sitting on her bed, surrounded by the pinks and whites in which her mother had decorated the room so long ago, she looked up the number for the Busy B Florist.

Charlene and Hank Bowers, who owned the business, were church members, and Tory had long felt she could trust Charlene. After all, Charlene had advised her through her first period and had dealt with her father in a way so that Tory's change in status had been seamlessly accepted in the household without a word. She was sure that Charlene had told her dad, but Tory was eternally grateful that she hadn't had to do it herself. There were some things that weren't meant to be discussed with fathers.

"Busy B. This is Charlene."

"Hi, Mrs. Bowers. This is Tory St. John."

"Tory! How are you doing, dear?" Mrs. Bowers called everyone *dear*.

"I'm just fine. Listen, I just wanted to know how much a dozen roses cost."

"Oh." Charlene paused. "Well, that depends on what kind of roses. But they're very expensive. Long-stemmed roses run about sixty-five dollars."

"Oh." Tory felt deflated. "I guess I couldn't afford that. I only have forty-six dollars and seventy-three cents saved from my allowance."

"If you're spending your allowance, dear, let me suggest a single rose in a glass vase. Thirteen dollars. And of course I'll throw in some greenery and baby's breath."

Tory thought about it. Given her budget, she didn't really have much choice. "All right. One rose then. I guess I need to come over there and pay you first?"

Charlene chuckled. "Your credit's good with me, dear. I'll just put it on your account. What color rose? And who do you want it to go to?"

"A red rose, please. And send it to Ruth Ardmore, please? At her office at the church."

"Sure." Charlene's voice was warm. "She must have done something very nice for you."

"Oh, she's just a nice lady."

"She certainly is. We're all glad she came to St. George's. Now what do you want the card to say?"

Tory hesitated, thinking rapidly. "Just sign it from a secret admirer. And don't let her know it came from me, please? Please?"

Charlene hesitated. "Tory? Are you sure you know what you're doing?"

Tory drew a deep breath and forced herself to be firm, the way her father sometimes had to be firm. "Mrs. Bowers, I am in a very difficult position, and this is the only way to get out of it. But of course, if you don't feel comfortable, I can get a flower somewhere else."

"I won't hear of it. I just hope Ruth doesn't misunderstand this."

"What's to misunderstand? It's almost Valentine's Day. If she misunderstands, I'll tell her I sent it."

"All right then. She'll have the flower tomorrow morning."

"Thank you!" Smiling, Tory hung up and hugged herself. Sometimes Cupid needed a hand. Humming, she went to make the dough for the pizza crust.

Chapter Two

Michael St. John was reading the morning paper over his coffee when he realized that Tory was being unusually quiet. Ordinarily she bounced around, interrupting him every couple of minutes to tell him something, asking if he liked the outfit she'd chosen for school, wanting to know if he was going to be home in time for dinner. This morning she got her bowl of cereal, came to the table, and didn't say a word.

He waited a few more minutes, then lowered the paper and looked at her over it. "Tory? Is something wrong?"

She was absently using the spoon to push Cheerios around in the pool of milk. When he spoke, she looked up slowly. "Not really," she said quietly. Too quietly.

He felt the pang of fear that went with knowing that life could steal the ones you loved. Any time Tory grew too quiet, he remembered how Eve had changed in the months before her death. As always, he stifled the pang, telling himself he was overreacting. "Don't you feel well?" he finally asked.

"I don't . . ." She shrugged. "I guess maybe I'm coming down with something. I feel kind of strange."

The worry sprang immediately to the fore. "Queasy? Achy?"

"Maybe a little queasy. And tired. Can I stay home today?"

Tory never asked to stay home from school. Now he was *really* worried. "Sure," he said quickly. "Of course you can. But I don't know if I want you staying alone. I'll see if I can get someone to come watch you."

Apparently she didn't like that idea, because she wrinkled her nose. "Dad, I'm thirteen! And you're only going to be next door. If I need you, I could just shout out the window, for crying out loud!"

Now *that* sounded like Tory. His anxiety eased considerably. "Well . . . all right. But you have to promise to let me know if you feel any worse. If you need to vomit, or anything."

She gave him a small smile. "If I need to vomit, I probably won't be able to tell you until afterwards. Gee whiz, don't get into a tailspin. I'll be *fine*."

"You probably will," he agreed. "But I'm going to take your temperature, and if you have a fever, you're *not* going to stay here alone."

She sighed, the sigh of a teenager who has to endure so much from a parent that words just can't begin to describe it. He had to lift the paper quickly to hide his smile.

"I'll get the thermometer," she said, and got up from the table.

"Thank you."

She returned with the thermometer, made a big show of shaking the mercury down, and popped it pointedly under her tongue. Two minutes later she showed it to him. Ninety-nine.

"That doesn't even count as a fever," she said.

"Maybe not." He hesitated. "All right, but if you start to feel chilled or anything, you have to promise to let me know right away."

"I promise."

"Why don't you get a pillow and blanket and curl up in front of the TV. Maybe watch a movie."

"I guess I could do that." She got up again and disappeared. A couple of minutes later he heard her arranging things in the living room. He had to force himself not to go out there and help her. She was growing up, he reminded himself. And by her own admission she wasn't feeling all that bad. Nor was a temperature of ninety-nine a catastrophe. Nothing like the terrible fevers she had gotten when she was sick as a small child, and she had certainly survived those.

He made himself wait a few minutes, then he peeked in on her. She was watching something on the Disney channel, and he smiled. Not *entirely* grown up yet.

In the bathroom, he shaved and found himself studying his own reflection. Not bad for thirty-eight, he decided, turning his head back and forth to try to see his profile. There was a little gray hair mixed in with the dark brown these days, and some lines that hadn't been there a decade ago, but nothing he could really complain about. And why the heck was he worrying about *that* all of a sudden? For years he'd wished he could look more mature because it would help him in his work as a priest. People weren't inclined to take much advice from someone who looked wet behind the ears.

So finally he had maturity in his appearance, and people were listening to him, and now he was worrying about aging?

He shook his head at his own silliness, but before the gesture was even complete, he found himself thinking of Ruth Ardmore. Well, of course, he thought. Having Tory press him to take Ruth out to dinner had got him thinking about himself as a man, that was all.

Finishing his ablutions, he went to his bedroom, where he changed from pajamas into his clerical collar and a gray suit. He had a love-hate relationship with that collar, which could become very uncomfortable in the Florida heat, but his flock expected it of him. Besides, he had earned that collar through hard work, sacrifice, and determination, and he spent every day trying to be worthy of it.

It bit at his neck a little, as it always did when he first put it on, but in a few minutes he'd forget it was there. He checked on Tory one more time before he left, then walked across the strip of mowed lawn that separated the dwelling from the church and his office.

The early February morning was cool and a little misty from the nearby bay. He paused a moment to enjoy the hibiscus blooms Evelyn had planted along the walkway, then entered the office wing of the church.

St. George's was a small Episcopal parish, not too large to feel familylike, but large enough to afford its own full-time priest, as long as the priest was content with a middle-class income. Michael St. John was more than content. If he'd wanted to make lots of money, he would have pursued an entirely different vocation.

He stepped into the front office and found Ruth Ardmore already there, busy talking to someone on the phone. He paused a moment to look at her, thinking that she'd gained a little weight since she had come to St. George's, and she looked a whole lot better now. She had been a ballet dancer in her former life, and as nearly as he could tell she had been little but skin, bones, and muscle when he had hired her. Now, he figured she must weigh all of a hundred and five, dripping wet.

But there was a softness to her face now that he found appealing, and her curves were ever so slightly more pronounced. And he liked the way she had stopped wearing her dark hair severely drawn back and now let it curl softly around her face. Damn, why had Tory even *suggested* taking her out to dinner? He didn't need to be thinking of his secretary as a woman!

She saw him and smiled, waving with her fingers. He waved back and went on into his office to scan his appointment book. It was with relief that he discovered his morning marriage-counseling appointment had canceled. Somehow he didn't feel like listening to the Maxwells argue about whether the dog should be allowed to sleep on the foot of their bed. It was his opinion that the Maxwells, after thirty-five years of marriage, preferred arguing with one another to every other possible activity. Without their arguments, their main entertainment would be gone.

He also wished they wouldn't keep trying to turn him into a referee. His every suggestion that they see a professional marriage counselor fell on deaf ears, however. Understandably, since Michael didn't charge for performing his pastoral duties. Every now and then he wondered wryly what would happen if he *did* start charging. He'd probably have a lot of free time.

He allowed himself a moment to daydream about calling Father Tom Ledbetter over at St. Stephen's to see if the Catholic priest might be able to slip away for a round of golf on this misty morning, then abandoned the idea. Tom didn't have any more spare time than he did, nor did Bill Carver, the pastor at First Baptist. They were all lucky if they could slip in a round on Monday morning once a month. And of course golf, even on public courses, was expensive.

He pushed temptation away and reached for some papers to get to work on, but Ruth interrupted him.

"Father Michael? Do you have a moment to spare?"

He looked up with a ready smile. "You know I do. You canceled my first appointment."

She returned his smile and stepped into his office. "Remember I asked you about setting up an exchange to accept donations of used furniture and the like to be borrowed by members of the congregation who have a need?"

"I certainly do. I even mentioned it two weeks ago in the announcements, if you recall. Any luck?"

She nodded, looking quite pleased with herself. "There's quite a bit of interest. Only now we have the problem of where to store all the things people want to donate. And we'll definitely need some real room. I already have offers of a used couch and some beds, a dinette set . . . well, you get the picture."

"I see no reason we can't use the parish hall temporarily. But before we accept anything, I'd better go ahead and talk to the vestry tonight about it. Sounds like we might have to add on some kind of storage room."

She looked concerned. "That won't be a problem, will it?"

He felt a twinge of amusement. When she had first started working for him, Ruth had been very uncertain about how to treat him. She wasn't Episcopalian, and everything had been foreign and new to her. She'd gotten over most of her uncertainty with him, but she held the vestry, who pretty much dictated the running of the church, in something approaching awe.

"Trust me," he said. "There's no reason they should have a problem with this, but if they do, we can use my garage for storage and I'll build some kind of storage room with my own two hands."

The smile she gave him made him feel about ten feet tall. He suddenly had a ridiculous urge to pound his chest, and the mental image made him grin.

But all she said was, "Thank you, Father."

He went back to looking over plans for the youth group's Valentine's Day picnic, the organist's suggestion for hymns next Sunday, and a note telling him that the Westcliffes were back in town from New York but hadn't been able to attend service because Renée was confined to a wheelchair after a stroke. He called immediately to make an appointment to visit them.

At some point he became aware that he could hear Tory talking quietly in Ruth's office. Immediately wondering whether something was wrong, he rose and went to look in.

His daughter was sitting there, dressed in jeans and a sweatshirt, helping Ruth fold the bulletins for the Sunday service. "Tory? Are you all right?"

She nodded. "I'm fine, Dad. I just got bored. I don't see why we can't have MTV."

"We've been over that a dozen times."

"I know." She wiggled in her chair. "It never hurts to make sure your position hasn't changed."

"Well, it hasn't, and it isn't likely to. How are you feeling?"

"The same." She gave him a hangdog look that his instincts said was entirely too practiced. "Ruth says it's okay if I hang out here for a little while. Maybe then I'll go back and take a nap."

He didn't believe it for a moment. Tory hadn't taken a nap since the day she turned three, not even when she was sick. He began to wonder if she was faking this illness.

But before he could question her—and probably not achieve a darn thing—the door opened and Charlene Bowers stepped into the church offices. She was carrying a single red rose in a beribboned green vase.

"Good morning, Father," she said cheerfully. Charlene was invariably cheerful. "Good morning, Tory, Ruth. How are you all this morning?" She put the vase on Ruth's desk.

Ruth looked at it with surprise. "Who is this for?"

"You," Charlene said. "But don't even bother asking me. I promised not to tell."

Ruth opened the card and read it aloud. "From a secret admirer?"

"That's it," Charlene said.

For Michael St. John, that moment turned into one of those defining moments of life. He looked at Tory and saw that she was grinning. He looked at Charlene, and saw that she looked uncomfortable. Then he looked at Ruth and saw her pleasure, surprise, delight, and curiosity. And more, he saw a softness in her face that caused him a serious pang just below his heart.

Ruth reached out a finger and touched the velvety edge of one rose petal. "It's beautiful," she said softly. "No one's ever sent me a rose before."

Tory pushed forward on her seat, so that she was sitting on the edge. "I thought ballerinas got lots of flowers."

"Oh, after a performance, yes. I got lots of flowers in my heyday." She smiled at Tory. "But no one has ever sent me a rose for no reason at all."

"Well," said Charlene, in a slightly sterner voice than was her wont, "I wouldn't place too much significance on it. You can never tell about people who do things anonymously."

Tory made a face at her. "I think it's romantic."

"You would," Charlene agreed.

Ruth looked at her. "Can't you tell me, Charlene?"

Charlene shook her head. "Fool that I am, I made a promise. Just don't set too much store by it, is all."

But Ruth touched the flower again, a soft smile on her face. "It's really very lovely."

Michael no longer felt like beating his chest. Instead he felt a very strong, very un-Christian urge to rip somebody's head off.

Tory, ever a master of manipulation, chose that moment to say, "Dad, why don't we have Ruth over for dinner tonight? She just has to come back at seven for the vestry meeting anyway.''

Any other time he would have given her a stern lecture for putting both Ruth and himself on the spot by asking like this. Any other time he would have reminded her that she was pretending to be sick. But this time, he looked at the rose and said, ''Sure. I think that's a great idea. How about it, Ruth?''

Ruth hesitated visibly, and Michael felt his heart doing a strange plummet, almost as if he were rising too fast in an elevator. But then, much to his amazement, he saw Ruth look at Charlene, and saw Charlene give a quick nod.

''That would be wonderful,'' Ruth said. ''I'd really like that.''

Tory looked triumphant, and Michael could have kissed Charlene Bowers.

''You know, young lady,'' Michael said sternly to his daughter late that afternoon, ''it was wrong of you to ask if Ruth could come over to dinner when she was right there. You put me on the spot.''

They were in the kitchen preparing beef stroganoff for dinner. Tory was washing mushrooms while Michael sliced them.

''I know, Dad. I'm sorry. I guess I forgot because I was sick.''

''And that's another thing I want to talk to you about. You weren't sick this morning, were you.'' It wasn't a question.

She gave him a wounded-doe look. ''Are you accusing me of lying?''

''The possibility has crossed my mind more than once today.''

''But I had a fever! You saw the thermometer.''

Michael looked down at the mushrooms he was slicing. He was losing control, he realized. Losing control of his daughter. The thought panicked him. Just as she was about to embark on the most peril-fraught years of her life, he was losing what control he had. God help them both!

''I didn't appreciate being manipulated into inviting Ruth to dinner,'' he said sternly. *Liar*, a little voice whispered. ''I explained to you that there are very good reasons not to put her in such a difficult situation.''

"This isn't the same, Dad. *I* asked her, and she's my friend. It's nothing like a date.''

That was also true, but he wasn't in much of a mood to be placated. "I'm still her boss, Tory. Don't ever put her in this position again.''

"Oh, don't be such a fuddy-duddy,'' his daughter said, slapping another handful of washed mushrooms in front of him. "Bosses invite employees over for dinner all the time, and employees invite bosses over. Everybody does it.''

"When did you become an authority on what employers do?''

"My dad is a priest, remember? The vestry is kind of like *your* boss, and they invite us over to dinner all the time. And don't tell me it's any different, because if they decide they don't like you, you'll be looking for another church.''

"But this *is* different.''

She shook her head mutinously. "If I'm here, it's not any different at all.''

God help me, Michael thought. Not only was he raising a difficult daughter, he was raising one who was too damn smart for her own good—or for his, because he couldn't think of a single, logical counterargument.

"That's all the mushrooms,'' she said, giving him another handful. "I'll start the brownies for tonight.''

He watched her cross the kitchen and pull out the box of brownie mix, debating whether to press the issue any further. Let it alone, he decided. If she tried this ploy again, he'd just refuse to issue the invitation. How much more could she do, for heaven's sake?

Not much, he decided. Not much at all. Because she was *still* a kid, and she couldn't do anything without his cooperation anyway.

He turned back to the mushrooms, assuring himself that this would be the end of it. It was all the fault of that stupid rose that Ruth had received this morning, anyway. If he hadn't been stupid enough to feel jealous, he never would have allowed Tory to manipulate him so easily.

And of course, there was no reason to be jealous. No reason at all.

Chapter Three

Ruth Ardmore arrived at the St. Johns' house promptly at six. Michael had chosen the time, figuring it would give them time to eat a leisurely meal and then consign Tory to the kitchen with the dishes when the vestry arrived at seven. Somehow he didn't want Tory hanging around with the vestry in her present mood. She'd probably tell them just what she thought if any of them mentioned how much she'd grown.

Tory had insisted on using the fancy crystal and china, and he hadn't bothered to object. What was the point? They'd just have another disagreement, and he was no longer confident of his ability to win these arguments with his daughter. Best, he decided, not to make an issue unless it was really important. Boy, did his ego feel battered after today.

But Tory went further than the best dishes. She added candles, and then astonished him by making a centerpiece of floating hibiscus blossoms in a crystal bowl. He found himself looking at his daughter with bemusement, feeling as if she had somehow jumped through a time warp and come out ten years older since yesterday. He had never guessed she had such talents.

Which left him wondering uneasily what else he didn't know about her.

Tory, of course, managed to be busy with something when Ruth rang the doorbell, so Michael had to go play host when he would as soon have sent his daughter who, after all, had issued the invitation.

As befitted the vestry meeting to come, Ruth had worn a sedate business suit, but she had softened it up with an emerald-green blouse that wrapped across the front to create a soft, deep neckline. When she slipped her suit jacket off, Michael found himself catching his breath.

He had been celibate too long. There could be no other reason why the simple act of helping a woman out of her jacket had suddenly become so erotic. The glide of the silky material of her blouse under his fingertips as he helped slide her jacket from her shoulders and down her arms seemed to leap along his nerve endings. Nor could there be any other reason why a woman's smiling brown eyes, sparkling in lamplight, could suddenly seem so magical.

This would not do at all!

"Where's Tory?" Ruth asked, as if she had no other reason for being here. Which she didn't, he reminded himself. Tory had extended the invitation, and Ruth had accepted for her sake.

"Um . . . oh! She's in the kitchen. Dinner's ready, so why don't you just take a seat at the table while we bring it out?" *Smooth, Michael, really smooth,* he thought. *Why don't you just hurry her right back out the door?*

"Thank you." She walked over to the table. "Such a pretty setting!"

"Tory thinks you're pretty special," he said over his shoulder as he hung up her jacket. "She pulled out all the stops."

"Well, I think she's pretty special, too."

"I guess that makes it unanimous." Realizing that for the first time in his adult life he couldn't think of a damn thing to say, he hurried toward the kitchen. Only when he was inside, with the door closed behind him, did he realize he should have held out Ruth's chair for her. He wanted to slap his own head in disgust.

"Dad, what's wrong?" Tory stood at the stove, ladling the stroganoff into the chafing dish.

"Not a thing. Ruth's here. Go out and talk to her while I bring things out."

"No, it's okay," she said sweetly. "You go keep her company while I bring everything out."

Enough was enough. He put on his sternest face. "Now look, young lady. You invited Ruth. She is *your* guest. You go out and entertain her while I take care of everything here."

"But—"

"No buts. This time we'll do it *my* way."

Tory gave him a mutinous look, but she put the spoon down, pulled off her apron, and marched past him.

Michael stood in the blessed solitude of the kitchen, enjoying a moment's peace, until he heard the sound of Tory's and Ruth's laughter. *That little minx,* he thought in sudden discomfort. She'd probably gone out there and told Ruth something like, "Dad's in a panic. He hasn't had a woman over for dinner since Mom died."

His life had become an out-of-control roller coaster, he decided miserably. Of course he was panicking. He couldn't find the damn brakes!

And he damn well better get his butt in gear and get dinner out there before Tory had a chance to pull any more shenanigans. In fact, the thought of what Tory might do galvanized him into overdrive. He slopped stroganoff into the chafing dish, yanked the salad out of the fridge, and ran for the dining room.

He burst through the door in time to hear Tory saying, "I'd really like to get a puppy, but Dad says it wouldn't be right to leave a puppy alone all day."

Oh, God, was she dragging that up again? "Trying to make me sound like Genghis Khan?" he asked with forced lightness as he placed the chafing dish over the alcohol lamp and set the salad down. Where were the matches? He started looking through the drawers of the hutch.

"They're on the table, Dad," Tory said. "I got them out

earlier.'' She handed him a box of kitchen matches.

"Thank you.'' He was beginning to feel like a jerk.

"And I wasn't trying to make you sound mean,'' Tory said. "Ruth said she wants a puppy but she works all day. I was just agreeing.''

"Right.'' He took his seat, giving his daughter a glittering smile. "Shall we say Grace?''

His companions bowed their heads, and he found himself suddenly arrested by the sight of two dark, silky heads bowed in prayer on opposite sides of the table. It had been like that when Evelyn was still here, and awareness touched him with wistful sorrow. He hardly heard the words of his own prayer.

Conversation slowed while everyone was served, but Tory evidently felt none of the shyness her father was feeling.

"I hate vestry night,'' she told Ruth. "I get to serve brownies and coffee and then I have to go to my room.'' She cocked her head. "I guess it would be worse to stay for the meeting, though.''

"Probably,'' Ruth said. "They remind me of vultures.'' As soon as she spoke, she clapped a hand over her mouth. "Oh, I shouldn't have said that.''

But Tory was already laughing, and in spite of himself Michael grinned. "Why do you think that?'' he asked.

Ruth's cheeks were rosy. "I'm terrible! But . . . it's just the way they pick everything apart, you know? Like a vulture picking over carrion until there's nothing left but bones. They never just agree to do something, or agree not to do it. They discuss it to death. Pick, pick, pick.''

Tory giggled again, and Michael couldn't get rid of his smile.

"I can't say anything,'' he said.

"Of course you can't,'' Ruth agreed. "I'm so sorry I brought it up. I should never have said it!'' She turned to Tory. "Promise you won't tell anyone.''

"Of course I won't! I don't want you to lose your job.'' But she laughed again. "Vultures! That's exactly what they're like, Dad.''

He ought to put a stop to this now, but somehow he couldn't make himself scold Tory or Ruth. Instead he said, "They have a very important job, taking care of the church and all the church money. They have to be careful.''

"Of course,'' Ruth agreed soberly. Then she looked at Tory again, and the two of them burst into renewed laughter.

Michael watched them, experiencing a serious twinge of envy, wishing he could share their laughter. What was wrong with him today? He'd run an entire gamut of unusual emotions: envy, jealousy, panic, desire . . . Maybe he was hitting an early midlife crisis?

"This stroganoff is delicious,'' Ruth said warmly.

"Dad made it,'' Tory volunteered. "He's a great cook. When he has time.''

"Nobody beats Tory in the pizza department, though,'' Michael volunteered. "She even makes the dough fresh.''

"Now I'm *really* impressed.'' Ruth smiled at Tory. "I hate anything that has to do with dough. I wouldn't even dare.''

"It's messy,'' the girl agreed. "My friend's mom taught me how to make it, and she showed me an easier way to clean it up. But I still manage to get flour all over everything. I'll show you sometime.''

"In your dreams,'' Ruth said dryly. "I cook, but I don't do anything that has to do with dough.''

Michael thought Ruth was politely trying to escape what was coming with all the force of a roaring locomotive. He could have told her the attempt was useless.

"I'll show you how to do it,'' Tory said. "You'll see. It's not as bad as you think.''

But Ruth surprised him by agreeing. "You're on. You come over to my place on Saturday and show me. Just give me a list of what I need.'' She turned suddenly to Michael. "If that's all right with you.''

"Fine by me.'' It wasn't as if he questioned Ruth's character as a companion for his daughter. She might have lived in a considerably faster lane as a dancer, but nothing he had seen about her in the last six months would lead him to believe she would be anything but a good influence on Tory.

"Tell you what,'' Tory said, "I'll teach you how to do bread and pizza, and you can teach me a little bit of ballet, okay?''

Michael saw a wistfulness in his daughter's eyes then that

surprised him. She had never asked for dancing lessons, and had even pretty much dropped out of gymnastics in the past year. What was going on here?

He glanced at Ruth, wondering if she felt that Tory was imposing, and saw a shadow pass over her face, as if she were touched by a deep sorrow. Of course, she had had to give up dancing.

"Tory, I don't think Ruth wants to . . ." He trailed off, not knowing how to explain without getting into areas where he had no right to make assumptions. Areas that were private to Ruth.

"It's all right," she said. "Really. I can show you a little, Tory, but I'm not really set up to be a teacher of ballet. If you want to get serious about it, you'll need to find a studio with a good teacher."

Tory waved a hand. "I don't want to get serious. I just want to know a little of it."

"Well, I can manage that without any trouble." She smiled. "I still work out every morning, just to keep in shape, but I'm nowhere near the dancer I used to be."

"It must have been tough to quit," Tory said with a child's frankness.

"It was one of the hardest things I've ever done."

"Then why did you do it?"

Michael knew he should silence Tory, but he wanted to know, too, so he didn't say anything.

Ruth hesitated. "Ballet is very athletic. Like gymnastics. You do that, right?"

Tory nodded. "Not as much as I used to, but I know what you mean."

"It's pretty much the same thing. And as odd as it sounds, a dancer is starting to get over the hill at thirty. I might have gone on a few more years, but I had some serious ankle injuries, and they began to catch up with me. Younger dancers started getting the parts I used to get, and I knew it was time to go." She spoke matter-of-factly, but Michael could see the sorrow in her gaze.

"But that's life," Ruth continued briskly. "And getting older is better than the alternative."

"But you're still so young!"

"Yes, I am. I have a whole life ahead of me, and I intend to make the most of it. That's why I'm going back to college."

Michael sat up straighter, surprised. "Don't tell me you're quitting!"

Ruth shook her head, smiling. "No. I wouldn't dream of it. But I'm signing up for night classes. And I'm hoping that if I'm a very good secretary you might occasionally let me take a day class."

"Well, of course I will. No question of doing anything else!" He felt relieved. Entirely too relieved, he realized with a sense of unease. After all, secretaries came and went, and Ruth was no different from the rest, was she?

When dinner was over, Tory popped up from her seat. "I'll do the dishes," she said, as if that weren't her usual routine on vestry Tuesday. "You stay here and talk to Ruth, Dad."

Skewered, he thought. He looked at Ruth, wondering what they could talk about. She looked as if she felt as awkward as he did. Under other circumstances he would have defused the moment by making some light comment about Tory's matchmaking, but he couldn't do that with a woman who worked for him. Instead he had to sit there and pretend that Tory's matchmaking wasn't as obvious as the nose on his face.

Finally he seized on Tory as the only safe avenue of conversation. "I hope you don't mind giving my daughter a few ballet lessons."

Her lips curved gently, and again he saw the shadow of sorrow in her eyes. "I don't mind. I have to admit, I've been trying to avoid anything to do with ballet. I even turned down an opportunity to teach. Cowardly, huh?"

He shook his head, and said gently, "Losing something we love is painful. We all try to avoid being reminded."

"Still, I didn't have to lose it completely. I could have stayed on the edges and taught." She shrugged. "I was feeling rather bruised and selfish, I guess."

"Are you regretting the decision now?" God, he hoped not. He couldn't have said why, but it was extremely important to him that she not be thinking about going back to dancing.

"Surprisingly enough, not at all." She smiled. "Actually, I feel kind of excited about having a whole new life ahead of me. Ballet was my obsession for so long—since I was four, actually—and it's eye-opening to realize how much of life I missed."

He wondered what parts she felt she had missed, but decided it wouldn't be polite to ask. He didn't know her that well, after all.

But he was saved by the doorbell anyway. The first of the wardens was arriving: Jim Curts, a pleasant businessman of about fifty with a moon face and a balding head. He was wearing paint-spattered khakis.

"I forgot," he said with a deprecating smile. "Julie wanted the house painted, so I took the day off and got started. You know how that goes—change your schedule and you forget everything else you're supposed to do. Hi, Ruth. Still enjoying our Florida weather?"

Ruth and Jim moved into the living room just as the doorbell rang again. This time it was Marvin Bridges, a tall, lean man of sixty who said little but handled the church's finances with all the skill of an accountant, which he was. He nodded to Michael, murmured something about the beautiful evening, and went into the living room.

Following him were Ned and Bill Pierce, twins in their forties who were members of the vestry primarily because they were large contributors to the church. They owned a chain of restaurants and could always be counted on to come up with a large donation when some special program needed help. Michael was counting on them tonight.

With them came Mitch Dunn, a retired Army officer who couldn't contribute much financially, but who was always the first to lend his labor when something needed doing.

And finally, the senior warden arrived. Jed Weathers was a cantankerous man in his seventies who felt he owned the church because he had been one of the five founding members—and was the only founder left alive. Michael greeted him respectfully, fully anticipating that this man was going to be a major roadblock to Ruth's furniture exchange idea.

Jed didn't like changes that he didn't initiate himself.

When they were all gathered, pleasantries behind them, Tory appeared bearing a tray of brownies. "Coffee anyone?" she asked brightly, as she always did.

She endured all the comments on her growth, although Michael had a sneaking suspicion she wanted to remark that if she were growing as much as they seemed to think, she'd already be taller than a telephone pole. She brought the coffee in on a tray a few minutes later, then politely excused herself. Michael felt a wave of relief. Tory wasn't going to assert herself tonight.

The routine business was finished quickly; no one wanted to argue about matters they had all agreed to in the past, and everyone seemed eager to get home early tonight. Ruth took notes quietly, apparently all but forgotten. That was going to change, Michael thought grimly. He really didn't expect instant cooperation on this scheme of hers.

"All right then," Jed Weathers said finally. "Is there any new business we need to discuss?"

"Yes," Michael said. All heads turned attentively his way. "Ruth has proposed a furniture exchange for the less fortunate families in the parish. Specifically, we would accept donations and make them available to be borrowed by people who need them. You probably remember that I asked in the bulletin a couple of weeks ago whether people would be interested in making donations to such a program."

They all nodded, looking from him to Ruth and back. Jed Weathers's face was already settling into the hard lines that indicated resistance. Michael mentally took a deep breath and plunged in.

"The response from the parish has been very good. We already have offers of donations for—what was it, Ruth? Beds, dinette sets, a couch? Anyway, it seems we could get a program like this rolling with relatively little difficulty, and it would certainly benefit our poorer families. The Butler children, for example, are sleeping on the floor, and the Kerrs don't have anything to sit on except folding chairs. These are good families who are simply finding it impossible to make ends meet right now. Bob Kerr, you may remember, was laid off and is still looking for work. He had to sell just about everything he owned. There are plenty of other equally deserving families who have fallen on hard times because of layoffs, or because of a serious illness. And of course there are our youngest members who are on their own for the first time and are struggling to set up housekeeping. It would be a wonderful thing for all of them if they could simply borrow furniture until they're able to buy their own.''

Heads were nodding agreement—except for Jed, who looked as if he were tasting something very sour.

''In order to provide this service for our members,'' Michael continued, ''we need to establish a storage facility and some kind of clearinghouse for the donations. I thought we might use a corner of the parish hall for a while, or even my garage, but we're going to need to build a structure where this can be handled on a permanent basis.''

Jed harrumphed, drawing everyone's attention. ''I don't see why we can't put up a bulletin board for the use of people who have items they're willing to donate to needy families. It's ridiculous to expect us to bear the expense of warehousing.''

''The initial expense,'' Michael agreed cautiously, ''would be high, since we'll need some kind of storage facility. But after that, maintenance should be minimal. Besides, Jed, we can't expect people who are planning to get rid of furniture to hang onto it indefinitely. They certainly won't have the room. What we're trying to do here is get usable items into the hands of families that need them before their original owners sell them or throw them away. People might be willing to hang on to things for a week or two, but beyond that, we'd be asking a great deal.''

''You're asking an awful lot of this parish to set up a used-furniture store.''

''I'm merely asking the people of this parish to be generous to our less fortunate families. I'm asking for an act of charity that won't inconvenience anyone more than a little.''

''But the cost of building a storage room!'' Jed shook his head. ''We don't have that kind of money.''

''Then I'll build it myself.''

Jed's frown deepened. ''You need our permission to put up a building on church property.''

Michael looked around at the other vestry members, trying to gauge their reactions to the discussion. Not one face gave anything away. He took a chance. "I somehow think the parish won't object if I put it up myself. And I'm equally sure I can get materials donated. We have three members who own building businesses who I'm sure will help out."

Ned Pierce spoke. "Bill and I will supply the materials. Hell—begging your pardon, Father—it can't cost that much. And God knows we've got plenty of families who could sure use help like this."

Michael could have hugged him. "Thank you, Ned. I really appreciate it. I'm not expecting to build a very large building."

"Oh, make it big enough now, Father," Bill said with a smile. "We don't want to have to be building another one in a year. And if the parish," he added with a significant look at Jed, "doesn't want it on church property, we've got a vacant lot over on Clayborn that will do just fine. We were thinking about putting a restaurant in there, but after we bought it we realized the traffic pattern just isn't good enough. Letting the church use the land would actually be a benefit to us."

Ruth, Michael noticed, was beaming ear to ear. She had such a beautiful smile.

"Well, that takes care of that then," Michael said. "I guess it would be wise to set up a building committee to oversee the plans so I don't mess it all up."

"There'll be plenty of volunteers who'll want to help put it up," Mitch Dunn said. "You can count on me."

"Thank you."

"Now wait just one minute," Jed said. "There's other matters here that need consideration. Building permits cost money. Insurance costs money."

"I'll appeal to the congregation," Michael said.

Marvin Bridges cleared his throat. "I think this is a wonderful idea, Father."

"It's Ruth's idea. And it *is* wonderful." She blushed as Michael spoke.

Marvin gave her a smile. "I can foot the cost of building permits. And there's certainly enough in the church operating account to cover the additional insurance. I don't see a problem with that if everyone else agrees.''

Now Jed looked as if he'd swallowed a lemon whole. He glared at them all. ''And who's going to run this little operation?'' he demanded. ''Next thing you know we'll be needing a new full-time employee. Who's going to foot the bill for that, Marv? You? Or you, Ned?''

''I'll run it,'' Ruth said quietly, speaking for the first time. ''What I can't fit in with my regular duties, I'll volunteer time to handle.''

Jed scowled at her. ''You're not even Episcopalian!''

''What does that have to do with it?'' Ruth asked. ''Charity is charity. But just to put your mind to rest; I've been giving serious thought to joining the church. It's certainly one of the nicest, warmest, friendliest churches I've been part of.''

Stick that *in your craw,* Michael thought, looking at Jed. Then he turned to Ruth and gave her a big smile.

''I'll help,'' said Tory, from the doorway. ''I'm old enough to do stuff, you know. I don't have to spend all my time with the youth group.''

Michael felt his heart swell with pride, and he beamed at his daughter. She had such a good heart, even if she was scaring him to death half the time.

Tory came farther into the room. ''I know you don't like the idea, Mr. Weathers. But it's such a neat idea! I'm sure we'll have enough volunteers to make it work.''

''But more important,'' Michael said, feeling it was time to take the moral high ground on this, ''we have needy families. It's our obligation to help them if we can. I can't imagine how awful it must be to be unable to provide beds for your children, or chairs to sit on.''

''We already do a lot of charity,'' Jed said stubbornly.

''Be that as it may, we're not doing enough charity. Baskets of food two or three times a year don't amount to a whole lot. Which brings me to another plan I've been wanting to propose. I think we ought to start a regular food drive, collecting canned goods and money toward a church cupboard that can provide food on a regular basis to our neediest members.''

"Oh, for God's sake," Jed said disgustedly. "We'll have every drunken, good-for-nothing, ne'er-do-well joining up just to be taken care of!"

Jim Curts cleared his throat. "If that's all that worries you, we can make it a requirement that people belong to the church for a certain time period before they're eligible for food. But it seems to me a lot of us would like to be able to help others on a more regular basis. We just don't know what we can do. Father Michael and Ruth have some good ideas to get us started."

"Next he'll be wanting us all to hug and kiss," Jed said sourly.

"No," said Michael. "I just think that with very little effort we can do quite a bit more for our community. We've been so involved in building this church that we've forgotten that we need to take care of the physical needs of some of our members, too. Now, I'm not complaining. It's been wonderful to watch St. George's grow from a small group of people meeting in their living rooms to a full-fledged church with so many members. But I think we've matured, gentlemen, and it's time to take up new responsibilities. Why, if every member of our flock brought just a couple of cans of food with them on Sunday, we'd surely have enough to feed our neediest families."

Mitch Dunn nodded. "I'm sure we could. Even I could manage that in addition to my tithe, and as you all know, I'm not a wealthy man. As for the furniture exchange, well, I've had plenty of building experience over the years, and I'm able-bodied enough to move furniture. I'd feel a whole lot better about myself if I were doing something more practical to really help people out."

Heads were nodding, and Jed seemed to realize he was losing ground, not gaining it. "You'll do what you want, I guess. But don't come complaining to me when it gets to be too much to handle and you can't get people out of bed on Saturday morning to help out. I know human nature too well to believe anything like this can work."

Michael usually made a point of not disagreeing too strongly with Jed Weathers, but this time he felt he had to.

"I'm sorry, Jed, but I have to disagree. Some people are

unreliable, it's true. But most people who make commitments keep them. If the parish is interested in these projects, we'll have enough volunteers. I'll put it to the members on Sunday, and we'll see what kind of response we get.''

To that not even Jed could disagree.

When Michael closed the door behind the last vestryman, he turned to find Ruth standing in the foyer, looking almost shyly at him. He was relieved to note that Tory was nowhere in sight. He wasn't up to any more of her hijinks today.

Ruth spoke. ''I just wanted to tell you . . . I thought it was wonderful the way you handled Jed Weathers.''

St. George could hardly have felt any bolder after he slew the dragon. Michael felt his chest swell. He managed a deprecating shrug. ''It was nothing. Sometimes we just have to do what's right. Lately I've begun to feel that this parish has been focused for so long on its own growth and development that we've lost sight of our larger mission. Of course, we're really not all that big yet, so we have to be cautious about what we take on. But we're certainly big enough to handle these few things.''

''I think so. All it takes are willing hands.''

''That's a very good philosophy. And true of most things.''

She smiled then, that warm, beautiful smile he saw so rarely. ''Well, I need to go now. Thank you for the lovely dinner.''

''Let me walk you to your car.''

Florida had some of the most beautiful nights in the world. It was just a little chilly, and the fronds of the palms in front of the church clattered softly in the breeze. The leaves of the live oaks in his front yard whispered quietly, and the Spanish moss Evelyn had loved so much swayed gently from their branches. Overhead, the day's earlier cloudiness had cleared away, leaving a sky strewn with stars so bright that not even the street lamps could wash them out.

''Did your boyfriend send you that rose today?'' Michael asked, and immediately wished he could snatch the question back. He didn't want to sound too interested, but on the other hand, he was intensely curious.

"I don't have a boyfriend." She gave a little laugh.

"I find that very hard to believe."

"It's true." She tossed her head almost defiantly. "I just don't have the patience for it anymore."

"Patience?"

They reached her car and she faced him. "I figured out a long time ago that there are very few men worth all the effort of trying to build a relationship. And right now I just don't have the time or the interest."

He looked down at her, wondering what secrets her dark eyes held, at which he could only guess. "Somebody gave you a bad time?" It was none of his business, and he really shouldn't have asked, but the downside of being a priest was that you got used to asking questions other people wouldn't.

"Several somebodies." She shook her head slightly, as if brushing away an annoying memory. "As a rule, men are selfish. Right now *I* need to be selfish. I need to get my life on course before I have time to cater to anybody else."

"He must have been a bad somebody," Michael said, letting go of the subject.

"Not really. He just couldn't think of anyone but himself."

She unlocked her car door and climbed in. Before she closed it, she looked up at him one last time. "Working at St. George's is teaching me that people can be generous. Even men." Smiling, she closed the door, waved, and drove off into the night.

Michael stared after her, then tipped his head back and looked up at the stars while the breeze tossed his hair. He wondered if Evelyn had thought he was one of those selfish people.

God, he hoped not. But when he remembered the hard years while he was in seminary, and his early years at St. George's when they had lived hand-to-mouth, he wondered.

Tory was picking up the cups and napkins in the living room when he came back inside. "Honey, I can do that," he told her.

She shook her head. "I'm tired of sitting in my room and I don't feel sleepy."

He picked up a couple of cups and swept some brownie crumbs into them.

"I'm really proud of you for standing up to Jed Weathers, Dad."

"Everybody stood up to him tonight, even you."

She flashed him a grin. "I sure did. The whole youth group will want to help out, you know. We've been talking about how we'd like to do something useful. We just couldn't figure out what. We're just kids, after all."

"But you keep telling me you're not a kid anymore."

She wrinkled her nose. "I'm not. But I'm still not grown-up enough to do a lot of things. Helping out with the furniture exchange is something we all can do. And the food pantry, too. And maybe even with building the storage place."

"Only if it doesn't interfere with your schoolwork."

"It won't."

"And it's nine-thirty, so you'd better get to bed."

Obediently, she put the dishes in the kitchen, kissed him good-night, and disappeared into her room.

Michael stayed in the kitchen, rinsing the cups and putting them into the dishwasher, thinking about Ruth the whole time.

Chapter Four

On Thursday, Tory left the schoolyard at lunchtime with two of her friends, and together they walked to a nearby supermarket. There was no question that she was disappointed in her dad's reaction to the rose she had sent Ruth. She had hoped it would make him jealous enough to do something himself, but he hadn't. Not even having Ruth over to dinner had seemed to loosen him up a whole lot.

Well, there was still a week until Valentine's Day. It was time to escalate.

For eight dollars, she bought a heart-shaped box of chocolates that was wrapped in red cellophane, and a mushy card that she had one of the other girls sign ''Your secret admirer.'' That ought to make her dad nervous, she thought triumphantly. And if it didn't . . . well, she had more than twenty dollars left, and she'd get another five this Saturday as allowance.

And this time, Charlene Bowers wouldn't be standing there telling Ruth not to make too much of it! Sheesh! Charlene had all but undone what Tory had been trying to do.

Tory swore her friends to secrecy, but of course the minute

they got home after school they told their mothers about Tory's plot to make her dad jealous enough to ask Ruth out. The mothers, both romantics, thought it was cute, and before long phone lines all over were humming with the tale.

Charlene Bowers was on the receiving end of one of these calls, and it so tickled her that she started to put together a floral bouquet to send from the secret admirer. First thing in the morning, she promised herself, Ruth Ardmore was going to have a desk full of flowers. Ruth, she was convinced, would make an excellent wife for Father Michael and a wonderful mother for Tory. Hadn't she been saying so to her husband for months now? It was time Father Michael remarried.

After she got home from school, Tory waited impatiently until her father went out on a call and Ruth went to open the parish hall for the youth group meeting. Then she slipped across the yard and deposited the candy and card on Ruth's desk.

When Michael returned from his call, he entered the church office to find Tory sitting in an armchair, reading one of her textbooks. On Ruth's desk in plain sight was the candy and the card.

He paused, looking at them. "Somebody brought something for Ruth?"

Tory looked up, pretending disinterest. "I guess," she said, and returned her gaze to her book. The worst thing about her dad was that he could tell when she was lying, and she didn't want him looking into her eyes right now. "I'll bet it's the same person who sent the flower." At least that wasn't a lie.

"Probably."

Her father's voice sounded so strange that Tory looked up, wondering what had made him angry. But he was already heading into his office. A few seconds later, he stuck his head out. "Why aren't you studying at home?"

"What made you so grumpy?" she asked, grumpily. "I just wanted to be sure to give Ruth the list of stuff she needs to make pizza on Saturday. Besides, I've got the youth group meeting in half an hour."

"Oh." He disappeared into his office. Moments later he looked out again. "I'll give her the list."

"Da-ad! I want to do it. This is *my* date with Ruth. If you want one, ask her out!"

"Minx."

"Crabapple."

"Imp."

"Grump." She grinned and he grinned back. *Whew*, she thought when she heard him settle behind his desk. Maybe it *was* getting to him. She preened for a few minutes, thinking how very clever she was.

Ruth returned shortly and was clearly surprised when she saw the candy and card on the desk. "What's this?"

Tory shrugged, unable to muster a bold-faced lie. "Don't ask *me*."

"This is terrible," Ruth said.

Tory's heart quickened. "What is?"

"Chocolates. I love them. But all the years I was a dancer I had to be so careful about my weight that I never ate them. I may go home tonight and be an absolute pig."

Michael had once again come to the door of his office. "You're as slender as a reed, Ruth. I don't think they could harm you." But Tory thought he was looking at the box as if it held poison.

Ruth opened the card first, read it, and blushed.

"What does it say?" Michael asked.

She handed it to him.

He read it. "A little juvenile."

Ruth snatched it back. "It's sweet. Be nice or I won't share my candy."

Tory sat up straighter. She hadn't considered the possibility that Ruth might actually let her have a piece of chocolate. And she adored this kind of candy.

Michael was looking at Ruth as if she were a perplexing puzzle. "I thought you didn't want a boyfriend right now."

"I'm not looking," she agreed, casting Tory's hopes into the pits, "but this is sweet and flattering anyway. And who knows? If St. George rides up on his white horse, I just might reconsider."

Michael looked glum, which cheered Tory considerably.

Ruth tore the cellophane off the box, opened it, and offered it to Tory. "Help yourself," she said. "I really don't want to eat all of these and I know I will if you don't rescue me."

Tory took two and bit into the first one, savoring the chocolate creme filling. Michael accepted one.

"Yummy," Tory said through a mouthful of chocolate.

Ruth selected a piece for herself and bit into it, looking as if she had just tasted heaven. "Mmm," she agreed happily.

Michael ate his, looking as if he didn't at all enjoy it. Then he excused himself to get back to work. Tory watched him go, with a sinking heart. She had never imagined that her own father could be so dense. Couldn't he see how tickled Ruth was by this secret admirer? Couldn't he take a hint that Ruth was interested in the possibility of romance? What did she have to do to goad him into action? Spend the rest of her allowance on flowers or balloons?

Balloons. Why hadn't she thought of that before? A bouquet of "I love you" balloons might just do the trick. Or maybe a bag of those little candy hearts with all the mushy Valentine's messages. Given the limits of her finances, she couldn't exactly be extravagant.

"Aren't you going to the youth group meeting?" Ruth asked.

Tory looked up from the book she'd been blindly studying to realize she had lost track of time. "Oh! Yeah! I need to see about getting the guys to volunteer for this furniture exchange thingy."

"The more the merrier," Ruth said with a smile. "I have a feeling I'm going to need all the help I can get."

"You sure will," Tory agreed, bouncing to her feet. "Mr. Weathers doesn't like the idea, so you can bet he'll do everything possible to make it difficult for us."

"Tory!" said Michael reprovingly from the depths of his office. "You are not to talk about people that way, particularly the senior warden."

Tory made a face. "I'm just telling the truth, Dad, and you know it. And you taught me never to lie."

Before he could retort, she had skipped out of the office, leaving nothing behind but the sound of her laughter.

•   •   •

"Ken Redfield called," Ruth told Michael just before she left for the day. "He said he and his wife are redecorating and they want to donate a complete bedroom and living-room set to the exchange."

"Great. That's really great."

Ruth tilted her head, looking curiously at him. He felt as if her eyes were seeing past his calm façade to the unpleasant feelings roiling inside him. "Unfortunately, they want to move the stuff out in a week. We're not going to have a storage space by then."

"We can probably fit it all in my garage. But first, why don't you just check with some of the people in the parish who could use some of the furniture. Maybe we can just get it directly to them."

"Good idea. First thing in the morning. Do you have some names for me?"

He nodded, wondering how it was that Ruth seemed to be growing more and more beautiful with each passing minute. Was this the same woman he had thought looked too scrawny and bony to be attractive when he had first hired her? "I've got some ideas. I'll have something for you."

"Thank you." She started to turn away, hesitated, and looked back. "Father? Are you feeling all right?"

If he'd exercised even an ounce of the common sense he believed he had, he would have said that he was just fine. Instead he blurted, "I'm uneasy about this secret admirer of yours." He was embarrassed the instant he spoke, and his discomfort only grew when Ruth looked amused.

"Really?" she asked. "Why?"

"Because . . ." He hesitated, looking for a way to explain his discomfort. "Well . . . it's just that these days a woman can't be too careful. There are stalkers out there, and some guy who doesn't want to tell you who he is . . . well, I'd be cautious in your shoes."

"Candy and flowers are hardly threatening," she told him, a smile flickering in her dark eyes. "In fact, they're a traditional way to get a woman's attention. As for who this person is, I suspect he or she will tell me soon enough. There'd be no point in doing this if he didn't want me to know eventually."

"Just be careful, Ruth."

She cocked her head and smiled. "I've dealt with big bad wolves before, Father."

"And why don't you call me Michael? At least when none of the parish are around."

"Oh, I can probably manage that. See you tomorrow." She gave a little wave and left.

He felt like a fool. Pure and simple. Making a mountain out of a molehill of flowers and candy, for the love of Mike. He had to get a grip here before he did something really asinine. He also had to get over to the parish hall for the youth group meeting before they began to wonder where he was and send out a search party.

Rising, he organized his papers into the neat stacks he preferred to find when he arrived in the morning. When he passed through Ruth's office, he noticed that she had left the box of candy on her desk. For some reason that made him feel like smiling.

"You know, Dad," Tory said the next morning at breakfast, "you'd better do something before this other guy gets Ruth."

Michael lowered the newspaper just far enough to be able to see his daughter over the top edge. He wondered how she could look so angelic when she was giving him a royal case of heartburn. "Ruth will do as she wants."

"Sure." Tory lifted a spoonful of cereal to her mouth, then paused. "But you know, if you don't show any interest in her, you'll never have a chance."

"I don't recall ever expressing any interest in her. Even to *you*."

Tory sighed, put her spoon down in the bowl, and propped her cheek on her hand. "Are you really so old that you don't see how beautiful Ruth is?"

Michael felt stung, and seriously annoyed. "Of course she's beautiful! And I'm not old. But that's not the point here."

"Of course it is. If you think she's beautiful, how can you stand by and watch some other man come on to her?"

Michael snapped the paper closed and looked at his daughter. "What kind of language is that? 'Come on to her.' Where are you hearing that?"

Tory shrugged. "At school, of course. Guys come on to girls all the time."

"At *thirteen*?"

Tory eyed him sadly. "Boy, you're really out of touch. I got asked to go to the movies twice this week."

"Oh, my God."

"I only said no because I knew you'd hit the roof. It's just the movies, Dad. On Saturday afternoon. No big deal."

No big deal that his daughter was being asked for dates by young males he probably didn't even know? "Of course it's a big deal. And you're too young to date anybody, even at the movies."

"All the girls do it, you know. But that's okay. I know you'd have a cow."

"Tory—"

She interrupted him. "Besides, we're not talking about me, we're talking about you. Don't you *like* Ruth?"

"Of course I like her. But that's not the issue."

"Sure it is. If you like her and you think she's beautiful, you ought to at least take her out to dinner."

"I explained already."

"Somehow I don't think Ruth is that much of a wimp. She wouldn't hold it against you if you just asked."

"I'm not going to ask, and you're going to drop this subject permanently."

"So you *are* a wuss."

He was not going to dignify that with an answer. "You're going to be late for school."

"I have five minutes yet."

"Then use them eating your breakfast. Otherwise, keep your mouth shut."

"Boy, what made you so mad? I was just trying to understand!"

"Then understand this, young lady. Ruth is my employee, and I will not date an employee. Period."

Tory got up and carried her bowl to the sink. Then she headed for the door. On her way out, she glanced back long enough to say, "Rules were made to be broken."

The last word, he thought. Just like her mother. Always the last word. Then he realized what she'd just said. Good grief, where was she getting these ideas?

He lingered longer than usual over the paper, oddly reluctant to go to his office. Of course, he realized. Tory had finally succeeded in making him aware of Ruth as a woman, and he was so uncomfortable with the realization that he was reluctant to face Ruth. Like a kid who'd suddenly developed a crush, he was reluctant to see her for fear she would realize it.

Ridiculous! Slapping the paper down, he went to get dressed. Tory and her machinations . . .

He was crossing the yard toward the church just as the Busy B Florist van pulled up in front of the office. Charlene Bowers waved to him as she climbed out, then went around to the back of the van. Michael watched with a sinking stomach as she pulled out a huge floral arrangement in a red cut-glass vase.

Charlene smiled at him around it. "Somebody's really determined to get Ruth's attention."

"Another one?"

"Sure enough."

"The same guy?"

"So it seems."

"Who is it?"

Charlene shook her head. "Now I can't tell you that, Father. A secret is a secret, and I don't want it getting around that I can't keep my customers' secrets."

"But you said she shouldn't take this guy seriously."

Charlene cocked her head toward the bouquet she was carrying. "This is a serious bouquet."

He couldn't deny it. The profusion of flowers was beautiful and probably outrageously expensive. "Someone from the church?"

"I'm not going to play twenty questions. Would you mind opening the door?"

He held it open for her, his mind running rapidly through the list of eligible bachelors in the congregation who might be able to afford an extravagance like this. He came up with too many for his peace of mind. Young, handsome men with plenty of money. Men who didn't come with all the headaches of priesthood and parish attached.

And why was he even thinking of this? He wasn't in the running. He wasn't even interested in being in the running.

Of course not!

Ruth was overwhelmed. He could tell from her face. A kind of wonder seemed to fill her eyes as she looked at the huge bouquet. "Oh, my!" she said. "Charlene, who is it?"

"Can't tell," Charlene said. "You'll find out in due time."

The bouquet took up residence on a filing cabinet, from where it spread its perfumes throughout Ruth's office. The fragrance even spread into Michael's office, a constant reminder that some young Don Juan was doing a good job of rattling his secretary's wish to remain uninvolved at present. St. George on a white horse indeed! That was probably the next step in this strange courtship.

Disgruntled, he forced himself to go to work on his sermon. For his text he chose James 3:16: "For where there is envy and selfish ambition, there will also be disorder and wickedness of every kind." He wrote nearly three pages of unaccustomed ranting before he realized he was ranting at himself for his own unworthy feelings.

Reaching for his Bible, he chose a more suitable text for a Sunday when he was going to ask his flock to volunteer on two major projects. James 2:15–17 said it all: "If a brother or sister is naked and lacks daily food, and one of you says to them, 'Go in peace; keep warm and eat your fill,' and yet you do not supply their bodily needs, what is the good of that? So faith by itself, if it has no works, is dead."

Now that was far more in keeping with the spirit he hoped to encourage in his congregation. As for *his* devils, he would just deal with them in private.

On Saturday afternoon, he drove Tory over to Ruth's apartment. He was rather surprised at the nice complex in which she lived, far nicer than he would have expected on her current salary. She must have saved quite a bit from her income as a dancer, he decided.

Tory was bubbling over with excitement at the prospect of spending a few hours with Ruth. On the one hand, he was delighted that she had found a respectable older woman to be a friend to her just as she was entering a very difficult stage of life. On the other, he was worried that it might only lead to grief when Ruth moved on, as she was bound to eventually.

And of course, he wasn't really looking forward to going home alone on Saturday, which was a traditional time for Tory and him to rent some really awful science fiction movies and scarf down hot dogs and chips in front of the TV. But this was just a sign of Tory's maturation, he reminded himself. Those times with his daughter were going to become fewer, as she steadily enlarged her own world of activities and eventually left home for good. He'd better start getting used to it.

"Please stay," Ruth said when he turned to leave after dropping off Tory. "We certainly aren't going to eat all this pizza by ourselves. Besides, we need a royal tester to make sure it won't kill us." Her eyes were dancing with mirth.

"Tory's a great cook," he started to say, conscious that his daughter had wanted this time alone with Ruth.

"Stay, Dad," Tory said. "Come on. If you go home, you probably won't even make dinner for yourself."

He considered disputing the image of himself as a helpless bachelor, then thought better of it. If he was honest with himself, he really wanted to join them.

"Please," Ruth said again, stepping back to open the door wider.

"Thanks."

Ruth's apartment was attractive in a very different way from his own home with its comfortably battered furniture. She had used bright primary colors for upholstery and wall ornamentation, and the whole effect was of lightness and brightness. An extensive collection of crystal animals was highlighted on an étagère.

"Help yourself to the stereo," Ruth said, indicating it with a wave. "Would you like something to drink?"

"No, thanks. I'm fine."

"Well, feel free to wander around while Tory and I whip up this pizza." Then she led Tory away to the kitchen.

Michael stood in the middle of the living room with his hands in his pockets. He was accustomed to being in other people's homes, and in his role as pastor, he was quite comfortable. This was different, though. He was feeling like excess baggage. He spent a few minutes studying the crystal animals, particularly admiring a sea turtle as it emerged from its shell, and a leaping dolphin.

He discovered she had two bedrooms, quite an extravagance for someone who was living alone. The doors were standing open, giving him a clear view. Her bedroom was decorated in the same bright colors, with a rainbow on the duvet. The other room interested him more. She had turned it into a small studio, with a mirrored wall in front of which was a dancer's barre. The carpeting had been replaced with a smooth tile floor. In the corner stood a small stereo system.

But what really got his attention were the posters on the other wall, show bills basically, many of them featuring Ruth in costume and announcing her various roles in *Don Quixote, Swan Lake*, and other shows he didn't recognize. He was uncomfortable as he realized that he knew nothing at all about ballet, something that was a very big part of Ruth's life.

He was enchanted, though, by some of the photographs of her. In one of them she couldn't have been much older than ten or eleven. She was wearing a tiara, and from what he could see of the set behind her, she must have been dancing in *The Nutcracker*.

Behind him was a closet full of toe shoes and tutus, and on the shelf above were leotards in every color of the rainbow.

Her career had shrunk to this one little room in an apartment, and he couldn't help but feel sad for what she had left behind.

From the kitchen he heard Ruth and Tory's laughter. Drawn to it, he wandered that way and leaned against the doorjamb, smiling as he watched them. Flour powdered the counter and dusted the fronts of their bibbed aprons.

Ruth spied him and smiled. "Beating this dough to death is cathartic."

"But not too much," Tory warned her. "If you knead it too much the gluten gets all stretched out and the dough gets like rubber bands. You'll never be able to spread it on the pizza pan."

Ruth regarded Michael wryly. "I have no idea what gluten is. Do you?"

"I'm ignorant."

"It's stuff in the dough," Tory said. "Kneading stretches it out. Too much kneading and you won't be able to do anything with it except make a loaf of bread."

"I can live with that," Ruth told her. She turned the dough, folded it over again, and pushed into it with the heel of her palm.

"I really think that's enough," Tory said, clearly enjoying her turn in the driver's seat. "Use the rolling pin on it now to roll it out as big as the pizza pan. Wait . . . sprinkle some flour on top of the dough, and rub some on the rolling pin."

Michael continued to watch, grinning as the dough developed a mind of its own, at first refusing to roll out flat, and then developing holes as Ruth tried to lift it onto the pan. Finally Tory stepped in and made short work of it. She was enjoying showing off.

And Michael enjoyed watching them. They were serious at times, and at other times dissolved into giggles. He always loved to see Tory have fun, but he was also delighted that Ruth genuinely seemed to be enjoying herself. He had thought she was just humoring Tory, but her pleasure seemed to be real.

They ate together at a small dinette while Tory talked vivaciously. One thing about his daughter, Michael thought, was that she made conversation easy for everyone around her. All you had to do was listen.

"You know," Tory said suddenly as the meal was drawing to a close, "a bunch of kids in the youth group would really like to learn some ballet. They were thinking it would be neat to learn a little so we could put together a show and maybe raise some money. What do you think?"

Ruth's silence was all the warning Michael needed. He

glanced at her, and saw real pain flickering in her eyes.
"Tory, I don't think Ruth wants to get involved in something
like that. I hope you didn't volunteer her."

"Oh, no! Of course not! She told me she couldn't teach
much . . ." Tory's voice trailed off as she looked at Ruth.
"I'm sorry. Did I say something wrong?"

"No, of course you didn't," Ruth hastened to assure her.
"The problem isn't you. It's me."

"What do you mean?"

"Just that maybe it's time I grew up." Ruth gave her a
small smile. "I'm acting like a child."

"Well, that's okay," Tory told her. "Dad says we all need
to keep alive the child inside us."

Ruth gave Michael a smile. "Your dad's right. But I really
don't want to keep alive the child who feels like throwing a
temper tantrum because she had to give up something she
loved. I don't want to keep the child who is having a terrible
time dealing with disappointment."

"So you've been avoiding dancing because it reminds
you?" Tory asked.

"Sort of. It's silly, though, because I work out every
morning and dance, just for myself."

"So do I," Tory confided. "I'm not good enough to be a
gymnast, but I still use time before school every morning to
work out and do my routines." She shrugged. "I was kind
of disappointed when I realized I wasn't good enough."

So that was what had happened to Tory's gymnastics. Michael's heart went out to his daughter. But then he wondered
why she had never talked with him about it. Was he spending
too much time taking care of his parishioners and not enough
taking care of Tory?

"Then you *do* understand," Ruth said warmly. "It's hard
to give up something you love. But I'm being childish about
it."

"Perhaps," said Michael, treading gently, "your problem
isn't as much disappointment as it is that you feel you're no
longer as good as you once were. Maybe that's what really
hurts, and it's why you don't like to be reminded. Maybe,"
he suggested cautiously, "you no longer feel you're good
enough."

Ruth nodded slowly, considering. "You're probably right. It's not only that I'm not as good a dancer, but that I'm not *good enough* as a dancer."

"Well, you'd certainly be good enough for *us*," Tory said firmly. "I mean, sheesh. I had to quit gymnastics, LuEllen has two left feet, and Shawna has never danced anything in her entire life."

"In short," Michael said, "the youth group wouldn't be a critical audience. And maybe you're being too critical of yourself."

Ruth looked wry. "I'm a perfectionist."

Tory looked glum. "Then we'd probably just drive you nuts."

"No, I wouldn't be a perfectionist about you guys," Ruth said. "Why should I be? You'd just be learning."

"Then maybe you shouldn't be such a perfectionist about yourself," Michael told her. "Maybe you should give yourself the same understanding you'd give other people."

"You're probably right."

"He always is," Tory complained. "He's always giving advice, and people are always telling him he's right. He's gonna get a swelled head."

It was impossible not to laugh. Ruth had a beautiful laugh, Michael thought, and it was nice to see the shadows gone from her eyes for a few minutes.

Ruth and Tory were very nearly the same size, so Ruth lent her one of her own leotards to wear while she taught the girl the basic ballet positions. Tory didn't want him to watch, but Michael found an unobtrusive vantage point from which he could watch the two of them at the barre. Tory's gymnastics training had certainly given her enough flexibility to give her an edge in learning the five basic positions.

And Ruth . . . well, she was incredibly graceful, a delicate reed swaying gently as she moved through the five positions in time to music she had put on the stereo. Watching her, Michael began to feel like a slug inside his own body.

But something else began to stir within him as he watched Ruth at the barre. He fell into a daydream in which he crossed the room to her, slipped his arms around her from behind, and began to kiss her slender, graceful neck. He imagined her leaning back against him, could almost feel her slight weight against his chest, could almost hear her soft sigh at the touch of his lips.

The knock on the door came as a rude shock.

"Michael?" Ruth called. "Would you mind getting that?"

"Not at all."

He opened the front door to find a tall, slender man with long blond hair dressed in slacks and a cotton sweater. He was holding a flower arrangement in one hand and a bunch of balloons in the other. He looked at Michael with surprise, then said, "Is this where Ruth Ardmore lives?"

"Yes, it is."

"Is she here? I'm an old friend of hers from the Huddleston Ballet."

Michael promptly invited him in, although he felt a surprising twinge of jealousy accompanied by a strong urge to tell the man he had the wrong address. This must be the secret admirer. Throttling him, however, was out of the question.

"Ruth?" Michael called out to her as he walked toward her miniature studio. "An old friend of yours is here."

Ruth emerged from the room with a curious Tory right behind her. Around her neck she had draped a towel.

"Todd!" Her face lit with delight, and she hurried across the room to embrace him.

Todd, thought Michael. Of course it would be Todd, a nice trendy name. For one of the few times in his life, he wished he were capable of violence. Or maybe he *was* capable of it—to judge by his current set of wishes, he certainly was—and was just deluding himself that he wasn't.

"Oh, what are these?" Ruth asked, stepping back to look at the flowers and balloons.

"I found them right in front of your door," Todd said, handing them to her. "Somebody likes you."

So he wasn't the secret admirer. Michael felt a rush of relief followed by serious deflation as he realized that the mystery man still had to be coped with.

Ruth set the flowers on the coffee table and let the bouquet of balloons float up to the ceiling. "What brings you here?

Why didn't you let me know you were coming?''

"I wanted to surprise you. I have to go back tomorrow night, but I thought we could have some fun.''

My exit cue, Michael thought. He glanced at Tory and found she was looking poleaxed. So much for her machinations, he thought grimly. This was one hell of a lesson for her. "Tory, go get dressed. We have to leave now.''

Ruth turned instantly to him. "Oh, no! Please, you don't have to leave.''

"Not on my account,'' Todd agreed equably.

Michael shook his head before Tory could put in her two cents. "No, really, it's time for us to go. It's been fun, Ruth. Really. But there are some things I need to do.''

Pouting, Tory left the room.

He offered his hand to Todd. "Michael St. John. That little imp was my daughter, Tory. Ruth was giving her some lessons.''

Todd looked quickly at Ruth. "I thought you swore you weren't going to do that.''

"I'm allowed to change my mind.'' She looked at Michael. "I wish you didn't have to go.''

There was something in her face, something in her eyes, that made his heart lurch sharply. He could have sworn she really wanted him to stay. *Don't be a fool*, he told himself. It was just wishful thinking on his part. She couldn't possibly want him to stay, not with stud Todd here for a visit.

Tory emerged from the bathroom in her own jeans and T-shirt, and handed the leotard to Ruth. "Thanks, Ruth. I had a lot of fun.''

"So did I, Tory. We'll have to do it again, soon.''

"Sure.'' Tory didn't look as if she held out much hope. In fact, she looked downright depressed as she walked with Michael back out to the car.

They were nearly home before Tory spoke. "You have to do something, Dad.''

"About what?''

"About Ruth.'' She looked at him, and he was surprised to see the sparkle of tears in her eyes. "Did you see those flowers? The balloons?''

"Todd didn't bring those—"

"It doesn't matter," she interrupted. "It doesn't matter who sent them. What matters is that if you don't do something, we're going to lose Ruth!"

Chapter Five

Life was the pits sometimes, Michael thought. His daughter wasn't speaking to him. Not only had she been upset when they came home last night, but she had discovered the big bouquet of flowers in Ruth's office that Charlene Bowers had delivered Friday morning. The look she had given her father was full of disappointment and hurt.

He told himself that the decision to date a particular woman had to be his alone, and that Tory's opinion in the matter was significant only if she couldn't stand the woman. He certainly wasn't going to allow his daughter to select a girlfriend for him, let alone a wife.

It didn't make him feel any better.

Since Evelyn's death, Tory had become the central focus of his life, along with the church. He had tried so hard to make up to her for the loss of her mother that sometimes he wondered if he had tried too hard. He supposed he cared entirely too much, but he couldn't stand to see her unhappy or hurt, and was willing to go to almost any length to protect her. But he couldn't always make her life perfect, and apparently this was one of those times.

He ached for Tory. He ached for himself. Both of them, emotionally speaking, were like rudderless ships on a huge sea sometimes. Evelyn's loss had left them both with needs that no amount of prayer could satisfy. Tory needed a mother. He needed a companion and lover. The loneliness in each of them could be fulfilled by nothing else.

But he seriously doubted that any woman could step into Evelyn's shoes as a mother for Tory. Not that Evelyn had been a paragon of motherhood that no other woman could match. But she had been *Tory's* mother, and no other woman's voice, touch, or embrace was going to give Tory the same sense of security she had derived from the mother who had cared for her in earliest childhood. How could it?

But maybe he was being unfair to Tory. Maybe she realized that no one could ever take Evelyn's place. His daughter confounded him sometimes, displaying an amazing maturity and wisdom only to turn right around and do something utterly childish.

Ruth was certainly the first woman Tory had ever expressed an interest in having as a stepmother. Perhaps the child was being more discriminating than he realized. Perhaps she wasn't expecting a relationship that would replace Evelyn. What if she had simply found someone she loved enough to welcome into the role? What if Tory had already made the necessary emotional adjustments?

And what if the whole problem here was that he had not?

When Tory went to bed, he sat in his study looking at the framed portrait of Evelyn that he kept on his desk. He hadn't been letting go, he realized. He had told himself that he had adjusted and moved on, but he hadn't. Somewhere deep inside, he had clung to the memory of his late wife, feeling that he would be unfaithful if he so much as looked at another woman. Feeling that it would be somehow sacrilegious to bring another woman into his life to take Evelyn's place.

No woman could take Evelyn's place. Nor would any woman even want to try. Any woman who wanted to come into his life would have to want her own place in his heart and life, one carved to fit her and her alone. Why should that make him feel disloyal?

It occurred to him that he could probably use some of the

counseling he was often called on to give his flock. Maybe he needed to get his own head screwed on straight here.

It was possible, he reminded himself, to love many people at the same time. It was possible and even laudable to have a heart big enough to encompass many loves. And each love was separate and unique, crafted for one person and one alone. Loving another woman would not in any way be disloyal to the memory of Evelyn. After all, Evelyn was gone, their marriage severed by the scythe of death. He was, by all the laws of God and man, free to love again.

Had he let his grief shrink his heart into a shriveled husk? Or was he simply afraid?

Afraid, he decided presently. He was afraid. Everything else was an excuse to cover the fact that he was afraid of the pain that went with loving and losing someone. He wouldn't really feel disloyal if he loved again. Evelyn had even told him before she died that she wanted him to remarry, that she hoped he would find with someone else all the joy and dizzying delight they had known. She had been that generous.

Maybe it was high time he got his act together.

Of course, that didn't solve any of the problems that went along with falling in love with your secretary.

On the way to bed, he paused to look in Tory's room. Asleep, she appeared much younger, looking all of seven or eight. But in the end, maybe she was wiser than he by far.

Monday morning turned into a madhouse. For some reason Michael couldn't fathom, it seemed as if half the women in the parish were dropping in "just to see how things were going." They clustered around Ruth's desk, talking in murmurs and giggling about her secret admirer. They made a great show of admiring her flowers, and at least a dozen of them poked their heads into his office to ask him if he didn't think it was romantic, and wasn't it wonderful that someone was courting Ruth this way.

He managed to smile and nod and agree, all the while thinking that he'd like to rip the guy's head off. Nor was it any comfort to realize he was being irrational. Irrationality was no excuse for thoughts of murder and mayhem.

And there was only one reason he was being irrational. The thought absolutely panicked him, but the simple fact was that he had become more than ordinarily fond of Ruth in her time here. It terrified him to think that some man might take her away, and it terrified him to realize that he was terrified. He didn't even want to think about what that meant.

Around noon, Charlene Bowers showed up with another bouquet. When she saw him, she smiled and shrugged, leaving his curiosity unappeased. At two-thirty she was back with yet another bouquet.

"I don't know what you've been up to, Ruth," she said, "but you've sure got somebody all hot and bothered."

Ruth nodded slowly, looking in utter amazement at the new bouquet.

"You ask me," Charlene said, "it'd be cheaper if he'd just take you out to dinner."

"I wish he'd tell me who he is," Ruth answered.

Michael felt as if a fist squeezed his heart. He stood in the doorway of his office and looked around at the bouquets. The place was beginning to look like a florist's shop—or a bridal bower. How could he compete with a man who had this kind of money to spend on flowers?

When Tory arrived after school, she was nearly crushed by the sight of the new bouquets. If her father had been there, she probably would have given him a hard time, but he had gone out on hospital visits and Ruth was alone in the office.

"More flowers, huh?" Tory asked glumly, sitting in the chair across from Ruth's desk.

Ruth nodded, looking up from the letter she was proofreading to study Tory. "What's wrong, hon?"

"Oh, just all these flowers."

"I thought you said they were romantic."

"The rose was romantic," Tory said stubbornly. "This is overkill."

Ruth nodded slowly. "I kind of agree with you."

"Who is this guy anyway?"

"I don't know."

"He could be some kind of sleazoid, you know."

"I know." Ruth smiled. "Then again, it could be Tom Cruise."

In spite of herself, Tory giggled. "Yeah, right." But just as quickly, she sobered. "I don't want you to go away, Ruth."

Ruth's face softened. "I don't want to go away either. And I'm not planning to."

Tory felt a wave of relief take her tension away, but as quickly as she let go of it, it returned. It was easy for Ruth to say that right now, but what if some Tom Cruise *did* suddenly turn up and sweep her off her feet? "Do you like my dad, Ruth?"

"I like him very much."

"How much?"

Ruth blushed faintly. Tory saw it and was heartened. "I like him a lot, okay?"

"If he asked you out to dinner, would you go?"

Ruth's color heightened. "Tory, I don't think this is something we ought to be discussing."

"Why not?"

"Because your dad is my boss."

"That's what he said."

Ruth was silent for a long while, looking at the screen of her computer. Finally she said, "When did he say that?"

"When I asked him why he didn't ask you out to dinner. He said he couldn't because he's your boss, and it would make you uncomfortable. Would it?"

There was another long silence that kept Tory on tenterhooks. When Ruth spoke, she seemed to be choosing her words with care. "It would depend on why he asked me, Tory. I would hate to think he was doing it just because *you* want him to."

"He wouldn't. He's told me more than once that his romantic life is his business, not mine."

"Oh. Why? Have you had a lot to say about it?"

"I didn't like the other women he asked out. He said it was none of my business."

Ruth hesitated. "I expect he'd feel differently if he wanted to marry one of them."

"Oh yeah," Tory said airily, as if it were a foregone conclusion. "Of course it would be different. Then he'd be picking a stepmom for me. I already told him I approve of you, though."

Ruth's cheeks reddened even more. "Um . . . thank you."

"I mean really, Ruth. If he asked you, would you say yes? To dinner I mean?"

Ruth looked almost wistful as she said, "I can't answer that, Tory. He hasn't asked me himself."

Tory scowled. "What about that guy who came to visit you this weekend? Are you going to marry him?"

A surprised laugh escaped Ruth. "Oh, goodness, no," she said. "Absolutely not. He's just . . . a friend. Like a brother."

Tory nodded, relieved. "You mean he's gay. That's good." Grabbing her books, she departed, leaving Ruth gaping behind her.

When Michael got home from his last parish visit he found Tory in the kitchen cooking up a storm. *Uh-oh,* he thought as he looked around. Trouble was brewing. Tory was after something.

"Hi, honey," he said. "I'll just run in and change, then I'll come help."

"It's all under control, Dad. Roast chicken, biscuits, gravy, and salad. It'll be ready in about twenty minutes."

"Sounds good." He dropped a kiss on her forehead, then went to prepare for a dinner that he figured was going to be a wrestling match. Tory hated roast chicken. The last time she had made it for him, she had wanted his permission to spend the weekend with a friend's family on their boat. He wondered what she wanted this time. A trip to Fort Lauderdale over spring break? A European vacation with a friend?

It was appalling to realize that he was beginning to look at his daughter with dread, as if she were a time bomb ticking away with an uncertain fuse. Ridiculous as it was, he was beginning to feel as if he ought to duck whenever she came into the room.

And there was definitely an ulterior motive to that chicken she was probably pulling out of the oven at this very minute. He wondered if she would allow him to eat before she dropped the bomb.

He changed into jeans and an old chambray shirt that by rights should have fallen apart years ago. The elbows were looking pretty thin, but so far they hadn't given up the ghost. Comfort clothes. At the rate Tory was going, she was going to have him hunting for a security blanket and sucking his thumb.

He entered the dining room feeling like a man on his way to execution. The roast chicken was already there on a platter next to the bowl of salad, and he reached for the carving knife and fork, figuring he could use cutting up the bird as an excuse not to face his daughter immediately.

He was just placing thin slices of breast meat on Tory's plate when she came from the kitchen bearing a basket of biscuits and a pitcher of gravy.

"We're all set," she said brightly as she put them down and took her seat.

He said Grace, reminding himself how thankful he had always been for the daughter beside him at his table. While she could occasionally be troublesome, she had been the biggest blessing of his life, and he thanked God for her.

She even displayed a surprising amount of discretion by not bringing up whatever it was she wanted until after he was replete and happy.

"Wonderful dinner, Tory," he told her sincerely. "You really went all out."

She grinned. "I even have dessert. Vanilla-bean ice cream and chocolate syrup."

He groaned. "Don't do this to me! I'm stuffed!"

"But ice cream is special, remember? You told me once that since it melts, it fills in all the cracks between the rest of the food in your stomach."

He found himself smiling, remembering the occasion very clearly. His mother had cooked a meal that Tory had loathed, and she had claimed to be full after only a few mouthfuls. When time for dessert had arrived, his mother had tried to tell Tory she couldn't have any because she was full. He had stepped in and explained why ice cream was different, much to Tory's delight—and Tory had gotten her ice cream.

"So what's up?" he finally asked as he and his daughter sat eating heaping mounds of ice cream.

"What do you mean?"

He cocked an eye at her. "Tory, I wasn't born yesterday, and I've been your father for thirteen years. I know when I'm being manipulated."

She flushed faintly. "I thought maybe I could get you to reconsider dating Ruth."

"I already explained my problem with that."

"Yeah, but . . ." Tory hesitated. "It would be different if you knew she wanted to go out with you, wouldn't it?"

"The subject has never come up, so I—" He broke off sharply, looking at his daughter with dawning horror. "You didn't."

"Didn't what?"

She looked innocent. Too entirely innocent to be believable. "Tory . . ."

She shrugged. "All I did, Dad, was send her that first rose and that box of candy."

"*You* sent her the rose? The candy?" Stunned, he could only stare at her.

"Well, it seemed like the thing to do. I wanted to make you jealous."

And succeeded all too well, he thought grimly.

"I spent most of my allowance on that stuff. Oh, and the card, too."

"Does anybody else know about this?" He was beginning to have a horrifying vision of the entire parish laughing at him behind his back while his daughter played John Alden to his Miles Standish. Well, that wasn't exactly right, but it was close enough. Oh, hell!

"Well, Charlene Bowers knows I sent the rose, but I didn't tell her why."

"Thank God for small favors!"

"Don't get mad, Dad. It was just a rose! Apparently nobody thought very much of it, not even Ruth." She looked crestfallen. "And she didn't even take the candy home."

"What about all the other flowers?"

Tory shrugged. "Somebody has more money than I do."

He looked down at the ice cream melting in his bowl and tried to rein in his annoyance. In her own inimitable fashion, Tory had only been trying to help.

"Dad? You're not going to let him get her, are you?"

"Who?"

"The guy who's sending all the flowers."

"Tory, Ruth isn't something on a store shelf that I can purchase at will. She's a human being, and she is the only person who has a right to say who 'gets' her."

"Well, somebody else is going to get her if you never even let her know you're interested!"

"Who said I was interested?"

"You don't have to say it! I can see it in the way you look at her!"

Oh, God. Michael felt his cheeks redden, and couldn't even find enough brain power to frame a denial. His daughter could see it. His innocent, thirteen-year-old daughter could see it. Then it must be obvious to the whole damn world. He wanted to find a rock to crawl under. The whole parish was probably buzzing about it.

Tory pushed back from the table and stood, her ice cream forgotten. "I didn't just get a crazy idea, you know. I knew you liked her a lot. It's obvious, Dad. And it's obvious that she likes you just as much! All I wanted was for you to give it a chance! Does that make me a bad person?"

She was gone, leaving him to deal with the outraged dregs of his dignity and his wounded self-image. He had a sudden mental image of himself as a slavering, dirty old man lusting after his secretary. Had Ruth seen it? Did she even suspect how much he wanted her? There was no hole deep enough to hide in.

Tory sulked in her bedroom for the rest of the night, leaving him no distraction from his unhappy thoughts. He cleaned up from dinner, washing all the dishes by hand, just to have something to do. He tried to watch television, which he normally avoided, but couldn't concentrate on mindless comedy and drama. He broke out a new novel he'd recently treated himself to, but not even high suspense could engage him.

And every so often he found himself staring at the telephone.

It's obvious that she likes you just as much.

He tried to tell himself that Tory was just imagining it,

but that was hard to do when she'd apparently figured out his feelings while he was still hiding from them himself.

But why would Ruth be interested in him? From his perspective, he had a few very important disadvantages. First there was his job, which often required long, odd hours and made great emotional demands on him. Ruth knew all of that. She had seen it repeatedly in the last six months. It was enough to turn most women off, that and the thought of having to become an adjunct to his career simply by marrying him. The spouses of politicians, soldiers, and clergy members deserved to be on payroll themselves.

Then, there was his moderate income. That was all it was and all it would ever be. He wasn't a pauper, but he probably wouldn't ever be able to afford a new car rather than a used one of recent vintage. Ruth was driving a better car than he, a snappy little Mazda.

And then there was Tory, a wonderful girl to be sure, but still a girl verging on the difficult teen years. A stepmother would have her hands full, even one that Tory adored. Most women wouldn't want to step into that minefield.

But Ruth knew all this as well as anyone could know it. She had been his right hand for six months, and she knew his daughter almost as well as he did. Could she still be interested?

His mouth was dry and his heart was beating heavily as he realized that he was seriously thinking about picking up the phone and calling her. What would she say? Would he ruin everything by putting her in an uncomfortable situation? What if Tory was wrong?

He sat for a long time, trying to talk himself out of calling, and trying to talk himself into it. He felt the same way he had as a child when standing on the tree limb above the swimming hole, afraid to jump but wanting very much to take the plunge like all the other kids. He remembered so clearly standing there, clinging to the limb above, frightened and exhilarated, and telling himself to just do it. He had jumped finally, and had never hesitated again.

What did he have to lose? *Plenty*, said the cautioning voice in his head. *A great secretary for starters.*

But now that he had realized just how drawn to Ruth he

was, that excuse was feeling pretty thin. How could he go in to work every day, wondering what might happen if he just had the guts to ask?

He reached for the phone, taking a deep breath to calm himself. Slowly he punched in her number.

"Hello?"

"Hi, Ruth. It's Michael St. John."

"Michael! Is something wrong?"

"No . . . no, nothing. I just wanted to . . . talk. Is it too late?"

The worry left her voice and was replaced by amusement. "It's only nine-thirty. I'm good for another two hours."

He laughed a little nervously. "I won't need that long."

"Oh." She was silent, apparently at a loss.

"I, um, wondered if you ever found out who your secret admirer is."

She gave a little laugh. "Actually, I'm beginning to hope I never find out."

"Why?"

"Because it's beginning to seem a little—pushy? I don't know exactly how to explain it, but it's making me uneasy. And I've got to wonder if this guy is a little weird. One bouquet followed by a dinner invitation would make sense. This is off the wall."

A deep tension in him let go, and a bubble of happy relief filled him. "I kind of thought so myself."

"I know you did. You warned me." She hesitated. "It's hard to call it stalking, but that's what it's beginning to feel like."

His heart slammed. "Do you think someone is following you?"

"Oh, no! Nothing like that. I mean, other than flowers, nothing has happened. But it's still beginning to make me feel closed in."

"Maybe you shouldn't be alone until we find out what's going on here."

Her reply was dry. "I don't have any other alternative."

His heart was now doing a rapid tap dance. "You could stay here. Tory's a great chaperon, and we have a guest room."

He thought he heard her sigh, but he couldn't be sure. When she spoke, her voice was warm and wistful. "I wish I could, Michael. Really. But your parish would be appalled. You'd be out looking for another job before you knew what hit you."

He wanted to argue with her, but knew it was hopeless. She was right; he lived in a virtual fishbowl, and appearances were everything.

"Can you call someone to stay with you?"

"No one I'd want to. But I'll be okay. This guy hasn't done anything threatening, after all."

He wanted to race to her rescue like St. George on a white charger, but he knew he couldn't. These might be modern times, but the standards expected of a priest were still medieval. God forbid he should be caught doing something more than half his congregation had done at one time or another. "I don't like it," was all he said.

"Well, if something scary happens, you'll be the first person I turn to. In the meantime, we might as well just expect the best."

They wandered off onto other subjects. She confided that she had grown up knowing she was going to be a ballerina, that she had been schooled in dance since the age of four. "It wasn't only my obsession, it was my mother's. She was my first teacher."

"Was she a dancer, too?"

"Yes, except that she never made the big time. So her dream for me was to dance for a major ballet company. And I did."

"How did you feel about that?"

"Oh, I was as obsessed as she was. I never wanted to be anything else."

"Maybe because you didn't have the opportunity. I wonder about that myself."

"You were raised to be a *priest*?"

"Basically. Both my mom and dad dreamed of it. You know, the way some folks dream of their kids being doctors or lawyers. My dad was a frustrated priest, I guess. It was always something he wanted to do, but couldn't for a variety of reasons—primarily that it costs a lot of money to go to seminary, and not many people with four kids can manage it.''

''But did you have other options?''

Michael thought back. ''I don't know. I didn't think so. But, like you, I didn't really want them, I guess. I just always assumed that I'd grow up and become a priest. I don't remember ever wanting to do anything else—except for one brief period when I wanted to be a fireman.''

''What little boy doesn't?'' Her chuckle was warm, and it reached all the way to his heart. ''But you're happy with your work now?''

''I wouldn't do anything else.'' He waited, fearing that she would disapprove in some way. But she didn't.

''I'm glad, Michael. You're a very good priest, and people really love you.''

But what about you? But he left the words unspoken, instead stilling the rush of yearning that filled him. He was still amazed by his feelings for her, and the way they had sprung on him full-grown before he had even known he was tumbling head over heels. And he still hadn't asked her for that date.

He postponed the question a little longer. ''Did you ever think of doing anything else?''

''Briefly.'' She gave a little laugh. ''When I was about six, I mutinied and told my mother I was going to be a nurse. It didn't last long.''

''And now?''

''I think I'm going to go to nursing school, actually.''

''That's wonderful!''

''Well . . . right now I can go nights, but eventually I'm going to have to go full-time.''

''So you're leaving me.''

And then she said the most wonderful thing he'd heard in a long time. ''I don't want to leave you, Michael.''

He should have done the selfless thing and assured her that she had to meet her goals and that he could find another secretary. Instead he said, his voice hushed, ''I don't want you to leave either.''

There was a long silence on the phone as the two of them hung suspended on a heartbeat. Michael teetered on the brink of doing something that would change his life forever. He knew that once he spoke the words, regardless of her answer, things would never be the same. Then he drew a deep breath, and like that little boy standing on the tree limb so long ago, he took the plunge.

"Would you like to go out to dinner?" he asked. "With me?" It wasn't the most graceful of invitations. He sat there with a racing heart, wishing he had found a better way to say it, hoping against hope that she wouldn't turn him down.

She caught her breath; the sound was audible even on the phone.

"Yes," she said. "I'd love to."

Chapter Six

Michael dragged himself to the table for breakfast. He and Ruth hadn't hung up the phone last night until well after midnight, and he was definitely feeling the lack of sleep. Not that he regretted it; beyond any shadow of a doubt, he had discovered a kindred spirit, and he had talked to Ruth as he hadn't been able to talk to anyone since Evelyn died.

The first sight that greeted him was Tory's hangdog face. His daughter was very unhappy with him and she wanted him to know it. He let her suffer for a while as he fixed a bowl of cereal for himself and scanned the newspaper. From time to time she sighed heavily, but he refused to take the bait. After what she had put him through this last week, he deserved his pound of flesh, un-Christian though the feeling was.

She wasn't eating anything, but finally, apparently realizing that he wasn't going to make a fuss about it, she went to get herself a bowl of cereal. It was as she was coming back to the table that he decided to put her out of her misery.

Without putting the paper down, he said, "I have a date tonight."

There was a sudden crash. He lowered the paper immediately and saw that Tory had dropped her cereal bowl. The
bowl itself was plastic and didn't shatter, but the rest of the
kitchen looked as if there had been an explosion of milk.

Tory was aghast. "Oh, I'm sorry, I didn't mean to . . . I
was just so shocked . . ."

"It's all right," he hastened to assure her, giving himself
a mental kick for being such a crabapple this morning. He
was already rising from the table, and when she reached for
the paper towels, he waved her away. "I'll take care of it.
You need to eat something before you go to school."

He wiped off a chair for her to sit on, and brought her a
fresh bowl of cereal himself. Then he got the sponge mop
and started pushing the mess together. The dripping kitchen
cabinets would have to wait a few minutes.

"Uh, Dad?"

"Yes?" He was at the sink rinsing out the mop, preparing
to run over the floor once again.

"Who are you going out with?"

"Ruth."

"Oh."

Her subdued response astonished him enough that he
turned around to look at her. "I thought that's what you
wanted."

"It was."

"*Was?*" He wondered if God would ever give him the
ability to understand his daughter. "What do you mean,
'was'?"

"Well . . . you're not just doing it because I put you on
the spot, are you? I'd hate that."

"No . . . What do you mean you put me on the spot?" His
mind was already sorting through a thousand horrifying con-
jectures.

"Just that . . . well, I was such a stinker about it."

"Believe me, nothing you did had anything to do with me
asking Ruth out." Except to make him so jealous he couldn't
see straight.

"Oh. I was kind of wondering. I mean it's all my fault
that she got all those flowers."

A creeping sense of dread began to fill him. "I thought you said you didn't know who sent them."

"That was before I talked to Suzi last night." Suzi was Tory's oldest and closest friend. "She told her mother about the card and candy I got for Ruth, and why I was doing it."

"I thought you were the only one who knew!"

"Well, I sure didn't think Suzi or Carol would tell anyone! They knew it was a secret!"

"But Suzi told her mom."

"And her mom told a lot of other people. Apparently they started sending flowers to Ruth to make you jealous. Everybody thinks you should marry her, Dad."

"Thanks for the information. I've never heard a better reason for marrying anyone!"

"Gee whiz, do you have to get so mad?"

"It never makes me very happy to discover the whole parish is laughing behind my back."

"Nobody's laughing at you! They're all just trying to help you!"

"By trying to make me jealous? It seems like a very strange kind of help to me."

Tory shook her head and jumped up from the table. "Would you ever have done *anything* about Ruth if we hadn't made you jealous?"

Before he could marshal a response, she was gone, flinging out the door in a high dudgeon. Her mother had been able to do that. In fact no one had ever been better at it than Evelyn. Except possibly Evelyn's daughter.

Tory's mood had improved considerably by that evening when he was getting ready to leave. She helped him decide which suit to wear and vetoed a couple of his more sedate ties, insisting that he needed a touch of color. Since he didn't own anything approaching a tasteless or loud tie, he let her have her way and agreed to the burgundy and blue stripes.

As he was leaving, she stood at the door grinning. "Just don't forget your table manners."

"I have excellent manners."

"And don't drool all over her."

What was the world coming to? he wondered as he got in

his car. Even his mother wouldn't have been so blunt.

When Ruth opened her door to greet him, he was suddenly breathless. She looked stunning in a royal blue silk sarong that left no doubt as to her supple curves. But even better, she was prettily flushed and her eyes were sparkling in anticipation. The sight warmed him.

"Where are we going?" she asked as he helped her into the car.

"I thought we'd go to a seafood restaurant out on the beach. It's a long drive. If you'd prefer something nearer . . ."

"Oh, no!" she said almost breathlessly. "The beach would be wonderful."

It was a forty-five-minute drive, but the time wasn't wasted. They picked up their conversation of the night before, eager to share themselves. They talked of their childhoods, their interests, and their hopes for the future.

And it was wonderful, Michael suddenly realized, to have a woman in the car beside him again. To smell her perfume instead of slightly musty upholstery.

"We've had so many calls on the furniture exchange that I can't believe it," Ruth told him. "Not just people who want to donate something, but people who want to help build a storage facility, or help run it. And the food pantry—well, people are already asking where they can drop off canned goods."

"We'd better get the ball rolling quickly then. I don't want to lose the momentum. Just tell people to bring things to my garage." He found himself smiling. "You know, we have a pretty good congregation."

"You certainly do."

"And I have a pretty good secretary."

"I think so."

They laughed, enjoying the moment.

"It's nice to be planning things again," he told her. "I think—I think since Evelyn died that I've been in a kind of holding pattern. The church has been growing, of course, and that's taken a lot of time and effort, but I haven't really put a lot of effort into planning new projects, the kind of thing that gives you something to work for and look forward to. I guess I've been drifting.''

"I'm sorry about your wife,'' Ruth said after a few moments. "Losing her must have been painful.''

"I felt as if my heart had been ripped out by the roots. Except for Tory, I'm not sure I could have carried on.''

"I just can't imagine how awful it must have been. I'm so sorry you had to go through that.'' She paused. "What was she like?''

"Very much like Tory, only more mature. I suppose I could say she was a saint, but she wasn't. She was terribly impatient at times, and she had a tendency to nag. But I loved her dearly.''

He glanced over at her. "And this isn't a very good subject of conversation for our first date.''

She turned and looked straight at him. "I just want to know if you're over her, Michael.''

He took a minute to answer, wanting to be sure that he was truthful and accurate. It was too important to both of them to just dismiss her query. "Yes,'' he said finally. "I'm over her. Truly.''

He thought he heard Ruth release a long sigh, but he couldn't be sure.

The restaurant he had chosen was just across Gulf Boulevard from the beach. It was a nice place, with small dining rooms and linen tablecloths, very different from seafood places that crammed everyone at long picnic tables. This place had atmosphere. Ruth ordered grilled salmon, while he had the broiled fisherman's plate. She wrinkled her nose.

"I hate grouper,'' she told him, commenting on his choice.

"What about catfish?''

"That I can deal with.''

"Pan-fried in cornmeal batter,'' he suggested.

"Seasoned with lemon pepper and poached,'' she countered.

"Now we've got a serious problem,'' he told her jokingly. "Different tastes in food.''

"If that's the only thing we disagree about, we're lucky.''

After dinner they decided to take a walk on the beach.

Ruth wanted to just walk across the highway, but he shook his head.

"I did that once," he explained. "Those condos across the way are private property. Some singularly unpleasant man came out on his balcony to yell at me for crossing the parking lot."

"You're kidding!"

"Afraid not. I think it's terrible that all these condos and hotels have gone up on the beach side of the highway, but that's the way it is. We'll drive a little way up the road to a public parking lot and avoid unpleasant property owners."

"Unpleasant rich people, you mean."

"Well, it *is* private property."

"But the beach is public."

"Yes, it is. But is it worth getting yelled at?"

"Oh, I suppose not." She gave a little laugh and shook her head. "It just sometimes seems to me that wealthy people try to hoard all the natural beauty of the world for themselves and keep it from the less fortunate."

"They do. However, if they want their beach replenished from time to time, they have to share it with the multitudes."

Ruth stopped in the ladies' room to remove her stockings. "Since I have to go barefoot in the sand. I can't see any reason to ruin a brand-new pair."

It was already dark, though, and most of the public parking lots were closed. Michael found one that was open until ten, however, and fed quarters to the hungry meter. Then, hand in hand, they crossed the boardwalk over the dunes and sea oats, and stepped into the cool sand.

For Michael it was as if someone had suddenly thrown a switch, turning the night into instant magic. There was no moon, but there were plenty of stars strewn in the sky overhead. The waves of the Gulf of Mexico lapped gently at the shore, a quiet lullaby of sound. Gulls were scattered over the beach, hunkered down into the sand, sound asleep. From time to time one would stir and adjust its wings, but other than an occasional ripple of their feathers caused by the wind, they might have been carved from silvery driftwood.

And he was with Ruth. Her hand in his was small and warm, and her fingers curled trustingly around his. Everything else seemed to recede into insignificance.

He spoke. "I found out who's been sending you all the flowers."

"So did I."

"Really? When?"

"Yesterday." She laughed. "All those women who stopped by were there to see the flowers they'd sent."

"Why didn't you tell me?"

She shrugged and then laughed again. "If I'd told you, would you ever have gotten jealous enough to ask me out?" Still laughing, she tugged her hand from his and started running down the beach.

He waited a moment, giving her a head start, loving the way her laugh sounded floating back to him on the breeze. Then he set off at full tilt, his longer legs devouring the distance between them. He suddenly didn't mind that the whole parish had been interfering in his life. This felt so *right*. And it absolutely thrilled him that Ruth had gone along with them because she wanted him to ask her out.

He caught up with her and ran beside her for a little while, but then he reached out and grabbed her hand. Laughing, she swung around toward him, and suddenly they were face to face and breast to breast.

The magic of the night was inside Michael now. He looked down into her face, a pale blur in the darkness, and felt his heart pick up a new rhythm, one of anticipation, hope, and excitement.

"Michael?"

He could hardly hear her murmur his name over the steady lapping of the waves, but he heard the hope in her voice. The anticipation. The wistfulness.

He had promised himself that he wouldn't move too fast. They needed to take their time and let their relationship develop slowly. Neither one of them was ready to leap . . .

But his common sense was being swept away by forces more powerful than the wind that was shifting the grains of sand on the beach. The stars above seemed to be in her eyes, and seemed to be in his heart as well. He wasn't moving too fast, he told himself. No way. He'd been with this woman five days a week for the last half-year. That was more than most people had before the first date.

"Michael?" she said again, her voice tremulous. "Don't you think it's time to sexually harass me?"

He felt a twinge of dismay to realize that apparently Tory had confided his motive for not asking Ruth out—he was going to have to speak to that child about not discussing family matters outside the home—but it was swept away by a surge of longing as intense and undeniable as a tidal wave.

Reaching out, he drew her closer still, wrapping her snugly in his arms, almost as if he felt that if he just held her tight enough she would never go away.

Oh, it felt so *good* to have a woman in his arms again, a woman pressed tightly to him. To have Ruth in his arms. Because it had to be Ruth. In all these years he had never wanted anyone else, and he felt a flicker of panic that she might go away, too.

Ruth tipped her face up, inviting him closer still. There was an instant, just an instant, of perfect clarity when he knew he wanted to imprint every detail of this moment on his mind, so he would never, ever forget.

Then, in the next instant, he was awash in sensation: the feel of her, the fragrance of her mixed with the scent of the sea, the taste of her . . . Oh, God, the taste of her.

He wanted to be gentle, to take exquisite care with her, but it had been so long! Her mouth was sweeter than nectar, tasting faintly of the liqueur she'd had after dinner. Her lips were soft, eager, and welcoming, and her tongue, when it touched his, was playful and enticing. He forgot himself, sinking into her, thirsting after her, as if she held the answers to all of life's mysteries.

When he realized in his heart that she was not going away, that she was as eager and impatient as he, he loosened his hold on her and let his hands roam her back, feeling the warmth of her, the strength of her. She had such a delicate neck, and such a slender build that it was a delight to feel just how strong she was. When his hands had traced the curve of her spine, they spanned her waist, measuring her smallness. Then slowly . . . slowly, they slid up her sides until his thumbs rested just beneath the gentle swell of her breasts. Her heat. He could feel her heat. And he knew that if he lifted his thumbs just a little higher he would feel her eagerness just as surely as she must feel his pressed against her belly.

A sound alerted him that they were not alone. Awareness crashed over him in a chilling wave, causing him to draw quickly back. Ruth was breathing heavily, her eyes closed, and her hands clung to his suit jacket, unwilling to relinquish their hold. She wanted him as much as he wanted her. The realization filled him with joy.

But the sound, recognizable as footsteps now, drew nearer. Reluctantly, he pulled back even farther and scanned Ruth quickly to be sure she didn't look too disheveled. No. She looked simply beautiful.

A soft sound of regret escaped her, and she opened her eyes, looking at him with wonder.

"Someone's coming," he said.

She nodded slowly, almost dreamily, and accepted his extended hand. Together they turned to continue their walk and approached an elderly couple who were striding along the sand.

"Oh my God!" Michael said softly.

"What?"

"It's Jed and Cecilia Weathers."

"Who . . . ? Oh no!"

But there they were. The senior warden and his wife were both clad in shorts and shirts, shoes in hand as they walked down the beach.

Maybe the Weatherses hadn't seen much, Michael thought. Maybe he'd heard them soon enough to save Ruth from embarrassment.

But no.

"Hello, Father," Jed said cheerfully. "Hi, Ruth. Glad to see you're out enjoying the beautiful evening."

"It certainly is beautiful," Michael agreed. He glanced at Mrs. Weathers, expecting to see disapproval, but all he received was a benign smile.

"It certainly is a night for lovers," Jed said.

Michael felt hot color creep into his face for the first time in years, and he was grateful that the night hid it from Jed's too-knowing eyes.

"Glad to see you're taking advantage of it," Jed continued. "Finally. Good night."

The Weatherses walked past them a few steps, then Jed turned to look over his shoulder. "High time the two of you woke up. We'll be expecting a May wedding."

Michael stared after them, stunned. Then he looked at Ruth. "Do you suppose they were sent to see what we're up to?"

"That sounds paranoid."

"You're right."

She laughed. "But I think that's exactly why they're here."

"But how would they know ... Tory!" Understanding dawned. "I'll bet that little dickens told them where we were coming to dinner."

"It wouldn't surprise me. I stopped being surprised when I found out the rose, candy, and card were all from her."

Michael looked down at her. "She's very determined to have you for a stepmother. Just so you're warned."

"No warning necessary. You only need to warn me about bad things."

His heart was suddenly so full he thought it would burst. "We need to take things slowly."

"Six months wasn't slow enough?"

His heart swelled even more. "You said you didn't want a relationship."

"I said I'd make an exception for St. George on a white horse." She stepped closer, her lips curved in a gentle smile. "I should have said St. Michael."

He felt a glimmer of uneasiness. "I'm no saint."

"I've figured that out, Michael. I spend forty-five hours a week with you, remember? I've seen you angry, I've seen you sad, I've seen you preoccupied. And what I haven't seen—well, I've heard about that from Tory."

Michael shook his head. "That girl. She's getting to be entirely too much of a handful. God knows how I'm going to survive the next few years."

She stepped closer. "Take me home. Please? I'm getting cold."

At once, he took off his jacket and draped it over her shoulders. She was right; the breeze was getting chillier as the night deepened. They hurried back to the car.

They were silent throughout the trip back to her apartment, as if neither of them wanted to disturb the tenuous understanding they had reached. As if both of them were aware that they were on the brink of a momentous decision, and neither of them wanted to make a misstep.

When they stood at the door of her apartment, he realized how desperately he didn't want this evening to end. When she invited him in, he stepped inside eagerly, with a certainty that it was time.

As soon as the door was closed, he drew her back into his arms and kissed her. She melted eagerly, clinging, her hands restless on his back. He could have stayed like this forever.

Forever. The word seemed to flood through him, quelling all his doubts. *Forever*. It wouldn't be long enough.

He lifted his head and looked down into her face, loving the slumberous look in her eyes and the puffiness of her lips. "I love you," he said.

Her eyelids fluttered open wider, and she surprised him with a soft laugh. "Well, it's about time."

"What?" He looked down at her, puzzled by her reaction and afraid of what it might mean.

"I've been in love with you since August at least," she told him. "I've been head-over-heels crazy about you, and I'd just about given up hope that you'd ever notice me."

"I noticed you. I just didn't want to face what it meant." He traced the curve of her cheek with his finger. "You're sure? Because I couldn't stand it if you change your mind later."

"I'll never change my mind about you. Or my heart."

That was all he needed to let joy fill him. Smiling so wide his cheeks hurt, he asked, "Ruth, will you marry me?"

"Of course I will."

Then he swept her up into his arms and carried her to the couch where he could hold her while he told her just how much she meant to him.

A long time later he glanced at the clock and winced. "I'd better call Tory and tell her not to wait up."

Tory sounded groggy when she answered the phone. "Don't worry," she said. "I'm not waiting up. But you'd better get home before dawn or everybody will be talking."

"Tory!"

"I'm not a child anymore, Dad. You'll just have to get used to it. So, are you and Ruth going out again?"

"By the way, are you the one who sicced Jed Weathers on us?"

Tory groaned. "I did no such thing! He called tonight and wanted to talk to you. I just happened to mention you'd gone out to dinner with Ruth. He asked where you'd taken her so I told him. Honest, Dad, I wanted to tell him to mind his own business, but I figured you'd get really mad at me if I did."

"I would have."

"So what was I supposed to do? Don't tell me he came looking for you to talk about business."

"No. He just turned up on the beach where Ruth and I were taking a walk."

"Gee, talk about nosy! So are you going out with Ruth again?"

"What did you just say about nosiness?"

"Da-a-ad!"

Ruth had a hand over her mouth, trying to hold in the chuckles, and finally Michael relented. "Actually," he said, "Ruth has agreed to marry me. Be careful you don't scare her away with your hijinks."

But Tory ignored the insult, instead concentrating on the important stuff. "Well," she said, "it's about time!"

For C.,
Who Changed
My Life

———♡———

Kate Freiman

Chapter One

Judd Blackburn returned his old friend's formal bow, then looked across the open expanse of Bob Lee's Kung Fu Academy as he caught his breath from an hour of sparring. A small group of women stood motionless near the entrance, looking back at them.

"Ah! My self-defense beginners," Bob told him, slipping the rubber knife into his pocket. "Gotta go. It's later than I thought."

Judd grinned. "Isn't it always?"

He followed Bob across the gym, indulging his curiosity about the group of women waiting for their first lesson. There were six, no, seven of them, a couple of them probably in their late teens, gawky and giggly between themselves. The other women, not so obviously uneasy, looked to be in their forties or fifties maybe. Except for the tall blonde in the gray sweats.

Judd slowed to take a closer look. From this angle, the blonde was definitely worth a second look. Nice. Very nice. Elegant, even in sweats. A *lady*, not a *babe*. She could be either married, or a shrew, or both, but there was only one way to find out, and he intended to do it. His return to Toronto to make peace with his family after seven years on the West Coast didn't require him to become a monk. He was young, healthy, unattached, and as human as the next guy.

In a couple of easy strides, he caught up with Bob. "Need any help?" Judd tried to sound casual, but he knew the instant his friend saw the blonde.

Bob snorted. "Go hide your ugly mug before you scare them away. Especially that one," he said with a smirk.

Undeterred, Judd grinned back and fell into step beside him. The blonde was studying the framed certificates on the wall. When Bob stopped and greeted the women, she turned and looked their way. Hazel eyes met his and grew round. Suddenly, the last ten years seemed like yesterday, and he was sitting in an English class at the University of Toronto, staring at the woman who had turned his entire life upside down.

Caroline stared into the startling blue eyes of the dark-haired hunk sauntering toward her like a tiger investigating a possible meal. There was no point in looking around, pretending she didn't know he was looking at her. Ten years folded back on themselves, and she felt again the jolt of seeing him for the first time—felt again the momentary loss of composure those eyes could cause in any woman healthy enough to be breathing. At that moment, Caroline was still breathing, but barely.

He gave her that slow, lazy smile that had never failed to inspire highly inappropriate awareness, and said, "Don't I know you?"

His low voice pointedly excluded everyone else in the little group of women clustered around the instructor, at the same time that it attracted their curious attention. Flashing her a killer grin, he added, "Ms. Lassiter's English class, U of T, nineteen eighty-eight, right?"

The words *I* am *Ms. Lassiter*! formed in her mind, but before she could say them, she realized he hadn't recognized her. Not really. She could tell the truth, or the whole truth. But if she admitted she'd been his English instructor at the University of Toronto ten long years ago, he would know immediately that she was starting down the slippery slope toward middle age. With her thirty-fifth birthday on the horizon, age was a very sore point these days. So, caught in his gaze like a deer in headlights, she simply nodded.

His dark brows rose a fraction. "I thought so."

He held out his right hand. Automatically, she put her own into it, then smothered a gasp at the heat that sealed his firm hold and seemed to travel up her arm. The pinpricks of heat tingling in her cheeks intensified.

"Judd Blackburn. Sat in the back," he reminded her, totally unnecessarily.

Judd the Stud, some of her lustier female students had dubbed him. Caroline had deliberately refused to speculate about the truth of that title. She could picture him clearly, always in the farthest corner seat: long-legged, slim-hipped, broad-shouldered, black hair styled quite a bit shorter than the thick curling locks now tied back from his chiseled features. His blue eyes had always watched her with disconcerting intensity, exactly the way they did now. Well, no, not exactly. At first, his expression seemed to be daring her to make him interested in the course. Later, after they'd begun the unspoken dialogue of his essays and her answering comments, he'd watched her as if he wanted to devour her words—or her.

"I remember," she managed to answer. Just call her the mistress of understatement!

Judd still held her hand. Caroline gave a little tug. He resisted just a second, his expression part dare, part amusement, before releasing her. Obviously, he hadn't changed much in a decade. Well, *she* had. She'd gained self-confidence, self-reliance, self-respect. She was at the Kung Fu Academy to add self-defense to that list, starting right now, although she'd originally had physical self-defense in mind. Still, she pressed her palm to her thigh to ease the tingling of her nerve endings.

"You haven't told me your name," he said, his voice the kind of intimate baritone that could probably seduce a houseplant, let alone a woman who considered herself immune to a calculatedly sexy grin and sizzling gaze.

Caroline recognized her second chance to tell him the

whole truth, but she hesitated, the *age* demon landing on her shoulder again, and she quickly decided against it. It was a harmless fib, she rationalized. Not really a *lie*. A version of the truth. What woman, red-blooded or anemic, in her right mind or not, would admit her real age to a younger man who was this attractive?

"Caroline Yates," she told him, hoping he wouldn't catch her little deception. Even if he did, another ten years would probably pass before she saw him again.

To her relief, the smile lines fanning out around his eyes deepened. "Hello, Caroline Yates. Are you in this class?"

She nodded, vividly recalling the way she'd challenged him with nearly those same words when he'd stood lounging in the doorway the first day of the term. He'd had the nerve to answer that his presence depended on how interesting the teacher was. Just what a barely experienced instructor wants to hear over the sound of her own knees knocking.

"Good. I'm helping Bob teach it."

That was an unexpected development, and in light of the edginess Judd Blackburn caused her, not an especially welcome one. He was so intense, so attractive, it was unnerving. Waiting for class to begin just now, she'd watched him working out with Bob Lee, and found herself reacting with breathless awe at his strength, his agility, his grace. He was definitely not the kind of man a woman—especially his *aging* former English teacher—wanted to fall on her rear in front of.

Caroline glanced toward the women gathered around Bob Lee, who was openly watching them, and obviously amused. She felt her cheeks burn. "Why would he need help?"

Judd gave her a rather predatory smile. She wondered if Little Red Riding Hood had felt this way when she found the big bad wolf grinning at her. "Someone has to be the bad guy for you to fend off. You know, 'Hi, I'm Judd, and I'll be your assailant for today.' "

Caught off guard by his sudden clowning, Caroline laughed up at him. His gaze locked on hers until she looked away, unwilling to continue the game. Before she could move out of range, he took her bare elbow in his large, warm hand and gently guided her toward the group. It occurred to her to pull her arm out of his light grasp, but he released her first.

"Is this what you do? Teach martial arts?" she asked, hoping to put the teacher-student relationship between them, even if their roles were reversed. Anything to create distance.

"Nope. I study martial arts. Now, seven is an odd number, and you'll need a partner for some of the skills you'll be learning." He flashed a boyishly guileless smile she knew she'd regret trusting. "So, I'll be your partner. In honor of our class reunion."

Caroline could have sworn she saw Bob wink at Judd. Deliberately, she drew herself up to her full height and wrapped her composure around her like a mental shawl. She was determined to ignore the man at her side, even though he radiated heat and sheer animal magnetism. Or rather, because of it. Just because she liked tigers, she wasn't foolish enough to enter a cage with one.

Why would she lie to him?

Ten years ago, she'd taught him to refuse the easy answers, to dig deep into his heart and soul to pursue truth, but she'd just now twisted the truth herself. She couldn't know it, but ten years ago, she'd shown him the way to recognize his own lies and those of others. She'd changed his whole damn life with that one English class. She'd inspired him with her respect for honesty and integrity. Yet here she was, handing him a whopper of a lie.

He was going to find out why. That was something else she'd taught him. Learn what made people tick. He usually did.

Standing a little to one side of Caroline, Judd crossed his arms over his midsection and watched her concentrating on Bob's words and gestures. She was pretending he wasn't there. He felt his mouth kick up at the corners. Caroline Lassiter Yates didn't know it yet, but that little lie, that little omission of the truth, was like waving a red flag in front of a bull. He already had his head down, his feet stirring up the dirt.

•   •   •

She'd been nervous enough about this venture, Caroline mused. Having Judd Blackburn looming over her, breathing down her neck while she tried to focus on the martial arts instructor, made her that much more aware of being out of her element. There was an air of controlled physical power about these two men that she seldom—no, *never*—encountered at the university. Wrestling with ideas, with research and academic politics, with paperwork and overwork, was a far cry from learning to wrestle with would-be muggers. And if she didn't start paying attention, she wasn't going to learn anything, except how to fall.

She liked Bob's gentle manner and clear directions, even though she suspected she'd never remember everything. Maybe she'd catch on without hurting herself or anyone else. After very sensible introductory remarks about not allowing themselves to get overconfident, Bob led them through a series of warm-up movements, many of them familiar to her from her own fitness activities. Then he sent them to sit on the floor in pairs for more advanced stretches. Before she could catch the attention of one of the women who had also come to the class alone, the heat of Judd's fingers manacled her wrist.

"C'mon, partner." When he leaned down and spoke close to her ear, his breath kissed her cheek. Her skin continued to tingle with tiny aftershocks even after he'd straightened and led her toward a mat.

The two-person stretches were also familiar, but she wasn't prepared for the sudden intimacy of doing them with a man she hardly knew—a man who radiated feline sensuality and a powerful sexual energy that was probably extremely contagious under the right circumstances. A man whose gaze didn't seem to miss a single nuance of her discomfort, if the amused expression in his eyes was any clue. Now, as she sat facing him on their mat, mirroring his spread-legged position, with his bare feet against the soles of her own, Caroline seriously considered bolting for the door and forfeiting the cost of the class. Then he held his hands out to her and she recognized the dare in his eyes.

With her pride on the line, she reached her own hands toward him. He grasped her wrists in a grip that required her to wrap her hands around his wrists. Had she thought his fingers circling her wrist earlier had created a heat wave? How naïve! Right now, she was being engulfed by a lava flow of warmth that was working its way up her arms and stinging her neck and cheeks with an embarrassing blush.

"Tell me if I go too far, or too fast," he told her in a low tone that had to be deliberately seductive, even though he looked perfectly, innocently earnest. "I'll stop whenever you say."

No one—certainly, no man who looked like Judd Blackburn—could be as innocent as he looked just then. She gave him her best skeptical look, but he didn't appear ready to cave in. So she simply nodded curtly.

For a moment, Caroline thought Judd was having second thoughts about tormenting her. Then he nodded back and drew her toward him millimeter by millimeter, his feet against hers, anchoring her legs in a wide V. She closed her eyes as he gently increased the pull on the muscles of her inner thighs, her arms, her back and waist. The stretching felt paradoxically wonderful and awful, and heightened her awareness of how open, how vulnerable and receptive her body was in that position. Receptive and more. With her torso angled toward him, her hands, trapped under his, now hovering over his thighs, she could be beckoning to him, reaching for him.

Alarmed by where her thoughts were straying, Caroline opened her eyes to discover that her gaze had also strayed. Oh, dear! Who would have thought sweatpants could be so . . . revealing? The man was . . . he had. . . . What was left of her breath escaped in a tiny gasp and she lifted her eyes to find him watching her with a knowing expression. Was there no safe place to look? Apparently not. She closed her eyes.

"Caroline? Are you okay?" Judd's voice came from distractingly close to her ear. "I don't want to go too far, the first time."

"You already have," she muttered.

Instantly, he released the tension holding her, letting her ease backward until she was almost sitting upright again. When she opened her eyes, he was regarding her with that same bemused expression. "You're pretty flexible. You must work out."

She felt herself blushing like a teenager. "I run a few times a week, and I've been doing yoga stretches for years."

"Yeah, yoga is good. Helps keep you young."

Just then, a slight warning twinge in her lower back made Caroline wince. Young? That was a cruel joke, even if he didn't have a clue!

"Ready for me, now?" Ignoring his double entendre, she gave a brief nod. Judd beckoned her to move forward. Uncertain what he had in mind, Caroline hesitated. "Come closer and put your feet up here," he told her, dropping his hands to the insides of his thighs just above his knees.

How gullible did he think she was? "Pardon me?" she said, as frostily as she could.

Judd had the nerve to look surprised. "Caroline, I'm six-four. If we go foot-to-foot, I'm not going to get any kind of decent stretch. The higher you put your feet on me, the better leverage I'll get."

She glanced at his long, muscular legs, spread in a wide V under the black sweatpants, then met his eyes. The tingle of heat in her cheeks was almost as embarrassing as the realization that he was right, and it was her mind wallowing in the gutter, not his.

"Oh."

It was a reasonable request, she understood now, but before she could grudgingly comply, Judd was grasping both of her bare ankles in his big hands. He tugged her closer toward him, sliding her on her bottom along the mat. Caught off guard, Caroline barely managed to smother an undignified yelp and regain her balance. She found herself sitting between his widely splayed legs, gaping at him as he arranged her feet against the insides of his legs. For a stunned moment, all she noticed was that his hands on her ankles were deliciously warm, the muscles of his legs were impressively hard, and that her insteps had just become incredibly sensitive erogenous zones.

Suddenly aware of her disappearing dignity, she snapped her mouth shut and glared at him. Did he have a clue how he'd violated her personal space? His eyes sparkled but he kept his expression perfectly neutral as he held out his hands, palms up. After another moment's hesitation, Caroline placed her palms in his. Judd caught her forearms in a warm, secure clasp.

"Ready?" That simple word, spoken softly in his low, intimate voice, hinted at hidden layers of meaning, which the teasing light in his eyes invited her to explore. But if she accepted his invitation to satisfy her curiosity, how much would she unknowingly reveal about herself? How would she explain the little white lie she'd already told him? That little fib had seemed so harmless when she'd uttered it, but now it grew steadily larger and darker in her mind with every passing moment in his company. One lie, no matter how small, really did beget other lies.

And so she lied again: "Ready."

Chapter Two

Judd couldn't resist rattling Caroline's cage. He could see she was trying to convince both of them that she was ready to touch him, to let him touch her, and it wasn't happening. But she wasn't willing to let him see that she was even a little shaken by the prospect of getting so close to him. He wanted to spark a reaction, *really* break through that control of hers. Every time he thought he had, she recovered so quickly. It might be childish of him—okay, it *was* childish of him—but he wanted to shake her up, wanted to see her reacting to him the way he was reacting to her. Ten years ago, he'd just been playing; he hadn't known what he wanted back then. Now, he wanted to know that his touch was making her as aware of him as hers was doing to him.

"Okay. Go for it," he told her. Her first try was too weak to move him. He squeezed her forearms gently, until she finally met his eyes. Hers were wide and wary. He offered a smile he hoped looked innocent and reassuring. "Give it your best shot, Caroline. I'll tell you if you go too far."

She went still and gave him the kind of look that told him *he* already had. He bit back a grin. She kept looking at him but didn't say a word, just gave a short, impatient-sounding sigh. He felt her muscles work when she started to pull him toward her. Closing his eyes, he let her draw him forward, let his body flow into the widening stretch, let his senses open to the woman in front of him.

When he drew in a long, deep breath, his head filled with the faint musk of her skin. Sometime earlier, she probably had used a floral perfume, but it had faded, blended into a scent no one could bottle. The closer she drew him, the more that delicious scent surrounded him.

The warm pressure of her delicate, narrow feet against his legs heightened the impact of stretching, all the way to his groin. His libido immediately translated those sensations into an arousing image of her legs locked at the ankles, around his back. The rush of heat to his loins warned him that his control was slipping faster than water down a drain.

Pressing his torso forward and down to maximize his stretch and get his mind off Caroline, Judd exhaled sharply and lowered his chest another inch or two.

"Are you sure you should go that far?" Caroline asked, her voice much closer than he'd expected.

He opened his eyes and stifled a groan. Aw, hell! Any closer and he'd be in her lap. "You're right; that's far enough," he muttered, sitting up. What was left of his reason prompted him to release her arms. In the mirrors lining the room, he caught a glimpse of Bob's sly grin and scowled back. "I think we're done."

Quick as a cat, she pulled her feet away from him, stood and dusted off her seat. By the time he'd gotten up, she was already walking toward the others. Judd followed her, admiring her graceful movements, and wondering if he'd just killed his chances of seeing her again.

Caroline tried to focus on Bob's words, but her entire nervous system seemed to be short-circuiting. Ridiculous, she scolded herself, but she couldn't deny the astonishing thrill, the tingling awareness that those few minutes of close physical contact with Judd had aroused.

Poor choice of words, she noted wryly, just as he came up behind her. Determined to ignore him, she squared her

shoulders and forced herself to concentrate on Bob's explanation of their first sparring exercise. Circling, he was saying,
keeping your opponent at a disadvantage, makes defending
yourself, or better yet, escaping, easier. He barely glanced at
Judd over her shoulder, but she sensed some unspoken com-
munication between them. Seconds later, both men were facing each other in front of the group. Like wary, suspicious
tomcats, they circled around an imaginary center, while Bob
described how his attacker, Judd, couldn't reach him without
leaving himself open to a defensive strike. It sounded very
good in theory, Caroline thought, but she felt more than a
little skeptical of her own ability to keep Judd at bay if he
continued to close in on her.

Too soon, the class was pairing off again, and Caroline
found herself facing Judd across about six feet of floor. She
looked at him, uncertain of what to do next. Before she could
blink, he had closed the distance between them and caught
her left arm in his right hand, startling a gasp from her.

"Pay attention." A slight edge of menace tinged his low
voice. "Watch my eyes. Always watch the eyes."

How could she look away, she wondered, when his eyes
smoldered like that?

He released her arm. "Watch my eyes, but stay aware of
my entire body, not just my hand."

How could she *not* be aware of his entire body? It was
the kind of body that commanded awareness.

"Keep moving away from my attacking hand or foot.
Open the door. Force me to circle to close the door. And
look for a way out. Remember, it's always better to escape
than to fight."

She couldn't agree more. Breathlessly, Caroline nodded.
There was no mistaking how serious he suddenly had become about self-defense. A fierce intensity had replaced the
earlier teasing glint in his eyes. She'd assumed, watching him
sparring with Bob before class, that Judd was also a student.
He'd said as much, himself. But it was evident that he'd
spent much of the past ten years perfecting his skills. Come
to think of it, she wondered as she stepped sideways, what
had he been doing for the past decade? Where had he—?

A flash of motion, and once again he'd caught her before

she could process the information that he was about to pounce. This time, he'd pinned her upper arms to her sides and was holding her so close to his big body that she could feel his heat even without touching him. His hands held her gently, yet when she tried to pull away, she couldn't escape. Annoyed, she glared up at him. He glared back.

"The bad guys don't wait for you to get into position," he growled softly at her.

Chastened, she stopped glaring. "You're right. I'm more of a sitting duck than a moving target." She hoped a smile would soften his expression. "Shall we try again?"

The smile didn't work. He dropped his hands and stepped back. "If you're not serious about this, don't waste your time and mine."

His challenging words echoed her own from the distant past—the beginning of the written dialogue that had lasted the length of her first teaching term. He'd turned in a scornfully brief note instead of the assigned essay. She'd written nearly those same words in response. From then on, his essays had subliminally seduced her with his insights, dazzled her with his ability to express himself clearly yet elegantly without showing off. Now, although he didn't know it, he was turning the tables on her.

"Point taken," she answered softly.

This time, she saw him coming toward her and quickly circled away from his right hand. He followed her, closing the distance between them, and she circled away and back, opening it again. They practiced until Bob called them back to the group to watch him demonstrate intercepting an attack. She watched the way he and Judd sparred in slow motion, simultaneously trying to learn the patterns of their motions while appreciating the beauty of their movements.

"Practice slowly, in control," Bob told them as the pairs took their places. "If you get through your partner's defenses, don't try to punch. Just try to touch your partner's chest."

Caroline refused to meet Judd's eyes until the heat stinging her cheeks subsided. When she did look up at him, his expression revealed that he was trying to subdue his amusement at her expense. Taking a quick breath, she straightened her

shoulders and faced him squarely. An unfortunately contagious grin deepened the lines fanning out around his eyes.
She couldn't help smiling back.

"Hmm. The stakes are higher. I guess you'll be paying
more attention this time," he murmured, his grin widening
a little as if daring her to deny it.

Caroline opened her mouth to reply, but just in time, saw
his arm moving toward her and raised hers in an awkward
attempt to copy the blocking movement Bob had demon-
strated. Her wrist met his forearm, and in slow motion, she
circled away, out of his formerly easy reach. He smiled, and
she wondered whether she was imagining a touch of pride
in his eyes.

The minutes flew by as Judd practiced with her, correcting
her mistakes, adjusting her position and her movements with
gentle patience. He managed to get inside her defenses several times, but stopped just short of actually touching her
chest. Still, the sight of his strong hand hovering mere inches
from her breasts was enough to send her pulse racing.

Then something totally unexpected and wonderful happened. She caught herself laughing in delight at the surprise
on his face after she ducked out of reach without his help,
and realized she hadn't had so much fun in ages. Much too
soon, Bob was thanking them for coming. The class was
over, and she was torn between wanting to linger with Judd
and knowing that she should escape before he figured out
her embarrassing deception.

Judd watched Caroline smile at the other women, then at
Bob, and realized he didn't have much time if he was going
to keep her from walking away right that minute. He resented
her lying to him, but he liked what she did to his libido,
which had been hibernating for much too long. He wanted
to know why she was hiding her identity, and he wanted
to . . . well, that could wait until he'd satisfied his curiosity.

He stepped into her path. She blinked up at him and a
wash of pink colored her cheeks. If he'd known her any
better, he would have given in to the temptation to stroke
his fingertips over the fine satin of her skin.

"How about going someplace close for dinner," he asked,

hoping he sounded more casual than he felt. When several seconds passed and she hadn't answered, he added, "We've got ten years to catch up on."

Her hesitation was lasting too long. Damn it! She was going to say no. Her smile was fading. Her whiskey-colored eyes reflected a nervousness he knew he'd caused. Was she worried that he'd confront her with her lie? Or that she'd have to call on self-defense skills she didn't have yet? When she gave a quick glance over her shoulder at the wall clock, he knew he'd lost the first round.

"I, um, I'm not really dressed right for anything . . ." The pink in her cheeks darkened, but then, unbelievably, she smiled. *Hallelujah!* "I guess . . . if it's someplace very casual," she said softly. "But I have to be home early, to finish some work," she added in a rush.

He was probably grinning like a jack-o'-lantern, but he didn't care. "No problem. Give me ten, no, make it five minutes to shower." If he kept her waiting too long, she might slip away.

A slight smile teased her lips. He wondered how long before he could persuade her to let that smile tease *his* lips. She nodded. "All right."

He headed for the locker room, peeling his shirt off as he went.

Caroline hugged her parka to her chest and tried to concentrate on the framed articles about kung fu and the popularity of martial arts that lined the wall outside Bob's office. The printed words blurred unintelligibly, but no one looking at her would be able to tell that she didn't have a clue what she was reading. It didn't really matter, as long as she appeared absorbed, casual, unconcerned about the prospect of embarrassing herself terribly when Judd inevitably caught her in that lie.

And if he didn't catch her, she was going to have to confess, or her conscience was never going to stop nagging her. Sir Walter Scott probably said it best, about deception and tangled webs. So what should she do? Just blurt out the truth now? Or in the middle of dinner? Or wait until after coffee?

Oh, lord! She felt so foolish! He'd think she was trying to impress him. To flirt with him. To—

"Hi! Ready?"

Judd's softly spoken greeting startled a squeak out of her, which of course made her blush like a schoolgirl. Honestly! If she kept reacting like that to his every word, gaze, or touch, he probably wouldn't believe her when she confessed to her real age. Or else he'd think—accurately—that she needed to get out more.

"Ready," she confirmed, unfurling her jacket. Judd took it from her and held it for her to shrug into. It wasn't her imagination that she felt the light pressure of his hands on her shoulders for a second before he stepped away. Predictably, heat rushed to her face even as she was turning to say, "Thank you."

He zipped his own parka, then cupped her elbow in his hand. She fell into step beside him, waving with her free hand when Bob called good-bye to them.

"Let's see," Judd said when they reached the door to the street. "Our best choices around here for dinner are Chinese, Vietnamese, Thai, deli, or fish and chips. Any preferences?"

When Judd opened the door for her, a blast of cold air swirled down her neck. She shivered and wrapped her arms around her middle. The promised mid-January cold snap, following the too-brief January thaw, had apparently arrived, along with the evening darkness, while she'd been taking her first self-defense lesson. "Deli," she suggested. "The best one in Chinatown is right across the street."

"Good idea. Good timing, too. The light's about to change."

Judd drew her arm through his, pulling her close to his side. She told herself that the shivers rippling through her were only due to the chill, damp wind battering at her, but she knew that wasn't totally true. There was something exciting, something tempting, something just a little scary about the way their bodies fit together, even with their jackets muffling the exchange of heat, the press of hips and ribs and arms.

Caroline was too cold to resist when Judd hustled them into the six-lane-wide crosswalk. Two minutes later, they were peeling their jackets off in the overheated New York–style delicatessen and sliding onto the red vinyl benches of a booth. A waitress dropped two huge laminated menus on their table as she passed by with a tray loaded with sandwiches. Caroline picked up a menu and felt something bump her knee. Judd's knee. She started reading at the top of the hot soup column. Something nudged her foot. Judd's foot. She peeked around her menu at him. He was studying his menu intently, but she saw the corners of his lips twitch. What a rogue! Hiding her own smile, she turned her attention back to choosing something to order.

When the waitress returned to the edge of their table, she angled herself toward Judd, giving Caroline the opportunity to watch her. The woman's heavily made-up eyes seemed to devour Judd, who was still studying the menu.

"What can I get you, hon?" she asked him, as if Caroline were part of the furniture.

Judd looked at Caroline across the table and smiled. "Do you know what you want?" he asked.

Yes, she thought. *I want to be younger. I want to be self-assured around you. I want to feel your touch again.* "I'll have a cup of the barley-mushroom soup, and half a sliced turkey sandwich." So it wasn't what she wanted, but it was what she needed.

The waitress's lips pursed. She made a note on her pad, said a quick, "Okay," and turned her attention back to Judd. "And you, hon?"

He set his menu down on the table. "I'll have the barley-mushroom soup, too, and a roast beef sandwich."

"You want a bowl? Not enough in a cup of soup for a man your size." The waitress's tone implied she liked her men big.

"Make it a bowl."

"What kind of bread? The rye is especially good today."

"Okay, rye. Caroline? Rye bread for you, too?" She nodded. "Rye for the lady, too."

"Mmm. And how do you like your roast beef, hon? Rare?"

"Sure. Rare."

"And to drink?"

"Upper Canada Lager for me. Sweetheart?" Caroline glanced at him to discover that he was, indeed, speaking to her. She gave him a questioning look, which he answered with a wink. "What are you drinking, love?" He reached across the table to catch her hands in his.

Even realizing that he was trying to hint to the waitress that he wasn't interested in her flirtation, Caroline felt her face grow warm. "Oh, ah, uh, a diet Coke, please."

With an aggrieved expression that telegraphed her comprehension, the waitress picked up their menus and spun away. Determined not to let Judd fluster her any further, Caroline tried to tug her hands out of Judd's grasp, but he tightened his hold just enough to make it impossible. Puzzled, she looked at him. He looked back, but the laughter that had lurked in his eyes a moment before was gone.

"No wedding ring. Anyone special in your life?"

This was her chance to make it clear that she wasn't interested, that she wasn't pathetic and desperate, or predatory like the waitress. This was her chance to show Judd she was independent, and liked it that way. "Counting my cat, or not?" she asked dryly.

He grinned. "Depends on the cat." His grin faded, his blue eyes darkened. "But that doesn't answer my question. Are you seeing anyone, living with anyone? Because if you are, I'll just say it was nice seeing you again after all these years and cut out after dinner."

"And if I'm not?" Oh, she shouldn't have asked! Not with his eyes so serious, not with her voice gone husky, not with his thumbs rubbing softly over the backs of her knuckles. Not with her little white lie growing larger and darker with every passing minute.

"If you're not," he answered, his voice so intimately quiet that she had to lean toward him to hear, "I suggest you prepare to be."

Chapter Three

At his declaration—warning? promise?—the bottom fell out of her stomach. *Involved?* She and Judd? *Involved*, as in . . . well, he probably didn't have anything like a bank robbery in mind. He was implying that he was as interested in her as she was in him. Maybe more so, since he didn't know she was an impostor. He wouldn't have any need for the caution, guilt, and embarrassment that was churning inside her. Was he teasing, leading her on, extending a hand only to pull it back when she reached out? That had happened before, but no, his bright blue eyes gazed at her with open directness, underlying the solemn tone in which he'd spoken.

Was she prepared? Caroline smothered the nervous giggle rising in her throat. *Prepared* was the precise opposite of the condition she was in at the moment! Was she interested? Willing to explore the possibilities of getting involved with Judd Blackburn? Oh, yes! But first, she had to be honest.

From experience and observation, she knew that romantic relationships faced enough obstacles without the additional handicap of deceit, no matter how innocently it started. Now, before she was free to answer his question—which was more like a challenge, but that was immaterial right now—she was definitely obliged to confess her deception. Judd had a good sense of humor; hopefully, he'd laugh off the situation, so they could go on without her little secret festering between them. If he couldn't laugh off her foolishness, if he didn't want to continue pursuing a relationship with her because of it, they were both better off knowing that now. Later would be too late.

Caroline took a fortifying breath, but before she could open her mouth to explain—and apologize—Judd said, "I'll be back in a minute. I promised my sister I'd call her around now." He gave her a quick smile, slid out of the booth, and was moving toward the back of the deli before Caroline could gather her newly scattered wits.

She watched him walk away, fascinated by her first real glimpse of him in jeans and a plaid flannel shirt. The jeans hugged a pair of calendar-quality masculine buns and showed off long-muscled thighs and tightly lean hips. The shirt framed broad shoulders, and its soft folds disappearing into the waistband of his jeans hinted at the tapering of his torso. And every woman Caroline could see from her vantage point seemed equally fascinated. Some gave him only a quick glance, but several let their appraising, appreciating gazes linger until Judd was out of sight down the corridor toward the sign for phones and restrooms.

When one of the women and several men in the deli actually glanced speculatively at her, as if assessing her relationship with the gorgeous man who'd just disturbed their equilibrium, she nearly laughed out loud in agreement. Yes, indeed, what was she, an aging, rumpled, unremarkable English professor, doing in the company of a man who looked like a soap-opera bad boy grown up? Darned if she knew!

Seeking a diversion, Caroline fished in her purse for her Day-Timer. Flipping it open to today's date, she ran down her list of things to do, checking off what she had already accomplished, underlining what was left on the list. Oddly enough, she noted wryly, there was nothing on her list that referred to making a fool of herself. Well, some days were just meant for overachieving, she mused.

"Any day is fine with me." Judd's voice startled her out

of her reverie. He was standing beside the table, eyeing her
Day-Timer.

"Pardon me?"

He slid into the booth across from her, seeming to fill her
vision so thoroughly that everything around him faded into
blurry scenery. Did he know how he dominated the space
around him? Of course he must know, and use it to his advantage, no doubt.

"Aren't you looking for places to pencil me in?" His low
voice vibrated with laughter.

She rolled her eyes. "Your modesty is overwhelming! I
was checking to see what I had left to do this evening."

He grinned. "Ah! You said something about having work
to do for tomorrow. What do you do?"

Here it comes, she thought. The moment of truth. Time to
bite the bullet and face his—what? Anger? Disappointment?
Amusement? Pity? Well, she deserved them all, didn't she?
Even so, she sincerely hoped he would take her confession
with better grace than she suspected *she* would, if the shoe
had been on her foot instead of his.

"I'm an associate professor of English at U of T," she
said, watching his blue eyes, waiting for his reaction, weigh-
ing how to apologize without sounding totally pathetic.

Judd nodded solemnly, as if he understood some profound
truth about her career. "So Ms. Lassiter's class influenced
you, too?"

That wasn't the reaction she was expecting! Caroline
nearly let her jaw drop in astonishment. What did he mean
by that? Obviously, he still believed her to be a classmate,
but . . . What did he mean, about the influence part? And
what *too*? Was he saying . . . ?

"I mean, you're following in her footsteps," he explained
before she could find her voice to ask. "It's funny, but I
almost didn't take that course. The one on popular lit. What
did she call it? 'Love, Death, and Alternate Realities,'
right?" Numbly fascinated, Caroline nodded mutely. Judd
offered a sheepish grin. "I come from a long line of
hereditary bean counters, but I'm the black sheep. My business grades weren't going to get me into a respectable MBA
program. I figured a reading list of romance, mystery, science

fiction, and fantasy would be a no-brainer. The plan was to ace the course, and bring up my grade-point average in business admin., but I got hooked on popular culture instead." His eyes took on a faraway look. "Lassiter was the best prof I ever had."

Caroline swallowed hard. This was obviously not the best time to blurt something like, *Why, thank you! And guess what? I'm Ms. Lassiter! I told you my married name because you're so darn gorgeous that my vanity overcame my common sense.* Oh, hell!

"So do *you* teach English somewhere?" she asked.

He gave her an odd look, shook his head, and said, "No." She waited for him to elaborate, but that was all he seemed willing to say. Just *no*. How interesting. Apparently, she wasn't the only one harboring some kind of secret.

With her curiosity piqued by his sparse answer, Caroline opened her mouth to ask what he *did* do, but the waitress appeared with their soups and drinks. This time, the woman skipped the endearments toward Judd, but showed him her interest by giving him an extra handful of cracker packages. His wink at Caroline almost made her laugh, but her urge to giggle was more from nerves than amusement. What was she going to do now to bail out of this situation?

Judd lifted his beer glass to his mouth and, closing his eyes, took a deep swallow. Caroline took the opportunity to study the way his throat moved, the way his long, dark lashes fanned out against his skin, the way his strong hand curved around the glass. In the instant before he set the glass down and opened his eyes, she found herself staring at his sensual mouth, at the way his lips glistened, at the way his tongue slid across his full lower lip to catch the last errant drops of golden beer. As if he could feel her gaze, his eyes focused on hers even as his lids were opening. Embarrassed at being caught, Caroline lowered her gaze to the cup of steaming soup in front of her, all too aware that the sudden heat in her cheeks had nothing to do with the temperature of her soup.

"I was thinking of dropping in on Ms. Lassiter, but she isn't listed on the faculty anymore." Judd's statement chased her curiosity about his occupation right out of her mind. Who cared what he did for a living, when she was facing the possibility of major embarrassment? Apparently oblivious to her agitation, Judd lifted a spoonful of the rich soup in his bowl and shrugged. "Think she took early retirement? She's probably old enough by now, don't you think?"

Caroline's mouthful of soup slid down her throat wrong, sending her into a fit of coughing. With tears in her eyes and her paper napkin over her mouth, she tried to catch her breath. When Judd started to rise, she waved him away with her free hand, but she didn't mean she didn't need his assistance. She meant, *Come one inch closer, and I'll hit you for that remark!* Retired? *Retired?* He must have thought she was over the hill ten years ago! He must have been nineteen, maybe twenty, when he'd taken her course. She must have seemed ancient at twenty-four for him to figure she was retired already. Oh, lord! And there she was worried that he'd think she was old *now!*

"You're sure you're okay?" he asked when she finally composed herself. She glared at him through the film of tears still filling her eyes, but nodded. "Good." He scooped up another spoonful of soup, and she watched his lips close around it, watched him swallow, but this time, she wasn't thinking about how sensuous and seductive his movements were. This time, she was thinking she'd like to sprinkle some arsenic in his soup.

Somehow, Judd managed not to laugh at the gamut of reactions showing on Caroline's face. Oh, man! He was bad! But he wasn't ready to reveal his occupation, and she obviously felt guilty about her little lie. Damn, she was cute, blushing like that. He would love to know whether she was blushing over her guilty conscience, or over the way he'd caught her staring at his mouth. She didn't voluntarily give away much of what she was feeling. Too bad. There was a lot of fire hidden under that cool exterior, fire he intended to stoke and sample. Eventually. For a moment there, he'd thought she was going to give him the truth—between the eyes, probably—after he dropped that comment about early retirement. But no such luck. Well, hell, he had to admire her self-control at not rising to the bait.

He guessed he could change the subject now, give her some time to recover. "So, Caroline Yates, tell me about yourself. Have you ever been married?"

Her dark honey brows went up. "Yes. Why do you ask?"

"Just wondering how anyone would be foolish enough to let you go." That wasn't what he'd thought he was going to say. He'd planned to tease her a little more with questions he already knew the answers to, dangle her a while longer, then tell her that he'd known she was Caroline Lassiter from the instant he'd seen her in Bob's gym. Funny thing, though. As soon as the words were out of his mouth, he realized he meant them.

With her soup spoon halfway to her lips, she gave him a very skeptical half-smile. "Do you practice lines like that in front of a mirror, so you can keep a straight face?"

This was getting to be fun. "Not anymore," he answered. Her tiny snort of laughter made him grin. "I hope your ex hasn't soured you against all men."

He kept his tone light, but he meant what he said. He was tired of bitter, vengeful women, and nervous about the wounded ones. Several times in the past decade, he'd imagined he could fix the damage a past relationship had done to women he'd been involved with. And every time, no matter how badly burned they claimed to have been, he was the one who'd ended up getting singed. It would be a real letdown if Caroline turned out to be one of those all-men-are-evil kind of women, because he'd probably feel compelled to change her mind, and get strangled by his own good intentions yet again.

To his relief, she smiled. "Not at all. I don't hate anyone."

Still smiling, she took a sip of her Coke. Judd let himself watch her lips close around the edge of the glass, watch her lick the drops off her lower lip, the way she'd watched him. He wanted his stare to make her think of what it would feel like to taste his mouth, the way her stare had set him to thinking. From the telltale wash of pink in her cheeks, he'd succeeded. Good to know he hadn't lost his touch.

"Actually," Caroline said, an odd tone in her voice, "I take that back. There is one man I think I hate. Or at least hold a grudge against."

The sudden flash in her whiskey-colored eyes hinted again at the fire hidden inside her. There was a story here. He could feel his curiosity kicking into gear, but he forced himself to wait for her to explain. After a brief pause while she closed her eyes, she looked directly at him and gave a tiny, self-conscious kind of laugh. "I suppose this sounds far-fetched, but the only man I've ever hated is Thomas Black, because he's responsible for my divorce."

If she'd thrown her cold drink in his face, she couldn't have shocked him more. Somewhere inside his head, he heard a little voice saying, *She didn't really say that. She couldn't really mean that.* But she had. She did. It was all he could do to keep his chin from hitting the tabletop.

The oversexed waitress *would* have to pick that exact moment to come by with their sandwiches. And she had to know if they wanted ketchup or mustard, and which kind of mustard. Finally, they were alone again. Caroline seemed so interested in her sandwich, he wondered if she even remembered her odd comment. Comment, hell! Accusation! She couldn't have picked a better way to set a fire under him.

"Thomas Black, the writer?" he asked, spreading mustard on his sandwich, trying to look and sound casual. He wanted to be sure they were talking about the same Thomas Black. "The one they call Canada's answer to John Grisham?"

Caroline nodded. Transfixed, he watched her slender fingers lift the bread from the top of her sandwich and delicately spread mustard over the sliced turkey filling with her knife. He remembered how he used to watch those fingers wrapped around a piece of chalk, writing on the chalkboard in perfectly rounded script. Her lecture notes had become his gospel. Damn it, he didn't want to know that his goddess of enlightenment had feet—or a heart—of clay. He wanted her to tell him the truth, but he didn't want to be disillusioned.

"So you know Thomas Black?" he asked, knowing damn well that she didn't. She couldn't. But that didn't always stop people from claiming anything from friendship to kinship with the elusive writer of a half-dozen runaway bestsellers, and another one due to launch on Valentine's Day, barely four weeks away. Nuts—often greedy nuts—charging plagiarism, threatening to sue for breach of nonexistent contracts. Women claiming to be Black's wife, fiancée, mother, sister, bearer of his children—legitimate or otherwise—threatening to sue for desertion, alimony, child support. Caroline couldn't be the type for that, but then again, she had lied about who she was, and still hadn't tried to confess and set the record straight.

With her mouth full of turkey sandwich, she shook her head. He ignored his own sandwich and waited for her to swallow and speak. Would she lie again?

"Not at all," she told him. At least she was telling the truth now, he thought. She gave a soft, self-conscious little laugh. "In fact, I wouldn't know him if I fell over him. I guess no one would, except his mother. From the little I've heard about him, he gives no interviews, allows no photos."

"So I've heard." She nibbled the corner of her sandwich. "So what's the connection?"

"Unbelievable as it sounds, my ex-husband quit his job, asked for a divorce, and took off for the wilds of Alaska and the Northwest Territories because of Thomas Black's first book."

She was right. It sure sounded unbelievable, but for reasons he didn't feel like examining, he wanted to believe whatever she told him. He framed his next words carefully. "Black's first book was set in Vancouver and Hong Kong. Alaska wasn't even mentioned in it."

Caroline shrugged and took another bite of sandwich, driving him nuts while she chewed. Finally, she swallowed another sip of her drink and wiped her lips with her napkin. "I wouldn't know. I never read it. I never saw the film based on it. I never read any of his other books, or saw those films, either. I refuse even to hold one of his books in my hands." She shrugged again. "It's kind of embarrassing to be so stubborn about it, and be teaching a course on genre literature, a . . . a lot like Ms. Lassiter's''—her cheeks went pink again— "but I've painted myself into a corner, and here I stay, me and my grudge." She gave him a quick, rueful smile.

While Judd was trying to process that information, Caroline said, "My ex was one of the most reliable, dependable, generous men ever to walk the earth. We grew up next door to each other. My father abandoned my mother and me about the same time his father died. Our mothers were partners in a catering business, and they worked very long hours. Jeff practically raised his three younger sisters, and looked after me as well. He was the kind of guy who always had time to do something for anyone who needed help. Little kids, little old ladies, lost kittens and puppies. I don't think he ever said no to anyone for the first thirty years of his life.''

Judd decided it would be churlish and rude to tell Caroline she was making him ill with her praise of her ex-husband. No guy was that saintly. Not that he wouldn't mind having a woman like Caroline think he was. What guy wouldn't? But this guy had to have some flaw. After all, the bozo walked out on her because of a Thomas Black novel, of all the flimsy excuses. He couldn't wait for her to explain *that* one!

''Jeff and I, well, I guess we got married because we were so used to being together. *I* was so used to depending on him. It was a natural progression, although that makes it sound rather heartless, and it wasn't. We did care about each other. Still do, I guess, although we only keep in touch with Christmas and birthday cards.''

Caroline looked at him as if her belief in the best of her former marriage was important. She didn't start speaking again until he nodded, signaling he understood, although he wasn't sure he did. ''Jeff loved photography, but I thought it was just a hobby. He always said he'd never make a living taking pictures, which was why he became an accountant. He got a great job with an investment company, and I finished my doctorate, and we helped his sisters go to university, and sent our mothers to Arizona to retire.''

Caroline paused, her eyes downcast. Judd waited, watching her fingertip trace a bead of water sliding down the side of her glass. Finally, she looked up at him. Her sad little smile wrenched at his heart. He had a bad feeling about how her story was going to end.

''And then one day,'' she continued, ''out of the blue, Jeff announced that a man calling himself Thomas Black, from a wealthy, prominent Toronto family, had written a thriller that had debuted near the top of the *New York Times* bestseller list and had been optioned for a movie. According to the urban legends about this guy, his family threatened to disown him if he didn't use a pseudonym to protect their privacy.''

''I've heard that story, too. But what's that got to do with your ex running away?''

Caroline sighed. Judd wanted to reach out and hold her hands, but they were tightly clasped together in front of her, as if to hold her together. ''Jeff took Black's success as a wake-up call. This man writing as Thomas Black was younger than Jeff, but had followed his dreams straight to the top. Jeff decided that if he didn't follow his own dreams of photographing the Arctic, starting immediately, we might have children, and that would tie him down so he would never get his chance.''

Caroline blinked and smiled, but her lips trembled slightly. Judd wished he had the right to kiss them into relaxing. ''So that's how Thomas Black broke up my marriage.'' There was no mistaking the hurt underlying the breezy tone she used to finish her story. Crazy as it sounded, she believed it.

Judd reached across the table, prying her hands apart gently but firmly. Holding them in his, he stroked his thumb over the backs of her hands, feeling inadequate. Her fingers stayed curled tightly in his palms for a long moment, but when he continued stroking and waiting, she finally rewarded his patience by opening her fingers and laying her hands on his. She smiled at him, a wistful smile that took his breath away.

Once upon a time, Caroline Lassiter had played a unilateral and unknown role in his life. He'd adored her for the way she'd made him feel, but she'd never given him any reason to believe she knew. She'd never even acknowledged the impulsively inappropriate Valentine's Day flowers he'd sent her ten years ago. The last time he'd seen her, after exams at the end of that year, she'd been wearing an engagement ring.

He'd kept the idealized memory of her like a talisman, a charm worn hidden under clothing, warmed by body contact, powerful because of its secret existence. He'd exploited it commercially, yet its magic continued strong in his mind. Over the past ten years, he'd occasionally imagined what it would be like to meet her again, just like this, to be free to tell her how she had changed his life. He'd pictured her reactions, ranging from coolly sophisticated amusement to passionate arousal at the notion of playing the muse. He'd never imagined, however, that she would hate him.

Judd studied a deep scratch in the battered Formica tabletop and pondered his dilemma. This probably wasn't the right time to confess that *he* was the Thomas Black who had ruined her marriage.

Chapter Four

Judd was looking at her as if he were sorry he'd ever asked her to join him for dinner. No wonder! How could she just blather on like that, about such an embarrassing part of her personal life, to a man who was practically a stranger? Caroline couldn't explain it to herself in any logical way. She could blame it on how intently Judd looked into her eyes when she spoke, how interested he seemed to be, how easy he was to talk to. However, it wasn't like her to blame her own actions on anyone else, so she must have needed to tell him that much about herself. Why? Because he was . . .

No, shame on her! Because she wanted to start with a clean slate? Yes, well, an *almost* clean slate. There was still the little matter of her real identity, and the longer she left that to be told, the worse it was going to seem. The trouble was, every time she looked into Judd's eyes, the words she should say got stuck, or evaporated, or simply changed into something else entirely.

But . . . Oh, she had said too much after all! He was still looking at her so strangely, so . . . uncomfortably. And who could blame him? She probably sounded terribly immature, or worse, positively neurotic, blaming her divorce on a suspense writer no one had ever seen!

"I'm sorry," she said hastily, feeling the heat of rising embarrassment. "I shouldn't have dumped all that on you."

He shook his head. "Hey, look on the bright side. Now that it's out of your system, you don't have to dump it on me during our first date." He flashed a playful grin. "Right?"

She studied his face for some sign that he was only teasing, but when he didn't start laughing and announce that he was only fooling, she answered with a cautious, "Um, right?"

"Good. So, that's settled. You're divorced, uninvolved, gainfully employed, discriminating in your reading habits, you have a cat, and your own house."

He looked very pleased with his glib summary of her life, which sounded rather dull recited like that. Yet she hardly knew anything about him at all. But before she could point out that imbalance between them, he spoke again.

"I'm tied up tomorrow night with some family obligations, but how about Saturday?"

It was like watching a hawk floating lazily on thermal currents one moment, then suddenly swooping out of the sky like a rocket, intent on its chosen prey, and realizing you're it. Caroline suppressed the urge to duck.

"Well, I . . ." *Yes or no?* she prodded herself, unable to recall any other situation when she'd been so lost for the right words, so unsure of her own thoughts. "Saturday?"

He raised the last part of his sandwich toward his mouth, then paused to meet her eyes. "I'm staying with family until I can move into my apartment. So Saturday morning I have nephew duty. My sisters', Victoria and Emily, combined monsters. They think it's cool to use me for a trampoline." His grin belied his aggrieved tone. "I'll pick you up about eleven-thirty. We can start with lunch, then play the rest of the day by ear. I'll make reservations for dinner. Is Marcel's Bistro still around?"

Caroline nodded. She couldn't fault Judd's taste. Marcel's Bistro was a fixture on King Street West, a charming old-world French restaurant near theaters and concert halls. It wasn't fancy or expensive, but it was rather romantic. Judd certainly seemed confident about how Saturday would turn out!

"Good," he sort of grunted around a mouthful of sandwich, then swallowed. She tried not to be too obvious about watching his sensual lips, his exposed throat. "I need to get some kitchen and bed stuff, for the place I'm renting. I gave away all my old stuff before I moved. Would you think it was sexist if I asked you to come with me after lunch? You know, make sure I don't forget anything important, or get all the colors and sizes wrong, that kind of thing?"

There was no mistaking the undercurrent of amusement in his tone. How could she resist giving his chain just the tiniest little jerk? "Yes, I'd think it was *terribly* sexist," she told him with as straight a face as she could muster. At his indignant expression, a chuckle escaped her. "But yes, I can help you through the ordeal of shopping." He sighed as if he hadn't been confident she'd agree. His uncertainty was rather flattering, Caroline decided. At least he didn't think she was predictable. "In exchange for a favor from you."

"Sure, anything. Name it," he said, temptingly eager.

Oh, what imp was perching on her shoulder today? Caroline couldn't remember the last time . . . no, she had *never* flirted like this before, and so what? It was *fun*! She batted her eyelashes at him, in her best Jessica Rabbit imitation, and smiled sweetly. "Paint my house?"

Judd blinked, and his jaw dropped. Then a low rumbling laugh shook his shoulders as he shook his head. "Guess I should have asked first, what kind of favor?"

She decided to take pity on him and stop teasing. "Nothing so taxing, honest. The class went too quickly for me to assimilate some of the things Bob was saying. Do you think you could talk me through the self-defense movements Bob taught today, so I can do a few stick drawings for reference? And maybe tape-record a description of the movements to play back later while I practice?"

"I can do better than that. I've got drawings already done for all of those movements, and more. I'll walk you through them a few times before your next class. Much better to practice correctly, instead of trying to learn by listening."

Oh, no! Did Judd think she was fishing for a way to see him again? Not that she wouldn't want to, but she didn't want him to think . . .

"Oh, really, that's not necessary. I don't need to take up your time for something as trivial as that. I'm sure there are books and videos. It's just that Bob mentioned that you two studied together years ago, and that you understand what he teaches. I mean, it's just a basic self-defense course. I'm not planning to get into martial arts the way you obviously have. Really, I don't—"

"Caroline, relax. I'll help you practice after you help me buy dishes and sheets, okay?"

Judd reached across the table, took her hand in his, and smiled into her eyes. As she gazed into the depths of his blue, blue eyes, the sensation of reality slipping sideways swirled over her. She hardly recognized herself. His fingers enclosed hers in a warmth that made tiny sparks tingle wherever their skin touched. She lowered her gaze to their joined hands and couldn't help wondering whether he could cause the same kind of hot-cold sparks by touching her any-where else. And when she raised her eyes to meet his again, she knew he'd read her thoughts as clearly as if she'd spoken them—as clearly as she read his, reflecting, magnifying her own. The shock of awareness burrowed into her, then flared along her nerves with searing swiftness.

"I don't know you," she whispered, staring wide-eyed at him. "I don't know anything about you."

The steadiness of his answering gaze was more unnerving than reassuring. "You will," he promised in a low, intimate tone. "Everything you need to know." Judd's expressive lips curved up into a slight smile. "All my secrets."

She wanted to believe him. She wanted this fantasy en-counter to become real. She wanted to learn all his secrets, wanted to savor the process of discovery, without being caught in her own secrets. This was an arsonist's pleasure, she found herself thinking. All the ingredients for a major conflagration coming together. The secret thrill of the pos-sibilities. The mental images. The anticipation of the moment of striking the match, the first contact, the sputter of the new flame. The uncertainty. Will it catch? No! Yes! Oh, yes!

Catch and climb and grow, consuming everything weaker in a pure celebration of energy.

Alarmed at a sudden image of herself as a phoenix not quite ready for the flames, Caroline shivered and tugged her hand out of Judd's grasp. "I really do have to get home," she said, much too breathlessly. "I have to finish preparing tomorrow's lecture notes, and, well, there's paperwork, and I have to feed Shoo, my cat, or she'll never forgive me." Her words tumbled out, giving away how flustered she was, and Judd, damn him, merely smiled knowingly. "I . . . can we get the bill?"

So far, so good, Judd thought as he walked beside Caroline toward the parking garage on the side street between Chinatown and Kensington Market. Or rather, so far, not so bad, he amended. She still wasn't telling the truth about who she was. But now, neither was he, thanks to one of those twisted quirks of fate that would be so improbable in fiction that he'd never get it past his editor. Until they'd gotten over all the initial getting-acquainted stuff, he'd have to be creative telling her about himself. He'd rather tell her the truth, but he didn't think she was ready yet.

On the other hand, they were connecting on some interesting visceral levels that definitely held promise. This time, he intended to take every advantage fate was offering by bringing them together again. This time, he wasn't going to give up as easily as he had ten years ago.

The wind picked up, slapping them with cold. Beside him, walking with her head down and her hands in her pockets, Caroline shivered and her arm brushed his. Now that was an opportunity to take advantage of, he thought, and wrapped his arm around her shoulders, urging her closer. She stiffened for a second, but he maintained the pressure until her shoulders relaxed and she nestled against his ribs. Mmm. She smelled nice. It would sure be better not to have a mattress's worth of padding between them, but then, without all that insulation, she probably wouldn't feel safe enough to let him hold her. This would do for now.

•   •   •

"There's my car," Caroline told him, reluctantly stopping beside her aging road dirt–colored Volvo. She had several reasons to be reluctant, she noted. For one, her car was in dire need of washing, which she took to be a reflection on its neglectful owner. For another, now she would have no further excuses to huddle in the shelter of Judd's embrace.

At least he hadn't released her immediately, she consoled herself, as the lack of his body heat let her feel the cold. She fished her key ring out of her pocket and fumbled the car key into the door lock. Judd put his hand over hers while she was unlocking the door. Startled, she looked up to find him much closer than she expected. So close, in fact, that he seemed to fill her vision.

"Lock your doors after you get inside," he murmured, making the warning sound like an endearment. Fascinated by the way the dim lighting around them made his eyes appear almost black, she simply nodded. "Until Saturday." His intimate tone, the intensity of his gaze, his closeness, made the simple words sound incredibly seductive.

"Until Saturday," she repeated, her own voice strangely husky.

"Good." The word came out in a whisper that seemed to carry layers of meanings she wasn't ready to uncover.

Judd bent toward her slowly, as if giving her time to consider, as if giving himself time to reconsider. Caroline stood still, arms at her sides, her face tipped up toward him, and let her eyes drift closed. Time slowed while she waited, while she absorbed the warmth of his body, while she memorized his scent and the sound of his breathing. His jacket brushed hers, making a soft rustling sound that somehow muffled the evening noises of Spadina Avenue three floors below. She felt his hand cup the back of her head, felt the heat of his palm, the firm pressure of his fingers. His breath whispered warmly over her cheek, her lips. And then his lips touched her cheek softly, sweetly, briefly—much too briefly. She felt as if she'd been tenderly enclosed in a net of possibilities, teased by promises of sensual and spiritual delights, elevated above the prospect of a first real kiss in a dank and dark public garage. It was sweet of him to be so respectful, but at that moment, she didn't care about their location, and the fact that they were virtually strangers.

"Better go," he said gruffly, startling her when he moved away. "Don't want your cat holding a grudge because her dinner's late."

Caroline opened her eyes to find Judd staring down at her face with an unnerving intensity that didn't match his light words. He reached past her hip to open the car door, and stood waiting silently until she sank into the driver's seat and turned the key in the ignition. He shut the door firmly and stepped back, hands jammed into the back pockets of his jeans, an unreadable expression in his eyes. As she drove away, she glanced in the rearview mirror; he was already out of sight.

But, as she discovered several hours later when she lay under the covers listening to Shoo purr and feeling too restless to sleep, out of sight was not out of mind. She'd never reacted to a man the way she had to Judd, and she felt almost like a stranger to herself. With her ex-husband there had been none of the nerve-racking, skin-tingling, mind-boggling excitement, the subtle sparring of flirtation, the sense of wonder and newness that bubbled up inside her whenever she thought about Judd. None of the men she'd dated in the past four years had inspired the kind of fascination, that degree of eagerness, that Judd had in a few hours.

That kind of uncertainty, with its inherent excitement and emotional risk, had always frightened her. It was like rafting in white water without a rudder, without a paddle, without a life jacket. Danger, gambling, traveling without a map were not for a woman who needed security, certainty, the safety of knowing ahead of time how things would work out. Judd had probably simply been flirting when he'd implied that he intended to pursue her in any sort of serious way, but her reactions went beyond amused, detached participation. She was going to have to do some serious thinking about her own intentions, before things between them heated up any more.

By Friday afternoon, when Caroline snapped the latch on her briefcase and closed her office door, she'd firmly resolved to keep her head—and her body—under control. Only a fool would risk her heart and her self-respect because a man she barely knew made her pulse race. And in this day and age, a woman who let her hormones make her decisions risked more than her feelings. No jumping into bed right away for her, thank you very much! She would make her position crystal-clear to Judd, and if he didn't agree, that would be too bad. Her mind was made up.

So why, a half-hour later, was she standing in her neighborhood drugstore, facing an astonishing variety of brands, features, styles, colors, and even *flavors*!—Good grief! She had to get out more!—of condoms?

Chapter Five

When the doorbell rang at eleven thirty-two Saturday morning, Caroline's heart—or maybe her stomach—did a wild flip. Calm, she told herself, pausing inside the door to her entry hall. Breathe slowly and deeply. She drew in a slow breath. The bell rang again. Her breath rushed out. She didn't feel any calmer, but if she didn't answer the door soon, Judd was either going to leave or freeze.

She swung open the door and his presence filled her vision. How could he be even better looking than she remembered? Taller, broader of shoulders, longer of legs. And that smile! He smiled right into her eyes, his own eyes sparkling with light, like sunlight glinting off the bluest ocean.

A blast of frigid air swirled through the doorway. ''Hi,'' she gasped. ''Come in while I get my jacket.''

He stamped last night's dusting of snow off his boots and followed her inside. Caroline felt her senses spring into full awareness of him. She felt his attention as distinctly as if he'd run his hands over her in a gentle caress. It was unnerving, this heightened sensitivity, this giddiness and lack of control over her reactions. And the unexpectedness, the illogicalness of it all. Why Judd? Why her? Why now?

She turned and looked up into his face, saw him smile at her as if he were truly glad to be with her, and thought, *Why not?*

''Caroline, are you having second thoughts about spending the day alone with me?''

His caution reminded her of the way young men at universities were being counseled these days, on how to proceed in dating rituals. They were being advised to ask permission for every action, no matter how small, from hand holding to kissing to every step of making love. Immediately, Caroline regretted that thought. She'd been in a restless state of aroused confusion—or confused arousal, she wasn't sure which anymore—since Thursday afternoon's encounter with Judd. The mere fleeting thought of her secret—and colorful!—stash of condoms in the bedside table was enough to make her feel flushed and chilled at the same time. Considering actually using them with—or more precisely, using them *on!*—the attractive, earnest man waiting for her to answer his simple question, threatened to turn her into a babbling idiot. Anyone reading her thoughts would think she was a fifteen-year-old, not a thirty-*something*-year-old!

She was a socially inept coward! No wonder she'd jumped at the chance to marry Jeffrey Yates. Poor Jeff had never been exciting enough to make her insides quiver. He had been her self-appointed protector, her friend, her companion, eventually her husband. He'd given her stability and predictability—at least until he'd given more of himself than he could afford—but he'd never been her lover. And, sadly, she understood now, she'd never been his. The realization that she had been profoundly insecure, petrified of being alone, dependent on but never in love with Jeff burst through her musings with astounding clarity. Poor Jeff! No wonder he'd run away, chasing after his dreams. He must have sensed how she felt, even when *she* hadn't, and must have felt smothered by the mistake of their marriage.

''Caroline?'' Judd's voice yanked her back to the present, with its giddy excitement and uncertainty. She refocused her gaze, and found him studying her. ''Are you all right? You looked like you'd gone into a trance.''

The prickling heat of a blush raced up her neck and cheeks. Hastily, she nodded. "Yes, I'm fine. I just . . . I just was thinking, and I . . ." She *what*? Had let her mind wander from going shopping to the realization that Thomas Black's first novel didn't have a thing to do with her divorce? If she tried to explain the way her train of thought had leaped that many tracks, Judd would be backing out the door faster than she could blink.

She began again. "I'm sorry. Sometimes an idea pops into my head and distracts me like that. My students say it's amusing. I think they hope I'll drift off while I'm doing final grades and give them all nineties." She smiled, hoping she'd distracted him enough that he wouldn't press her to tell him about the idea that had absorbed her attention, because at the moment, her mind was blank. It was still before noon, but she figured she'd already met her embarrassment quota for the day.

To her relief, he grinned back. "Happens to me all the time, but I'm usually the only witness. So, while you were lost in space, did you decide how you feel about being alone with me all day?"

Caroline felt her own smile widen. "Yes, I'm fine to be alone with you and several thousand other shoppers."

Judd's low chuckle rewarded her agreement, but it was such a sexy sound that it didn't do much to soothe her rattled nerves. The moment she picked up her jacket from the chair where she'd placed it, Judd took it from her and held it for her. She hesitated for a second, trying to remember the last time a man before Judd—a date, not the maitre d' of a restaurant—had held her coat for her. It wasn't a major gesture, but as Judd's fingertips grazed the sensitive skin at the back of her neck, then set her scalp tingling when he lifted her hair free of her collar, she decided it was a shame more men didn't think to do it more often. Or maybe it was a shame more women didn't think to encourage it.

"Is this the unforgiving feline?" he asked, his lips so close to her ear that his warm breath tickled her.

Caroline watched her big calico cat pad down the staircase and pose for Judd, her neat white paws perfectly aligned in front of her white bib, her long fluffy tail curled around her body, her tiny ears aimed forward. "Yes, that's Shoo. She can usually find it in her heart to forgive my neglect, as long as my apologies come in edible form." Shoo blinked her amber eyes as if in agreement.

"Mmm. Very sensible," he murmured, his lips brushing the edge of her ear. "And very pretty." His fingers combed through her hair, sending shivers down her spine.

"Th . . . Thank you." She didn't think he was referring to Shoo, but she didn't want him to think she was vain, or lacking in manners.

Judd stepped away from behind her. "We better go. Victoria warned me the parking lots fill up pretty quickly with the after-Christmas sales."

"I just have to get my boots from the front closet," she told him. He followed her, then leaned against the wall while she pulled on her boots. "Where do you fit in the sibling order?"

He held the door for her, then closed it and gave the handle a shake, testing the lock. "Victoria is the oldest, and I'm the baby." He gave her a wicked look that told her just what kind of baby he must have been. "Poor Emmy was the filling in the family sandwich. What about you?"

"Just me."

"Sounds lonely."

"Sometimes," she conceded. "But it was nice to be the center of attention." Except, having said the words, she realized that she had never really been the center of anyone's attention. Was that one of the reasons she responded to Judd the way she did? Because he made her feel special, if only for the present moment? And if so, did that make her pathetic and needy, the way she'd been with Jeff, or just plain normal and human?

Looking up at the clear blue sky, noticing the sunlight sparkling on windows, the pigeons huddled on a neighbor's roof, and another neighbor's silver standard poodle trotting jauntily down the street, Caroline decided that she really didn't want to dwell on her weaknesses. It was a beautiful day, she was going out with a very handsome, very nice man, and she intended to enjoy herself. There would always be time later, when she was alone, to reflect on whether she'd grown up at all in the past decade, or still had to work out the same problems.

There were four sport-utility vehicles, representing several different manufacturers and price ranges, parked directly in front of her house, and two others across the street. Toronto probably had more four-wheel-drive vehicles than the entire rest of Ontario, Caroline mused. She wondered which one of them would belong to Judd. He cupped her elbow and led her across the street, which narrowed the field to the two Pathfinders, one red, one black. But to her surprise, he continued past them, stopping at a nondescript brown sedan.

"You thought I'd be driving one of those flavor-of-the-month SUVs, didn't you?" His tone was amused, not accusing, and his eyes sparkled.

"Well," she hedged, then laughed lightly. "Yes, I did."

He slid his arm around her shoulders and turned her away from the brown sedan. "Well, you were right. The red one's mine," he announced, laughter lurking in his voice.

Feeling foolish for being so transparent, Caroline refused to laugh with him. Or tried not to. After he let her in on the passenger side, he climbed into the driver's seat, started the car, and buckled his seat belt, all without looking at her. Then, while shifting into first gear, he glanced sideways at her, his expression so boyishly unrepentant that she couldn't keep her own laughter from bubbling up out of her.

"So," she began after she'd caught her breath, "what have you been doing the last ten years?"

"I stayed in Toronto for a few years, graduated, worked in a job I really hated for a couple of years, then moved out to Vancouver Island. I was there almost seven years."

She watched him flick on his left signal, glance over his shoulder, and change lanes across Avenue Road with an easy grace. "Where on the island?"

"Outside Victoria. I had a little house on a few acres, with all sorts of wildlife around. It was very peaceful." He gave her a rueful look. "Maybe a little too peaceful."

"Is that what brought you back to Toronto?"

"No. My dad had a mild heart attack a couple of months ago, and when I came home for Christmas, I decided it was time to come home again."

If she hadn't liked him already, that would have tipped the scales in his favor. "Did you have to give up your job to move back?"

At first Caroline thought she was imagining the change in his manner. Before now, he'd been glancing at her while answering her questions. Now, he kept his eyes focused directly forward, concentrating on oncoming traffic as they waited to turn left onto Cumberland Street and the upscale Yorkville shopping area. He seemed to be hesitating an unusually long time for a question that really only required a yes-or-no answer. And he'd reacted much the same way on Thursday, over dinner, when she'd asked about his work. How odd.

They stopped at an intersection, waiting for a wave of assorted pedestrians to finish crossing so he could turn left. He peered so intently and silently through the windshield, while the southbound cars whizzed steadily past them, Caroline was certain he was stalling about answering her question. But why?

Finally, he made the turn, then negotiated the short distance to an indoor parking garage, steering around illegally parked Jaguars and other luxury cars, dodging conspicuously dressed pedestrians, whether in furs or designer jeans, who stepped into the street as if they expected traffic to stop for them.

"Well, not really. I . . . I was, uh, I'm a, uh, a consultant, so I can work almost anywhere I want, as long as I, uh, can get to a phone and fax."

Caroline suppressed a smile. If she had a nickel for everyone she knew who was a consultant, she could take early retirement the way Judd thought she already had! "What kind of consultant?"

"Research," he announced suddenly. He shot her a sidelong glance. "Research and specialty writing." Another glance away, then back at her. "And some teaching."

"Ah," she responded, amused that he'd seemed reluctant to confess something so ordinary. It wasn't as if he were an assassin or a crooked accountant or a breaking-and-entering specialist. Then again, maybe it was the very ordinariness of his work that made him hesitate, assuming that she wouldn't be impressed by his real occupation. Men could be such odd, competitive creatures! Still, she decided, giving him a smile intended to be reassuring, seeing that tiny chink in the armor of his self-confidence was rather endearing. Maybe he'd see it as a trade-off when he discovered who *she* really was.

Nearly four hours after he'd parked on the roof level of the exorbitantly expensive Yorkville garage, Judd drove north on Avenue Road toward Caroline's house, grinning, he was sure, like an idiot. And why not? Caroline was everything he'd imagined—hoped—she'd be: witty, curious, gentle, self-confident, and very, very sexy in an oddly innocent way—as well as what he hadn't expected: foolishly touchy about her age. He couldn't think of any other reason why she'd lie about who she was, especially since it would be so easy for him to find out from the University faculty office. But hell, he didn't care. It was one of those female things that made them so interesting. His sister was always claiming to be younger than her younger brother! Caroline would confess eventually. And to make her feel better, he'd tell her he'd known right away. Then they could have a good laugh over it, and get on with things.

He stole a look at her as he waited for a break in the southbound traffic so he could turn. She looked lost in thought, her hazel-gold eyes soft, staring out the windshield without seeing the street, he'd bet. Daydreaming about him, he hoped. Maybe wondering, the way he was, if anything would develop from the self-defense practice they were about to do. He knew what *he* wanted to have develop. He was aching to hold her, to kiss her, to lose himself in the heat simmering just below her cool, calm surface. He wanted to ignite some of that passion within her, and hear her cry out in wild pleasure. He was willing to let her set the pace, let her tell him when she was ready for more than casual, not-quite-accidental touching.

But hell! If she could be as decisive about a relationship with him as she'd been about helping him buy dishes, sheets, and towels, it would be like standing in the path of a tornado! The prospect of that made him grin even wider.

• • •

"Don't bother changing," Judd said in answer to her question. They were in her living room after their shopping safari, because Judd insisted that this was as good a time to practice her self-defense skills as any. "Bad guys don't wait till you're wearing comfortable clothes. You're better off knowing what to do in a normal situation. Elevators, stairwells, parking garages, any inside places, or the middle of the sidewalk on a sunny day."

Caroline suppressed a shudder. "That's why I signed up for Bob's class. My next-door neighbor was mugged right on her own front walk, at about four in the afternoon. Some guy sauntered up to her, grabbed her purse, and knocked her down." She wrapped her arms around herself. "What scared me was that it could have been me if I hadn't stopped at the grocery store on my way home. I saw him running away."

Judd settled one lean hip against the arm of her living-room sofa, his expression grim. "Okay, let's street-proof you. We'll run through the basics Bob taught first, and then I'll show you some street-fightin' tricks."

"Rats! My brass knuckles are in the shop." Caroline grinned playfully.

He caught her by the upper arm so quickly that she never saw him move. His fingers held her gently, but when she struggled, she couldn't break his grip. Astonished, she stared into his eyes. His cold answering stare frightened and paralyzed her. They stood immobile for a long moment, her heart beating painfully against her ribs, her breath coming in shallow gasps. Misgivings flashed wordlessly through her mind.

And then, suddenly, he gave her a very self-satisfied grin. "Here's what you do to break this hold and get away." He tipped his head to one side. "Hurting me back is optional."

She considered kicking him for scaring her, but she forced herself to relax and focus on what Judd was saying and the ways he was moving her arms and feet. Maybe she could even convince him that she'd known all along that what he was doing was part of the lesson, not his sudden and inexplicable transformation into a rapacious beast. Except that with every touch, every breath that carried the scent of his skin, she found it harder and harder to concentrate.

"Okay," he said after they'd gone through the movements

several times in slow motion. "Walk past me, like you're window shopping on Bloor Street."

Caroline walked down the center of the floor. She was several steps past where she'd left Judd when she felt him grab her shoulder. She forgot which way to turn and smashed into him, her senses assaulted by the heat and hardness of his body.

"Oh!" she gasped against his chest.

"Mmm," he grunted. "You pack a wallop, babe, but a hug isn't gonna stop a mugger." He released her, steadied her. She felt her cheeks burn and had to force herself to meet his eyes. "Here. Let's walk it through."

For the next hour, using his hands and voice, Judd showed her how to counter various kinds of grabs and holds. His fingers left trails of fire wherever they touched her, even through her clothes. Every time he held her against his chest, she felt her responses escalate. Her nipples tingled and budded under her silk undershirt. The thought of Judd's strong, gentle hands closing over her breasts kept flashing into her mind despite her efforts to pretend he was a mugger more interested in her purse than her body. She couldn't decide whether she was relieved or disappointed when he suggested they take a break so he could explain some new techniques.

"Well done," he murmured when they'd worked through the new blocking and evasive movements. "But don't get overconfident."

Judd was standing mere inches away from her. A little out of breath, Caroline smiled up at him. He gave her a brief answering smile, then leaned toward her and pressed his lips to her forehead. He didn't touch her anywhere else, but she felt the contact everywhere. For a long, trembling moment, she stood unmoving, feeling the warmth of his lips radiating into a sizzling aura of awareness. She heard the ticking of her antique mantel clock, the *whoosh* of passing cars, the surging of her own pulse. She felt the earth rotate. When he broke the contact between them, everything became a little colder. She had to clench her fists to her sides to keep from reaching out, drawing him back. Not daring to reveal her response to such a simple gesture, she closed her eyes.

"I'm going to take my own advice," he said softly, "and

not get overconfident.'' Caroline looked up to find him gazing at her, the expression in his eyes a reflection of her own
confusion and surprise. ''I'll pick you up at seven-thirty tonight. Wear something you can dance in. There's a club I
want to take you to after dinner.''

Unable to find her voice, she nodded. Judd moved toward
the front hall in his socks, with Shoo winding herself around
his ankles. Caroline followed them, smiling at the way her
cat flirted shamelessly, while he put his boots on. Endearing
himself to feline and human, Judd paused to lift Shoo into
his arms and stroke her into a frenzy of purring and paw-
kneading that left his shirt covered with silky white hairs.
Caroline raised her hand to try to brush them away, but he
was out the door so quickly that she didn't even make contact.

Shoo stood with her front paws braced on the glass of the
storm door, meowing plaintively as she watched Judd saunter
down the walk toward his car. Caroline picked the cat up so
she could close the door.

''I know exactly how you feel,'' she told Shoo. ''I just
wish I knew what to do about it.''

The one thing she *did* know was that Judd would have to
know the truth about her before the evening was over.

Sometime after midnight, Judd walked Caroline to her front
door, keeping her tucked close to his side even though the
press of her hip and shoulder against him was driving him
pleasantly crazy. They were definitely due for some steamy
good-night kisses. All evening, he'd teased them both with
little touches, long, smoldering looks, and slow, close dancing. It was the kind of teasing that lovers could afford to do,
knowing that they'd be able to satisfy their aching hunger in
each other's arms. He didn't for one minute expect Caroline
to take him into her bed on their first date, but he wanted
her to be thinking about it long after they'd said good-night.
He sure as hell would be!

Caroline angled toward him, and even through their coats
he felt her breast press against his side. Immediately, his
body responded with a rush of heat that stole his breath. She
tipped her head up to look into his face, and the expression

in her eyes, the slight tilt of her lips, made him wonder whether she'd been doing her own brand of teasing all night, too. Given his constant state of semi-arousal, he wouldn't be surprised if she had.

"Would you like to come in?" she asked, echoing his silent wishes. "I can make some decaf coffee, or offer you a cold drink."

There was a touching hesitation, a note of uncertainty in her voice, that made it hard to know what she wanted him to answer. But she wouldn't have asked if she didn't mean it.

"Sure. Decaf sounds good."

Her smile told him he'd made the right choice, but he didn't give a damn about coffee. If he didn't taste her kisses soon, he was going to explode. He managed to curb his impatience while she unlocked the door, but the instant she shut the door behind them, he made his move. First, the buttons of her coat, one at a time, from throat to knees. Deliberately, he let his fingers skim over her curves, watching surprise turn to desire in her eyes. When the coat was unbuttoned, he used the open lapels to draw her closer to him, until his knees bracketed hers and her body arched back, letting her look up at him, pressing her to him. The delicate musk of her skin surrounded him. The rush of blood to his loins told him she wouldn't have any doubts as to how she was affecting him. The effort to keep from pulling her closer sent tremors through his muscles. Finally, he stopped trying and lowered his face toward hers.

She whispered his name against his lips, and then her arms came up around his neck. He captured her lips as he slid his hands inside her coat to grasp her waist. The black dress she wore was as soft and slinky as it looked, and her body inside it was lean and supple. Her lips parted under his, and he tasted her. She was even sweeter than he'd imagined.

He tore his mouth away from hers and buried his face in the side of her neck, breathing in her scent and tasting the delicate spice of her skin. When she made a soft sound and sagged against him, as if her knees had buckled, his hunger turned into a tiger, clawing at him for satisfaction. An answering growl rose in his throat as he covered her mouth with his again. Her tongue met his, parrying, inviting, caressing, and he dragged her with him so he could collapse against the wall before he fell with her.

Then Caroline broke away so suddenly that he nearly did fall. Stupidly, breathlessly, he gaped at her.

"Judd, I'm sorry." She sounded as if she were about to cry. "I . . . I can't . . . There's something I have to tell you, before . . ." There were tears in her dark eyes now, and it was his fault. "Judd, this was a wonderful day, but I'll understand if . . . if you decide you never want to see me again after I tell you . . ."

He decided he'd better help her out or they'd be stuck in the hallway all night. He caught her hands in his and brought them to his lips. Her eyes widened as he kissed her hands.

"It's okay, Caroline. I knew all along."

Her hands stiffened in his. Uh-oh.

"You knew *what* all along?" No mistaking the suspicion in her voice. Her jaw clenched and her eyes narrowed.

This wasn't going the way he'd anticipated. He trailed little kisses across her rigid knuckles, pausing briefly to dip his tongue into the crease between two fingers. The tiny tremor he caused sent a brief jolt to their joined hands, but her jaw didn't soften. He better get this over with quick, so they could get back where they'd left off. He couldn't remember the last time a woman's kisses had made his knees weak, and he liked it.

He gave her the simple truth. "I knew right away that you're my old English teacher, Ms. Lassiter."

Maybe he shouldn't have used the word *old*. The sparks in her eyes looked serious. Damage control time. He tried a coaxing smile, but her expression held. By some mysterious process, *he'd* ended up on the defensive. Why was it always so much easier to deal with women when they were figments of his imagination, characters in his novels? At least it would be easy to prove he understood her motives and didn't hold her little white lie against her.

"I figured you were trying to hide your age by pretending to be a classmate," he explained.

"How perceptive."

He grinned. Now that was out of the way, they could go

back to kissing. The fact that he still had his own whopper of a lie to confess could safely stay on the back burner. He'd tell her before they became lovers, but after he was pretty sure she'd forgive—

He never saw it coming. Without any change in expression to signal her intentions, she nailed his instep with one of those sexy but lethal spike heels. No doubt about it, he thought with a wince, he was one hell of a good teacher!

Chapter Six

Caroline froze in astonished dismay. She'd just spiked Judd's foot! The hope that she'd missed anything sensitive died when his surprise turned to a grimace. The blood that had rushed from her head at his blithely insulting announcement flooded back, stinging her cheeks. Her paralysis of embarrassment suddenly dissolved in the heat of her blush.

"Oh, Judd! Oh, I'm so sorry!" The words came out about an octave higher than her normal voice. "I've never done anything like that in my life! I didn't mean to hurt you. Please, take off your shoe and sock and let me—"

"Hey, it's okay. Relax." He spoke gently, but firmly, startling her into momentary silence. That was when she noticed they were still holding hands. "You have learned well, Grasshopper," he added with a slight smile, and through her agitation she realized he was imitating the masters of David Carradine's character, Kane, on the TV series _Kung Fu_. His smile widened. "I sorta deserved it." The tiny lines around his eyes deepened. "And you just gave me one hell of a compliment."

She was stuck in her front hall with a lunatic! "Compliment? Are you nuts?'' she practically yelled at him. ''I just could have broken one of those tiny bones in your foot!''

He gave a dismissive little snort, then tugged her toward him. Caroline tried to resist, but when she realized she really wanted him to hold her again, she gave up and let him slide his arms inside her coat to pull her snugly against his big, hard—Oh, was he ever!—body. Still, she felt confused by his reaction and wary of his motives. Not even Miss Manners had rules for this situation, she was sure.

''Yeah, I probably am nuts, but that's got nothing to do with anything right now.'' His low voice rumbled near her ear, his breath tickling her skin seductively. ''I'm a black belt in kung fu, and you took me by surprise. As your teacher, I'd say that's a compliment.'' He tightened his arms and pressed a warm kiss into the curve of her neck. ''A slightly painful compliment,'' he added, a laugh lurking in his voice, ''but I've taken worse hits.''

''I'm so embarrassed,'' she mumbled against his chest.

''About stomping me or lying about your age?''

Well, he certainly wasn't mincing words! ''Both,'' she snapped back. He didn't have to be so cheerful about her humiliation. ''I didn't want you to think I was an over-the-hill spinster. And I guess I'm old-fashioned enough to be concerned about dating a younger man.''

''Can I make a suggestion?'' His warm breath stirred her hair over her ear, and tickled awake sensitive nerves that sent a shiver of pleasure down her spine.

''Mmm. What?''

One of his hands slid down her back, teasingly close to her bottom. Against her belly, his body was hard with arousal. Caroline fought the urge to press herself closer and make a suggestion of her own. But her mind wasn't ready, even if her body insisted it was. She'd be damned if she was going to get herself trapped into a one-night stand just to prove she was as attractive as any younger woman.

''Let's continue this discussion tomorrow afternoon,'' he said. ''Do you ice skate?''

Surprise that he wasn't suggesting they continue their conversation in her bed, mingled with relief that he actually wanted to see her again in spite of her foolish behavior, made her feel light-headed. All her self-preservation instincts went on alert, warning her not to let herself care so much, so quickly. But other, equally primal instincts clamored to take over and destroy her caution. She'd taught enough classes on romance novels to understand that she recognized Judd as a suitable mate. What woman wouldn't?

There was no point in denying that she was very attracted to Judd, and had been ten years ago, too. But back then, professional ethics, fear of taking chances, and her assumption that Jeff expected to marry her had combined to convince her that her interest had been a passing fancy. And it probably had been . . . then. Both of them were very different people than they'd been ten years ago. If she'd allowed herself to follow her impulse after that term had ended, who's to say that she and Judd wouldn't have broken up even more quickly than she and Jeff had?

He eased her away from him, still holding her waist in his strong hands. They were large enough to make her feel small, feminine, protected, not feelings an independent professional woman was supposed to enjoy, but Caroline liked the way Judd made her feel anyway.

"Caroline? Do you ice skate? I haven't been skating at Harbourfront, and my nephews say the rink on the edge of Lake Ontario is 'way cool.' Okay?"

She found her scattered wits and nodded. "Yes, I skate. That sounds like fun."

"I want to get to know Toronto again, and I want to do it with you." He tipped his head to one side, regarding her so solemnly that she felt a twinge of guilt for noticing the double entendre. Then he winked, and her guilt dissolved. He meant to do that, the rat! "Interested?"

Caroline smiled. An affirmative answer would definitely have two meanings. With all the trouble one lie had gotten her into, she was perfectly happy this time to tell the truth. "Yes, I am." He rewarded her with a quick kiss on her mouth that left her smiling even more. "I'm afraid I don't get out enough to show you all the other 'way cool' facets of Toronto, but I'd like to help you explore."

He answered with a kiss that this time lingered sweetly, a lazy exploration of her lips with his, until her long-banked sexuality flared. Breathlessly, she opened her lips under his, welcoming his tongue with her own. He started to pull her closer, then paused and groaned against her mouth. With softly clinging kisses, he slowly drew back. When he lifted his head, she gazed into his eyes in dazed need, grateful that he had the fortitude to stop them before she made another wrong decision.

"I'll pick you up about three tomorrow. Dress warm."

With Shoo winding around her ankles in a bid for food and affection, Caroline watched Judd stride toward his Pathfinder. She didn't move until his taillights blinked and disappeared at the end of the street. Then, as a smile tugged at her lips, she locked her house and made her way upstairs, thanking the powers that be for giving her another second chance, and for making Judd a generous and honorable man.

Caroline looked up from a stack of essays and her gaze landed on the calendar on her office wall. February thirteenth, only four weeks since her first date with Judd. Four weeks of spending nearly every evening and all of her days off with him, except when he'd gone out of town on business. Four weeks of exploring Toronto like kids locked in a toy store overnight, from concert halls and theaters to the Science Centre and the Royal Ontario Museum and the Art Gallery of Ontario. Four weeks of sampling every imaginable kind of cuisine, from the most rustic pub rollicking with live Irish folk music to the most sophisticated fusion of French and Chinese cooking at an exclusive restaurant in a narrow renovated Victorian house. Four weeks of daydreaming and forgetfulness and thinking about Judd when she should have been concentrating on other things.

She was in love.

She was in love, and it was the most exhilarating, scary, wonderful, validating, and vulnerable feeling! She wanted to tell the world, and she wanted to keep it her secret. She wanted Judd to know, but she was afraid to tell him. What if he didn't feel the same way? What if he did, but didn't want to commit himself to a real relationship? Caroline wanted to think about marriage, about children, about the future. What if Judd didn't want any of those things? What if all he'd ever intended was an affair? What if he broke her heart?

Caroline shook her head. Where was this *what-iffing* coming from, so much of it rather pessimistic? And not much of it based on any kind of evidence. For one thing, and it was probably the most important, if Judd only intended to have an affair with her, he was certainly taking his time about it! She'd never been so frustrated or confused in her life. Last weekend, intoxicated by his kisses, she'd very nearly demanded he stop teasing and make love to her—but she'd lost her nerve at the last second.

Ah, well, this train of thought wasn't getting these essays graded. Summoning her willpower, Caroline made her way through the stack of papers, finishing a couple of hours later. With her stomach reminding her that she'd skipped lunch to meet with some of her students, she packed away her work and prepared to go home for a solitary evening. She had a date with a face mask that was guaranteed to make her face glow—or so the woman at the cosmetics counter had promised.

By tomorrow, she probably wouldn't need help glowing! Judd would be back tomorrow from New York City. On Tuesday, before he'd left, he'd invited himself to her house Saturday for a home-cooked dinner, which he promised to cook. No wonder this was the first Valentine's Day in years about which she'd felt even remotely romantic. Except for the one memorable time Jeff had sent her white roses and a surprisingly romantic card, then proposed to her, he'd always dismissed Valentine's Day as commercial and artificial.

But why dwell on Jeff when she could be thinking about Judd? Was he as attracted as he seemed? After all, that wasn't something a man could, um, fake. Perhaps he didn't want to rush her, Caroline mused as she stepped outside into biting cold wind and swirling snowflakes. She wrapped her coat tighter around her, wishing it could be Judd's arms enfolding her in his warmth. Perhaps she'd find the courage to let him know that she wouldn't mind being rushed. But would she *ever* have the courage to discover whether the green fluorescent condom really did glow in the dark?

*   *   *

Judd barged through the airport exit and yanked open the back door of the first taxi in line by the curb. Impulsively, he gave the driver Caroline's address. He'd missed her like crazy, but that wasn't the primary reason he'd decided to fly home early. All he seemed to be able to think about was how much he wanted her in his arms, in his bed, in his life. But first, he had to crawl through some broken glass, figuratively speaking.

He couldn't satisfy his gnawing hunger for her, with his lies of omission about to blow up in his face. When she learned who he really was, she'd feel betrayed. She probably wouldn't feel very rational. He couldn't count on her sense of humor to help him smooth this over. He needed to set the stage carefully. One wrong step, one false note, and he could lose her. And the hell of it was, he wouldn't be able to blame her if she told him to get lost.

The timing couldn't have been much worse. When he and his publicist had planned this promotional escapade, with his family's consent, he couldn't have anticipated that Caroline would walk back into his life. He hadn't planned on falling in love with probably the only woman on the face of the earth who had reason to hate him. Prolonging the lie was out of the question. Even if he didn't confess, Caroline would find out soon enough.

He wouldn't be able to keep lying to her even if he wanted to. He'd never intended his pretense, his charade, to go on this long. There just hadn't seemed to be a good time to tell her about his secret identity. Now, of course, he could see all the opportunities he'd missed, but it was almost out of his control. Assuming she didn't see posters of his face plastered all over bookstores for the Valentine's Day launch of his newest hardcover, someone would recognize him. If she didn't catch him next week in his first-ever television interview, a pretaped exclusive with Barbara Walters, she'd probably see him on Letterman a few nights later. Or chatting with Rosie O'Donnell during the day. If she somehow managed to miss all that, there were the book sections of the local newspapers.

Like the old saying, he could run, but he couldn't hide. Anyway, he didn't want to run. He loved her, and he intended to make sure she didn't get away. All he had to do was convince her that she could believe him now, when she shouldn't have believed him before.

The taxi stopped for a red light next to an open flower shop. Valentine's Day was tomorrow, but right now he needed all the sweet-talking, romantic buttering up he could muster for the coming evening.

Judd opened the car door and stuck his foot out just as the car started to roll in anticipation of the green light. When the dome light came on, the car lurched to a stop. Judd lost his balance and swore under his breath. The driver shifted to glare at him over the seat. "Wait for me," he barked, before the driver could say what was obviously on his mind. "It's a damn emergency!"

He skidded across the slushy, crowded sidewalk, dodged a yappy little frou-frou dog on a rhinestone leash, and stopped short at the array of black plastic buckets holding roses. Dozens and dozens of fresh roses, in all shades of red and pink. Guys in suits and wool coats, and guys in work clothes and quilted jackets, were buying red roses by the armful. But he didn't want red or pink or yellow roses. He almost conceded defeat, but as he pivoted in desperation, he saw exactly what he wanted in a corner of the front window display.

Cradling his roses, wrapped carefully to protect them from the biting chill, he got back into the taxi. It was Friday the thirteenth, but it just could be his lucky day.

Caroline felt the claylike substance on her face with hesitant fingertips. She was afraid if she touched the mask even a tiny bit too hard, her face would crack. The stuff was cool and plasterlike, so it must be ready to wash off. Setting her book down, she left her cozy corner of the sofa to go upstairs and wash her face. Shoo, curled in front of the big living-room radiator, woke and stretched, looked at Caroline, and dashed out of the room. Caroline tried to laugh but she couldn't move her jaw.

The doorbell rang when she was halfway up the stairs. She froze, heart pounding, frantically trying to decide what to do. At eight in the evening, it could be a neighbor, a canvasser, a friend who happened to be in the neighborhood. Whoever it was couldn't see her clearly, but could probably see movement through the leaded-glass door panes. At about fifteen-second intervals, the bell rang three more times. Not responding was rude. But she couldn't answer the door dressed in her rattiest robe, with this greenish-gray plaster stuff on her face! If she just stood there like a statue, whoever it was would go—

"Caroline?"

At the sound of Judd's bellow, her heart leaped and sank at once. Her first impulse was to rush down the stairs to let him in. Oh, no! She couldn't! She looked like a freak! Caroline stopped at the foot of the stairs. But he must have come back from New York early. To see her? Oh, that was so sweet! How could she turn him away? She started to smile at the prospect of seeing him almost a day sooner than she'd expected, but the hardened face mask held her muscles immobile. That was enough to help her decide. Potential humiliation tipped the scale against opening the door. She couldn't let him see her like this, no matter how much she wanted to be with him!

Standing behind the inner door, she called, "Judd, I can't see you now," as clearly as she could without actually opening her mouth, which made her sound as if she were chewing cotton.

"Caroline, what's wrong?" Judd bellowed back.

"Nothing." Her answer came out as a sort of loud mutter. "I'm getting ready for bed."

"It's eight o'clock."

He had a valid point, but she could hardly sigh in defeat with her face encased in dry mud. Never again would she do something this bizarre for the sake of vanity! Never! "Right. Can you wait five minutes?" Now she sounded as if she had no teeth!

"No, damn it, I can't wait out here five minutes! I'm freezing, and so are your roses!"

Roses! He'd brought her roses! Should she laugh or cry? "Okay," she called back, opening the inner door to the small foyer, which was several degrees colder. Judd's silhouette loomed in the window of the outer door, distorted by the privacy ripples in the glass. "But you have to promise to count to twenty before you come in. I'll be right back down." She turned the deadbolt knob, then paused. "Promise?"

"I promise. Hurry up!"

Gathering her robe in her free hand, Caroline unlocked the door and fled toward the stairs without looking backward. Behind her, she heard Judd counting: "One, two, four, six, ten, twelve." That cheat! It would serve him right if she let him take a good look at her in her plaster mask, looking like a character from *Tales of the Crypt*! But it wouldn't be sweet revenge, because she'd probably never see him again.

Judd slammed the front door against the wind and cold. She made the mistake of hesitating for half a heartbeat. His footsteps on the hardwood floor of the front hallway came closer much too quickly. Caroline clutched her robe and grabbed at the handrail to pull herself up the stairs faster. One stair from the top landing, her foot caught in the edge of her robe and she almost fell. The yelp she made came out strangled by the plaster on her face.

"Caroline, wait!" Judd was right behind her on the stairs, obviously mistaking her flight for something more sinister than vanity. Now she'd have to explain, and he'd laugh at her for trying to make herself look younger. Mortified by that scenario, she tried to bolt. If she could just get to the bathroom and lock the door, she could wash the mask off before he had a chance to appreciate the full horror of her appearance.

The next thing she knew, he'd caught her and they were falling together onto the carpeted upper landing. His strong arms secured her, his lean body twisted, and he rolled onto his back under her. She found herself lying on his chest, her legs tangled with her robe and his legs. One of his thighs ended up wedged very intimately between hers, threatening to part her robe. Her breath came out in a startled rush, but somehow, she had the presence of mind to duck and hide her face against his shoulder. That was when she smelled the cool, delicate scent of the roses they'd crushed between them.

"Oh, Judd! The roses!" Her voice came out in a muffled wail.

His hands were moving slowly and deliberately over her upper body as if he were feeling for injuries, but her body reacted as it always did whenever he touched her. Desire warmed her blood, melting her bones, waking the nerves of her skin and making her aware of the emptiness inside her that longed for him. Liquid fire pooled low in her belly, stirred by the way his thigh pressed between her legs.

"Forget the roses. Are you all right?" Caroline nodded with her head still pressed against him. "Why did you run away like that?" She shrugged. "You aren't afraid of me?" Indignantly, she shook her head. "Good." His roving fingertips slid along her neck, teasing under the collar of her robe. Suddenly, his fingers stilled. "Oh, my God! You're cracking!"

Chapter Seven

Caroline felt as if all the starch had melted out of her. There was no escape now, never had been, she supposed. It was Tinkerbell versus Godzilla: not exactly even odds! All her own fault, of course. How could she have forgotten Judd's martial arts expertise, his agility and strength, not to mention his persistence? Why hadn't she simply flung open the door, waited for him to stop laughing, and let him sit in the living room while she washed the goop off? If love was going to make her this stupid, perhaps she should think twice about it!

But this was no time for second thoughts. With his fingers under her chin, Judd gently but unavoidably lifted her face toward him. She squeezed her eyes closed and waited for his reaction. After a long silence, she heard a muffled snicker. Her wince made the dry mask around her mouth crack. Judd's snicker turned into a snort. The tension of the taut muscles of his belly transmitted the heroic effort he was making not to laugh. She was grateful for that little favor.

"I'd like to get up," she told him, the muffled-through-cotton sound of her voice ruining her haughty tone.

Suddenly, she was surrounded by shaking so powerful she thought it was an earthquake. Or hoped it was an earthquake. But no, it was Judd, laughing too hard to make a sound at first. Then he wrapped his arms around her and howled. Resisting his embrace only made little bits of dried face mask flake off onto his soft black shirt. Finally, she stopped trying to pull away and lay in his arms, waiting for his laughter to simmer down enough for him to hear her when she told him to leave.

But that didn't happen. Instead, he rolled them over so he was lying above her, and his body was pressing even more intimately against hers. When she opened her eyes, the light and laughter in his beautiful blue eyes was all she could see. He lowered his head as if to kiss her, then apparently thought better of it, snickered, and lifted his head again to look at her.

"Oh, Caroline! I love you!" All she could manage was a strangled gasp. She waited for more laughter to follow, but his expression was suddenly serious. "Aw, hell, I didn't mean to spring it on you like this. I was going to wait till tomorrow, do the Valentine's Day thing and make it romantic. But . . ." His chuckle tightened his belly against hers in a rather tantalizing way. "But I couldn't help myself. I guess I'm just a sucker for a woman in dry mud."

Caroline appreciated his effort to smooth her ruffled pride, but she knew better than to give in to wishful thinking and take his declaration of love at face value. "Let me up and I'll shower this off," she mumbled.

She thought he was pushing himself up from the floor, but he was only releasing her enough to look into her eyes again. She tried to maintain her tattered dignity, but the expression in his eyes was too wicked. The next thing she knew, she was laughing, in a muffled way, through the remains of the face mask.

Her laughter stopped on a startled gasp when she felt Judd trace her collarbone with his fingertip. And then his fingers slid down to the upper swells of her breasts. He'd never touched her like this without at least a layer of clothing between them. Her nipples hardened in answer to the sparks of sensation his fingers created with each teasing stroke. His thigh wedged more firmly between hers, pressing upward with a suggestive rhythm that sent desire rippling through her.

"What have you got under this robe?"

His voice was a husky whisper that somehow fanned the flames already licking at her nerves. Caroline knew she was at a turning point in their relationship, knew which way she wanted to go, and sensed he was going to take his cues from her. She put her hand on his and guided it under the opening of the robe, watching his eyes darken as his palm cupped her breast and her nipple beaded hard in tingling response. His eyes closed and his lips parted in a silent gasp. He held himself still, barely breathing, for a long moment. She watched the pulse surging at the base of his neck. Saw him swallow. Wondered what he was thinking.

Judd opened his eyes. "Caroline, I do love you," he told her in a husky, hushed voice. "It's not just something I'm saying because I want to make love to you." He gave her a crooked grin. "Although I kinda think they go together. Don't you?"

She wanted desperately to kiss him, but all she could do was gaze back into his eyes and nod. His grin widened.

"You said something about a shower a few minutes ago." With the grace and agility of a panther, he disentangled their bodies and rose to his feet. Feeling considerably less graceful and agile, Caroline accepted the hand he extended to her and let him pull her upright. "Sounds like a plan to me." With his hands on her shoulders, he ducked as if to kiss her mouth, hesitated, then finally dropped a quick kiss onto the top of her head. "Go on."

Watching Caroline walk away, Judd discovered he was shaking inside. His body was throbbing with sexual arousal, but that wasn't why he felt stunned, felt like he was about to jump without a parachute. Truth was, that's exactly what he'd done, and now he was falling without knowing what kind of landing waited for him.

He'd told Caroline he loved her. He'd told her he wanted to make love to her. But he still hadn't told her the secret he'd been keeping from her, and he had less than four hours to a deadline that could literally be the death of any feelings she had for him.

There was only one thing to do.

The door at the end of the hall closed behind her. He leaned against the wall to think. The memory of the way she'd placed his hand on her breast rose to tempt him. No mistaking the meaning of that gesture. He'd file that away for the book he was outlining right now, that was beginning to lean toward a very strong love story in the subplot. If only he could outline his life the way he planned his novels, he might know what to do next, and how it would turn out. Then again, when had he ever followed his outlines? His characters always threw him curves when he tried to make them do what he wanted them to. Real live women, he knew, were even less predictable than fictional characters, but it was worth it to try.

When he worked out his plots, he paced, so that's what he did now. On his second trip up and down the carpeted hallway, Shoo appeared out of the shadows and trotted along with him, meowing up at him as they paced.

"You know her better than I do," he caught himself murmuring to the little cat. "Should I tell her before or after we make love?" Shoo planted herself in his path, forcing him to stop. Her fluffy tail whipped back and forth as if she didn't think much of his idea. Squatting, Judd lifted the cat, who curled against him purring like a sports car; then he rose and resumed pacing, now stroking the cat's silky fur.

"Okay, here's the deal, cat," he muttered. "I can make love to her first, and tell her the truth after she's convinced how I feel, or I can tell her first, and risk her not wanting to see me ever again." Shoo offered no opinion, but Judd decided to interpret her delicate drooling on his hand as a vote for love first, secrets later.

"Well, now, if her door is locked, that's a sign that I have to tell her first," he told the cat as they approached the bedroom door. The knob twisted easily and the door opened enough for him to pause and listen, his heart pounding like a jackhammer. From behind a closed door across the bedroom, Judd heard the sudden spraying of water, followed quickly by a muffled yelp. He grinned, guessing Caroline hadn't waited for the water to heat up enough.

"Same rules," he informed Shoo on his way across the bedroom. Glancing at the neatly arranged floral quilt and pillows, he wondered if Caroline had stopped to make her bed before going to shower. "Is that a good or bad sign?" he asked Shoo, whose sudden increase in purr volume seemed to indicate that it was a good sign. "Okay, if she's locked this door, that's a sure sign that I'm supposed to confess first." Anticipating that the door was locked, he approached the bathroom door, put his hand on the knob, turned it, and found himself opening the door. The sound of spraying water, the scent of vanilla, the warmth of the steam, invaded his senses.

Suddenly, he was quaking inside again. Leaving Shoo outside the bathroom, Judd stepped inside and shut the door behind him. Through the rippled glass shower enclosure, he watched Caroline's form moving under the running water. The blood rushed to his loins so quickly that he felt lightheaded. Within seconds, he was hard and heavy and hungry for her.

He could still turn back, Judd told himself as he said her name softly. He could even tell her now, through the shower door. He *should* tell her now. But he needed her to believe he loved her, or else he could lose her. How could he convince her that his heart was honest, even if his tongue hadn't been? Words were the tools of his trade. He could make them do whatever tricks he wanted, even bend the truth to suit his purposes. But actions couldn't lie. At least not as easily as words.

Caroline's silhouette went still behind the shower enclosure. "Judd?"

"Yeah." It wasn't too late to tell her. "Caroline, I have to—"

The shower door slid open, revealing her naked and more beautiful than he'd dared to imagine. She was a sea nymph, with the water streaming over her pale skin and her wet hair fanning out in dark gold ribbons of wet silk. His breath caught and his mind went blank. His body took charge, hungry and heavy with the need to sink into hers and bind her to him in a way he'd never felt before. Her eyes were wide, and the hand she held out to him trembled. He took a step toward the shower.

She gave him a shy smile that went straight to his heart. "You probably ought to take off your clothes."

On some level, Judd knew he was functioning enough to undo buttons and zippers and shoelaces, but his awareness stayed acutely focused on the woman waiting for him. Nothing else mattered at that moment, and that moment was all that existed.

Caroline felt reality fracture and shift into another plane where time slowed and senses heightened, where gravity turned to lightness and the entire universe became focused on the joining of one man and one woman. Her ingrained shyness, her emotional fears, even her sense of herself, evaporated, transformed into the certainty that she and Judd must bind themselves together in a physical celebration of the new feelings germinating between them. Even with her limited experience of relationships, Caroline knew Judd was right: loving and making love went together. But it had been so long since she'd considered herself a focus of desire that she found it hard to believe Judd wanted her as much as she wanted him.

When he kicked off his jeans and turned toward her, she had to stifle a gasp of surprised admiration—and sudden trepidation. His lean, smooth-muscled body was beautiful, and there was no doubt that he desired her. A lot. A lot more, in fact, than her extremely tame experience had prepared her for. She had neither skill nor technique to call on, and desperately didn't want to disappoint him.

Suddenly, Judd was standing under the shower with her, so close that the water was all that separated them. Thoughts of technique flew out of her mind when he touched her shoulders with gentle fingertips. His hands came up to bracket her face and hold her for his kiss, a sweetly tentative bonding of softened lips that deepened and grew hungry with every passing second. Shakily, Caroline reached up to clasp his shoulders for support. The movement lifted her breasts, and his step forward brought their bodies together completely, with her breasts flattened against his chest and his hard, heavy manhood cradled against her belly. The feel of his pulse pounding there fueled the flames of desire licking at her bones, melting them, sending the honey of arousal to welcome their joining. A whimper of frustrated need escaped her throat.

Judd slowly drew his lips from hers. He wrapped his arms around her and held her tightly. To her astonishment, his powerful body trembled against her. "Oh, sweetheart, I would make love to you right here, right now," he murmured, "but I didn't bring protection into the shower."

"Then we better turn off the water," she managed to say.

That seemed to be her last coherent thought for a long while. Judd released her long enough to shut off the shower, then scooped her up in his arms as if she were as light as a child. He carried her past the towel bar so she could grab bath sheets, then strode to her bed. When he set her down to dry her, he certainly didn't seem to think she was a child. His sensual stroking turned her nerves to live wires that sparked with every touch. Even her scalp tingled when he blotted the water dripping from her hair. Every wakened inch of her body clamored for him to repeat his caressing tour without the towel between her skin and his fingers.

As if he could read her mind, a moment later he was doing just that, his gentle caresses wringing cries of delight and desire from her that she muffled by pressing her mouth to his. When she could stand no more of his teasing, Caroline wrestled the towel away from him and began her own exploration of his magnificent physique as she dried the water remaining on his heated skin. Soon, her hands replaced the towel. She discovered the doeskin smoothness of his skin, stretched taut over muscles as hard as marble, but alive with the blood pulsing within him, echoing within her, with the insistent force of a bass drum. Without warning, Judd bent his head to meet her lips, and Caroline felt the world spinning around her.

"Do you have anything, or shall I . . . ?" he murmured into the side of her neck. Kneeling over her, he pinned her arms above her head with gentle hands and trailed kisses to the aching tip of her breast.

The sensations he created with his mouth sent Caroline

arching off the mattress. "Night . . . stand . . . drawer," she gasped.

She felt him moving, reaching, returning to her, but between caressing and kissing him and receiving his caresses and kisses, she felt disconnected from reality. "Next time, Caroline," he whispered. "Next time will be slower. Promise. But I don't think I can wait much longer."

"Don't . . . wait," she told him, her voice caught between a gasp and a sigh. "Oh, no, don't wait!"

He was so careful, so reverently gentle, so sweetly focused on her that their joining brought tears to her eyes. Again and again, he brought her, trembling and keening, over the brink of overwhelming pleasure, until she didn't believe she could endure any more sensation. As if he knew the exact moment, Judd gave one final thrust that seemed to reach right to her heart, and the growl that echoed around her told her that he, too, had found release. Now it was her turn to soothe the shudders that wracked his body, until they both caught their breath. For a long, dreamy time, he held her curled in his arms. Caroline floated between sleeping and waking, absorbing his heat, until she felt his desire stirring and turned to welcome him again.

When Judd awoke at ten the following morning, he couldn't recall ever feeling so damn good before. What a night! What a woman! No doubt about it, he was the luckiest—

Oh, hell! His luck was about to run out.

Chapter Eight

In a heartbeat, his smug lassitude turned to guilty panic. Judd clapped his hands over his eyes and groaned. Oh, God, he was an idiot! What had happened to his careful plan to break the news to Caroline before making love to her? Sitting up in the bed, he caught a glimpse of a dangling white and orange tail twitching from under the edge of a curtain. Ah! He could blame it on Shoo! Last night, she hadn't uttered a single syllable to persuade him to leave Caroline's bedroom before he made a fatal mistake.

Before he could formulate a sensible plan that wouldn't hurt Caroline or get him tossed out into the snow, Caroline came out of the bathroom. Her eyes met his and the glow that washed over her sent his new good intentions into full retreat after his old ones. There she was in faded jeans and a white Toronto Blue Jays ''Back2Back World Champions'' sweatshirt, her hair still damp, no makeup—and no mud, either!—smiling as if just looking at him made her happy. She made him feel so . . . so . . . so *good*! He was going to have to finesse his confession somehow. He'd never forgive himself for hurting her.

"Hi!" She came to the side of the bed. He caught her hand and brought it to his lips. Her skin was soft like cream, and smelled like vanilla. "Go back to sleep if you want. There's nothing in the house for breakfast. I usually do my grocery shopping on Saturdays. I'll run out and—"

"You don't have to wait on me." He was so mad at himself, he almost snapped at her. Not a good sign. "Let's go out for breakfast or lunch or something. Just give me a few minutes to shower. Okay?"

Her sweet smile made him feel even worse about letting his deception drag on until after they'd made love. The only thing stronger than his guilt was his fear that she wouldn't understand, wouldn't forgive him, when she heard the truth. Well, he'd find out when he confessed at breakfast. If he waited any longer, the news was going to hit the fan all by itself, and it would be out of his hands. He preferred to maintain control when and where he could.

It was a perfect day. The air was bitingly cold, but the sun was bright and the sky was a clear blue with a few fluffy white clouds. Walking along crowded Yonge Street arm in arm with Judd, Caroline wanted to jump and laugh with joy, and tell the world that she was in love with the most wonderful man.

But . . . there was always a *but*, wasn't there? Judd seemed preoccupied this morning. It was much too early in their relationship to expect him to make any kind of commitments or promises, but she didn't know what she'd do if he was having second thoughts. Throwing herself at his feet wasn't an option, even if it was a temptation. But she felt too excited, too emotionally fragile, to know how to deal with anything more discouraging than one of those "let's not go too fast" conversations she was much better at doling out than at receiving.

Passing the third convenience store with tubs of fresh-cut roses and carnations causing pedestrian congestion, Caroline remembered she hadn't thanked Judd for the roses he'd brought last night. Well, she thought with a rush of heat to her cheeks, not in so many words. Impulsively, she stopped and tugged at his arm to make him pause.

"I almost forgot—" she began, but he pulled her around so she was facing the opposite direction, startling her into puzzled silence. He was scowling at something past her, but when she tried to turn around to see what could be causing him to look so displeased, he tightened his hold on her arm so she couldn't. Caroline waited for what she considered a reasonable time, but he didn't offer any explanation of his odd behavior. "Judd, is something wrong?" she finally prompted.

He seemed surprised by the sound of her voice. "Uh, no. No, nothing's wrong." He met her eyes, then looked past her again. "I, um, let's go to that place we just passed for breakfast."

"It's not nearly as good as the one on the corner," she pointed out, suddenly feeling inclined to be stubborn.

Now he looked into her eyes, his expression puzzled. "What were you going to say?" She must have looked as confused as she felt, because he added, "A minute ago, you said you almost forgot something."

Caroline stared at him. Something was very wrong, and she didn't have a clue what it could be, except that it was behind her and he didn't want her to see whatever it was. Either that, or he'd suddenly gone stark raving mad.

"I started to say I forgot to thank you for the roses. They're beautiful, and most of them survived," she told him, unable to fight the blush creeping up her neck again as she vividly recalled how they'd crushed the blooms between them. "White roses are my favorites."

He touched her cheek with cool fingertips, and the look in his eyes made her forget everything else. "You didn't thank me ten years ago, either, when I gave you white roses on Valentine's Day," he said.

Once again, Caroline felt reality shifting under her. She clung tighter to his arm and stared into his eyes. "*You* gave me white roses ten years ago?" He nodded. Caroline shook her head. "No. Please say you didn't."

"But I did. I had a hell of a crush on you back then." He grinned a little sheepishly. "I wrote a really mushy card, and paid a kid to deliver them."

She felt ill. "The card . . . Do you remember what it said?"

" 'For C., who changed my life. J.' Remember how you used to sign your comments on my papers with your initial?" He gave a little snort of laughter. "I was so sure you were interested, and just being discreet."

Her knees buckled. Judd caught her by both elbows and hauled her into his arms. "Hey, it was just a crush," he murmured. "I got over it." He pressed a soft kiss against her temple. "Now I'm in love, which is something altogether different."

Caroline wriggled out of his embrace and stared up at him. "Oh, Judd! Jeff gave me white roses, with a note that said . . ." He shook his head. She didn't know whether to laugh or cry, but she believed him. "Oh, my God! That rat! He stole your roses and your note and passed them off as his! We got engaged that night." And she'd lost her virginity, but she wasn't about to confess to that, too. The curse Judd growled under his breath summed up her feelings succinctly. "Oh, lord! When Jeff asked me for a divorce, he said something about being sorry for the roses, but under the circumstances, flowers didn't seem very important."

A group of teenagers jostled past them, bumping her. "I need to sit down," she told Judd. "After that discovery, I definitely deserve to have breakfast where the bagels are fresh and they don't burn the coffee. Come on. I can't think out here."

With her emotions somewhere between stunned and outraged, Caroline turned to tug Judd toward the bakery café on the corner. She took several steps down the sidewalk, then stopped short in front of the bookstore next to the café and gaped. Judd's face looked back at her from full-color posters—dozens of posters—covering the entire window, except for the center poster, which announced the unveiling of Thomas Black's latest thriller, and of Thomas Black himself. Or rather, of Judd Blackburn.

Her breath caught in her chest. This had to be a mistake, a joke . . . But this was Valentine's Day, not April Fool's Day. She felt a hand on her arm. Numbly, she looked over her shoulder at Judd.

"Caroline? I can explain—"

"I can't believe I felt so guilty for not telling you the truth, and all this time *you* were lying to *me*!" Desperate not to cry in public, in front of Judd, Caroline broke away from his grasp and tried to run. That was, she understood, what she did best.

She'd underestimated him. Before she could take more than one quick step, he caught her shoulder and stopped her. Without stopping to consider possible consequences, she did what he'd been trying to teach her. Using her hurt and anger for strength, she swung her elbow backward, hard, ramming Judd's solar plexus with satisfying force. A strangled noise behind her told her she'd finally done the movement right. She wanted to keep walking, but her feet wouldn't obey her. What if she'd hurt Judd?

"Lady, are you okay?" a man asked.

"Taught her everything she knows. She's fine!" Judd's voice came out in a wheeze. "I'm the one who can't breathe!" She almost laughed out loud at how petulant he sounded.

"Hey, pal, you want me to call an ambulance?" another man offered.

The sounds came to her muffled through shock. But a moment later, when Judd said, "Caroline, give me five minutes to explain. Then you can walk away if you still think you should," she heard him clearly.

They stood in front of the window filled with his photograph, close enough to talk privately, not close enough to touch. Even with the sun shining, Caroline felt the cold from her head to her toes. She huddled in her parka and stared at Judd's chin, not ready to meet his eyes, for fear of what her own might reveal.

"I was going to tell you after the first self-defense class. I wanted to let you know how much your course did for me. You literally changed my life. But after you explained how Thomas Black caused your ex to take off, I've been trying to figure out a way to tell you the truth so you wouldn't hate me." He gave a shrug and shook his head.

Caroline stared at him in disbelief. "But I don't really blame Thomas Black for Jeff wanting a divorce! Jeff and I got married for all the wrong reasons. He just used Black's first novel as an excuse.''

Judd stared back. ''Well, hell, if you knew that, why didn't you say so?'' he demanded indignantly.

''Because I felt silly enough talking about it the first time!'' she snapped back. ''What was I supposed to do? Send you a press release? Until a few minutes ago, Thomas Black was a total non-issue in my life.''

''Yeah? So how come you never read any of my books? I sent you a copy of the first one—''

She clapped her hand over her mouth to keep from yelping. Enough people were staring at them already. ''*You* sent me a copy?''

''Here we go again,'' he muttered. ''Yes, I sent you a—''

''I thought it was from Jeff, rubbing salt in my wounds, so I didn't even finish unwrapping it.''

''Then you never read the dedication?'' His voice was curiously soft, gentle. She shook her head. ''Or the dedications in any of the others?'' Again, she shook her head. ''I have something to show you, then, but I promised to explain. Will you let me?''

Now Caroline nodded. She risked a look into his face and saw that he was smiling. When she gave him a tentative answering smile, he opened his arms. After a brief hesitation, Caroline moved into his embrace and let his warmth flow through her.

''My father hated the thought that his only son and heir to his name and the family business wanted to write books. We finally struck a deal. I gave him my time as one of the vice-presidents of one of the family companies until I sold the first book. Then I was free to leave, but I promised not to use my real name or reveal my identity, so he wouldn't be embarrassed.'' Caroline felt Judd's powerful body vibrating with tension. ''I didn't care about his feelings, but I didn't want to hurt my mother, so I agreed. My agent and publisher got a lot of mileage out of the whole secret identity thing, so it ended up working in my favor anyway. But after my father's heart attack, he had a change of heart and decided he was proud of his prodigal son after all.''

"But you couldn't tell me, because you thought I hated your alter ego," Caroline concluded.

He leaned back so he could look into her face. "Dumb, huh?"

She nodded. "Almost as dumb as me trying to pretend I wasn't an older woman."

His lips twitched, a warning that he was holding back a smile. "Think you could learn to love a callow youth like me?"

She smiled. "If I had the right teacher, I probably could."

Judd ducked his head and brushed a quick kiss across her lips. "Come inside the bookstore. I want to show you something."

He led her past two clerks who were staring open-mouthed at him, and halted at a pyramid of hardcover copies of the latest novel by Thomas Black. Judd picked up one of the books and placed it in her hands. The book was heavy, its cover smooth and cool, and she felt a ridiculously sentimental urge to hug it.

"Open it to the dedication page," he instructed her. She lifted the cover, but he stopped her. "Wait." She looked up at him, but he was signaling to one of the dumbfounded clerks. "Bring me a copy of all the Thomas Black books you've got. Paper or hardcover, doesn't matter."

After a moment of scrambling and thumping in the depths of the store, the two clerks came running with armfuls of books, which they piled up with touching reverence. Then, elbowing each other, they retreated down the aisle. Judd turned back to her and smiled. "Okay, open any one of them. Open all of them. But before you do, will you marry me?"

Caroline thought her heart had stopped. "Is this a trick question?" He shook his head. "No more secrets?" Again, he shook his head. Her heart began beating again, racing. Through the sheen of tears filling her eyes, she saw how nervous Judd looked and smiled. "Well, then, yes, I will." He reached for her, but she held up the book in her hands. Laughter that was partly joy, partly excitement, bubbled up inside her. "Wait! Reading the dedication page was your idea."

She opened the book and silently read the dedication. Judd

handed her a different book, open to the dedication. One after another, she read the dedication in every one of his novels, until her tears made the letters swim and blur. Finally, setting down the last book, she looked at Judd with tears streaming down her cheeks.

He smiled and pulled her into his arms. With his lips brushing her ear, he whispered the words she'd read in every book he'd written: ''For C., who changed my life.''

Send Me No Flowers

Sherry Lewis

For Randy
with love

Chapter One

David Randolph leaned back in his chair and gazed around the crowded restaurant while Barry Slocum rambled on about the case they'd been assigned to litigate at the end of the month. Barry hadn't missed a beat all through the meal—not when their server placed their plates on the table, or when she cleared their meals away, or even when she brought the check.

"They didn't give us much time," Barry said, peering at David over his glasses. "We only have a month to get ready for trial. Think you can do it?"

David nodded. He could, even though this type of case wasn't his favorite.

Barry marked his place with one finger and closed his file. "I'm still not sold on having you as my junior counsel on this case. You're too new to the firm to handle something this size, and I don't know why Gottfried ever assigned you to it." He talked as if David's previous years in practice counted for nothing.

David cocked an eyebrow at him. "Thanks for the vote of confidence."

"You joined the firm a month ago. You haven't been with us long enough to become familiar with the client. And it's not exactly the type of case you were working on at your last firm."

David couldn't deny that. He'd spent the first years of his career defending mom-and-pop businesses against corporate aggressors and he hadn't completely adjusted to representing the other side. He said only, "I've been here six weeks. I moved to Colorado Springs before Christmas."

"Well, those extra two weeks certainly make a difference." Sarcasm filled Barry's voice and his frown deepened. "I just hope you can do it."

David sent him a thin smile. "I'll do my best."

Reopening the file, Barry cleared his throat and began again. "As I said earlier, we have to prove this case by a preponderance of evidence. That means our exhibits will have to be flawless, and I'm going to need some research on the Federal Rules of Evidence before next week."

It was a cinch Barry didn't intend to do the research himself. David added a note to his nearly full notepad and gazed around the restaurant again. It was only the first of February, but he saw suggestions of Valentine's Day wherever he looked. Vases of red carnations graced each table. Red and white candles flickered inside crystal bowls on narrow wooden ledges. Even their server wore a heart-shaped pendant around her neck.

The decorations had caught him off guard when they'd walked in. David hadn't given Valentine's Day much thought since his divorce. In fact, he hadn't spared much thought for romance of any kind during the past few years.

"Their argument is that, according to ERISA . . ." Barry's voice cut into David's thoughts and pulled him back to the present. He made notes until Barry finished at last and excused himself for a moment.

Leaning back in his chair, David glanced out a nearby window. Snow covered the patio now, but it would make a pleasant place for lunch when the weather turned warmer—if it ever did. Already he longed for the heat and sunshine of Phoenix, and he missed the relative freedom he'd had as a partner in the small firm he'd left to accept this job.

He told himself he wasn't having second thoughts. He'd made an informed choice and he'd stick behind his decision. Working for smaller firms hadn't brought in any money, and he certainly hadn't built a name or earned the respect of his peers.

Not that making a name for himself had ever been high on David's list of priorities. But since he and Virginia had divorced, and since they'd had no children, his career was the only thing he had left. He might as well make *something* of himself before he became an old man.

Enjoying another mouthful of dessert, he started running through Barry's commentary again and mentally organizing himself when something a few feet to his left captured his attention. Inside a narrow doorway, a woman with long brown hair reached for something at her feet. Her hair fell over her shoulders and tumbled halfway down her back when she stood again.

David lowered his fork to the table. There was something familiar about her—the shape of her hands, the way she moved, or the glow of her hair when she stepped into the winter sunlight streaming through a window.

She stood just inside a small bookstore he'd noticed when he and Barry arrived at Ristorante Veneto for lunch. He'd been surprised to find one of Colorado Springs's finest restaurants hidden behind a red brick house with white trim, huge awnings, and a sign naming it Every Book & Cranny. Finding the two businesses joined by a connecting door surprised him even more.

The woman tucked a lock of hair behind one ear and turned to speak to someone David couldn't see. His stomach knotted and his heart began to beat faster when her profile came into view. He knew the woman couldn't be Shawna— not here, not now—but the resemblance was remarkable.

He hadn't seen her in seven years, since Kevin Monroe spirited her away to Boston shortly after their marriage. He hadn't thought about her in a long time, yet now that he'd seen *this* woman, the memories of Shawna came rushing back.

They had worked together in a small law office for two years in Phoenix. David had been a new attorney, Shawna a reluctant paralegal. They'd quickly become friends, but while David's feelings had deepened as time passed, Shawna's had not.

They'd never dated—at first, because they were friends; later, because she'd been in love with Kevin—but they'd spent hours working on cases together. David had often wondered what they'd have been like together as a couple.

Laughing silently at himself, he realized Barry had returned and now stood over him. "Can you have it on my desk by Monday?"

David hadn't even realized Barry had been speaking to him again. He'd been too distracted. "What?"

"The *brief.*"

"You want me to draft the trial brief in less than a week?"

"That's what I said. Haven't you been listening?"

"Of course, I have," David lied.

Barry narrowed his eyes. "And you understand the direction Gottfried wants us to take with the case?"

David nodded toward his notepad. "I've written it all down."

Barry adjusted his glasses. "Good. Gottfried wants to meet with us this afternoon when we get back into the office."

David nodded slowly, trying to anticipate Gottfried's questions and mentally adjusting his week's schedule to allow time for drafting the brief. He stole one last glance at the doorway and once again, the woman captured his attention. She shook her head, pointed toward something, and stepped out of his line of vision. Just as well, he thought. He needed to keep his thoughts on the case and the upcoming meeting with Gottfried.

But seeing her and remembering Shawna had all but shattered his concentration. Maybe the bookstore was what brought Shawna back to mind so sharply. She'd spent many lunch hours in Phoenix browsing the bookstores, and she'd talked often of owning her own bookstore someday. David had encouraged her to take the risk, but she never had. She hadn't believed she could succeed in her own business, and Kevin had only reinforced her self-doubt.

From somewhere nearby, a woman's laugh carried over the noise of the other diners, the clink of glasses, and the clatter of silverware. Low and slightly husky, it sounded so familiar that David jerked upright in his seat. He paused in the act of returning his notebook and pen to his briefcase and stared at the now-empty doorway.

Barry clicked his briefcase shut. "What is wrong with you?"

"Nothing."

Scowling, Barry flicked a glance at the doorway. "What is it? You see a book you've been dying to read, or something?"

"No." David managed an embarrassed laugh. "It's nothing, really. I just thought I saw someone I knew. An old friend."

"That's very nice," Barry said. "But if it's not too much bother, could we *please* get back to the office now? I have a client coming at one-thirty."

"Of course." David picked up his pen, but when the woman laughed a second time, his hand froze. She couldn't be Shawna after all these years, He was seeing things. Hearing things.

He stood and picked up his briefcase, only vaguely aware that Barry was issuing more instructions. He struggled to concentrate, but he couldn't ignore the growing need to go after her, if only to prove she *wasn't* Shawna. It would only take him a minute or two. He could slip into the bookstore, take a closer look, and prove to himself she was a figment of his imagination so he could get back to work.

"Why don't you go on ahead. I'll meet you back at the office," he said quickly and hurried away before Barry could object. He brushed past a waiter, crossed the restaurant, and ducked through the doorway into a tiny room lined with shelves. To his right, a half-flight of steps led down to a wide landing. Across the landing, an identical set of steps led up into another room, and he could see at least two more book-filled rooms beyond that. But he couldn't see the woman anywhere.

He turned right toward the landing and studied the store as he walked. In the larger rooms, wicker chairs with flowered cushions formed cozy-looking places for customers to sit while they browsed. Every inch of wall space had been covered by shelves crowded with books—paperbacks, coffee-table albums, children's books, recent releases in hardcover, and old leather-bound volumes. Alcoves sprouted off rooms and former closets had become book-filled cubbyholes. The owner had certainly chosen an appropriate name for the store. David had no doubt Shawna could have spent hours in a place like this.

He stepped down to the landing and glanced to his left. The woman stood near a cash register on the main level, another half-flight down. Changing direction abruptly, he descended into a large room that housed the store's main entrance.

Now that he'd found her, his mission seemed slightly ridiculous. She stood with her back to him, talking to a saleswoman with striking red hair. Unless he tapped her on the shoulder or headed outside, he wouldn't be able to see her face.

The saleswoman glanced up as David approached. She smiled and turned back to the woman, but she must have said something about him. The woman stopped talking and turned to face him.

Her smile faded for a second, then widened into a familiar grin. "David? I don't believe this. Is it you?"

"Shawna?" Feeling a little self-conscious, he laughed. "I saw you from the restaurant in back, but I'd almost convinced myself I was seeing things."

She spread her arms, as if to give him a better view. "Well, you're not." She looked wonderful. Her clear brown eyes sparkled. Her face seemed to glow with happiness— more happiness than he'd expected her to have with Kevin Monroe for a husband.

"No," he said. "I can see that now."

He hesitated for a moment, then gave in to the urge to wrap his arms around her.

She returned his embrace, nestling her cheek against his chest and sighing with contentment.

David had intended the gesture as nothing more than a friendly hug, but the touch of her cheek, the softness of her sigh, and the scent of her perfume stirred something inside that he thought he'd put behind him years ago.

He straightened his shoulders and stared down at her. He'd forgotten how beautiful she was. He'd put aside his old feelings and gone on with his life. But all at once, the memories flooded back, and he let his mind wander back seven years, to the days when he'd longed to hold her exactly like this.

❤ *Chapter Two*

Shawna Wells took a step away from David so she could see him better. She couldn't believe he looked exactly the same. He still towered over her by at least eight inches. Still had the flat stomach, broad shoulders, and thick brown hair that had always caught women's eyes. Only a few tiny smile lines near his eyes acknowledged any passage of time.

Behind her, Heather cleared her throat in a signal too obvious to miss. In the two years she'd known Heather, they'd grown almost as close as she imagined sisters must be.

Grinning, Shawna introduced her friend, then slanted a glance at David. She'd missed him, but she hadn't known how much until she saw him again. She'd thought of him often, but until she heard the deep timbre of his voice, she hadn't realized how much she'd wanted him near while she got over her divorce.

"I can't believe you're here," she said again. "What are you doing in Colorado Springs?"

"I moved here just before Christmas. I'm working at Gottfried and Samuelson now. What are *you* doing here?"

She ignored the question and whistled softly. Gottfried and

251

Samuelson? Maybe he *had* changed. "Very impressive. But I thought you swore you'd never work for a big-name firm."

"I did," he admitted. "I changed my mind. I decided it was time to make something of myself."

Her smile faded. He didn't sound like the David she remembered. "Make something of yourself? What on earth for?"

"For the hell of it, I guess," he said with a shrug. "But you haven't answered my question. Why are you here?"

Leaning against the counter, Shawna tried not to let his evasive answer bother her. Seven years had passed. She couldn't expect him to share confidences as easily as he once had. "I've been here two and a half years."

"You live here, then? That's great. Are you working somewhere close? Maybe we could have lunch together sometime."

"Very close. In fact, I work right here."

"Here?" David studied the room again. "I could tell it was your kind of place as soon as I came in the back door."

"Could you? Why?"

He shrugged. "I don't know. It looks like the kind of store you'd like."

"You're right," she said with a laugh. "And it's not just my kind of place, it *is* my place."

Almost in slow motion, his eyes widened and turned from blue-gray to a clear, deep blue. A pleased chuckle started deep in his chest and worked its way to the surface. "You *did* it? You actually bought your own store?"

"I did it, believe it or not."

Letting out a whoop, he lifted her off her feet and twirled her around the limited floor space. "I'm so proud of you."

She laughed aloud. His reaction didn't surprise her. She'd known how pleased he would be for her. "So—?" she asked, sweeping the room with one arm as they circled. "What do you think? Do you like it?"

"Like it? I *love* it." David stopped spinning and lowered her to the floor again. Glancing over his shoulder, he pulled his arms away and stiffened. "Listen, I've just finished a business lunch at the Veneto. I'd love to stay and talk for a while, but I've got a meeting with one of the senior partners.''

Shawna shook her head quickly to set his mind at ease. When she wasn't helping customers today, she had to contact the local romance authors who'd agreed to participate in the open house she'd scheduled for Valentine's Day, call publishers and warehouses to check her orders for the authors' newest releases and backlist titles, and shelve yesterday's shipment from her main distributor. She'd be lucky to make any progress before Heather went home in another two hours.

''I have a thousand and one things to do today,'' she assured him. ''I couldn't talk for long, even if you could.''

''At least give me a number where I can reach you. Maybe we can get together for dinner one of these nights.'' He hesitated briefly, then added, ''All of us.''

For the first time since he'd walked into the room, Shawna realized that a new job and new city might not be the only things different in David's life. ''All of us? Are you married?''

The question felt funny leaving her lips. Though he'd dated in Phoenix, he'd always been a confirmed bachelor— or at least claimed to be. She couldn't imagine him married.

He shook his head slowly. ''I was for a while. I'm divorced now. I meant you'd probably want to bring Kevin.''

Something she couldn't identify worked its way up Shawna's spine, but she didn't take time to analyze the feeling. ''Kevin and I aren't together anymore. We've been divorced three years.''

David smiled, just as she'd known he would. He'd never made any pretense of liking Kevin. ''Divorced? That's great.''

She mock-frowned. ''It didn't feel great at the time.''

David flushed. His smile faded as he raked his fingers through his hair. ''No. I'm sure . . . I mean . . . Sorry.''

She couldn't help but laugh at his expression. ''It's okay. I'm over it now.''

His smile returned, and relief replaced the embarrassment on his face. ''Good. You're well rid of the bum.''

''I knew you'd be brokenhearted.''

"Devastated." He sobered again. "Are you seeing anyone special? Someone you would like to bring along?"

"I'm not dating anyone right now." She had no plans to, either. After watching her mother fade into the shadow of her father's personality, she'd vowed to avoid the same kind of relationship. She'd thought Kevin was different, but it hadn't taken long to realize he could have been her father's clone. And the few men she'd dated since had convinced her that all men eventually behaved the same way.

Behind her, Heather made a choking noise—her editorial comment on Shawna's current attitudes and lifestyle. Shawna tried to ignore her, but David slanted a curious glance in her direction.

Shawna knew what he'd see on Heather's face—that all-too-familiar expression of disapproval—and, given half a chance, she'd launch into the lecture about how Shawna had been alone too long and how much she needed love in her life. Shawna had heard it so many times, she could almost recite it verbatim.

Determined to stop Heather before she could get started, Shawna turned to face her. But Heather's expression surprised her. Shawna had seen this look before, too—usually when a good-looking man walked into the store, or on those rare occasions when she let Heather persuade her to go out. David had captured her interest.

Pushing her gorgeous red hair from her forehead with one hand, Heather smiled into David's eyes. "I've just had the most incredible idea. Shawna and I are going to a party this Friday. How would you like to go with us?"

He'd refuse, Shawna knew he would. They'd always shared a dislike of loud parties.

To her amazement, he smiled. "I'd love to. When and where?"

Shawna didn't even try to hide her confusion. "You would?"

"Sure. It sounds great."

"*Great?* You're kidding? When did you start liking parties?"

David smiled slowly. "I don't, but if you're going to be there, I'll come along. You're going, aren't you?"

"Well, yes, but—" She broke off and sighed. She didn't want to explain how Heather had coerced her, or why she'd been so reluctant to agree in the first place. "Yes."

"What time, and where do I meet you?"

Heather sent David one of her most winning smiles—the one that inevitably got her what she wanted. "We haven't worked out the details yet. Why don't I give you my number? Call me Thursday, and I'll let you know what we decide."

Obviously charmed, David smiled back. "Fine."

While Shawna watched, Heather pulled one of the store's business cards from a holder, wrote her number on its face, and pressed it into David's hand. Battling a flash of irritation, Shawna watched him study the card as if he wanted to imprint Heather's number into his memory.

Almost as an afterthought, he held the card out to Shawna. "You can give me your number, too, if you'd like."

How kind of him, she thought almost bitterly, then pulled herself up short. Her reaction surprised her. She'd always wanted to see him with a woman who'd appreciate him. She'd always wanted him to be happy. So, why did Heather's interest disturb her? Why did she resent his interest in return?

Because Heather floated through life, flirting easily, and gathering men everywhere she went—that's why. She wouldn't appreciate David—not the way he should be appreciated. He deserved to build a life with someone interested in lasting love, not just in having fun for a few months before moving on to the next romance.

Biting back all the responses that rose to her lips, Shawna jotted her home number on the back of the card. Then she returned the card to him and tried to push aside her disloyal thoughts.

After all, Heather might surprise her. She might recognize David's loyalty, his compassion, and his intelligence. She might value his thoughtfulness, his sense of humor, and his great big generous heart. But she'd probably look past the real David and concentrate on his looks and position.

As David dropped the card into his breast pocket, he shot an anxious glance at his watch and took a step away. "I've really got to get back to the office, they'll be waiting. But I'll see you Friday, okay?''

He looked so concerned about leaving that Shawna battled another flash of irritation. ''Okay.''

''I'll call you.''

When she realized he spoke to her, not Heather, her spirits lifted a notch. ''Great.''

He crossed the room, took the steps up to the landing two at a time, and disappeared into the mystery section.

Heather stared after him for a moment, then smiled slowly. ''What a great guy.''

''Yes.'' Shawna slid behind the counter and crossed to her desk. ''He is.''

''Good-looking, nice, *and* an attorney.''

Exactly the reaction Shawna had expected. She flicked a troubled glance at Heather. ''He's not your type.''

''Not my type?'' Heather stared at her, open-mouthed. ''Are you crazy? He's *exactly* my type.''

Shawna started to shake her head, but when she realized what she'd been about to say, she stopped and laughed awkwardly. Listen to her. She sounded just like David had when Kevin first showed an interest in her.

Disturbed by her reaction, she pressed her fingers to her forehead and shrugged. ''Maybe so.''

''Don't you want me to go out with him?''

Deliberately avoiding Heather's gaze, Shawna dug through the papers on her desk for her list of romance authors and their phone numbers. ''I didn't say that.''

''No, you didn't. But that's what it sounds like.''

Shawna couldn't explain her reservations without hurting Heather, and she wouldn't intentionally hurt her friend for the world. Working up a smile, she forced herself to look into Heather's eyes. ''If you're interested, go out with him.''

''Do you really mean that?''

''I really mean it.'' Shawna lifted the receiver and tapped one finger on her list. ''Now, I've got to get to work. And so do you.''

''Yes, boss.'' Heather started toward the landing. ''I'll be in the children's section if you need me.''

Shawna lowered herself into her chair and punched in a

number from her list. Leaning back, she waited for the first author to answer. But she didn't want to think about authors or Valentine's Day or romance novels. For the first time in years, she wanted to remember Phoenix.

She couldn't believe that she and David had run into each other after all these years. She couldn't believe how incredible he looked. She couldn't believe he'd actually been married. And she couldn't help noticing that without him, the store suddenly felt a little empty.

Chapter Three

David sipped a lukewarm beer and tried to ignore the pounding headache he'd had all day. Cigarette smoke drifted from nearby tables as music resounded from the walls and combined with conversation and laughter to make his ears ring.

He'd worked all week preparing for trial, and he wanted almost more than anything to spend a few hours unwinding. But he'd promised to come to the party, and he'd kept his word. He'd made a big mistake. Not only did Shawna look incredible in her slinky black dress and heels, but again he'd felt the stirrings of desire. Not only had he spent the past hour watching her with some tall, blond man who bore an unfortunate resemblance to a Norse god, but even Heather had deserted him.

Waving away a waitress who approached his table, he sipped his beer again. He couldn't explain, even to himself, why he didn't get rid of the room-temperature brew and replace it with a cold one. For some reason, he almost relished his misery.

When he'd agreed to come tonight, he'd been half-hoping to discover that Shawna had changed over the years. That she'd grown less intelligent, less caring, less beautiful. Instead, his heart hammered in his chest each time she drew close, his mouth dried when he looked at her, and every passing moment drew him further under her spell.

Now, she sat at a table across the room from David, beneath a spray of red and white balloons and a banner wishing someone named Val a happy early birthday. She laughed at a comment from the Norse god, then flashed an apologetic smile at David.

David smiled back, but his mouth felt stiff, and he battled an unwelcome surge of resentment toward the man he'd started thinking of as "Thor." Watching her with someone else brought back memories of the times he'd had to watch her with Kevin. He'd known Kevin was wrong for her from the beginning, but his hands had been tied. He felt nearly as helpless now.

As the music from one song died away, the band switched to a slow, romantic number. Several couples moved onto the dance floor and began swaying to the music.

Scowling, David took a long swig of beer, then pushed the bottle away. Why *had* he come tonight? Why did he insist on sitting here like a lump and growing more morose by the second? If Shawna wanted to hang on Thor's every word, David would find someone else to dance with. He stood and searched the barroom. Surely, he could find at least one interesting woman here.

"David?" Heather's hand touched his shoulder a fraction of a second after her voice reached him.

He smiled as he turned. "I wondered where you'd gone."

"I needed to say hello to some old friends." She flicked a glance at the crowded floor. "Do you want to dance?"

Anything to take his mind off Shawna. He nodded and said, "I'd love to."

When she took his arm and walked beside him, her breast brushed against him. She smiled into his eyes as she turned into his arms, but for some reason, even such intimate contact couldn't drive Shawna from his mind.

Heather tilted her head back and showed her neck to its best advantage. "Are you having a good time?"

He glanced at the table Shawna and Thor shared. "Sure."

Heather followed the direction of his gaze. When she looked back at him, her smile had been replaced by a thoughtful frown. "No, you're not."

"I'm having a *great* time."

"Liar."

He searched her eyes for a moment and caught a flicker of amusement. "Okay," he admitted. "I'm lying. I'm not what you'd call a party animal."

"Neither is she." She nodded toward Shawna. "In fact, I practically had to resort to blackmail to get her here tonight."

David stole another glance. Shawna and Thor had moved onto the dance floor. She fit snugly into Thor's arms, and he looked enraptured. Growling, David told himself it didn't matter. He'd been attracted to her once, but that was long ago, long over, long dead and buried.

"Who's her friend?" He thought he'd kept his voice casual, but Heather's slightly widened eyes told him he hadn't succeeded.

"Bob Armistead. They dated for a while a few months ago."

"Really?" David didn't like hearing that Thor was an old flame, but he liked even less the shaft of jealousy that knifed through him. The Norse god chose that moment to pull Shawna closer. David pivoted again and tried to focus on the woman in his arms.

Heather smiled. "They broke up when he started talking about marriage. She's determined not to get married again."

"After Kevin, I'm not surprised."

Heather pulled slightly away and studied him in silence for a few seconds. Without warning, she stopped dancing. "I think you and I need to talk."

David stumbled a little and stopped. "About what?"

Flicking one last glance at Shawna and Thor, she tugged on David's sleeve and turned away. "Come on, I won't bite you."

More wary than curious, he followed her through the crowd, helped her with her coat, and shrugged into his own. Keeping one hand on the small of her back, he trailed her through the crowd and out onto the sidewalk.

Outside, February hit him with a vengeance, but the fresh

air felt wonderful after so long inside the smoke-filled bar. He pulled in a breath and waited for Heather to speak.

She walked several steps away from the door, letting muted music and an occasional burst of laughter mark the time before she spoke again. Her breath formed thick clouds in the frosty air. "You're in love with her, aren't you?"

David barked a laugh. "In love? No."

"Don't lie to me, I can tell just by watching you."

He backed a step away and held up both hands as if to ward off her accusation. "Believe me—"

"Save it, David. Your emotions are written all over your face." She glanced over her shoulder at the bar's entrance. When she faced him again, he could see concern in her eyes. "I'm tired of seeing Shawna alone. And I'm tired of seeing her so bitter because of her father and Kevin. Until tonight, I thought she should get back together with Bob. Now, I'm not so sure."

"Why not?"

"Because I think you'd be better for her than he would."

Her honesty disarmed him, but he understood much better why Shawna liked her so much. Still, she'd jumped to an erroneous conclusion, and he didn't want to leave any misunderstanding between them. "That's flattering, but—"

"Just admit it. You're in love with her, aren't you?"

David wanted to deny it again, but Heather's wide eyes and guileless smile tore the truth from him. "I'm attracted to her. I always have been. But there's nothing more to it."

Laughing softly, Heather shook her head. When a gust of wind dropped the temperature even further, she folded her arms across her chest. "Okay. If you say so."

"It's true. We're friends, that's it."

The wind lifted the hem of Heather's skirt and ruffled her hair. "There's one sure way to change that."

David drew back and stared at her. "How?"

"Tell her how you feel."

He laughed again and took a couple of steps backward. "I don't think so."

She followed him. "I do."

"Tell her *what*?"

"That you're attracted to her. That you want to get to

know her again. Ask her out, for heaven's sake.''

''I don't think so,'' he said again.

Heather held his gaze for a long moment. ''There's a reason you've found each other again.''

He knew where she was going with this, and he wanted to stop her before she could get started. ''Coincidence.''

''I don't believe in coincidence, and if *you* do, you're fooling yourself.''

David took a step away and stared at the sidewalk. Chunks of ice lined the pavement and the wind swirled old snow into the equivalent of dust devils. *Coincidence*, he insisted silently. But he couldn't ignore the fact that even though they'd been through seven years, two marriages and two divorces, they'd both ended up in Colorado—together.

Something stirred in his memory—the day Shawna had announced her engagement to Kevin—and his heart dropped, just as it had then. A familiar ache weakened him. *Had* he been in love with her? He thought about how often he'd been lost in her smile during a case, how many times her eyes had held his captive across a cluttered desk. He shook his head, as if he could rid himself of the memories. When that didn't work, he glared at Heather for putting the idea into his head.

''Even if I *did* love her, she's obviously taken with Thor.''

Heather laughed aloud. ''*Thor?* I love that. It fits.'' She sobered again and stared at him until he gave in and met her gaze. ''She's not taken with him. She's just too polite to tell him to back off.''

''They look pretty cozy.''

She lifted her eyebrows. ''Jealous?''

''No. I just don't want her to fall in love with someone who's obviously so much like Kevin. He's got the same arrogant outlook, the same cocky attitude . . .''

Heather laughed. ''No, you're not jealous at all.''

He scowled at her. ''I told you—I'm attracted, but it's been a long time. I don't know her anymore.''

She flicked a glance at the heavy door, as if she could see Shawna through it. ''I guess she has changed since the divorce.''

Yes, she had—at least, in some ways. ''I certainly hope you don't say anything about this to her.''

"Don't worry." She patted his arm gently. "I won't give you away. It's your secret, not mine."

"There's no secret."

But she laughed again and turned toward the door. "This isn't an accident, David. You and Shawna have been given another chance. Don't throw it away." She tugged open the door and let the music and laughter rush out to surround them. "At least think about it."

Before he could say anything else, she slipped inside and let the door bang shut behind her. The party sounds muted once more, the wind picked up and nipped at his ears, and David was left alone in the frigid February air with nothing but his thoughts.

Chapter Four

Shawna tried desperately to keep her eyes on the door through which David and Heather had disappeared, but with Bob tugging her this way and that to the music, she couldn't keep the door in sight. She told herself to be grateful for Heather's interest in David—after all, she'd kept him company after Bob latched onto her. But she didn't like imagining what was going on outside between them.

"So—?" Bob shouted over the music. "What do you think?"

With effort, Shawna tore her attention from the door and forced herself to focus on Bob. "What do I think? About what?"

"Dinner tomorrow night." Bob sounded slightly irritated. "Haven't you been listening?"

She hadn't, but she tapped one finger to her ear and made a face. "The music's too loud."

Bob's eyes narrowed as if he didn't believe her. "I asked you to have dinner with me tomorrow. Do you want to, or not?"

Shawna hesitated. She'd enjoyed Bob's company when

they'd dated before, until he'd grown serious and started talking about a lifetime commitment. Obviously, he wanted to take up now where they'd left off. "I don't think that would be wise."

Slowing, Bob pushed her gently away so he could see into her eyes. "Why not?"

Shawna frowned in annoyance. He still couldn't take no for an answer. "I don't want to get serious with anyone right now."

He sighed heavily, as he always did when things didn't go his way. "You've been divorced for three years. Don't you think it's time to put Kevin behind you?"

"This isn't about Kevin," she said. "It's about me. I'm not ready for that kind of relationship yet."

"When do you think you *will* be ready?"

"I don't know." Struggling to hold back her rising irritation, Shawna gave in to the temptation to look at the door again. Where *were* Heather and David?

"We're good together, Shawna. You're beautiful and smart. The people I work with like you . . ."

When the outside door opened in the middle of his comment, and Heather slipped inside—alone—Shawna pulled away and tried to look apologetic. "Will you excuse me? I need to talk to Heather for a minute."

"Can't it wait?" Bob reached for her again. "I want to spend time together and solve these problems between us."

Shawna didn't want to spend any more time rehashing the past. "No," she said, keeping her voice firm. "It can't wait."

She didn't give him another chance to stop her. Slipping past dancing couples, she left the dance floor. It seemed to take forever to work through the crowd, but she reached their table at last and dropped into a chair beside Heather's.

"Where's David?" Shawna had to shout to make herself heard over the music.

"Outside."

"Outside? Why?"

"He's thinking."

"Thinking?" Shawna didn't know whether to laugh or worry. "It's freezing out there."

"He's a big boy. If he gets cold, he knows how to get back inside." Heather scanned the room, located a waitress, and signaled for another round.

Shawna didn't want another round. She wanted to find David and leave. She'd had more than enough for one night. "What were you doing out there?"

"Talking."

"About what?"

"Don't worry," Heather said. "I changed my mind. You're right—he's not my type."

"Really?" Relieved, Shawna leaned back in her seat, then scowled and bobbed forward again. "I wasn't worried."

Heather smiled, but she didn't say anything.

"I *wasn't*. I just want to get out of here."

"You want to leave?" Heather's eyes rounded. "Why?"

"Because Bob's trying to make a comeback, I have a headache, and I'm tired," Shawna shouted as the music died away and the band left the stage for a break. Her words echoed in the sudden silence.

Heather pulled a bill from her evening bag and handed it to a waitress who materialized beside them. "I'm not ready to leave. Why don't you and David go ahead? I'll find a ride home or take a cab."

"Are you sure?"

"Positive."

Shawna wouldn't argue. She glanced at the outside door again. "What's he thinking about?"

"Who? David?"

"Yes."

"I don't know," Heather said with a careless shrug. "Why don't you ask him?"

"Maybe I will."

As Shawna stood, Heather lifted her jacket from the back of her chair and handed it to her. "Don't forget your jacket. It's cold out there."

As she walked quickly across the empty dance floor, Shawna slipped her jacket on. Outside, the wintry air burned her lungs. She wrapped her arms around herself and looked in both directions along the sidewalk. She didn't see David until a shadow near one corner of the building defined itself into his familiar shape.

"David?"

He stepped into the glow of a streetlight. "Yeah?"

"What are you doing out here?" Her sudden attack of nervousness surprised her.

"Thinking."

"That's what Heather said. Did she offend you somehow?"

"Not at all. Quite the opposite, in fact."

Shivering in a sudden blast of icy air, Shawna backed against the building and bit back her next question. She knew she shouldn't pry. Obviously neither of them wanted to talk about it, but she couldn't help being concerned.

While she considered what to say next, David took another step toward her. "Where's . . . Bob?"

"I don't know." A gust of wind whisked down the neck of her jacket. She tugged her collar a little tighter.

David closed the distance between them and shielded her from the wind. "He's not the right guy for you, you know."

He'd met Bob only for a minute—certainly not long enough to form an opinion—but he was right, just as he had been about Kevin. "I know."

David let his eyes travel slowly across her face. His expression changed, suddenly so intense that her breath caught, her heart lurched, and her mouth grew dry. She forced herself to look away. "Are you having a good time? Do you want to stay?"

"Do *you*?" This was the David she remembered. He'd always been more concerned with her needs and desires than his own.

"No, I don't."

"All right. Let's get out of here. Where's Heather?"

"She's staying for a while."

He cocked one eyebrow at her. With the moonlight accenting his features, he looked incredibly handsome. Sexy, even. He took her by the arm and led her along the icy sidewalk. "Well, then. I guess it's just the two of us."

Far too aware of his touch, Shawna scolded herself silently for letting two glasses of wine affect her reason. But her knees threatened to buckle and she couldn't keep from stealing glances at him as they walked.

What was she thinking? David was a friend. A dear and trusted friend. She'd be a fool to let a little alcohol and the soft glow of moonlight turn her thoughts in any other direction—even for a moment. Taking a shaky breath, she tried to pull herself under control, but she had an uncomfortable feeling that she'd never look at David as merely a friend again.

David maneuvered his Grand Am through the nearly deserted streets. Snow from the most recent storm gusted across the road and spattered against the windshield, and the scent of Shawna's perfume filled the car. On the passenger side, Shawna leaned her head against the seat and tapped her fingers in time to Aretha Franklin's "Natural Woman" on the radio. She looked beautiful sitting there. Relaxed. Contented. Completely the opposite of the emotions churning inside him.

He cleared his throat and smiled at her. "So . . . what interesting things are there to see and do around here?"

"That depends on how far you want to drive and how much you want to spend. Have you been up Pikes Peak yet?"

"I haven't been anywhere but King Soopers for groceries and the gas station near my apartment."

She laughed. "Well, you've seen the best, then. Everything else I could tell you about would pale by comparison."

Some of his tension faded. "That's what I thought."

"You could visit Garden of the Gods or the Air Force Academy, and we have some incredible ski resorts nearby."

He made a face. "I don't ski."

"Neither do I, but you should learn. You'd be great at it."

"I don't want to ski. I'm not thrilled by the idea of broken bones." He smiled slowly. "But I'll learn if you will."

Her easy, comfortable laugh sent a whisper of warmth up his spine. "Not me. You know what a klutz I am."

"You're not a klutz."

"Oh, yes I am. Kevin always used to say I was the only

person he knew who could throw myself on the floor . . . and miss.''

''Kevin was an idiot.'' He tried to maintain the easy tone, but his voice came out low and tense.

Her smile faded. She looked out her window and remained silent for several seconds. ''What do you think of Heather?''

The question caught him off guard. From Kevin to Heather? He missed the connection. ''She's very nice.''

''Yes, she is.'' Surprisingly, Shawna sounded almost reluctant to agree. ''Are you going to ask her out?''

He flicked a surprised glance at her. ''No.''

''No?'' Her eyes widened, and she turned in her seat to face him. ''Why not?''

''You want me to?''

''No.'' Shawna flicked a smile at him and shrugged lightly. ''I mean, I don't care. If you want to . . .''

Her words, spoken casually, sent an unexpected shaft of discouragement through him. He tried to push it away. Why should it matter whether she cared or not? Pulling in a deep breath, he let it out again slowly. ''I'm too busy to date much.''

''Oh.'' Her scent reached him again, soft and slightly musky. Jasmine and cinnamon. Sweet and spicy at the same time, like the woman herself.

Something David couldn't identify darted across her face, but it disappeared again almost immediately. Disappointment? Maybe—for Heather's sake.

She fell silent again for a long time, but he couldn't stop thinking about what she'd said or about his reaction. She didn't care if he dated another woman. Without warning, he realized how much he wanted her to care. He wanted to take her into his arms and *make* her care.

Shoving the thought away, he glared out the windshield and kept his eyes focused on the street. That thought shouldn't have even crossed his mind. They were *friends*.

In spite of his resolve, he flicked another glance at her and asked the next question almost before he had time to think it. ''What about you and that guy at the party?''

''Bob?'' She sighed softly and her lips curved into a tight

smile. "We dated for a while. He's . . . aggressive. Persistent. Hard to get rid of."

"You want to get rid of him, then?"

She nodded slowly. "He's ready for a commitment. I'm not."

"Is that the only reason?"

As her curious gaze traveled across his face, he struggled to keep his expression impassive. "He's nice enough, I guess. But he's jealous, and I don't like that."

Jealous. David heard Heather's voice ringing in his head accusing him of the same thing. Was he jealous of Thor? Of Kevin? Or was he merely feeling protective of his friend?

He tried to convince himself of the latter, but he knew it wasn't true. He could lie to everyone else, but he couldn't lie to himself. He *was* jealous, and his feelings for Shawna ran deeper than he'd ever suspected, deeper than he'd ever admitted—certainly deeper than they should.

Chapter Five

Relishing the warmth of David's car, Shawna rested her head against the seat and studied his face as he drove. Why hadn't she noticed his strong profile before? Why hadn't she realized how sensuous his smile was? Surprised by her thoughts, she dragged her gaze away. Maybe the question should be, why did she notice them now?

She pulled in a deep breath and brought up the one subject she knew would keep her thoughts in line. "You haven't told me anything about your wife, you know."

David shrugged. He obviously wanted to look unconcerned, but his lips thinned as they always did when something upset him. "There's not much to tell. I met Virginia about six months after you left Phoenix. We were married three months after that. It didn't work out."

"Not much to tell? You loved her enough to marry her, didn't you? What was she like?"

David hesitated a few seconds. "She was young and pretty." He frowned at some memory. "She was an architect, and good at what she did."

"What happened?"

"Between us?" He darted a glance at her. "I wasn't right for her. I made her miserable."

"I don't believe that."

"You should," he said. "It's true."

She touched his arm, intending to offer comfort, but longing flickered inside her without warning. She pulled her hand away, forced a smile, and paraphrased a line from one of her favorite movies. It had often made David laugh in the past; maybe it would help now. "You know I'd rather walk on my lips than talk bad about anybody, but she doesn't sound too bright."

It earned nothing more than a thin smile. "I think the problem was, she was *too* bright."

"Any woman would be lucky to have a man like you." As soon as the words left her mouth, Shawna bit her lip. She'd said similar things to him before, but tonight her words seemed charged with hidden meaning.

He didn't seem to notice. "The trouble was, I got married for the wrong reasons. We had nothing in common. We ran out of things to talk about almost immediately. It was like we loved each other, but we didn't *like* each other, you know?" He glanced at her. "I know I won't make the same mistake twice. I don't want to get married again until I can marry my best friend."

Shawna froze. Surely he hadn't meant that the way it sounded. She watched emotions chase each other across his face as he realized what he'd said. She studied his hands, strong and sure, gripping the steering wheel, and she wondered for a moment how they'd feel against her skin.

Heat crept up her neck into her face and her breath quickened. Maybe Heather was right. Maybe Shawna *had* been alone too long.

She turned away and stared out the window as they put several streets behind them. She didn't trust herself to speak. If she didn't stop thinking this way, she would grow so uncomfortable around David that she'd have to make up excuses to avoid him.

He seemed willing to let the silence hang between them, until he turned into a parking spot in front of her condominium. Leaving the engine and heater running, he hitched himself around in his seat to face her. "Are you busy tomorrow? Would you like to show me the sights?"

In spite of her response to him, she wanted desperately to say yes. This morning, she wouldn't have thought twice, but by letting her thoughts veer out of control she'd put up a barrier between them. She didn't want it there. She wanted to feel comfortable with him again.

"I'm sorry," she said honestly. "Saturday's our busiest day at the store."

"Oh. Sure. I wasn't thinking." He frowned slightly. "I've got a brief to write, anyway. How about Sunday?"

"I can't. Weekends are too busy at the store. I've got Heather working for me, and two college students part-time, but I can't take off whenever I want to. I've got a huge shipment of books to put away, an open house to finish planning, flowers to order—and customers to help in my spare time."

His frown deepened. "Then how about lunch tomorrow? I'll be downtown anyway."

"I don't usually stop for lunch. I just eat a sandwich at my desk." She knew she sounded obstinate, almost as if she didn't want to spend time with him.

"Can you make an exception? We'll probably both need a break, and I'll work better if I allow myself to get out of the office for an hour in the middle of the day."

The suggestion tempted her. The expression in his eyes persuaded her. "All right. You've talked me into it."

"Great." He seemed to relax a little. "What time?"

"One o'clock? Heather and Nicole can go to lunch first."

The grin she'd always found so endearing in the past stretched across his face, but this time it made her pulse dance. "Perfect. Where do you want to go?"

"I'll let you decide, as long as it's near the store."

"Okay, I'll see what I can find. Do you have any preferences? Italian food? Mexican? Thai?"

In spite of herself, she laughed. "You know what I like, David. I haven't changed."

"No, you haven't." He placed a hand on her arm. "Shawna—"

His fingers scorched her skin and sent a spiral of heat

through her. She struggled to keep him from hearing anything odd in her voice. "Yes?"

He hesitated, almost speaking several times but stopping himself each time before the words left his mouth. After a moment, he stopped trying and held her gaze. His eyes bored into hers, as if he wanted to see into her soul. Leaning closer, he let his eyes wander from her eyes to her lips, and rest there.

For one split second, she thought he intended to kiss her. Her breath caught, her face burned, and her heart beat so loudly that she knew he must be able to hear it. Her senses screamed to life, and she needed all her self-control to keep from leaning toward him, turning her mouth toward his, and inviting his kiss.

He held her gaze for what felt like an eternity, silently assessing. Surely he could see her desire. He must know she longed for the touch of his lips, the feel of his hands, the warmth of his embrace.

Instead, he broke eye contact. "It's great to see you again."

"You, too."

"I'll walk you to your door."

Shawna could only nod. He'd seen the look in her eyes—she knew he had—and he'd pulled away. He'd made it clear he didn't want their relationship to change.

It didn't matter that her rational side didn't want things to change between them, either. His rejection hurt. She got out of the car before he could cross to her side and open the door. Walking quickly through the beginning flakes of a new snowstorm, she stayed a step ahead of him all the way to her door. Once there, she fumbled with the key and the lock until, at last, she managed to unlock the door and step inside.

David leaned against the frame, watching her. His posture seemed casual, but his smile looked as tense as hers felt.

"Thanks again." She could hear the strain in her voice. She willed him to say something to ease her embarrassment and make everything easy between them.

He said only, "I'll see you tomorrow." But he no longer looked happy and relaxed. She didn't wonder why. Given a few more seconds, she'd probably have thrown herself at him.

Murmuring a good-night, she closed and locked the door. But instead of turning out the lights and going into her bedroom, she leaned against the door and listened to the sound of his footsteps as he walked away.

Once before, she'd given in to a sudden, overwhelming physical attraction. She'd let flowery words and sentiment convince her that Kevin had loved her. Too soon, their marriage had turned into an imitation of her parents' empty one. She'd left Kevin with nothing more to show for their four years together than a broken heart and a shattered self-image.

Now that a little logic had found its way back into her head, she knew that kissing David would have been a huge mistake—even if he *had* wanted it. She couldn't allow the warmth and caring she'd always felt for him to turn into something else simply because she'd been alone too long.

Drawing a steadying breath, she flicked out the light and promised herself that the next time she saw David, she'd have put her fanciful thoughts firmly behind her.

Cursing himself the whole way, David hurried back to his car. Inside, he ground the engine to life and leaned his head against the seat back. He'd almost lost control. Almost pulled Shawna into his arms and kissed her.

He sat upright and glared at his reflection in the windshield. His life had been plodding along just fine until he ran into her on Wednesday. He'd been reasonably happy in his new job and fairly content with his new life. He'd known what he wanted and how to get it. But not anymore.

He could only imagine Shawna's reaction if he'd given in to the urge to kiss her. As it was, she'd looked like a frightened rabbit. He'd watched her eyes darken and her lips part, but she'd pulled away when he'd leaned closer.

Cursing under his breath, he told himself not to be a fool. Heather had forced him to acknowledge that he cared more for Shawna than he'd ever admitted. He'd almost let her convince him that Shawna would respond if he let her know how he felt.

Knowing Shawna as he did—or at least as he had once—

she might eventually do just that. But he didn't want some
sense of obligation on her part to lead them into a relationship like his with Virginia. He knew that this time *he'd* be
the partner who loved more than he was loved, but one-sided
relationships didn't work.

Growling at the snowflakes on his windshield, he flipped
on his wipers and backed the car out of the parking space.
He shifted roughly and pulled onto the street fast enough to
make the car fishtail for a few seconds.

Slowing, he drove along the icy roads and tried to put
Shawna's dark eyes, her soft, full lips, and her warm smile
out of his mind. But he'd come so close to stepping over an
invisible line beyond friendship, he honestly didn't know if
he'd have the strength to hold back next time.

Ridiculous. He *had* to hold back. He'd just have to find
some way to take his mind off her. Maybe he should find
something physical to do. Join a gym and work out, or . . .
Hell, maybe he'd even learn to ski.

He'd take a dozen cold showers a day if necessary—not
that they'd do any good. If his feelings hadn't dulled in seven
years, what made him think he could turn them off now?
Instead of trying and failing, as he surely would, he should
find a way to show her how he felt. He'd let her realize
gradually that he loved her, not hit her with the news like a
ton of bricks. And he'd find some way to win her love in
return.

Smiling to himself, he turned into his apartment complex
and parked his car. Yes, that's exactly what he'd do. He'd
think of some way to reveal himself—slowly. He could do
it. Patience had always been one of his strong suits.

As another thought occurred to him, he nearly laughed
aloud. Shawna had always loved Valentine's Day, and with
the holiday less than two weeks away, the idea forming in
his mind seemed the perfect solution.

Chapter Six

Shawna tugged the collar of her coat around her ears and trudged across the parking lot toward Every Book & Cranny. Morning sunlight reflected off the new powder and burned her eyes. Frigid wind whistled around her, bit through her nylons, and lifted her skirt.

Clamping one hand on the fabric, she chided herself for not waking in time to iron a pair of slacks. She'd scheduled herself and Heather to open the store together, but she was already half an hour late. She'd spent a restless night and had slept through her alarm—something she hadn't done in years. Heather was reliable, but if she'd stayed late at the party or had trouble waking, the store might still be closed.

Shawna turned toward the front door and breathed a sigh of relief when she saw the small OPEN sign in the window. Inside, she shrugged off her coat, hooked it onto the coat tree, and retrieved the morning mail from its basket. She let the warm air soothe her as she slipped behind the counter, but she'd have to go outside again soon to shovel the walks.

Lowering the mail to her desk, she scanned the store for Heather. When her fingers brushed something unexpected, she glanced down and found a single yellow rose on top of her author list. Yellow. Her favorite.

Dropping the mail on the corner of her desk, she picked up the rose and stared at it.

"Beautiful, isn't it?" Heather's voice sounded from the landing behind her.

Yes, it was beautiful. A bud just beginning to open. Perfect. And totally unexpected. Shawna lifted the rose and inhaled its fragrance. "Where did it come from?"

"Beats me. I was in the back when it came."

"You didn't see who brought it?"

Heather started down the stairs toward her. "I didn't see anybody come in the store."

"You didn't hear the bell over the door?"

"No."

Shawna frowned at her. She studied Heather's too-innocent eyes and the mouth that tried not to smile. "I don't believe you. You know something about this, don't you?"

Heather's eyes narrowed and indignation replaced amusement on her face. "Are you accusing me of lying?"

"No." Shawna glanced at the rose again. "No, I guess not."

"I hope not," Heather said as she slipped behind the counter and leaned to inhale the flower's scent.

Shawna touched the rosebud to her cheek and tried to remember the last time anyone had sent her flowers. "Who knows I love yellow roses?"

"Lots of people. You've mentioned it before."

True, but nobody had ever paid attention. "Who could have left it?"

"Beats me. Has anybody been acting interested? Or haven't you noticed?"

"Interested in me? No." Shawna started to put the rose down, then paused as an unwelcome thought formed. "Except Bob."

"Bob?" Heather made a face.

"I thought you liked Bob," Shawna reminded her. "I thought he was the perfect guy for me."

"I do like him," Heather said. "But . . . I don't know. After last night, I changed my mind."

Shawna propped the rose against her desk lamp and rested her hands on her thighs. "What did you drink last night? First, you changed your mind about David. Now, you're having second thoughts about Bob."

"I didn't drink anything odd. I just saw things more clearly, I guess." Heather leaned one hip against the counter and nodded toward the rose. "Has Bob ever sent flowers before?"

"No. But there's always a first time."

"I suppose," Heather said slowly. "And maybe it's from someone else."

For half a second, Shawna let herself toy with the idea of David as the mystery man, but this didn't sound like the work of a friend. A rose implied something more. "Nobody that I can think of. Any suggestions?"

Heather pushed away from the counter and snatched up a stack of books. "How would I know?"

"You pay more attention to those kinds of things than I do."

"I pay attention to men who flirt with *me*. I'm assuming *you* know who flirts with you."

Shawna flicked her a disbelieving glance. "You don't pay attention? Baloney. You keep a running list of potential boy-friends for me to consider."

"That's an exaggeration."

Maybe, but not much of one. Shawna sighed and touched the rose's stem. "It *must* be from Bob."

"Oh, come on." She could hear the exasperation in Heather's voice. "Bob's not the only guy in the world with a brain. Obviously, there's at least one other person who knows what a terrific woman you are. What about David?"

"David?" Shawna's voice sounded a little too sharp. She softened her tone and tried again. "If David sent me a rose for inviting him to the party, he'd have sent you one, too. No, it *must* be from Bob."

Heather rolled her eyes and sighed as if Shawna were try-ing her patience to its limit.

But Shawna refused to let her imagination run wild. "It's not as if there are men coming out of the woodwork, dying with unrequited love for me."

"Don't sell yourself short."

"I'm not selling myself short, I'm being realistic. Even if someone does act interested, I'm not. I don't encourage them."

"*That's* an understatement."

This was getting them nowhere. Shawna pulled the author list closer and dug around for a pen. "The rose is from Bob."

"Okay. If you're so sure, why don't you ask him? At least call to thank him." When Shawna hesitated, Heather laughed again. "It's not from him, and you know it."

Shawna didn't want Heather to see her uncertainty. She couldn't imagine Bob doing something so romantic, but nobody else could have sent it. She supposed Bob deserved a thank-you, even if she didn't want to get involved with him again.

But she still didn't want to call. He'd always ignored Shawna's fear of moving into a relationship too fast, and dismissed her concern about maintaining her own identity in the relationship as nonsense. Like Kevin, he wanted someone who'd fit into a space he'd created in his life. Shawna's hopes and dreams wouldn't matter to Bob, any more than they'd mattered to Kevin. After one conversation and a couple of dances, they were right back where they'd left off— with Bob in hot pursuit.

She refused to fall into that trap again. She squared her shoulders and told herself to buck up. She'd set him straight once—she could do it again. "All right," she said, slowly. "I'll call." She reached for the telephone, steeling herself to refuse Bob's next move—most likely an intimate gathering with friends so he could display her.

To her relief, the telephone rang four times without an answer. When his answering machine clicked on, she hung up quickly. "He's not home."

"I suppose you can always call later," Heather said.

Nodding without conviction, Shawna pushed aside a box full of valentine cards and dragged the phone closer. "In the meantime, I'm going to put it out of my mind and get to work. Did Lucille call about the flowers for the open house?"

"Not yet. So . . . tell me what happened when David took you home last night."

Shawna made a note to call Lucille, whose floral shop was only a few doors away from Every Book & Cranny. "Nothing."

"Nothing? Then why were you late this morning?"

"I didn't sleep well," Shawna said. "That's another reason I don't like parties. They leave me too keyed up."

Before Heather could respond, the bell over the front door tinkled and a new customer stepped inside. Heather hesitated for a moment. She obviously didn't want to abandon the conversation.

But Shawna did. She didn't want to discuss men or flowers or parties anymore. She had work to do. Ignoring Heather's pointed glare, she turned her attention to the author list. And she ignored the almost overwhelming urge to sneak one last peek at the rose.

A few minutes before one o'clock, David opened the door to Every Book & Cranny and glanced quickly inside. Nervous about seeing Shawna again after leaving the rose on her desk—and being caught in the act by Heather—he squared his shoulders and stepped inside.

Heather had promised not to say anything to Shawna, but David didn't know her well enough to trust her blindly. He didn't know what reaction to expect from Shawna.

Inside, Heather rang up a sale on the cash register. Several customers browsed in nearby rooms. Shawna sat behind her desk, chatting with someone on the telephone. She looked up as he entered and waved him toward the counter. She'd put his rose in a cup near the lamp, out of her way.

He leaned a hip against the counter and worked to avoid meeting Heather's gaze. But when the customer walked away from the cash register and Shawna hung up the telephone, he couldn't avoid her any longer.

Grinning at him, Heather leaned on the counter. "Shawna got a rose from a secret admirer this morning." She darted a glance over her shoulder at Shawna. "Didn't you?"

Relieved that she hadn't given him away, David lifted an eyebrow. "A secret admirer?"

Shawna scowled at the innocent rose. "It's no secret. I know who sent it."

He tried to look relaxed, but he failed miserably. His neck tensed. His shoulders stiffened. "You do? Who?"

"It's from Bob." She pushed the rose a few more inches away. "But I don't want to hear about it, okay?"

David's expression froze. *"Bob?"*

"Yes, Bob." Shawna tossed her head, almost as if she dared him to react. "The guy at the party last night."

"The Norse god."

She glared at him. "I'm warning you, David, don't start that. It's nothing."

Nothing? Trying to hide his disappointment, David stuffed his hands into his pockets. "All right. When a guy sends a woman a rose, it means nothing. I'll try to remember that for future reference."

"That's not what I meant," she insisted. "I meant, from Bob it's nothing. There's nothing between us anymore."

"That's too bad." He made no effort to hide his sarcasm.

Shawna rolled her eyes in exasperation. "Are you ever going to approve of the men I date?"

He shrugged. "If you ever date the right guy, I will." Out of the corner of his eye, he saw Heather grin. He turned to avoid meeting her gaze. One glance between them, and they'd give everything away.

To his relief, a flicker of amusement lit Shawna's eyes. "Maybe I should just let *you* pick out the next one." She leaned back in her chair and crossed her legs. The hem of her skirt fell back and revealed several inches of her thigh.

"Maybe you should." David had no idea how he managed to keep his voice steady.

"When pigs fly," Shawna snapped, but a note of amusement softened her words.

David reluctantly dragged his gaze away from her legs and worked up an exaggerated sigh. "That's what I figured. In the meantime, are we still on for lunch?"

"Yes, if you promise not to spend the whole time telling me what's wrong with Bob and why I shouldn't have anything to do with him."

"I promise." David couldn't think of any subject he

wanted to discuss less than Thor. "Instead, you can tell me all about this Valentine's Day party you're planning."

Shawna lifted her coat from its hook. "It's just a promotional idea to bring in customers. I don't really like Valentine's Day, but we've got a strong romance readership in this area, so I'm hoping it will be good for business."

"Sounds like a good idea. But I thought you loved Valentine's Day. When did that change?"

Pain flashed through her eyes, but it disappeared almost immediately. "When I grew up."

Heather let out a sigh. "When Kevin broke her heart."

Before David could say a word, Shawna shot a warning glance at her friend and led the conversation back to safer ground. "We're having close to a dozen local romance authors signing their newest books. I've got a caterer bringing in heart-shaped hors d'oeuvres, and we'll have romance novels everywhere."

"Hearts and flowers," Heather said with a dramatic sigh. "Soft music playing on the stereo. Cupids waiting to shoot arrows into lovers' hearts." She flashed him a mischievous grin. "You're coming, aren't you, David? There'll be romance in the air, romance in the food, romance *everywhere*. It'll be the perfect place to fall in love." Obviously subtlety wasn't one of her strong points.

David kept an eye on Shawna's expression. "It sounds interesting."

To his relief, she didn't react to Heather's broad hint. "To be honest, I hadn't envisioned it quite *that* way."

Heather wagged a hand at her. "That's because you've grown so cynical about love."

Shawna acted as if she hadn't heard. "We'd love to have you come, David, but please don't feel obligated."

We, she said. Not *I*. Not Shawna the woman, but Shawna the store owner. It wasn't exactly the sort of invitation David wanted, but he didn't hesitate to accept. "Of course, I'll be here. I wouldn't miss it." He tugged open the door and waited for her to step through.

She glanced at him as she passed. "I'm surprised. I didn't think romance novels were exactly your cup of tea."

"Hey, if it's important to you, it's important to me. What

kind of friend would I be if I didn't show up?''

Her warm smile melted his heart and made hope flicker again. Her eyes looked deep and full of mystery, her lips soft and inviting. He watched her pulse jump in the hollow of her throat and forced himself to resist the impulse to kiss her.

He closed the door and followed her down the sidewalk. He longed to undo everything Kevin had done to hurt her. He ached to take away the thorns in her heart. He wanted to protect her, help her learn to love again, and restore the trust and hope that had once been part of her. But he could only love her and stand beside her while she worked through the rest on her own.

With the god of thunder uppermost in Shawna's thoughts—no matter how often she protested—David couldn't afford to waste time. Heather had warned him that Thor could be persistent. This morning, she'd told him that Thor had questioned her after David and Shawna left the bar and that he'd left no doubt he intended to win Shawna's heart again. But that would destroy her.

After lying awake most of the night, David had decided he couldn't let history repeat itself. He renewed that promise to himself now. Even if Shawna didn't want him, he couldn't sit back and watch Thor finish what Kevin had started.

Chapter Seven

Too aware of David across the table from her, Shawna studied the menu and tried to concentrate on making a selection. The restaurant he'd chosen for lunch brought back fond memories of late nights and weekends at the office when they'd eaten Mexican food together in Phoenix.

A soft Latin ballad drifted from a loudspeaker, and piñatas danced from the ceilings. In the windows, surrounded by painted hearts, a variety of green plants spilled over the sides of colorful Southwestern pottery. Tantalizing aromas drifted from the kitchen and made her almost weak with hunger, and David's eyes, hands, and shoulders made her weak in other ways.

He lowered his menu and moved his water glass away. "Have you decided?"

"Everything sounds great, but I'll have the chili rellenos."

He leaned back in his seat and grinned. "I should have known. You want the usual, then?"

As it had since last night, his smile made her heart leap and his voice did something to her insides. Knowing he'd remembered her favorite dish touched her deeply, but she couldn't let emotion carry her away. She made a face at him. "And I'll bet you're having the large combination plate, right?"

"Right." He laughed softly. "You know me well."

She did know him well—that was part of the problem. She knew how he felt about everything, from politics to religion to food. She knew how he smiled, how he laughed, how his eyes looked when he was troubled. In the past, she'd been able to relax with David as she'd never relaxed around any other man. But already her absurd infatuation made her nervous and far too aware of hidden nuances behind every word she uttered.

She glanced around the restaurant again. "This place is great. Can you believe I've lived in Colorado Springs two and a half years, and I've never eaten here?"

"I believe it. You've probably existed on takeout at your desk since you bought the store."

She worked up a mock frown. "Are you implying there's something wrong with that?"

"*Wrong?*" He pretended to be horrified. "Absolutely not. You misunderstand me. Working through lunch, putting in ungodly hours, burning the candle at both ends, never seeing the light of day or breathing fresh air—it's the only way to stay healthy."

She knew he meant to joke with her, but something in his tone sounded serious. "Is that what you do?"

Nodding slowly, he scooped salsa onto a tortilla chip from the bowl between them, handed the chip to her, and prepared another for himself. "More often than I should, I guess. Especially since I moved here."

"Tell me the truth, David. Why *are* you working for Gottfried and Samuelson? In Phoenix, you always swore you'd never work for a large firm like that."

He shrugged lightly, but his smile faded. "It gives me something to do, I guess."

"So would basket weaving." She wedged the chip into her mouth. The salsa exploded in her mouth and left a pleasant tingle on her tongue. Perfect.

The expression in his eyes tugged uncomfortably at her heart. "I'm thirty-five years old, Shawna. I don't have a wife. I don't have children. My career is all I've got."

She loaded another chip with salsa. "So you're going to spend the rest of your life doing something you don't like?"

"The law's the law, isn't it?"

She tried not to let his evasive answer disturb her, but her efforts failed. "I can't believe you said that. You *love* working directly with people, not corporations. You have a natural ability to reach people, and I know how happy you are when you help someone win against the big guys."

He slanted a glance at her. "You're right."

"Then why are you doing this?"

"I told you. My career is all I've got. Maybe I just thought it was time to earn some respect. Maybe I got tired of struggling to make ends meet. Hell, I don't know. I made the decision, and here I am. Can we just let it go at that?"

She nodded reluctantly. She hadn't intended to offend him. "Yes. I'm sorry."

Reaching across the table, David covered her hand with his. "I'm the one who should apologize. I'll admit I'm testy—probably because I wonder whether I've made a mistake." He squeezed her hand, but so gently it almost felt like a caress.

His touch made Shawna's heart stutter and she searched his eyes, wondering whether he'd meant to touch her that way.

He gave nothing away. "You're right, I don't like representing corporations and I don't really believe I'm doing a whole lot of good where I am now. But, on the other hand, if I hadn't come here, I wouldn't have found you again."

In that case, she was glad he'd made the choice.

He opened his mouth to say something more, but his gaze locked on something behind her before he could speak. His eyes hardened and he drew his hand away. "Well. Look who's here."

Confused and disappointed by his sudden withdrawal, Shawna turned to check behind her. Bob stood just inside the doorway, dressed to kill as usual. He flirted casually with the hostess and scanned the restaurant, as he always did, to pick out a table. He noticed them almost immediately.

Shawna groaned silently. She didn't want Bob to join

them. Not when David had been about to say something important. She glanced back at David, but the moment had been lost. His expression had shifted to one she recognized from her early days with Kevin. Tight. Controlled. Even a little angry.

She flashed a resigned smile. "Bob."

"Bob," David repeated. Even his voice sounded stiff.

Within seconds, Bob reached their table. Like David, he looked slightly angry. Worse, he looked jealous. "Shawna." His hearty tone sounded forced. "What a surprise, finding you here."

"I'm having lunch with David. You remember each other, don't you? You met at the party last night."

David muttered something, and Bob's eyes narrowed. "Of course, I remember." He jerked his chin toward David, but made no move to shake his hand. "Are you two on a date?"

Shawna resisted the temptation to say yes. The lie might make him go away, but she wouldn't let herself use David like that. "No, just taking a lunch break together."

Bob forced out a relieved laugh. "Good. Then you won't mind if I join you." Without waiting for her response, he dropped onto the seat and draped one arm along the back of the booth.

Resentful of the intrusion, Shawna pulled slightly away.

David cocked an eyebrow at her, as if he expected her to do or say something. "Shawna?"

"Oh, Shawna doesn't mind, do you, sweetheart?" Bob dropped his arm to her shoulder and squeezed playfully.

Yes, Shawna minded. She didn't like him making assumptions about their relationship, but she'd dated him long enough to know how he reacted to even the slightest criticism, and she'd been the victim of his public displays of jealousy before. She refused to give him a chance to cause a scene that would leave her looking like some two-timing bimbo to the other diners—many of whom she recognized as casual customers of her own.

Part of her wanted David to protest, but she knew he wouldn't. Her more logical side liked him behaving like an adult in an uncomfortable situation. Fighting anger, she decided to tolerate Bob in public, but vowed to set him straight in private.

David watched Thor squeeze Shawna and fought back rising resentment. He tried desperately to keep his anger from showing on his face, but only because he knew Shawna wouldn't like it.

With his trial gearing up, he wouldn't have as much time as he wanted to spend with her. He'd counted on this lunch to move their relationship forward, not backward. But he forced away a surge of jealousy, dunked another chip in salsa, and tried to ignore Thor's easy possessiveness and Shawna's silence.

It didn't work. He had to fight down one tempting comment after another because he knew they'd sound cheap and malicious if he voiced them. But he wanted more than anything to knock Thor's stupid arm from Shawna's shoulder and drag her away so they could be alone again.

When the Norse god roared with laughter at some comment he'd made, David wedged a chip into his mouth and bit—hard. Shawna looked relaxed, almost as if she welcomed the jerk's attention. Maybe she did. Maybe she wanted a guy like Thor. And maybe David should forget saying anything to her, forget the roses, forget Valentine's Day—forget he loved her.

He laughed silently at himself and dipped another chip. Who was he trying to fool? He couldn't forget, even if he wanted to. When he flicked a glance at Shawna, the expression in her eyes caught him off guard. For a split second, she didn't look enraptured with Thor. If anything, she looked almost annoyed.

David tried not to let her see him smile, but he suddenly felt much better. He didn't have to forget anything. He loved her. He wanted to spend the rest of his life with her. And, with any luck, she'd soon realize she felt exactly the same way about him.

Chapter Eight

Shawna placed a stack of romance novels on the basement shelf, blew her bangs from her eyes, and dragged another box toward her. She shifted a bag full of white lace tablecloths to a lower shelf, repositioned a box of porcelain Cupids, and studied the results of her efforts.

Valentine's Day. Years ago, she'd loved it. She'd sent cards to almost everyone she knew, and she'd decorated her house at least two weeks in advance. But her enthusiasm had embarrassed Kevin and, after arguing about it for two years in a row, she'd grown to hate the day and the memories surrounding it.

Irritated with herself for letting her thoughts stray, she looked at the boxes on the floor and tried to concentrate on work and her impending dinner date with David.

She'd seen him only twice since that disastrous lunch six days before, and then only for a few minutes each time. In spite of his workload, he'd called every day, sometimes talking for a few minutes, others chatting for nearly an hour.

He'd called the previous day and invited her to have dinner with him tonight at Ristorante Veneto. On one hand, the invitation thrilled her. On the other, he'd said he wanted to discuss something important, and that made her uneasy. He'd sounded almost nervous, and her mind had raced since the call, trying to guess why he wanted to talk with her.

Logic reminded her of the blitz created by an upcoming trial—late nights and early mornings, with too little sleep in the hours between to keep her going. David would have endless exhibits to mark, copy, and circulate before trial. He'd be inundated with subpoenas to issue, lengthy pretrial documents to prepare and file, and last-minute settlement negotiations. On top of that, he'd have meetings, meetings, and more meetings to attend. But logic didn't wipe away her disappointment.

Prying her thoughts away from such disturbing topics, she tore open a box and studied the spines of the books inside. When she saw Celia Montgomery's latest release, she sighed with relief. Celia would be a major draw on Valentine's Day, but she'd attend only if Shawna could make her book available. It had been selling so well, Shawna had almost given up hope of getting it from her suppliers.

For the first time in days, her spirits lifted. As she pulled out a handful of books from the box, a single rose on one cover brought another set of never-ending questions flooding back. For the sixth day in a row, her secret admirer had left a yellow rose on her desk. For the sixth day in a row, he'd left no clue to his identity.

She still wondered if Bob might be the mystery man, but she couldn't imagine him letting the game go on this long without revealing himself. She'd started watching the faces of male customers, representatives from local distributors, even the mailman. But she'd seen no clue on any of their faces.

To be honest, the roses were starting to make her a little nervous. The only thing that kept her rational was Heather's secretive smile each time a new yellow rose appeared. Unfortunately, none of Shawna's attempts to draw out her stubborn friend had been successful.

As if her thoughts had conjured Heather from nowhere, footsteps sounded on the old wooden stairs behind her. When several seconds passed in silence, she straightened from her task and turned. To her surprise, she found David watching her. His lips curved in a lazy smile that made her heart race, and the intensity in his eyes sent waves of heat through her.

She glanced at her watch and groaned aloud. "I'm late, aren't I?"

"It's a little after six, but don't worry. You're obviously busy." He perched on a rickety table near the stairs.

She motioned to the stacks of boxes, some half-empty, some still unopened. "I lost track of time."

"I can see why." He tugged off his tie, shrugged out of his suit coat, and rolled up his sleeves. "What can I do to help?"

Embarrassed, Shawna shook her head. "Nothing. Just give me ten minutes to clean up and change."

She started toward the stairs, but he caught her arm gently as she passed. "You're busy. Let me help you finish. We can have dinner afterward."

Surely, he couldn't mean that. Kevin would have thrown a fit if she'd let anything come before a date with him. Bob would have pouted all evening. David *couldn't* be okay with this.

"It's all right," she said. "I can finish tomorrow."

"And get behind on tomorrow's work? Not on your life. I know how much you have to do before Valentine's Day." He swept the room again with his gaze. "Besides, a little physical labor at the end of a hard day will help me unwind."

"I have four days until the open house, David. I'll be busy from now until then, but I'll get it done."

"You don't want my help?" The expression on his face stunned her. Almost as if she'd hurt him.

"I didn't say that. I appreciate the offer more than I can tell you. But I feel horrible, especially since I know how hard it is for you to get away with the trial so close."

Grinning, David lifted a stack of books in his broad, sturdy hands. "Don't feel guilty. Your work is every bit as important as mine. Besides, if I get behind and find myself in dire need of an experienced paralegal, I know where to find you."

She laughed and shook her head. "I see how your mind works now. It's all a setup. You're trying to manipulate me back into a line of work I detest."

His smile faded so suddenly that she knew she'd said the wrong thing. "I'd never ask you to do anything you didn't want."

"I know you wouldn't. It was a joke—obviously in poor taste—but a joke. You know I'll do anything you need."

His eyes darkened and something that looked suspiciously like desire filled them. "Will you?" Even his voice sounded different—soft, deep, and incredibly sexy.

"Yes." The word came out little more than a whisper, and she couldn't shake the feeling that they were talking about something more personal than legal research. For a heartbeat, she wondered again if he could see something in her face, or whether he'd been stricken by a similar reaction to hers.

As quickly as it had appeared, the look vanished. "We can eat when we're finished here," he said. "It won't bruise my male ego. Hell, I won't even bad-mouth you to the other single guys in Colorado Springs."

She managed a tight laugh. "You promise my reputation will remain intact?"

"Unblemished," he vowed, sketching an X across his heart with two fingers.

She still didn't want to start their evening this way, but she recognized the determined look in his eyes and she knew better than to argue further. "All right, then. I guess you could unpack the boxes near the window and put the books on the top row of shelves."

"Your wish is my command." He bowed from the waist, crossed to the boxes, and started to work.

Shawna watched him for a few minutes, captivated by the play of muscles beneath his white shirt and by the slight frown he wore when he concentrated. At odd times over the past week, she'd glimpsed something in his expression or heard a note in his voice that made her wonder whether he felt something more than friendship. But now he seemed exactly the same as he always had.

He was her friend. Nothing more. If he'd wanted more than friendship, he'd have said something by now. She knew the routine. He'd manufacture excuses to touch her, drop thinly veiled hints, and make countless comments full of innuendo. But David did none of those things. Instead, he laughed, talked, smiled, and listened to what she said. And he avoided touching her, as if she carried some contagious disease.

Pushing aside a sinking sensation, Shawna turned back to her own stack of boxes. And she almost managed to convince herself that she was relieved, not disappointed.

David forced himself not to stare at Shawna as she lifted books from the last box in her stack and settled them on the shelf. He'd seen that flash of desire in her eyes when he arrived, and it had made his heart race with anticipation.

Working with her for the past two hours in the semidark basement, gazing into her huge brown eyes, and knowing that no one would see if he pulled her into his arms had almost been his undoing more than once.

As she stretched to reach the shelf, the denim of her jeans molded to her bottom and her T-shirt stretched across her back. Sucking in a sharp breath, David tried to glance away, but he couldn't tear his eyes from her.

He almost gave in to the urge to tell her everything right here, right now, but common sense returned and he decided not to. He'd spent six days planning tonight's dinner at Ristorante Veneto. He would set the mood with candlelight, music, and wine, and begin to show her what was in his heart. If she responded, he'd tell her everything on Valentine's Day.

Dragging his attention away, he broke down empty boxes while she studied the packing slip to make sure that every book listed had been delivered. When she lowered the document to the table and faced him, he noticed the smudges of dirt on her face, shirt, and fingers for the first time.

He knew she'd be horrified, but she'd never looked so beautiful to him. He imagined her crossing to him, wrapping her arms around his neck, and pulling his face down to hers. The image set him on fire, and he had to turn away quickly to keep her from guessing what he'd been thinking.

Her footsteps brushed the concrete as she walked up behind him. "I'm sorry this took so long. Maybe we should skip dinner tonight. If I look anything like that formerly white shirt of yours, we shouldn't go anywhere in public.''

David glanced at his shirt and frowned. Shawna might look charming; he just looked like a slob. She was right. They couldn't go out in public, especially not to one of the best restaurants in town.

''I guess Ristorante Veneto is out,'' he admitted. ''But if you think I'm going to skip dinner, you're sadly mistaken. I was hungry before. Now, I'm about to expire.''

Her laugh stirred his blood. ''Poor baby.'' She rubbed the back of her hand across her cheek and left another smudge. ''All right, I suppose I'll have to feed you.''

David had seen her dressed for success, for play, and for long weekends at the office, but he'd never seen her like this before. He liked the way her hair tumbled out of its clip and brushed her shoulders, the way exhaustion seemed to loosen something inside and make her movements even more fluid. He knew she didn't like anyone to see her like this, and being here with her felt almost intimate.

He smiled slowly. ''We could order in.''

''We could. But to be honest, I'd like to get out of here.''

''Why don't we call for Chinese and have it delivered to my place? We can be there in twenty minutes.''

She tilted her head and studied him for what felt like an eternity. His heart slowed as he waited for her answer. At long last, she smiled. ''Why not? I'll need a minute to make sure Franco and Nicole have things under control, then we can leave.''

''No problem.'' He meant it. He'd been dreaming of this night for days. He could wait another few minutes.

She started up the stairs, then turned back to face him. ''David?''

''Yes?''

''Thank you.''

''What did I do?''

She smiled softly. ''You're a wonderful friend.''

He returned the smile. ''So are you.'' And he prayed silently that she'd be willing to move beyond friendship to the relationship he'd begun to need.

Chapter Nine

Less than fifteen minutes later, David held Shawna's arm as they skidded across the ice toward the parking lot outside Every Book & Cranny. Shawna didn't draw away, nor did she seem uncomfortable with his touch. Air so cold it almost hurt bit through his pant legs and rushed up the sleeves of his coat.

He glowered at the night sky and muttered, "I can't believe how cold it is up here."

Shivering, Shawna drew the lapels of her coat closer. "I guess it *is* a little colder here than in Phoenix."

"A *little?*" He let out a disbelieving laugh. "It's freezing. And we're so high, there's no air."

"If you think *this* is high and cold, just wait until you get into the mountains. You haven't felt anything yet."

"In that case, let's not go to the mountains. Right now, all I want is to get back inside—fast."

She laughed up at him. "Wimp."

"*Wimp?* Good Lord, woman, even a polar bear would freeze in this weather."

"Oh, all right. Come on." Pulling away quickly, she

grabbed his gloved hand and tugged him after her.

David longed for the touch of her hand without the glove, but he figured the heavy fabric and insulation between them was a godsend—at least for the moment.

Laughing, he half-slid behind her along the sidewalk and took small steps to match hers as they crossed the parking lot. Once behind the wheel, he blew out a breath of iced air, jammed his keys into the ignition, and started the engine. Pushing the heat lever as high as it would go, he held one hand above the dashboard and willed the car to warm up quickly.

He felt Shawna watching him, smiling as if she found him amusing. "Tell me one thing. If you're so anti-winter, why did you move to Colorado? Besides money and fame, that is."

"I thought I wanted something different."

"What about the people you left behind?"

"Not an issue," he said. "I miss a couple of friends from the firm, but there's nobody who makes me lie awake at night battling homesickness." He slanted a sideways glance at her. "What about you? Did you ever regret moving to Boston?"

Her smile faded. "Yes, I did. Often."

He couldn't resist asking the question that had haunted him from the moment he'd learned about her divorce. "What happened between you and Kevin?"

She didn't speak for so long that he thought she might not want to discuss her marriage. "I used to be a dreamer," she said at last. "Don't ask me why, but I believed in true love that would last forever. I believed the love stories I read as a girl and the romance novels I devoured before I married Kevin." Her expression tightened. "Now I know better. It's far too easy to mistake lust and the heat of passion for real love."

David put the car into reverse and glanced over his shoulder as he backed the car around. "I suppose it is."

"I've been in love before," she said without looking at him. "I'd rather have lust, even if it doesn't last."

David wanted both. He let his gaze drift from the road for a second. "So, is that what happened with Kevin? You were attracted to him and then discovered you didn't love him?''

''*He* didn't love *me*,'' Shawna answered slowly. ''He wanted a wife who'd fit into a mold he'd dreamed up. I happened to have some of the qualities he wanted, but I don't think it would have mattered if he'd married me or someone else, as long as his wife was endowed with the sterling virtues on his list.'' She flicked a lock of hair over her shoulder and sighed. ''He turned out to be just like my father. My father doesn't see my mother as a person, just an extension of himself. Kevin's the same way.''

That didn't surprise David a bit.

She shook her head as if the memory defeated her, and looked out the window again. ''I don't know why I believed in happily ever after in the first place. I should have known better. I grew up knowing what happens after marriage.''

David stopped at a red light and faced her steadily. ''Your parents' marriage isn't the only kind there is, you know. Not all men are like Kevin and your dad.''

''No?'' She laughed harshly.

He could understand where her bitterness had come from, but he hated to see it. Keeping his face impassive, he concentrated on keeping the car under control as he accelerated again. ''Are you saying you don't believe in love?''

''No, I don't.''

His stomach knotted. If she didn't believe in love, he didn't stand a chance. He didn't want a fleeting physical relationship with her, he wanted forever. ''You should believe.''

''Why?''

He turned the fan on the defrost a notch higher. ''Because it exists. It's hard to find, I know, but it truly is out there if you wait long enough to find the right person. Someone who loves *you*, not an image of the perfect woman.''

Shawna laughed again, but the sound held no humor. ''You're still a hopeless romantic, aren't you?''

''I guess I am. There's nothing wrong with that.''

''Yes there is.'' She sounded almost angry. ''Hopeless romantics wind up with broken hearts. I learned my lesson. I'll never give myself so completely to a relationship again.''

''That doesn't sound healthy.''

"Well, it is. Letting romance sweep away common sense and blind you to reality—*that's* not healthy."

"You've just been in love with the wrong kind of guys."

"I hate to break this to you," she said, flicking an annoyed glance at him. "But *all* guys are the wrong kind. I don't mean anything personal by that," she added with a thin smile. "I know you guys can't help it. But men aren't capable of deep emotional commitment. They want a perfect woman, and it only takes a great pair of breasts or a firm behind to get them to forget every promise they've ever made."

Did she really believe that? David studied her expression, hoping to see a flash of playfulness. He didn't find one. "That may be true for some guys, but not all of us."

"Okay, okay," she said with an acid laugh, holding up her hands in surrender. "I can already see we're not going to reach an agreement, so maybe we ought to drop the subject."

"Maybe we should." David didn't like hearing such harsh sentiments coming from her, and he couldn't help adding another black mark in Kevin's book for taking away the softer side that had once been so much a part of her.

He let silence hum between them for a few minutes, then tried to change the mood. "So—? How 'bout them Broncos? Think they'll make the playoffs next season?"

As he'd hoped, his question brought some of the light back into Shawna's eyes. She sent him a half-smile and replayed an old joke they'd laughed about many times in Phoenix. "They might, if they get enough home runs and they don't foul out."

Remembering how many sports fans she'd baffled that way, he laughed aloud. Her smile widened. At the next traffic signal he turned and met her gaze again. "Truce?"

She removed one glove and extended her pinkie. "Truce."

After tugging off his own glove, David wrapped his little finger around hers and held it. If he'd had his way, he'd have held onto her forever. He loved seeing her smile. He loved knowing that he could make her smile or make her laugh. Every moment he spent with her only increased his desire to build a future together and to help her find herself inside the armor she'd constructed around her heart.

When the car behind them honked softly to indicate that the light had changed, David forced himself to let go of her finger and drive through the intersection. He stole another glance at her and vowed silently to find some way to make her happy—forever.

Determined to keep the mood light, Shawna stepped past David into his apartment and gazed around the room. David flipped a switch and lamps on either side of his leather couch gave off a soft, almost romantic glow. He flipped another switch and a gas fireplace in one corner of the room leaped to life. The room looked exactly like David: warm, comfortable, slightly sexy . . .

Her thoughts screeched to a halt when he came up behind her, so close they were almost touching. "I'm going to wash up and change out of this shirt. Do you want to borrow something to wear?" His voice reached into her heart, his scent filled the space between them, even the air pulsed in rhythm with her heart.

"I'd love to." She turned to face him and braced herself for the jolt of desire she'd learned to expect. "I feel like I've been rolling in dirt."

He grinned, but an intensity she'd never noticed before filled his eyes. "I'll be a gentleman and refrain from saying you look as if you have."

Shawna gave him a shaky smile in response. "Thanks. You know how bad I'd feel if you *did* say something so unchivalrous."

"Which is exactly why I'm keeping my mouth shut." He turned away and disappeared into what must have been his bedroom. A few minutes later, he emerged carrying two sweatshirts and two pairs of sweatpants. "Do these look okay?"

"They look wonderful." She tried to keep her fingers from brushing his as she took one set of clothing.

"Use my room. There's a bathroom attached so you'll have privacy, and I put out clean towels if you'd like to shower."

A hot shower sounded like heaven, but the idea of being naked anywhere near David's bedroom made images arise that she knew were better forgotten. She longed to feel his lips on hers and the crush of his arms around her. She ached to run her hands along the broad expanse of his chest, but she wouldn't jeopardize their friendship for a brief flare of passion.

David pulled slightly away. "You go first. I'll clean up when you're through."

Half disappointed, she worked up a weak smile. "Thanks. I'll only be a few minutes." Inside the bedroom, she closed the door and leaned against it, taking in this part of David she'd never seen before.

Dark wood gleamed from the headboard, dresser, bedside tables, and a rocking chair near the window. A gray spread with black-and-white geometric patterns covered the bed. He'd left a pair of jeans and his black-and-red plaid jacket on the arm of the rocking chair. Volumes of law books formed a stack on the floor near the bed, and a throw pillow lay forgotten on his dresser.

Intrigued, Shawna started toward the bathroom. As she passed the dresser, the clothes in her arms brushed against the pillow and pushed it to the floor. She stooped to pick it up and noticed a pile of change, what looked like a receipt, and a framed photograph that had been hidden beneath the pillow.

She touched the picture frame. He probably kept a picture of a woman in there—a love he'd left behind in Phoenix, or even his ex-wife. Unable to resist the temptation to see what Virginia looked like, Shawna turned the frame over.

To her surprise, she'd seen the picture before. It had been taken at one of the softball games they'd played together as members of the firm's team in Phoenix. She remembered the moment well. She stood in the foreground, laughing triumphantly after hitting her first home run. Behind her, one arm looped over her shoulder, David grinned into the camera.

Shawna stared at the picture, scarcely able to breathe, too stunned to form coherent thought. Why had he enlarged and framed *that* picture? But even as she wondered, she knew the answer.

Suddenly worried that he'd walk in and catch her snooping, she glanced at the door. With trembling fingers, she replaced the frame facedown and started to turn away. But the receipt caught her eye next. Big as life, the logo for Lucille's Flowers stared up at her, and Lucille's broad scrawl listed David's purchase as one yellow rose.

Shawna dropped the receipt and stared at the door. The roses were from *David*? This had to be wrong. He wasn't the type to send roses casually—especially for six days in a row.

She took an unsteady step away from the dresser and hurried into the bathroom, locking the door behind her. She closed her eyes and tried to catch her breath. Vaguely aware of the passing time, she undressed, turned on the water as hot as she could stand it, and stepped inside.

The water felt heavenly, but her mind raced as she stood beneath it. Over and over, the scene in the picture played through her mind. David's smile taunted her, his laugh teased her, and his eyes, deep blue and full of emotion, tormented her.

Lathering her hair quickly, she tried to decide what to do next. Yes, she'd felt a growing attraction for him, but she didn't want *this*. She didn't need a serious relationship. She certainly didn't want one. And she cared too much for David to let what they had die. Friendship could last forever, but love always died eventually.

She rinsed her hair and let the shower pelt her face and shoulders. She'd worked hard to protect her heart since the divorce. She'd only let herself relax with David because she'd believed in their friendship. She'd assumed he wasn't any more interested than she was in changing their friendship. She'd trusted him. She'd let herself become vulnerable, and he'd repaid that by lying to her and betraying her trust.

With effort, she ignored her anger and told herself not to let emotion dictate her reaction. Once she'd been all emotion, but Kevin had mocked her instinctive responses, and she'd learned the hard way to think before she spoke.

She turned off the shower and mopped her face with a towel. Sighing heavily, she ran through her options once more. If she confronted David and told him how she felt now, he'd laugh at her. A well-reasoned response would do more than passionate argument. So, she'd go back into the living room, pretend nothing had happened, and get through the evening somehow.

But her spirits fell as she pulled on David's sweatshirt. Sitting across the table from him, knowing the truth and saying nothing, would be one of the hardest things she'd ever done. Far worse would be the moment she had to tell him good-bye.

Chapter Ten

David leaned back in his seat and lowered his chopsticks to the table. Shawna had come out of the shower pale and shaken. At first, he'd explained it away as exhaustion. But he'd soon realized that something else was wrong. Horribly wrong.

He nodded toward the wide picture window that looked out of the dining room to the city below. "What do you think of the view? It's beautiful, isn't it?"

"Yes, it is." She didn't even look.

Frowning, he watched her pick at her food. "So, what do you think I should see first? Garden of the Gods or Pikes Peak?"

"It doesn't matter."

"Is there anyplace else I should see?"

She shrugged. "Estes Park. I love it there."

"I thought you said you didn't ski."

"I don't." She lifted a tiny bite of sesame chicken to her mouth. "I shop."

In spite of the tension between them, David laughed aloud. "You *shop*? I never thought you were much of a shopper, except at bookstores."

"I don't shop for clothes or makeup," she said, glancing away again. "But I love art, sculpture, and wood carvings, especially if I find something by a local artist."

She sounded a little better. Maybe she was only exhausted after all. "After Valentine's Day, why don't we spend a day in Estes Park. You can show me all your favorite places."

She shook her head quickly. "I don't think so. I really can't spare weekends away from the store, and you work during the week. I'll just tell you where to go if you're interested."

Without her along, David didn't care if he ever saw Estes Park, but he didn't say so. He listened while she talked about art galleries, jewelry stores, and a shop run by brothers who created masterpieces in wood.

She didn't look at him as she spoke. In fact, she seemed to go to great lengths to avoid meeting his gaze. *Something* had happened, but he had no idea what. At last, as if she sensed him watching, she stopped speaking.

"Go on," he said. "What else?"

"I . . . I don't remember. It's been a while since I was there last."

David tried to act as if there were nothing unusual in her behavior. "Why don't I take a day off after the trial. We can explore the town together."

"I don't . . ." she said quietly, but her voice faded to nothing before she could finish her thought.

His heart thudded slowly. His throat tightened. What had happened between his handing her the sweatshirt and pants and when she'd emerged from his bedroom, sleek and clean and more attractive than any woman had a right to look?

He forced himself to speak again, to keep her talking so he could figure out what was wrong. "You haven't said whether your secret admirer left another rose today."

"Yes, he did."

Her expression looked so tight that David wondered for a moment if she'd figured out he'd sent the roses. Impossible. He'd given no clue, no matter how badly he'd wanted to. He lifted one eyebrow in the way he'd long ago discovered brought a smile to her lips. "Really? Did he leave a card this time?"

This time, his efforts didn't work. Her lips thinned into a tight line. "No. Just a yellow rose, like all the others."

"Somebody's obviously taken with you."

Her eyes clouded and she forced a brittle laugh. "I don't know about that."

"Why not?" He lowered his chopsticks and stared at her. "You're intelligent, warm, funny, and a lot of fun to be around. Not to mention beautiful."

She focused on her hands, but her cheeks grew red.

He cocked his head to see her better. "Don't tell me nobody's ever told you that before."

Her eyes looked almost hard. "My mother did."

"That's not what I meant, and you know it." David leaned toward her and moved his hand so close to hers that their fingers almost touched. "Kevin must have told you how lovely you are."

"Kevin?" She laughed bitterly. "Not after we were married."

"Never?"

Shawna shook her head and looked away again.

David left his hand near hers and rubbed his forehead with the other. "Do you mind my asking what you ever saw in him?"

"I thought he loved me. He *told* me he loved me."

Her honesty caught him off guard, but it didn't answer his question. "Did you love him?"

"Of course I did . . . at first." She pulled her hand away and propped her elbows on the table. "What about you and your wife? Did you love her?"

"Not as much as I should have."

Her eyes darkened as if his answer angered her. "How long did it take you to figure that out?"

"Not long."

"Why did you marry her?"

This time, he avoided her gaze. "Let's just say it was for the wrong reasons."

"You don't want to talk about it?"

"No." He managed an uncomfortable smile.

"Okay," she said with a shrug.. "We won't."

He'd offended her. Pulling in a steadying breath, he forced

himself to answer. "I didn't realize it at the time, but I married Virginia to put something painful behind me. I knew almost from the first that I'd made a horrible mistake. I didn't love her, and she sensed it."

She met his gaze with a steely one of her own. "But she fit the picture you'd drawn for yourself of the perfect wife."

"No." He spoke too quickly. There was more truth in her statement than he liked. He'd only recently realized that Virginia's main attraction had been her physical resemblance to Shawna. "I was miserable. She was miserable. It wasn't the kind of marriage I wanted, and it certainly wasn't the kind of marriage she deserved."

Shawna didn't say a word.

David knew he was probably digging himself into a hole so deep he'd never get out. Following instinct, he brushed her fingers with his. Her hand felt warm and soft. Everything inside him tightened, and he realized suddenly what a mistake he'd made by being less than honest with her.

By trying to skirt the issue and hide the truth, everything he said sounded as if it had popped out of Kevin's mouth— or Thor's. In his own way, he'd been no better than either of them.

He didn't want a relationship defined by half-truths. Shawna deserved honesty. If he loved her, *truly* loved her, he'd offer nothing less. He brushed one knuckle softly with his thumb and tried to find the right words. She tilted her head; she was so beautiful that his breath caught in his throat.

Drawing a deep breath, he searched for the strength to tell her everything. He studied her face, ignoring the pounding of his heart, willing her to listen, and hoping against hope that she wouldn't reject him afterward.

Without warning, she pulled her hand away and stood. "I need to get home. Will you drive me back to my car?"

"Why? What's wrong?"

"Nothing." The word came out so sharp, it had to be a lie. "I have a headache."

David pushed away from the table and stood. "I'm sure I can find something for it in the bathroom."

She shook her head quickly. She looked almost frantic. "No. Just take me to my car. Please."

Desperate to understand, David reached for her again. "What's wrong? Was it something I said?"

She looked up at him, but her eyes had grown cold. "Something you *said*?" Laughing harshly, she took a step away. He watched her struggle with herself, then finally give up. "No, David. You didn't *say* anything. You played me for a fool. You tricked me. You sent me roses for the past six days, pretending to be my friend, and all the while you've been . . . you've been . . . I don't know *what* you've been doing."

David's heart almost quit beating. He wanted to defend himself, but he couldn't think of anything to say. He'd done exactly what she accused him of.

Her eyes narrowed. "You're not even going to explain?"

"Yes," he said slowly. "I can explain. I love you."

"Don't." She took another step away and shook her head frantically. "Don't say that."

But now that he'd opened the doors on the truth, he couldn't shut them again. "I've always loved you, Shawna. Even back in Phoenix. I just wanted to show you how *much* I love you. The roses were supposed to be romantic, not some cheap trick."

"You should have told me, David."

Did he only imagine it, or did her voice sound a little softer? "I know. I'm sorry." He took a step closer, but she backed away. "I love you, Shawna. We could have the best kind of relationship there is—partners, lovers, and friends."

She looked angry. "That isn't the way it works."

"It *can* be."

"No." She backed away another step. "I can't deal with this. Please, take me to my car."

He wanted to refuse, to make her stay and talk to him until they'd worked things out, but he couldn't. Asking that of her would be more of the same. "If that's what you want, I'll drive you back. But will you at least think about what I've said?"

He anticipated a vehement refusal. Anger. Hostility. Instead, she remained completely silent. She slipped on her coat, snatched up the bag holding her clothes, and walked to the door quickly. Anger defined every movement.

Heartsick, David started after her, but before he could get even halfway across the room she bolted outside. Thinking frantically, he trailed her to the car. Praying for a miracle, he drove as quickly as he dared on the icy roads. Willing her to say something, he pulled into the parking lot. But he still didn't know how to repair the damage he'd done.

Shawna pushed open her door and stepped outside almost before the car stopped moving. Without a word, she slammed the car door shut and climbed into her own car.

David watched until she backed out of her parking space, then drove behind her onto the street. For a split second, he thought about following her home and demanding a chance to explain. But common sense warned him to leave her alone—at least for now.

When she turned at the first intersection, he sat at the stop sign and watched as she drove away. No doubt about it, he'd done everything wrong. He'd been so determined to win her love that he'd made a mess of the whole situation. With another woman, his plan might have worked, but Shawna had too many unresolved issues to consider his gesture romantic.

He tried telling himself he didn't love her, after all. That he'd been knocked off his feet by passion, left off-balance by desire. But as he drove the empty streets, the emotions that had tormented him when she married Kevin came back to stalk him, and the fears he'd battled then descended upon him again.

His heart crashed, his stomach churned, and his mind blanked except for one thought. He'd just lost the only woman he would ever love.

Chapter Eleven

"You," Heather said as she twisted a roll of red crepe paper, "are the biggest fool I've ever met in my life."

Shawna didn't even look at her. They'd been arguing for almost half an hour, and her anger doubled with every passing minute. She crossed the room, twisting the streamer as she walked. "You don't seem to understand that David lied to me."

"He didn't *lie*," Heather argued. "He just withheld information. There's a difference."

Shawna let out a sigh of annoyance. "*You* might be able to justify his behavior. I can't."

"He loves you."

"He *lied*," Shawna insisted, and climbed onto a folding chair. The open house started in the morning, but her heart wasn't in decorating tonight. The hearts and flowers aggravated her already foul mood. "I trusted him more than I've ever trusted any man. I don't know how many times I talked with him about my stupid secret admirer. He had plenty of chances to tell the truth, but he lied."

Heather sighed heavily. "You're overreacting."

"I am *not*," Shawna insisted. "I trusted him to be honest with me, but he wasn't. All the time we were together, ever since he showed up again, he's been tricking me, keeping secrets, *lying*. I feel violated."

Snorting a laugh, Heather popped a piece of heart-shaped candy into her mouth. *"Violated?"*

"Yes, violated."

"I don't believe this. Do you know how many women would kill to have a good man love them the way David loves you?"

"Thousands, I'm sure." Shawna didn't even try to hide the sarcasm in her voice.

"Hundreds of thousands. Maybe millions." Heather took a step toward her. The crepe paper sagged to the floor.

"Will you please stay there and be quiet?" The words snapped out of Shawna's mouth. She didn't care. "Valentine's Day is tomorrow. We don't have time to do this twice."

"I'm perfectly capable of working and talking at the same time. You just don't want to hear what I have to say."

"You're right, I don't. In fact, I don't even want to think about David anymore." As if she could *stop* thinking about him. She hadn't thought of anything else since she'd driven away from him three nights before. The yellow roses he'd continued to deliver and the straightforward notes of apology hadn't helped.

Of course, she'd tossed them into the trash as soon as they arrived, but they'd done their job. She couldn't close her eyes without seeing his face. Every time the telephone rang, she grabbed for it, half-wishing he'd call.

With a scowl, Heather backed into place again. "All right. I'll stand here. But I won't be quiet. You're making the biggest mistake of your life. The man loves you."

"Love." Shawna snorted in derision. "If that's love—"

Heather cut her off. "It is, and you know it."

Did she? If he started off trying to trick her, what would be next?

"It's romantic," Heather insisted.

"It's manipulation."

"Only because you're comparing him to Kevin. But,

Shawna, he *isn't* Kevin, and you need to remember that.''

Shawna wanted to defend herself, but the words hit home. ''If that's love, he has a funny way of showing it.''

''At least he *does* show it. Good grief, I could see it in his eyes the first time he spent more than five minutes with you. You could have seen it, too, if you'd ever looked.''

''Why would I look?'' Shawna pivoted on her heel and faced her. ''He was my friend. I don't make a habit of staring into the eyes of every man I know just to see if he might be secretly in love with me.''

''No? Well, maybe you should start.''

''Don't be ridiculous.'' Shawna tried to shake a kink out of the crepe paper, but the kink only tightened.

''You think he tricked you,'' Heather said. ''Tell me what you wanted him to do. Drop to his knees and profess undying love the first minute he saw you again?''

Shawna glared at her. Now she sounded ridiculous. ''No, but the way he went about it was just . . . *wrong*. And your keeping it secret from me was wrong, too.''

''I didn't have any right to tell you. It wasn't my secret.''

That might be, but it didn't make her feel better. ''You're my best friend. You should have said something.''

Heather pushed back her hair. ''How long do you think I'd be your best friend if I raced around telling secrets? You ought to be thankful I never told *him* how *you* feel.''

Shawna flicked an irritated glance at her. ''There's nothing *to* tell.''

''You don't think so?'' Heather smiled softly. ''Come on, Shawna. I'd have to be dead not to see the way you look at him, or to hear the sound of your voice when you speak of him, or to miss the way you lunge for the phone every time it rings.''

''I don't lunge. I'm *trying* to be professional, to conduct my business the way it should be run. I don't believe in letting the phone ring off the hook when customers call.''

Heather laughed. ''Okay. If you say so.''

The laughter only increased her irritation. ''I'm glad you find the whole sordid mess so amusing. I'm thrilled you think it's all so unspeakably romantic—''

Heather's smile faded. "I don't think it's amusing, but I do think it's romantic."

"*Romantic.*" Shawna twisted the crepe paper streamer and stepped onto the chair again.

"You know, if you'd lose a little of that stubborn pride of yours, you'd think so, too."

Shawna stepped off the chair. "I'm not being stubborn, and I'm not proud. But he should have told me, Heather. He should have done it all differently."

"How?"

"For starters, he should have been honest with me."

"Why should he have been honest with you?" Heather demanded. "You weren't honest with him."

"I never lied to him."

"Yes, you did. And you've been lying to yourself, too. If you weren't, you'd realize he did tell you how he felt—several times. He just never said it aloud."

"*I'm* not the one who's been hiding a secret love for nearly ten years," Shawna interrupted.

"No." Heather adjusted a vase of cut flowers on a nearby table with her free hand. "But you did fall in love with him, and you never told him."

"I'm *not* in love with him," Shawna protested. "And even if I were, I didn't send him roses for a week and a half and never attach a card. I didn't listen to him wonder about the damned roses and keep my mouth shut when I could have set his mind at ease. I didn't—"

Heather waved one hand to stop her. "Fine. You're right, as usual." She sounded angry. "David did everything wrong, and you did everything right."

The anger in her voice brought Shawna up short. "I didn't say that—"

"Yes, you did," Heather insisted. "And I'll tell you what your next step should be."

Shawna hesitated a moment before asking, "What?"

"You should make a list of ways you find acceptable for a man to prove he loves you. You don't like what Kevin or Bob did, and with good reason. David did exactly the opposite, but you don't like that, either. So, make a list and post it right by the front door so the next guy who comes along doesn't miss it.'' Heather dropped the streamer and started to walk away, but when she reached the door, she glanced back. ''While you're at it, make a list for your friends, too. That way, we'll all know how to show you we care, and there won't be any misunderstandings.''

Before Shawna could say anything, she disappeared around the corner.

Shawna gave the streamer a vicious twist. Instead of spiraling the way she wanted, the flimsy paper tore in half. Biting back her immediate response, she dropped onto the chair and stared at the wall.

Heather was crazy. She was wrong. Shawna didn't put restrictions on the ways her friends could show they cared. She'd have accepted any way David chose to tell her how he felt, as long as he told her the truth.

When she realized how that sounded, her eyes widened and she stared at the wall in front of her. Was that true? Would she have accepted anything David had done? Or had she been blind to David because she'd become so accustomed to men like her father, Kevin, and Bob?

She buried her face in her hands and remembered a hundred small ways David had declared himself over the years— the way he'd always supported her dream, the way he'd always listened to what she said, the way he'd always been there when she needed him. She relived that horrible moment in his apartment when he'd confessed that he loved her and she'd rejected him. And she saw again the hurt on his face and the pain in his eyes.

Kevin had been angry when she asked for the divorce, but she'd never seen him hurt. Bob had been angry when she ended their relationship. In all her life, she'd never known her father to let anyone see him hurt. But David hadn't hidden his pain from her. He'd looked devastated, but even more, he'd been concerned about her.

At the realization, tears filled her eyes and a lump formed in her throat. She glanced around the room again, hoping Heather had come back. But she was still alone.

Dropping the decorations she held, she hurried from the room. But she'd waited too long. Heather had disappeared.

When she heard the side entrance close, she bolted upstairs to the landing. "Heather?"

Nothing.

She ran through the self-help area and into the children's section. "Heather, wait."

Outside, she heard Heather's Audi roar to life.

Wrenching open the side door, she stepped into the bitter cold. "Heather! Wait!" But Heather pulled from the parking lot onto the street.

Shawna watched her leave, battling tears of regret. The painful lump blocked her throat and threatened to choke her. Two of the most important people in her life lost in two days. That had to be some sort of record.

She watched the Audi's receding taillights and whispered, "You're right. I'm sorry."

But only icy wind and the sound of tires on the wet street answered.

Chapter Twelve

Shawna strolled through the crowded authors' room and tried to look as if she were enjoying herself. She smiled at customers, checked on authors to make sure they had what they needed, and tried to ignore the pounding in her head. Chatter filled the air and Pachelbel's Canon in D floated from the stereo. The melody had long been a favorite of hers, but today it made her heart heavy.

She couldn't complain about how the open house had gone. They'd sold more books than she'd expected. They'd helped more customers than she'd anticipated. Even the authors had had enough business to keep them happy. In fact, everyone looked happy—except Shawna.

She didn't want to see any more smiling couples, or smell another flower, or drink another cup of punch. And if she heard the word *love* again in this lifetime, it would be too soon.

As she turned to leave the room, a vase of cut flowers on the counter caught her eye. Both Heather and Nicole had received flowers from men they knew. Shawna hadn't received anything—not even David's rose.

David. She pushed aside rising panic and tried to look interested in something. But she couldn't stop thinking about him or wishing he'd come to the open house. She'd tried calling several times throughout the day to apologize, but each time, his secretary said he was out of the office. He might have been gone, but Shawna couldn't stop wondering if he was avoiding her.

She'd watched the door during his lunch hour, but each time someone who wasn't David entered the store, she battled disappointment. Now, with less than two hours until closing, she'd finally given up hope and admitted to herself that he wasn't going to come. And the ache inside her became almost overwhelming pain.

She wanted to get away from the customers, the authors, the horribly sweet punch, the heart-shaped hors d'oeuvres, the cloying scent of the flowers, the annoying decorations, and the irritating bowls of red, pink, and white candy. She wanted to stop smiling, block out the noise and laughter, and forget hearts and flowers and romance. But she couldn't.

With her smile frozen in place, she helped a regular customer locate a few books by her favorite authors. Holding back tears, she suggested a new romance by a first-time author to a new customer whose husband had been waiting patiently for at least half an hour while she browsed.

Finally, unable to keep up the pretense a moment longer, Shawna lifted a glass of punch from a nearby table and slipped into a long, narrow hallway lined on both sides with nearly full bookshelves. Blessedly, the hallway was deserted—at least for the moment.

She closed her eyes, sighed softly, and stepped out of the low heels that had probably already raised blisters on her feet. Wriggling her toes, she vowed to wear more comfortable shoes if she ever did something like this again.

But even the quiet moment couldn't soothe her aching heart or lessen her fears. Like a fool, she'd let apprehension keep her from being honest with David. She'd run away from a good and honorable man who loved her. She'd let the past block her path to the future.

She tried telling herself that she could apologize for everything and still save their friendship. But her heart felt like a block of concrete, and the only parts of her that didn't hurt were the ones that felt as if they'd already died.

Around the corner from where she stood, she heard the deep rumble of a man's voice, and Heather's voice answering. "I don't see her," Heather said. "But I think she went that way. Maybe she's in the mystery section upstairs."

Shawna's heart leaped with anticipation. David? Had he come, after all?

The man responded, but he still spoke too low for Shawna to hear what he said or identify his voice.

"I've got to help a customer," Heather said. "But you can look for her."

Forcing her aching feet into her shoes, Shawna abandoned her glass on a half-empty shelf and started back toward the end of the corridor. Now that he was here, a thousand things she wanted to say raced through her mind. She didn't know where to start or what to say first, but even that didn't dull her joy. It didn't matter what she said, only that he'd come to see her.

Just as she reached the end of the hallway, the man stepped into view. Shawna stared into his familiar face and bit back what she'd been about to say. It wasn't David.

Bob grinned when he saw her and held out a vase filled with a dozen red roses. "There you are. Heather said she thought you'd come this way."

No, no, no. This was all wrong. Even as her heart crashed, Shawna forced a thin smile. "I needed a minute alone."

Bob pushed the vase toward her and glanced over his shoulder. "Looks like you've had a great turnout."

She didn't want his roses. Compared to the yellow rose she'd been receiving daily, the display looked almost vulgar. But she took the vase to avoid an argument. "We've been busy."

"You must be pleased." Bob leaned against one bookshelf, effectively blocking her path. "Listen, Shawna. I've been doing a lot of thinking the past few weeks. About us."

"Us?"

Nodding, he looked deep into her eyes. "I don't understand why you're afraid to fall in love again, but I came tonight to tell you I'm willing to wait a while so you can work through whatever's bugging you.''

Shawna shook her head slowly. ''No.''

''Really,'' he said. ''There are people you can talk to about problems like yours.''

She stared at him for a long moment and thought about how different this conversation would be if she were having it with David. Bob would never understand her, but David had always understood, even when she couldn't put her feelings into words. She stared at the vase in her hands and slowly realized that Bob wanted to *fix* her. David had wanted her just as she was, but like a fool she'd sent him away.

''I don't want you to wait,'' she said softly.

''But I will.'' Bob touched her shoulder with one hand. Unlike David's, Bob's touch did nothing to her. No flashes of heat. No spirals of desire. No weak knees or trembling hands. ''Have dinner with me tonight after you close the store. We can talk about everything then.''

''Thank you, but I can't.''

His eyes clouded. ''I've got it all arranged.''

''Then you'll have to invite someone else.''

''What's the matter with you, Shawna? What are you so afraid of? Why do you keep running away from love?''

Shawna started to answer, then stopped and thought again about his questions. Smiling slowly, she faced him squarely. ''There's nothing wrong with me, Bob. I'm not afraid of anything, and I'm not running away from love. Not anymore.''

''Then why won't you have dinner with me?''

As the truth became more clear, her smile grew, her heart lightened, and her hands grew clammy. She handed the vase to him. ''Because I'm in love with someone else.''

Bob recoiled as if she'd hit him. If he hadn't looked so dismayed, she might have laughed aloud. ''Someone else? Who?''

''David.''

''The attorney?'' Bob snorted a laugh. ''Oh, come on, Shawna. You can't love *him*.''

''I do.'' She smiled broadly, certain for the first time that she meant it.

"You've run from love for so long, what makes you think *this* is the real thing?"

"He's not only the man I love," she said softly. "He's my best friend in the world. He knows me. He understands me. He accepts my weaknesses and applauds my strengths. I've run from love all this time because I never thought love like this existed. But it does. And now that I've found it, I'm not going to lose it. Not ever." She brushed past him as she spoke. "If you'll excuse me, I have things to do."

Without waiting for his response, she hurried around the corner and scanned the authors' room. To her relief, the crowd had started to thin. With luck, business would taper off from now until closing, and she could leave soon afterward.

When she saw Heather helping a gray-haired woman in the far corner of the room, she made her way through the crowd and took her friend by the arm. "I owe you an apology."

Heather stepped away from the customer and studied Shawna's face. "Did Bob find you?"

"Yes. And talking to him was the best thing I've done all day."

Heather's eyes narrowed. "Why?"

"Because, I've finally realized what I want—*who* I want to spend the rest of my life with. If you hadn't read me the riot act last night and sicced Bob on me tonight, I might not have figured it out for days, or even weeks."

Heather's sly grin lit her face. "You mean, you've finally realized what I've known all along?"

"Yes."

"And you're going to tell David?"

"I'm going to try to find him as soon as we close tonight."

"Bad idea," Heather said, shaking her head as she scanned the room.

Shawna's heart skipped a beat. "Why?"

"Don't wait. Go now. Things have slowed down here. Franco, Nicole, and I can manage without you."

Shawna almost laughed aloud. "Are you sure?"

Frowning, Heather propped her fists on her hips. "Do I look like I'm kidding?"

"No, you don't." Shawna laughed and kissed Heather's cheek. "And I'm not foolish enough to defy you twice in one week."

With Heather's wonderful, vibrant laugh still echoing in her ears, she raced into the main room, retrieved her bag from a desk drawer, and snagged her coat from the coat tree. Trying to hide her impatience, she waited as two new customers came in through the front door, then ran outside to the parking lot.

For the first time in her life, she knew what love was. She just hoped she hadn't waited too long to make things right.

Counting the rings on the telephone, David paced the length of his living room and dragged the phone's long cord behind him. He pivoted when he reached the dining room and paced back again.

He'd returned to his office a little before eight o'clock after an incredibly tedious twelve-hour deposition. Disgusted by Barry's interrogation techniques, he'd decided to quit Gottfried and Samuelson and go back to the work he loved. But all thoughts of a career move had flown out of his head when he found several messages from Shawna. No explanation provided. No message. Just her name and a check in the box saying she'd called.

Worse, he'd also found the Valentine's Day card he'd bought her and the note he'd scribbled to his secretary asking her to have the card delivered with a yellow rose, both abandoned where he'd apparently left them when Barry burst into his office at seven-thirty to insist they leave *that very minute*.

David had tried to reach Shawna from the office, but Franco had told him that she'd already left, and he'd overheard Nicole in the background saying something about Thor. Sick with dread, David had driven home quickly, ordered dinner in, and immediately started trying to reach Shawna at home. So far, he'd had no luck.

Now he cursed under his breath, slammed down the receiver, then picked it up again and redialed. Shawna *couldn't* have gone out with Thor, with his blond good looks and chiseled features, his Armani suits and Gucci loafers. Nicole *had* to be wrong.

Willing Shawna to answer—to *be* there—David listened to the phone ring. Closing his eyes, he begged every power in the universe to make what he dreaded most a lie.

Long after he'd lost count of the rings, he breathed a defeated sigh and slowly replaced the receiver. He stared at the wall and tried to decide what to do next. A minute later, a knock sounded on his door.

Snagging up the twenty-dollar bill he'd left on the table, he crossed to the door and jerked it open. To his surprise, he found himself staring at nothing. No pizza delivery man. No hot food. Just empty space. He didn't need pranks tonight, he wasn't in the mood. Battling anger, he backed up a step and started to close the door. When his gaze swept the welcome mat, he froze and stared at the single yellow rose in front of the door.

With his heart hammering, David picked up the rose and glanced slowly toward the outside stairs. Shawna stood there with her arms at her sides, her eyes wide and dark, the moonlight spilling over her shoulders and highlighting her hair.

Holding the rose, he straightened, but his knees threatened to buckle. He couldn't bring himself to speak. He couldn't make himself move. He waited for her to tell him what she wanted.

Her smile quivered and her hands trembled almost as badly as his own. She took a hesitant step toward him. "I came to apologize." Her voice sounded like music.

"Did you?" His own voice came out nothing more than an agonized croak. He longed to pull her into his arms and feel her against him, but he held back. He only hoped that the rose meant she'd changed her mind about everything.

She pressed her lips together, as if what came next was difficult for her to say. He waited, alternately wishing he could make it easier for her, and wanting to kick himself for loving her so much if she still didn't love him.

She moved another step closer. Close enough for her scent to reach him. "I . . ." She wiped away a tear with one fingertip. "I've been wrong, David. Very wrong."

His heart urged him to hold her. His head wouldn't let him. "About what?"

"About you. About me. About *us*. I ran away because I

was afraid. I rejected you because I didn't believe love really existed. But I didn't know what love was."

"And now you do?"

She nodded again. "Now I do. Love is what you feel for me, and it's what I feel for you. It's deeper than I ever imagined, warmer than I ever hoped. It's kinder and gentler than I ever dreamed." She wiped away another tear and stepped directly in front of him. "I love you, David. Please forgive me."

"I can't do that." He forced the words around the lump in his throat.

Shawna closed her eyes and sighed. "I guess I shouldn't have expected anything else."

Reaching for her gently, David pulled her into his arms and pressed a tender kiss to her temple. "I can't do that," he said again. "There's nothing to forgive."

Her eyes flew open. Hope filled them. "Yes, there is."

"No. You needed time and space. You needed honesty and trust. I should have told you how I felt—"

Smiling, she touched her fingertips to his lips so gently that his heart skipped a beat and the lump in his throat doubled. "You showed me in a thousand different ways how you felt. I just didn't look or listen. But tonight . . ." She laughed softly. "Bob came to see me at the store tonight. I'd been waiting for you to come all day, and when you didn't—"

"I wanted to come," he interrupted, "but I couldn't. I was in a damned deposition for twelve hours."

Relief replaced the anxiety on her face. "Thank God. I thought you were avoiding me."

"Never."

"I love you, David. I think I've always loved you."

The last of his apprehension vanished. All his dreams for the future sprang to life again. "I *know* I've always loved you." He tilted her chin and touched his lips to hers. When she responded, he finally released the hold he'd kept on the desire that had tormented him for so long.

She moved closer into his embrace, wrapping her arms around his neck and parting her lips slightly to welcome him. He let his tongue brush her lips, then delve into her sweet mouth. He moved his hands up her sides, almost to her breasts, before he realized they still stood in the open doorway.

He ended the kiss reluctantly. "I want you more than I've ever wanted any woman or anything in my life, but I'm not going to ravish you in the hallway."

She smiled, an incredibly sexy smile that sent heat soaring through his entire body. "I might ravish you."

Closing the door behind them, he pulled her into his arms. Passion roared to life and he kissed her again—deeper, longer, until they both gasped for air.

When they parted, Shawna smiled up at him. "I want to spend the rest of my life with you, David. I want you to be my partner, my lover, my friend—my husband."

His pulse roared in his ears. "Are you sure?"

"I've never been so sure of anything in my life."

"Would you still want me if I quit my job?"

Her sudden smile delighted him. "You're going back to a smaller firm?"

He nodded. "I have to, Shawna. I can't do this anymore."

She rested her head on his shoulder and sighed with contentment. "I want you, David. Whatever you do, wherever we have to go, I want to be with you."

He ran his fingers along her hips, then tilted her face with one finger, kissed her eyes, her cheek, her jawline. "You don't know how good that sounds."

"Maybe not," she said with a contented smile. "But I know how good it feels."

"Does this mean you believe in love again?"

"More than anything in the world." She sighed softly and leaned her head on his shoulder. "You know, I thought this would be the worst Valentine's Day I've ever had, but it turned out to be the best."

"For me, too," David said softly. "Happy Valentine's Day." He kissed her once more, tenderly, and looked deep into her eyes. "We're going to be so good together."

Smiling slowly, Shawna trailed her fingers along his cheek. "Yes, David. And we always have been."

Linda Francis Lee

__ BLUE WALTZ 0-515-11791-9/$5.99

They say the Widow Braxton wears the gowns of a century past...she invites servants to parties...they say she is mad. Stephen St. James has heard rumors about his new neighbor. However, she is no wizened old woman—but an exquisite young beauty. But before he can make her his own, he must free the secret that binds her heart...

__ EMERALD RAIN 0-515-11979-2/$5.99

"Written with rare power and compassion...a deeply compelling story of love, pain, and forgiveness."—Mary Jo Putney

Ellie and Nicholas were on opposite sides of the battle that threatened to rob Ellie of her home. However, all that mattered was the powerful attraction that drew them together. But selling the property would unearth a family scandal of twenty years past...and threatens to tear the young lovers apart.

__ CRIMSON LACE 0-515-12187-8/$5.99

High society in New York, 1896 —the story of a disgraced woman returning home and discovering a renewed hope for love...